THE CRIMSON DEATHBRINGER

A SCIENCE FICTION NOVEL

SEAN ROBINS

ACKNOWLEDGMENTS

I am going to keep it short, Oscar-acceptance-speech style.

I would like to express my deepest gratitude to:

My editors Margaret Diehl and Robert Smythe, whose suggestions and advice immensely improved my writing.

Everyone who helped me in writing my book. My beta readers, who helped shape a lot of my ideas, the members of the two writing communities I have joined (Writing Forums and Critique Circle) who freely offered feedback and guidance, and the Creativia Community (read family) who are the most supportive and passionate group of people you can imagine.

Jenna Moreci, who in her own words "writes books, makes videos about writing books and is super interesting."

Last but not least I must thank my wife Jenia, who motivated me to finally sit down and finish the book I had planned to write for years. How she did that is a long and funny story that I will tell you later.

PROLOGUE

Only a true warrior could appreciate the majestic beauty of the enemy fleet's flagship.

A warrior like me, thought General Maada, sitting in the cockpit of his single-seat space fighter.

Dwarfing all the other capital vessels in the galaxy, the Akakie starship was a work of art. An electroplated gold layer covered her sleek, stretched oval hull. The ship's twin side engines propelled the craft forward, lighting a bright blue flare behind her. Maada did not know the exact extent of her capabilities, but he had no doubt the enemy ship could easily obliterate a small planet. His space fighter seemed minuscule in front of her.

On a VR screen inside Maada's cockpit, the Akakie fleet commander said, "General, this is pointless. Look at the size of our armada and imagine the firepower of our starships. Your fleet has nothing but puny space fighters. You have no chance against us, and I assure you invading our territory is tantamount to suicide. Just turn that little ship of yours around and go home. Unlike you, we Akakies are peace-loving people, so we will be merciful and let you go. You can even keep all those planets you have already conquered and colonized."

"You talk too much," growled the general.

The Akakie commander had a point. Their technology was light years ahead of the Xortaags'. Their ships were not only significantly bigger; they had much more powerful armaments and heavier armor. That golden starship probably packed more firepower than the entire Xortaag fleet combined. Maada's situation did look hopeless.

Which was exactly how he wanted it to look. He had been preparing for this encounter for years, and the Akakie commander's over-confidence told him his plans had succeeded.

You filthy insects have no idea who you are dealing with, thought Maada. He dove in, laser bolts pouring out of his crimson space fighter's cannons.

The Xortaag fleet followed him.

CHAPTER ONE

"Jim, we've arrived," said my hover car.

"Thanks, Max," I said. "She'll be out in a minute or three."

"Liz has spent three hours in that beauty parlor just for a Christmas party?" asked Max. "You think maybe she's found out you're planning to propose tonight?"

"Not unless she can read minds."

"Honestly, you're kind of easy to read. Do you want me to tell you what you're thinking about right now?"

I smiled. "You have telepathic powers now? Neat trick, for a car."

"You're wondering if she *has* found out you're going to propose," said my overly perceptive car.

I held a finger up to my lips. "Be quiet. Here she comes."

Liz got in the vehicle. She was dazzling in an emerald green velvet bodysuit with strategic cutouts, crystal snowflake earrings, and thigh-high boots. I was in a smart tux with the color modifying to complement my date's ensemble. The tux seemed to think a satiny black was the right accompaniment. I disagreed, but my suit had already proved it had a better fashion sense than I did, so I went with it.

On our way to the nightclub we used to frequent a lot—a small, cozy place called Cubano Lito—my hover car chimed its notice tone. "I'm sorry, Jim, but we'll need to take a detour. SCTU has blocked Fifth Avenue between Washington and Lincoln streets."

"No problem, Max," I said. "We've got time."

"Something's up. Way too many SCTU soldiers around," said Liz.

"No surprise there," I said. "They're everywhere these days."

She was right though. Tonight, there were too many of them in the streets. Liz grabbed my arm when Max reached a roadblock guarded by Security and Counter-Terrorism Unit soldiers, all in full tactical gear and carrying assault rifles. An officer scanned my car and with a hand motion signaled us to continue. Max didn't need to be told twice.

Liz raised her middle finger toward the officer. Max anticipated her move and blackened her side window. Liz reacted by kicking the car door like a petulant child.

Max and I protested at the same time, "Hey!"

Max sent a text to my personal digital device. *Jim, can I please throw her out?*

I thought about it for a second; then I shook my head.

Liz tucked a lock of hair behind her ear. "I sometimes feel we live under Sauron's rule and there're bloody Orcs everywhere."

I laughed. "Nice one. I would've gone with the Galactic Empire and Stormtroopers."

"You guys really have to come up with more recent references," said Max.

"Come on, Max," I said. "You know how much we love the classics."

"Especially with all the garbage Hollywood produces these days," added Liz. "I honestly don't think they've made a good movie in ten years."

I blew out a noisy breath. "Ten years? Try fifty."

"Nothing beats the classics," said Liz. "Where do you think your name has come from?"

"Max or me?" I asked.

"I was talking to Max," she said, "but come to think of it, both of you."

"I know you aren't the hold-your-tongue type," I told her, "but make sure you don't criticize Zheng in front of others. His spies are everywhere, and comparing him to Sauron will get you a date with an SCTU officer"—I narrowed my eyes—"unless you *want* a date with one of them. Rumor has it Zheng has them genetically enhanced, which includes things like, eh, stamina."

Liz giggled. "Only if they are using *your* genes, Mr. Five-Times-a-Night."

"Am I blushing?"

"Nope. And by the way, didn't you say Zheng was like Hitler during the air force cadets' graduation ceremony, so loudly that half of the people in the room heard it?"

I feigned horror. "I'd never say such a thing about our supreme leader. I didn't say he was like Hitler; I said he was the reincarnation of Hitler. Huge difference."

Liz laughed and looked out of the car window. "I respect what the Resistance is doing, but I honestly hope Kurt von der Hagen doesn't pull something tonight and ruin our Christmas Eve."

I felt a lump in my throat when she mentioned Kurt's name. I took my PDD out of my pocket and checked the news. No assassination attempts. No bombing. No Resistance-related reports. Just another day in paradise. I tried to stop thinking about Kurt and his not-so-merry band of freedom fighters and focus on my proposal plans. Priorities.

A few minutes later Max pulled over in front of Cubana Lito and announced, "We've arrived."

I got out first and offered my hand to Liz. When I turned towards the club's entrance, I noticed two SCTU agents handcuffing a homeless man. The man wore a torn air force flight jacket. A cardboard sign hanging on his neck read "Disabled Air Force Veteran Says Fuck Chancellor Zheng!"

I chuckled. "Short, eloquent and straight to the point. We fighter pilots have a way with words."

The man wasn't struggling. He just stood there, shoulders slumped, looking like he'd accepted his fate. There was a small crowd of bystanders.

Liz put her hand on my arm. "I'm not normally the voice of reason, but maybe you don't do anything that ends with us spending the night in jail?"

"Didn't you just try to flip an officer off?"

"He wouldn't have noticed. We were inside a moving car."

I winked at her. "Don't worry. It takes only a minute."

I walked towards the two agents. "Hi. My name's Major Jim Harrison, and I'm an air force officer."

One of them gave me a dry look. "I know who you are, Major," he said. "How can I be of assistance?"

I smiled and extended my right hand. "I just wanted to say thank you for your hard work, protecting us day and night, especially on Christmas Eve."

He shook my hand, but his expression didn't change. I added, "Let me buy you a drink inside."

"There's no way we can get into the club without a reservation."

"Let me worry about that," I said.

The two agents exchanged a look and hesitated.

Liz joined us. "Come on, guys. It's Christmas."

"That it is," said the second agent. "We're on duty, but we can take a few minutes off and get a drink." He uncuffed the homeless guy, tore the sign off of his neck and said, "Keep this up, and you'll end up in the Coffin."

Liz shuddered.

"Max, take this gentleman to wherever he wishes to go," I called out.

The homeless man didn't even bother to thank me. He limped to the hover car without saying a word. His lack of gratitude made me wonder if he deserved to rot in jail.

I offered my arm to Liz. "Nicely done," she said.

"I should've gone into politics," I answered.

"How about a selfie?" one of the SCTU men asked me. "It's not every day we meet a war hero."

We left the two agents at the bar and went to the table I'd reserved in the club's second-floor balcony. Liz, who was a vegetarian, ordered a salad. I ordered a steak with fries, but I was so excited I'd lost my appetite. I barely touched my food. Liz noticed I wasn't eating and with concern in her eyes asked me, "Are you all right? Do you want to go back home?"

I didn't want her to suspect anything out of the ordinary was going on. I answered with the first excuse I could think of. "My New Year resolution's losing some weight, and I've decided to start tonight."

She tilted her head. "What are you planning to lose, muscle? You look like you're at zero percent body fat already."

I wasn't a very good liar.

After dinner, we went to Cubana Lito's dance floor. It was packed wall to wall with people dancing to booming Latino music. I wasn't much of a dancer (real men don't dance), but Liz, who was Afro-Hispanic and born in Cuba, was a natural. The two of us met some old friends, drank pina coladas, danced, and said Merry Christmas to a million people. We talked, bantered, and mercilessly made fun of other people. She laughed at my jokes and often came up with comebacks that in her British accent somehow sounded funnier.

"You know, being out with such a beautiful woman's good for my self-image," I told Liz. "All the other guys look jealous."

"You aren't too bad yourself," she said. "A lot of women keep checking you out."

I kissed her on the dance floor, her body pressed against mine, ignored our friends' get-a-room comments, and told her, "The past few months have been the happiest time of my life."

Toying with a lock of her curly hair, she gave me a coy glance and whispered in my ear, "For me too, honey." Her breath was warm and reminded me of what we'd be doing later.

Life was good.

We returned home at around two AM. I was tipsy, and with Liz pressing up against me and kissing my neck, I didn't realize we'd arrived until Max said, "Jim, we're in front of your home."

I owned a one-story Colonial house in Nassau County. Nothing too fancy, but not too shabby either. I got out of the car and walked through my small garden with its wintering rose bushes that looked like wooden candelabras to the front door with Liz holding my arm. I said, "Cordelia, I'm home."

A soft, feminine voice said, "Welcome home, Jim."

The door of my house opened. We entered the living room, laughing and kissing each other. Then the faint smell of expensive cologne hit my nostrils, and I found a tall, blond man sitting on my favorite sofa. He had piercing gray eyes and a completely unfashionable goatee, and he was wearing a long black trench coat. There were not one, but two freaking lethal-looking machine pistols next to him on the coffee table.

There were a few small blood stains on his shirt, my sofa and the floor.

Liz let out a tiny shriek. I put my arm around her shoulder and said, "Don't worry. Everything's fine."

"Hi, Jim," said the man. "It's been a while. Merry Christmas."

My heartbeat hadn't returned to normal, but pretending that it was an ordinary visit, I answered with an air of nonchalance, "Hi, Kurt. So nice of you to drop by. Just a few days ago I thought splashing some blood on my sofa would give it that gritty, rebel look."

Yep. Kurt von der Hagen, the legendary freedom fighter, tyranny-battling rebel, ruthless terrorist, deadly super-assassin (all depending on whom you asked), and the number one individual on every security agency's most wanted list was sitting right there in the middle of my freaking living room. Right when I was about to propose. King Kong wrench, thrown.

Liz looked at me with wide eyes. "Why're you two talking like you know each other?"

"Sweetheart, meet Kurt, whom I'm sure you recognize from all the wanted-dead-or-dead posters," I answered.

"Newsflash: He's my best friend. We've known each other since we were in elementary school. Kurt, this is my girlfriend, Elizabeth."

Kurt stood up, grimacing with pain and clutching his side, and in perfect Spanish—which I could mostly understand but couldn't speak—said, "It's a pleasure meeting you, Elizabeth. May I say you look absolutely stunning."

Liz looked lost for words, but one didn't become an acrobatic pilot/stuntwoman without fast reactions and the ability to think under pressure. "Charmed, I'm sure," she said in English, "but in case you haven't noticed, you're bleeding all over our furniture. Let's patch you up, and then you can tell me what Public Enemy Number One is doing in our living room."

I snorted. "Public Enemy Number One? Huh! John Dillinger ain't got nothing on Kurt. Mr. Super-Assassin eats the likes of him for breakfast."

"With all these references to classic movies, I confess half of the time I have no idea what Jim's talking about," Kurt said, "but I can already tell the two of you are perfect for each other."

Liz frowned at me. "You're 'best friends' with someone who doesn't watch movies?"

I held up my palms. "It's a very long story."

Liz had some medical training and had dealt with many wounds and injuries in her career. She went to our bedroom to bring her bag of medical tools.

"Cordelia?" I said.

"Yes, Jim?"

"What's going on outside?"

"Nothing much. All quiet," she said.

"Did anyone follow Kurt?"

"Not so far as I can see, and you know I can see a lot."

"Full lockdown mode," I said.

Half-inch steel sheets covered all my housed windows and doors. The only way someone could enter now was using explosives.

"This won't stop SCTU, you know," Kurt pointed out.

"True. But Cordelia can see them coming, and it'll give us more time to figure out what to do," I said.

Liz came back to the living room. Kurt took off his trench coat. I got my shoulder under his arm and helped him walk to our dining table and lie on it. Liz slashed Kurt's shirt with a pair of scissors. She unwrapped the piece of cloth around Kurt's waist and examined the bullet wound on his side. I tried to look over her shoulder.

"Give me some room," she told me. A couple of minutes later she added, "It isn't bad, but you're losing too much blood. Hold still."

She debrided the wound and started patching Kurt up.

"Before I forget, Cordelia?" I frowned. "Aren't you supposed to inform me if an armed man tries to enter my house?"

She asked with concern in her voice, "Jim, are you all right? Have you had brain trauma recently? Do you want me to call a doctor?"

Much like her owner, Cordelia was a wise-ass. Liz couldn't stifle a laugh.

Kurt flinched. "Don't make me laugh. It hurts too much."

Cordelia continued, "This is Kurt, your oldest friend. He's been in this house 523 times already. The last time he was here, he was covered in blood and heavily armed too, and he was accompanied by Allen, who was carrying a grenade launcher."

Liz laughed. "What? No bazooka?"

11

My face grew hot. Kurt pressed his lips together and averted his eyes. Cordelia had just reminded us of the last time we'd seen each other, nearly two years ago, right before Kurt started his campaign to bring Zheng down. He'd come to ask me if I'd consider joining the Resistance. I told him starting a revolution against Zheng was suicide and did my best to convince him not to go down that road either. I also said I didn't agree with his methods. I was a soldier, not an assassin. I'd killed plenty of people in combat, sitting in the cockpit of my fighter jet, but I just couldn't do it with a sniper rifle, or worse, a bomb, especially if innocent bystanders were at risk. I was a very good fighter pilot, but I'd make a terrible freedom fighter.

That was the day I turned my best friend down.

I rubbed my temples. "How did he get in?"

"He asked nicely," answered Cordelia.

"I need clean towels," said Liz, still working on Kurt's injury.

"On it." I darted towards the bathroom.

A few minutes later, Liz, putting fresh bandages on Kurt's wound, asked me, "So, how did you two end up being best friends?"

"We went to the same elementary and high school together, right here in New York," I said. "After my parents died, I spent most of my time in Kurt's house. You remember I once told you my father was a politician?"

"How can I forget? That's almost the only thing I know about your dad," said Liz. "You never talk about your parents, so I decided not to ask any questions."

"Good decision," said Cordelia. "Do *not* go there."

I ignored her. "Some thirty years ago, Kurt's father and mine used to work at what was then known as the United Nations. The two of them came up with the idea of the

12

United Earth. After my dad passed away, Kurt's father vowed to continue the work in his memory. You know how that turned out."

She did. Everybody knew. It'd be hard to miss the rise and fall of the United Earth's government unless you lived in a pineapple under the sea.

I looked at my best friend, lying injured and in obvious pain on my dining table. He looked older. No wrinkles or gray hair, but his eyes were weary, and a hardness had replaced their youthful joie de vivre. I remembered how ecstatic he was when his father Thomas von der Hagen was elected as Earth's first president after a worldwide election some three years ago on January 12, 2075. The entire world rejoiced. We all thought humanity had finally put its destructive tendencies aside and was ready to unleash its full potential. It was a global party from Sao Paulo to Tehran to Cape Town, Paris, Sydney, and San Francisco. The Unification was going to start a glorious era of peace, cooperation, advancement, and economic development for the human race that would last forever.

It lasted less than a year.

Thomas's fatal mistake was to appoint Graham Zheng, an influential American general of Chinese descent, as the director of SCTU. Right under Thomas's nose, Zheng gathered the most ruthless people on the planet around him and turned SCTU into an uncontrollable monster.

The dream of lasting peace on a united Earth died when Zheng put a bomb in Thomas's car, killing both Kurt's parents. Zheng executed all the United Earth's high-ranking government officials, declared himself ruler of Earth, and with the army and SCTU's support butchered whoever stood in his way.

Earth's national governments quickly fell in line. With

both the army and SCTU concentrated in North America, the USA and Canada didn't have a choice, and the East Asia Coalition was more than happy to support Zheng. Zheng bribed the other world powers by offering their leaders enormous economic rewards. With the major countries in the world in Zheng's pocket, the smaller countries' only option was to capitulate.

The national governments bowed down to Zheng, but ordinary citizens had a different idea. They fought back, spearheaded by Kurt and a French Canadian former Green Beret, Allen Jonson, who used to be Thomas's head of security. These two founded the Resistance, which later spread like wildfire all around the planet.

The Resistance wasn't a Gandhi-like pacifist movement. In the beginning, Kurt and his followers were hopelessly outmatched and outnumbered; they were a bunch of suicidal guys fighting the might of Earth's collective military and security forces. Kurt decided the only way to do this was an-eye-for-an-eye policy. He went on a rampage of political assassinations, sabotage, and general mayhem the likes of which had never been recorded in history, and he proved he was really good at it. I never understood how the mild, idealistic young man that I knew turned into a super-assassin. Allen trained him, and Kurt did have some military experience—he voluntarily enlisted during the war—but he had to have a natural inclination for violence to do it so well.

After Zheng's coup, I thought about leaving the air force, but flying jet fighters was my true passion. What else was I supposed to do with my life? It was the only thing I was really good at. Fortunately, the air force wasn't involved in the battle with the Resistance; that was the Security and Counter-Terrorism Unit's job. If one day we were asked to bomb a Resistance stronghold, I'd walk away, court martial or not. That was my red line. Since the coup, the air force's main function had been to stop national governments from thinking about secession, which would've caused another war, so I'd convinced myself by staying in the air force I was promoting peace. A few months after Zheng's coup, I met Liz, and my dilemma faded in importance. The stronger our relationship became, the less I thought about leaving the air force.

And now here I was facing all these questions on the night I'd planned to propose. The luckiest man on the planet, that was me.

Liz narrowed her eyes. "We've been together for a year and a half, and you never once bloody mentioned your friendship with Kurt?"

I lifted an eyebrow with such control that it would make Mr. Spock proud. "How was I supposed to bring this up? 'By the way, honey, you know this terrorist guy who's killing people left, right and center? He's my best friend.'"

"I'm not a terrorist," said Kurt, color rising in his cheeks. "I'm a freedom fighter. I only kill bad guys."

"We know," I said. "Still, a man's freedom fighter is another man's terrorist. Or was it the other way around? I don't remember."

Once Kurt stopped bleeding and it looked like he was in no imminent danger, a thought rose in the back of my mind. *You saved his life. That's great, but now it's time for him to leave. If he is caught here, both Liz's life and yours will be forfeit.*

But where was he supposed to go? Out on the street swarming with security forces? He was my best friend, and I still felt guilty for leaving him alone in the first place. Plus, there was no way Liz would allow an injured man to be sent to certain death, whatever the consequences.

It was Kurt's turn to tell us how he had ended up in my house. "I'd been after Palermo for nearly two years—"

Liz and I asked together, "Who's Palermo?"

Kurt rolled his eyes, and then sighed and said, "Cordelia?"

"Mike Palermo? Nobody important," she said. "Really. There's no reason for Jim and Liz to know him. He's only the director of SCTU and Chancellor Zheng's right-hand man."

"Tomorrow, I'm going to call the technicians and ask them to change Cordelia's personality from 'annoying' to 'docile,'" I said.

"On second thought," said Cordelia, "Palermo always works in the shadows, so there are very few people who know about him."

"He *worked* in the shadows," Kurt corrected her. "Two days ago..."

* * *

New York · December 23, 2077
(Two days ago)

The icy breeze stung Sergei Molanov's face, reminding him of Mother Russia. Armed with an STG 666 assault rifle and wearing a black tactical uniform, he was standing guard next to the main entrance of a luxurious mansion on a gloomy winter evening, wondering which of his many shitty choices in life had led him to his present situation.

On the surface, everything was great. He was the head of security for Mike Palermo, the director of the infamous Security and Counter-Terrorism Unit and one of the most powerful men on the planet. It was a cushy job, with a fat paycheck and out-of-this-world benefits. Plus, Sergei was really good at his line of work. He and his team had thwarted three assassination attempts by the Resistance in the past two years, and during one of those he'd taken a bullet meant for Palermo. A bullet shot by Kurt von der Hagen, leader of the Resistance, no less. That had raised Sergei's status to a level he'd never imagined possible.

Sergei knew what he'd gotten himself into when he accepted the job. He expected the director of the security forces in the most brutal dictatorship in history to be a hard, ruthless man. He'd gotten accustomed to the interrogations, torture, and executions he'd witnessed or heard about. This was war, and the Resistance had spilled its fair share of blood. This was especially true of von der Hagen, even though he'd nurtured a romantic image of himself as a freedom fighter in the public eye.

What had gotten under Sergei's skin was the bi-weekly visits to the three-story, eighteen-bedroom mansion where he was right now.

The mansion, built with utmost attention to quality and elegance, was a "gentlemen's club" called The Harem. It was run by the Russian mafia, and it was both expensive and exclusive. Rumor had it the girls who were forced into prostitution there were kept under the influence of drugs, and the clients were allowed to do whatever they desired. This was the place where Palermo, who had violent tastes to begin with, would let his sadistic imagination run free. Sergei, like everyone else on his team, believed the stories he'd heard about what was going on inside those walls, including the one about Palermo beating one of his "dates" to death.

Sergei's younger sister, Katia—a lovely girl whom Sergei

had adored—had been raped when she was only eighteen. She took her own life a few months later. Sergei hunted down the rapists, three young men from an influential family in Moscow, and killed them along with their bodyguards before fleeing to the US. Thinking about Katia made his knees wobble. He had to lean against a marble column to steady himself.

After all these years.

Standing outside this door and imagining other young girls experiencing the horrors that had led Katia to suicide was a torture Sergei could no longer tolerate. But he didn't have a choice. No one walked away from a man like Palermo and lived to tell the tale. If he quit his job, he was dead meat.

The door opened, and Palermo walked out, smirking, with a satisfied look on his jowly, high-colored face. His fleshy mouth always reminded Sergei of calves liver. There was a smear of blood on his right sleeve, next to his 24-karat gold cufflink. Thinking about that creature exercising his cruelty on a terrified girl made Sergei nauseous.

That was it. He couldn't take it anymore. He'd pack a bag and run away tonight, and to hell with the consequences. But first, he'd come back here and shoot up this diabolical place. He was a dead man anyway, and he'd done more than his share of bad shit. He might as well go out doing something right.

The cracking sound of the supersonic bullet's impact reverberated in the air. The top half of Palermo's head turned into a bloody mess, and a good chunk of his brain and a hot gout of his blood splashed on Sergei's face and neck. Palermo's body fell to the ground, twitching in death.

Okay. This should solve my problem, Sergei thought.

* * *

KURT, fifteen hundred meters away on top of a high-rise building, watched Palermo's head explode through his M-28 Sniper Weapon System's telescopic sight, punched the air and said, "Bull's-eye!"

Fierce joy rippled through Kurt. Eliminating Palermo was the Resistance's biggest victory. The thrill of the hunt was intoxicating. There was nothing he liked better than planning a meticulous operation, accounting for all the possibilities, and preparing for a one-chance-only long-distance kill shot. At the same time, niggling remorse dogged him. The bright, idealistic politician dreaming of world peace that he'd once been was now an assassin. He wished he could go back and take a different path, one where his talents and skills would work toward something nobler than kill after kill, but he knew it was impossible. This work needed to be done. Someone had to stand up to the vicious military dictatorship ruling Earth. Still, his heart ached. It was something he had to live with.

I'm glad Dad never saw me doing this.

Next to him, his spotter Allen chuckled. "Fourth time was the charm."

Kurt took off his fingerless gloves. "I wish I'd shot him on his way in. I might've saved a couple of girls some pain," he said while removing the suppressor. He put his sniper rifle in its case.

Allen scratched his gray beard and took a drag on his cigarette. "I still think you should've taken Molanov out too."

"And I still think not," answered Kurt, dusting freshly fallen snow off his black trench coat. "He's just a soldier doing his job. In another life, we'd be good friends. Let's go. Things are about to get really interesting around here."

The older man followed him. "You won't be so forgiving when we try to kill another one of Zheng's goons and Molanov stops us again."

Kurt opened the door leading to the stairs, thinking it'd been a good day at the office.

Behind him, Allen called out, "Wait up, boy! You know damn well my old knees play up in cold weather."

* * *

"So where's Allen?" I asked.

"I don't know," said Kurt. "We were seperated while escaping, and later I was shot. With no safe houses in the immediate area, I ended up here."

He talked a little more about the chase through the city streets, his evasion tactics and concern about Allen. Then Liz said she couldn't keep her eyes open anymore and retired for the rest of the night. This was probably an excuse to leave Kurt and me alone to talk and catch up.

"It's good to see you, old friend," I told Kurt, "but I honestly wish it was under less dangerous circumstances. I don't particularly wish for us to be put up against the same wall they'll put you up in front of a firing squad."

"I'm sorry, Jim, but I didn't have a choice. It was either this or passing out in the street. I feel much better though. I can go now."

He was lying; he was still pale as a vampire. It made him look younger, more innocent. As much as I wanted him out of here, I wanted him alive more. "SCTU hasn't kicked our door down yet, so I guess we're safe. You know my home's your home. Stay as long as you want. You need to get some rest." I wiggled my index finger at him. "But if I get executed over this, I promise my ghost will haunt you for the rest of your life."

Kurt smiled. "You still crack jokes when you're nervous, I see."

"And sad, and angry, and frightened. A joke a day keeps the doctors away. Want to catch some sleep?"

"Way too excited to sleep tonight," said Kurt.

"Want some beer?"

Kurt chuckled. "Does a bear shit in the woods?"

"We don't have any Paulaners though," I said. "In our defense, we didn't expect a visit from you."

Kurt was born and raised in New York, but Thomas was from Munich. Kurt had inherited two things from his father's birthplace. One was his love for a Bavarian beer called Paulaners.

"How're Bayern Munich doing these days?" I asked.

"Europe's Champions three years in a row, and Super League quarter-finals this year. They wiped the floor with the other teams in the group stage," he said with a hint of pride in his voice.

I grabbed a few bottles of beer. We made ourselves comfortable on my not-bloodstained sofa and clanked our bottles. Sipping my beer, I said, "I can't begin to tell you how sorry I was when I heard about Janet."

Kurt's bright eyes turned dull, and he stared into the distance. "She didn't have a violent bone in her body. I don't know what I was thinking when I let her join the Resistance."

Only then did I realize his cologne smelled familiar. It was Dior Men Dangereux. I was with them when Janet gave Kurt the same brand for his nineteenth birthday ten years ago.

"So how's your love life now?" I asked.

"Have been single since Janet was killed."

"Dude! Not for nothing, but that was two years ago. You can't be planning to live like a monk for the rest of your life."

Kurt responded philosophically, "There's no place for romance in the life I've chosen. It does get lonely sometimes, but this is the only way."

"Speaking of romance, I was planning to propose tonight. Thank you for ruining my perfectly laid plans."

He looked regretful. "You can always do it tomorrow night."

I shook my head. "Nah. I want to do the dinner and dance again, so I have to wait a few days. I might do it on New Year's Eve."

"Can I see the ring?"

"It's in the bedroom under my pillow," I answered. "I hope Liz doesn't find it by accident."

"She seems great, by the way."

"She is. You couldn't find a warmer, kinder and more caring woman. But just between you and me, we have a little bit of a Dr. Jekyll and Mr. Hyde going on in here. She's super volatile. She gets angry quickly and makes rash decisions. I know I just described all women, but—"

Kurt laughed. "That's sexist. All women aren't like that."

"Since when are you an expert on women, Mr. I-Have-Had-Only-One-Relationship-in-my-Life? Anyway, as I was saying before you rudely interrupted me, you have no idea how bad she gets when she loses it." I added, "Can I ask a super personal question?"

"Shoot."

"How many people have you killed?"

Playing with his goatee, he thought about it for a minute. "Hard to tell, with all the gunfights, explosions, and whatnot. I can tell you this though: Including Palermo, I've assassinated fourteen high-ranking government officials. This should be some sort of record."

Only half-jokingly, I said, "And how do you sleep at night?"

"Like a baby. I only kill evil bastards. My methods are brutal, and I don't kid around, but I never kill someone who didn't have it coming. Plus, I am doing humanity a favor."

I stifled a laugh. "How do you figure?"

"Zheng's regime will eventually fall. A war is coming. Keep in mind several countries didn't want to join the Unification even when it was a democracy. Japan, France, and Germany are already up in arms. A strong dictatorship can fight for years and bring down the whole world with it. If we manage to seriously weaken it, we'll expedite its inevitable downfall."

"Wow! Lots of big words there. Have you practiced this speech before?"

Kurt smiled. "I tell you something else too. The tide's turning. The way we're going, it's entirely possible we can topple the regime in the next couple of years ourselves, even without a war."

I didn't buy it. From where I was standing, Zheng's regime was way too entrenched to fall any time soon. That was probably just wishful thinking.

Changing the subject, I asked, "Do you still play?"

Kurt used to play the piano. I was sure he could've been a professional pianist if he hadn't become a politician. He grinned. "Do you honestly think I carry a piano with me from hideout to hideout?"

"I hope Allen's fine," I said. "Even though he never liked me."

"That's because you don't stop making fun of him," Kurt answered. "He's probably in a safe house now. That old fox isn't easy to catch."

* * *

New York - December 24, 2077

Allen knew something was very wrong.

He was in one of Resistance's safe houses, a small studio flat with a tiny window and cheap, battered furniture that looked like it'd been bought in a yard sale. Allen was sharing the place with Mark, a young man who had recently joined the Resistance. Mark kept walking back and forth and looking out of the window, his tall frame hunched. He was sweating profusely even though the room wasn't hot, and he kept sneaking furtive glances at Allen's Glock 55, which Allen had been dismantling and cleaning while sitting behind a small wooden dining table in one corner.

It looked like the younger man was trying to make a decision. Allen chose to move things forward. He put down the Glock on the table, leaned back in his chair and asked, "They got to you?"

Mark averted his eyes. His shoulders sagged. He muttered, "They've got my family," and took another glance at the dismantled gun. Then Mark pulled his own sidearm, cocked it, took a step toward the dining table, pointed the gun at Allen's head and yelled, "Don't move a muscle, old man!"

"Fatal mistake," said Allen.

Allen shot the young man from under the table, several times and in quick succession. Splinters of wood flew up in the air. Mark was hit in the chest and belly. He fell backward on the floor, blood gushing from his wounds.

Allen stood up, a smoking Smith and Wesson M&P Bodyguard in his hand. The muscles around his mouth twitched. With sadness in his voice, he told the dying man, "Ankle holster, rookie."

The door of the flat was kicked open with a loud bang, and several SCTU soldiers rushed in.

Allen's mouth went dry. Beads of sweat appeared on his bald head. Trapped in the small flat with no other exit, he was doomed. His adrenaline soaring, he took aim at the first soldier's head, right between his eyes. The barrel flashed, and the SCTU goon toppled. Allen shot another man. His gun clicked empty. The soldiers rushed him. He hit a man in the face using his gun like a club and kicked the second in the balls. Two other soldiers grabbed his arms. He went down under the weight of the attackers. They handcuffed him and stood him up. He kept struggling, but there were ten of them.

That was it then. Allen never thought he'd run forever. Still, he was disappointed that he'd let himself get captured, especially so soon after the Resistance's greatest victory, killing Palermo. He thought about Kurt and wondered if he'd managed to escape.

An SCTU captain, wearing the force's dark brown uniform, walked in and stood in front of Allen. "Where is von der Hagen?" he asked.

Allen spit out blood. "With your mother."

The officer nodded to a spectacularly big soldier, with shoulders wide as a bull. The giant swaggered closer to Allen and hit him in his belly, chin, and nose. Allen felt his nose break. With blood pouring out of his nostrils, he thought he was about to lose consciousness. These guys weren't kidding around.

He shouted, "Okay! Okay! I tell you! Jesus!"

The captain held up a hand, and the soldier stopped. Allen looked the officer in the eyes and smirked. "With your sister."

The captain rolled his eyes and was about to say something when a young SCTU lieutenant ran in and saluted. "Sir! We got him. He's hiding out with a Major Jim Harrison, an air force fighter pilot."

Allen thought, *Jim Fucking Harrison? Really?*

"*That* Major Harrison?" asked the captain.

"Yes sir, unless there's two of them," answered the young man. The captain gave him a hard look. He blushed and averted his eyes.

"Is he a Resistance member?" the first officer asked.

"Unknown, sir, but we don't think so," the lieutenant said. "He's an old acquaintance of von der Hagen. We interrogated him right after von der Hagen founded the Resistance, but he didn't seem to know anything."

The captain looked at Allen and flashed a satisfied smile. "Well, it appears today's our lucky day. Let's go."

He walked out of the room, followed by the other officer.

Behind them, Allen growled, "Yeah, you better run."

* * *

I WAS POURING a cup of coffee for myself when Liz, having changed into jeans and a t-shirt and somehow looking even sexier, joined us for breakfast. I'd just started sipping my coffee when Kurt said, "It's time for me to go."

Liz and I protested at the same time. "Absolutely not! Are you crazy? In the state you are in, you'll faint before taking five steps. You need rest. It's not safe out there."

Kurt looked at the two of us in surprise. "I expected Jim to react in this way, but I must say I'm touched by how much Elizabeth cares about me, given that we've just met."

"Don't flatter yourself," I said. "It isn't actually about you. Liz is obsessed with doing the right thing."

Liz laughed and punched me in the arm.

"I really have to go. I've set up a time and place to meet up with the other members of the Resistance. If I stay any longer, I'll lose the chance to contact them for a while."

I had no idea if he was telling the truth or wanted to avoid jeopardizing us any further.

Kurt put on his black trench coat, holstered both his machine pistols and shook my hand. "Thanks for everything. Maybe next time we meet we won't be living under Zheng's dictatorship."

I answered, "Who knows? If Zheng does go, maybe there'll be another President von der Hagen in office."

He hugged Liz. "It was a pleasure meeting you. Jim told me about your charity organization. I'll be making a hefty donation soon unless you don't accept a terrorist's money."

Liz beamed and flashed her dazzling smile. "Be careful, Kurt."

Kurt smiled back. "Careful is my middle name. How do you think I've survived this long? Don't worry. They'll never catch me."

"Jim?" said Cordelia.

"Yes?"

"Something's wrong," she said. "I've just found out someone has been tampering with one of my external cameras' feed."

"Which camera?" I asked.

"The one covering the front door."

With a deafening blast, my house door exploded inwards. Dust and smoke filled half of the living room.

A cold chill grabbed my heart, and I was rooted to the spot for a second.

Kurt didn't miss a beat. He pushed Liz behind a sofa, shouted, "Jim! Get down," and drew both his weapons. Two black-clad SCTU soldiers rushed in. Kurt shot them both. The sound of gunshots was ear-splitting.

We're so screwed.

I jumped behind the sofa where Liz was hiding. She grabbed my hand and despite the fear in her eyes calmly asked, "What're we going to do?

My ears still ringing because of the explosion, I scanned the room, keeping my head down. Kurt hit another soldier. His ammunition couldn't last forever. He took cover behind another sofa, the one that had his blood on it. Several bullets ripped through the sofa. It wasn't having a very good day.

All the stories I'd heard about the torture and abuse people suffered in Zheng's prisons rushed back to me, sending a chill down my spine. The image of Liz in a prison jumpsuit hit me like an eighty-ton tank. A woman as free-spirited and full of life as Liz wouldn't survive long in prison, and that was if the SCTU soldiers didn't shoot us first. The last thought made me shudder. I shielded Liz with my body, thinking feverishly, trying to find a way out of this mess or at least to save Liz.

Someone threw a gas grenade into the room.

I had an air force-issued M-25 handgun with two extra magazines in the closet in my bedroom. There were more soldiers surrounding us than the number of bullets I had, but anything was better than lying here in my living room waiting to die. Plus, if Kurt and I were both armed, there was a small chance we could create an opportunity for Liz to save herself. That way, at least there was hope.

A thought popped up in the back of my head. *Hope's a dangerous thing.*

Oh, shut up!

I looked in Kurt's direction to see if he could cover me while I ran to the bedroom to get my gun. He was looking at me. In his gray eyes, through the smoke, dust, and gas, I saw remorse and guilt. And the decision not to be captured alive by his enemies.

My blood running cold, I shouted," Kurt! No!"

Kurt stood up, sorrow clouding his features. He gave me a sad half-smile, dusted his trench coat off, sent me a small salute with one of his machine pistols, and with fire bursting out of both his guns' barrels, started walking towards the door.

I hesitated for a second; then I ground my teeth and ran out of my hiding spot, planning to tackle Kurt and stop him from committing suicide-by-cop. A hail of bullets hit the floor inches from me. I had no choice but to jump back behind the sofa. Helpless, I watched as Kurt, still shooting, disappeared in the thick, fog-like gas.

Liz called out, "Jim!"

I turned my head to find her on the floor, eyes wide with horror, clutching her chest and throat. Only then did I realize I had a hard time breathing.

The bastards had gassed us.

Watching Liz slowly suffocate made my whole body start to shake. I crawled to her, held her in my trembling arms, looked into her dark eyes and said, "Everything's gonna be all right. I promise I'll get you out of this; you hear me?" My breath was ragged and harsh. I was desperate for her to believe me, though I knew she was too smart for that.

Her face pinched with fear, Liz clutched my arm, holding on tight, and managed to whisper between coughs, "Save yourself. Go now. Leave me here."

Go where, exactly?

She closed her eyes. Her body shuddered and went limp.

I pulled her closer, face buried in her thick, sweet-smelling hair, and said, "I didn't give you your ring."

It was at that moment when I realized I was about to lose everything. My best friend was probably dead. My love was dying. I wouldn't last much longer myself. Despair swallowed me up whole. Every single muscle in my body tightened, and I started hyperventilating, partly because of the gas and partly because of the terror. I felt like I was being pulled into a black vortex, and resistance was indeed futile.

I gently lay Liz's motionless body on the floor, feeling blank inside. I covered my nose and mouth with my shirt, held my breath, and used the increasingly thick gas as cover to run to the bedroom. I got my M-25, loaded it, hid behind the bedroom door frame, controlled my shaking hands with sheer willpower, aimed and shot at the silhouettes I could barely make out in the living room. The gunshots echoed deafeningly in the confines of my bedroom.

I hit a soldier who went down screaming in pain. Another soldier shouted, "Man down! We've got a man down!" and ran to the side of his fallen comrade. I drew my lips back in a snarl and shot him too. The bullet punched its way through his neck, causing a gaping hole. He fell to the ground, a pool of blood forming around him.

I shot the sheriff, and then I shot the deputy.

Another soldier, wearing a black gas mask, stepped out of gas and smoke less than ten feet to my left. He was pointing a deadly-looking assault rifle at my head. I reacted a fraction of a second faster than he did and shot him in the forehead, right where the Mark of Cain would've been. The sight of his brain splattering all over my living room bookshelves filled me with a primal, savage satisfaction.

A bullet grazed my right thigh. A sharp pain lanced through my body. It was like being stabbed with a white-hot piece of metal. My knee buckled, and I fell to the floor, grabbing my injured leg. I hid behind the door frame for a few moments and took several deep breaths.

"Major Harrison!" someone shouted. "Put your weapon down and walk out with your hands above your head. This is your last chance."

"We know you're injured," said a woman. "We're ready to offer medical assistance."

These guys were trying to good-cop-bad-cop me.

"I'd rather suffer the end of Romulus a thousand times than accept assistance from you," I yelled back.

"What?" said the woman. She sounded confused.

"What's Romulus?" asked the man. "Is it a code name for the Resistance's headquarters?"

I burst into hiccupping laughter, which somehow made the sharp pain lancing through my wounded leg more excruciating. I didn't expect SCTU goons to understand *Star Trek* references. "Yes, it is, and you'll never find it." I wished I could see the look on their faces when they ran Romulus through SCTU's databases.

"That's it!" yelled the man. "I'll count to ten; then we'll come in, guns blazing. One, two . . . "

"Dramatic much?" I asked.

Resting the back of my head against the wall, I looked at

my blood drenched pants and thought about bandaging the bullet wound, but it sounded like a waste of time. I'd be dead in a few seconds anyway. I'd always imagined I would draw my last breath in a jet fighter's cockpit during an aerial battle, not in my own bedroom in a *Butch Cassidy and the Sundance Kid* style shoot-out. I looked around my bedroom one last time, thought about Liz, bit my lip, and inserted another magazine into my gun.

I shouted, "Say 'auf Wiedersehen' to your Nazi balls!" rolled on the floor and pulled the trigger several times at a fast pace. The M-25 thundered. Someone yelled in pain. Enemy bullets whizzed past my head.

Then everything went dark.

CHAPTER TWO

Commander Tarq watched his daughter walk towards him and both his hearts swelled with pride. Varina looked dashing in her white fleet uniform. All around, the Akakie war machine moved into high gear to defend against the incoming Xortaag invasion. Hundreds of shuttles and cargo ships were coming and going in preparation for the imminent battle. The sight of Alora Planetary Defense Force soldiers running around trying to be helpful made Tarq chuckle.

When she got close enough, Tarq tilted his head forward, and his two front antennae touched Varina's, sending a warm sensation throughout his body.

"Look at you, the fleet flagship's new helmsman," Tarq grinned. "You could not possibly have asked for a more prestigious assignment in your first year of service."

Varina narrowed her eyes. "You did not have anything to do with it, did you?"

"Of course not." Tarq tried to look offended. "Just in case you have forgotten, I am the commander of Special Operations Force and have nothing to do with the fleet."

"Really? 'I have nothing to do with the fleet?' You are going with that?" asked Varina. "You think I do not know *everyone* shakes in their boots when they hear your name?"

"I do not have a clue why. I am such a nice, witty and likable person!"

Above them, a space fighter nearly crashed into a cargo ship. The pilot avoided a collision by changing course in the last second. Tarq sighed. One day, the fleet personnel's inexperience would cause a serious problem. Fortunately, not today.

Pointing at the cargo ships and shuttles, Varina asked, "Is all this really necessary? Surely *Invincible* can deal with the Xortaag fleet on her own."

Tarq shrugged. "We figured as long as we were going to war for the first time in centuries, we should make it an overwhelming show of force. Plus, why not go all the way and put an end to this plague that has infected the universe for too long?"

"So for once I am off to save the galaxy, and you have to stay behind and watch," said Varina.

"Do not get cocky, young lady." Tarq feigned indignation. "Who do you think has devised our overall defensive strategy against the Xortaags?"

"I do not know. The fleet admirals?"

They both burst into laughter.

"Those guys cannot find their own antennae unless someone smarter holds their hands," said Tarq.

Varina laughed harder.

"And I am not going to stay behind," added Tarq. "I will be on board the command ship. There is no way I would miss our first battle in several generations."

"My shuttle is ready," said Varina. Their antennae touched one more time, and she walked away. Tarq waited until she waved goodbye and disappeared inside the shuttle.

Tarq went back to the Akakie command center. He sat at his station and brought up a holographic image of *Invincible*. Tarq had denied it when Varina asked, but he had pulled a lot of strings to get his daughter on that ship. With the enemy fleet getting closer to Alora, he was certain the safest place for a helmsman right now was the bridge of *Invincible*. Varina's old ship, *Dauntless*, was a fine vessel, but she did not have a fraction of *Invincible*'s firepower. Given how superior their technology was—The Xortaags did not even have starships, only single-seat space fighters —*Dauntless* was not in any real danger, but Tarq had decided to be cautious.

Tarq looked at *Invincible* with bright eyes. The golden ship was armed with several enormous, multi-barreled laser turrets, two blaster cannons powerful enough to vaporize a small moon, a few hundred missile launchers, and an impenetrable laser-based point-defense weapon system. Tarq's people had built her to be both magnificent and invulnerable; a giant, lethal killing machine serving as the embodiment of the Akakies' unparalleled technological superiority in the universe.

Tarq had dinner with *Invincible*'s captain a few evenings ago. During the meal, the captain bragged, "If the galaxy's best engineers combine the history's greatest achievements in military invention into a singular war machine, such a distinguished creation will pale into embarrassed insignificance beside my ship's awesome ingenuity and scientific superiority."

Tarq chuckled. The captain had never experienced an actual battle. The Akakies had lived in peace and prosperity for centuries, devoting their time and energy to art, enlightenment, technological advancements, and pulling pranks on each other. They were fondly known as galaxy's pranksters, and it was a point of personal pride for Tarq that he had a reputation for pulling off elaborate and sophisticated pranks. They lacked both the experience and the aptitude for war, but it was a moot point. With the Akakie science and technology significantly more advanced than the rest of the universe, nobody dared mess with them, and the few times that an enemy was stupid enough to try, Tarq's Special Operations Force had dealt with them with no need to involve the fleet.

Well, if the Xortaags want to commit collective suicide, we are happy to oblige, thought Tarq.

* * *

THE XORTAAG FLEET attacked three days later.

Aboard the Akakie command ship, Tarq touched the holographic display in front of him and zoomed on *Invincible*. With bulging eyes, he watched a crimson single-seat space fighter leading a few dozen similar but dark gray craft evade *Invincible*'s weapons and hammer her with energy bolts, causing dazzling explosions. Tarq gulped and clutched at his chest. The Xortaags' small space fighters were a lot more maneuverable and had much better weaponry than the Akakies' intelligence, gathered by Tarq's own agency, suggested. That triggered an ominous realization, given force by his recognition of who was piloting the blood-red vessel. Tarq knew that pilot. Everyone in the universe knew him.

He slumped onto his seat and buried his head in his hands. Everything he thought he knew about the enemy fleet's capabilities and tactics was wrong. He had been deceived. No, he had been a *fool*.

Even so, this is impossible, thought Tarq. *Invincible* was capable of unleashing a world-killing array of heavy weaponry. A thousand space fighters could not possibly be a match for her.

It was as if the pilot of the crimson space fighter heard Tarq's thoughts and decided to prove him wrong. The enemy vessel spit a deadly stream of laser bolts at *Invincible*, bringing about more explosions. Several sections of the starship were in flames.

Invincible lit space with countless white-hot energy bolts and filled it with thousands of missiles. The Xortaag vessels, and especially the devilish blood-red space fighter, zigzagged through the missiles and energy bolts with such skill that it made Tarq's blood boil with jealousy. One of the starship's blaster cannons came to life. It missed the targets and annihilated one of their own fleet's vessels instead.

What is the point of building the most advanced weapons in the galaxy if the people using them are so damned incompetent?

Biting his fingers, Tarq pictured Varina sitting at *Invincible*'s helm, desperately fighting for her life. He cursed under his breath and asked his assistant, "How did the Xortaag ships suddenly became so powerful? I personally observed their last two campaigns . . . Oh!"

Tarq paused for a second. "We saw what they wanted us to see."

Tarq's assistant, Lieutenant Barook, said, "My thoughts exactly." He pointed at the red fighter. "It seems you have finally met your match."

Staring at the crimson space fighter with burning hatred

in his eyes, Tarq murmured, "General Maada! I should have known defeating him would not be easy."

The contents of the file Tarq himself had prepared about General Maada flashed through his mind. Maada was the Xortaags' legendary warrior and military genius. The mere sight of his crimson space fighter would send shivers down the collective spine of the space-faring species throughout the galaxy. As the commander of the fleet, there was no need for Maada to lead the attack. He could have stayed safely in Xortaag's command ship and directed the assault from there. Instead, the General always deputized implementing strategy and coordinating the fleet to others and rushed to the frontline. Under Maada's command, the Xortaags had conquered more than forty planets, including a few far more technologically-advanced civilizations, exterminated all their inhabitants, and killed billions of sentient beings.

Underestimating the general had proved to be a fatal mistake.

"Stop biting your fingers. You are going to leave blood stains everywhere," said Barook.

Tarq looked down at his hands, and sure enough, he saw dark blue blood drops— drawn by his sharp teeth—on his fingertips. He wiped his fingers on the top part of one of his four legs and kept staring at his station's holographic display, desperately hoping for a miracle to save his daughter.

A frightened voice announced, "Here they come again!"

The crimson space fighter and its wingmen attacked *Invincible*, laser cannons blazing. Maada's vessel dove at high speed, pulled its nose up at the last moment, and did a firing run close to the starship, hitting her repeatedly from bow to stern. The gray space fighters followed it, raining deadly laser bolts on the Akakie ship. Energy bolt after energy bolt tore into her, scoring devastating hits. As soon as the Xortaag vessels veered off, a massive ball of multihued fire engulfed *Invincible*, and in a flash, she blew up into millions of minute glowing shards shimmering in dark space.

Five thousand sailors, vaporized. Just like that.

And Varina.

The thought of his daughter made Tarq feel his hearts were about to give out. His only child, who could not wait to grow up, was dead. Varina, who loved his pranks, and who never got tired of listening to the stories of how her father had saved the galaxy multiple times, was gone, and it was Tarq's fault.

The command ship was under attack. Someone shouted, "Brace for impact!" The vessel shook violently. Tarq did not pay any attention. He stared at what was left of Varina's ship, and overwhelming grief cut through him like a thousand sharp knives. Trying to use physical pain to block his mental anguish, he grabbed his two front antennae and pulled them so hard the agony made his vision blur. That worked. For a brief second.

His PDD beeped. It was a video message from Varina. With terror in her eyes, she said, "Father, we did our best," and then the message cut into static.

His daughter's last thought before being murdered by the Xortaags was how she had disappointed him.

The thought made his gut churn. He twisted his antennae as hard as he could. The severe pain pushed him to the brink of losing conscientiousness.

Barook approached him from behind, said, "This does

not help," and gently opened his fingers one by one, making him let go of his antennae.

A fleet lieutenant announced, "The fleet is retreating."

That was a diplomatic way of putting it: The Akakie ships were zooming away from the Xortaags at maximum speed. Despite the tragic situation, Tarq could not stifle a bitter chuckle.

"This is no 'retreat,' you moron," Tarq murmured under his breath, his voice so faint only Barook could hear him. "This is the worst every-Akakie-for-himself, save-your-own-exoskeleton, run-for-your-life tail-turning in history."

And the Akaki ships' crew could not even do that right. A starship veered off its course and ran into another one. Both ships blew up with a spectacular explosion. Tarq noticed the first ship to escape to safety was *Dauntless*. He covered his face in his hands and groaned. Barook put his hand around Tarq's shoulder in silence.

An explosion shook the bridge. Tarq looked at the damage reports coming in. For a moment, he wished Maada would come and finish what he has started. But then who would avenge Varina?

An admiral, wearing a white uniform almost identical to Tarq's but with fleet insignia, shouted into his communication device, "You cowards! Where do you think you are going? Get back in there. I will have all of you court-martialed for this!"

"It seems they are more afraid of Maada than you, Admiral," Tarq said, bleary-eyed.

The admiral took his frustration out on Tarq. With both pairs of his antennae standing erect in pure rage, he yelled, "And you, Commander Tarq. This is all your fault. You are supposed to be the greatest strategist ever lived. All this was your plan."

Tarq bared his teeth for one second, but he managed to control himself. Biting the Navy admiral's head off would not help anyone. He took a deep breath, steadied himself and replied, "And I paid the price for my mistake. Or has it escaped your attention that I have just lost my only daughter?"

"I have to point out the command ship is also, eh, retreating," said Barook.

The admiral froze; then he spun on his heels, ran to the ship's captain and started arguing with him.

Barook said, "It is safe to say you have made a lot of new enemies today."

With Varina gone, and their extinction in sight, that did not sound like such a big deal right now.

"I am the commander of Special Operations Force. Making enemies is literally in my job description," Tarq answered.

"Not to mention your affinity for playing practical jokes on highly influential people," said Barook. "You remember what you did to that poor admiral a while ago, don't you?"

Tarq chuckled bitterly. "You honestly think I remember everyone I have ever played a prank on?"

Tarq looked around the bridge. All other officers were glued to their various screens, watching what was happening in disbelief. He knew they were all thinking the same thing he was: Their catastrophic failure here probably meant the end of their species in the very near future. Unless they—more specifically Tarq himself, since he was the Akakies' chief strategist—came up with a brilliant plan and did it fast, they were about to suffer the same dreadful fate as the other races who had been in the Xortaags' way: enslavement for a few generations, followed by a comprehensive genocide, leaving every man, woman and youngling dead.

Tarq silently vowed, *not if I have anything to do with it.*

* * *

General Maada kicked the conference hall door open.

The four guards stationed inside the hall made no attempt to stop the general. They saluted, stared ahead and avoided eye contact.

"Wise choice," growled Maada. "I am certain you remember what happened the last time I stormed this hall."

The officer in charge, trepidation written all over his face, approached Maada. "General, with all due respect, His Highness is in the middle of an important meeting—"

Maada did not even bother to look at him. He drew his sidearm and shot the officer in the foot. The man made no sound. He folded, grabbed his foot and toppled to the floor. The smell of burned flesh filled Maada's nostrils. The guards did not move an inch and made no attempt to help their superior officer.

Pussies!

Deep inside Maada's brain, Crown Prince Mushgaana's voice said, "That was a bit too much."

Maada's anger coiled in his stomach. He had repeatedly asked Mushgaana to stay out of his head. He felt violated when Mushgaana, or any other members of the uniquely talented royal family, entered his mind and read his intimate thoughts.

Clenching his fists, Maada approached a big table at the center of the conference hall, where Mushgaana and five high-ranking diplomats who had just arrived from Tangaar were sitting. He ignored everyone and addressed the prince.

"I have just heard you have accepted the Akakies' peace proposal."

Mushgaana frowned. "Yes, I did."

"This is stupid," said Maada, raising his voice. "Have you lost your mind? We have the initiative now. We must push forward until we reach Kanoor."

One of the diplomats, a well-dressed young woman, sprung out of her seat. "You dare address His Highness in this manner?"

Maada glared at the woman. Nobody talked to him like that. His hand was moving towards his sidearm when another diplomat told the first one, "What are you doing? This is General Maada."

The woman's eyes widened, and she paled. She stuttered, "My apologies, General. In my defense, you look completely different in the news feeds."

Mushgaana laughed. "The general has no time for trivial matters like newsfeeds and interviews. We hired an actor to do that. But we did not want to scare people, so we decided to find someone without that scary beard and those terrifying scars."

The diplomats forced a laugh. Maada touched the scar on his left cheek. He was loyal to Mushgaana, but in moments like this shooting him in the face sounded very appealing.

Mushgaana continued, "Still, we cannot have you insult the commander of our fleet, can we?"

The diplomats sitting next to the woman pulled their chairs away from her. She leaned on the table to support her weight, lips shivering and face white. Everyone knew what was coming.

Maada stared at the crown prince, trying to get his attention, and thought, *Your Highness, if you want to melt people's brains for entertainment, it's your right, but I respectfully request you do not do it on my account.*

Anger flashed in Mushgaana's baby blue eyes, and for a second Maada wondered if the crown prince might hurt him. They had been in many successful campaigns together and formed a close friendship. Mushgaana was surely accustomed to his outbursts and did not take them personally. Then the general remembered Mushgaana could read his thoughts, and he blushed so hotly his olive skin became the same color as his fabled space fighter.

Mushgaana chuckled, obviously amused by his discomfort. The woman sank back into her seat, a palm pressed to her heart.

"The peace treaty is a ruse," said Mushgaana as if nothing had happened. "You know the Akakies are technologically much more advanced than we are, and our intelligence suggests the fleet we destroyed on Alora's orbit was probably one-third of their total forces. We caught them by surprise this time, but the next encounter will not be so easy. The treaty will give us the opportunity to do three things: reverse-engineer a few of the ships we have captured and build a new fleet, attack easier targets, and replenish and expand our current fleet. Once we are better prepared, we will invade the Akakie homeworld."

"Do you have a new target designated?" asked Maada.

With a flick of his wrist, Mushgaana brought up a holographic image. "Right there. The blue planet, third from the sun. And it is only the first of seven targets we have identified and are planning to hit one after another. Let me finish this meeting. After that, you and I must sit together and start planning our new campaign."

Maada glared at the crown prince. Mushgaana should

not have made the decision without consulting him first, but as the crown prince, it was his prerogative.

"Before you leave, let me share a military secret with these gentlemen and the lady," said Mushgaana. "A decade ago, when the confrontation with the Akakies started to look inevitable, General Maada figured they might be watching us. In our last three military campaigns, he made our fleet perform far below their ability. We took some losses in those battles, but it was worth catching the Akakies with their pants down."

The diplomats looked at Maada with admiration in their eyes. That made him uncomfortable. He bowed his head, turned and walked toward the hall entrance. The officer he had shot earlier was receiving medical attention. Maada stopped by him and said, "Sorry about that."

Grimacing in pain, the officer replied, "Not a problem, General. It is not the first time, and to be honest, it is kind of an honor."

Outside the hall, Maada rubbed the scar on his face and thought, *I should really learn how to control my temper*.

He nearly jumped out of his socks when, in his brain, Mushgaana said, "Have you ever considered therapy?"

CHAPTER THREE

A nauseating stench assaulted my nostrils as soon as I came to.

I was in a small prison cell, alone, wearing an orange jumpsuit. The cell was empty, except for a narrow, hard platform which was supposed to be a bed, a toilet, and a sink. It smelled of urine and vomit.

I couldn't remember when I'd passed out.

My right thigh was bandaged. With a slight limp, I walked to the cell's barred door and looked outside. I saw nothing but a few empty cells. I knew where I was: the Coffin. Zheng's infamous maximum security prison where SCTU imprisoned captured Resistance members along with the most dangerous death row inmates on the planet.

I sat on the bed and tried to process my situation. It was disorienting. One moment, I was at the top of the world. I had a career I loved, I was rich and famous, and I was in a loving relationship with the most amazing woman I'd ever met. Now I was on death row. Helping a member of the Resistance carried the death sentence. I'd helped their leader and shot a few SCTU agents to boot. They'd probably sentence me to five consecutive executions, each carried out by a different method. I was confident they would even invent a couple of new methods just for me.

It was not the thought of dying that tormented me. Not because I wasn't scared of death. If I had sat down and thought about it, I'd have freaked out. But I was very good at avoiding this particular topic. As a fighter pilot and veteran of two wars, I'd faced death several times in the past. Each experience had made the next one just a bit easier. What gnawed at my brain was losing everything I treasured. I thought about Liz, wondering if she'd survived the attack. Thinking about her possible demise caused an almost physical reaction—as if a limb had been torn from my body.

I'd met Liz at a party thrown by another pilot in my squadron. I'd had a few drinks and was tipsy, so at first, I didn't notice the gorgeous, Afro-Hispanic woman with the fancy British accent passionately discussing some political issue with a group of admiring young men, who I was certain didn't care about her political views. What first caught my attention wasn't her long thick black curly hair, her very expensive canary-yellow body-hugging dress, her smooth coffee-bean skin or her long, long legs—and I was a sucker for long legs. I noticed her when she said, "The needs of the many outweigh the needs of the few."

I'd always said if I ever found a girl who could quote Mr. Spock, I'd marry her in a heartbeat.

One of the men talking to her nodded and smiled like an old, wise guru. "Ah, Aristotle. How very fitting."

I approached the group and said, "Or the one."

Liz looked at me approvingly and repeated, "Or the one." Then her amazing eyes—dark brown with flecks of gold—widened. "You're Jim Harrison!"

The other guys gave me an exasperated look that told

me they knew they'd lost any chance they might've had with Liz the moment I walked in. I got this particular look all the time.

"The book or the movie?" I asked.

She smiled, opened her bag and took out her PDD. She touched the screen a few times and gave it to me. I looked at the screen and saw my book's cover. I read out loud, "*Nights of Thunder; the Adventures of Air Force's Youngest Flying Ace.*"

I winked at her. "That's me all right."

A few months before the Unification, China, Korea, and Japan, who didn't want to join, formed their own alliance called the East Asia Coalition. You couldn't have a United Earth if a third of the population didn't sign up. The provisional government of Earth imposed severe economic sanctions on them. The Eastern Coalition responded by going to war with the rest of the world. The war ended with both sides making major concessions, and the Unification became official.

During the war, my squadron was deployed in the Philippines. I shot down thirty-two enemy aircraft. I was only twenty-five at the time. Later, I wrote a book about my experiences during the war. As luck would have it, seven months after the war and right when my book was published, a dictator seized power in one of the ex-Soviet Union republics and declared independence. The United Earth Air Force sent its most decorated fighter pilots to show the dictator the error of his ways, and I ended up adding another sixteen kills to my tally in less than two weeks (yeah, I was that good). This helped my book sell a few million copies and got me a movie deal, on top of a couple of documentaries that had already been made about me. I was a big deal.

I gave her PDD back. "Did you like it?"

"Yes. You're funny, Mr. War Hero. But I thought you were kind of cocky and full of yourself. Now is your chance to prove me wrong."

Who was I, as a perfect Southern gentleman, to prove a beautiful woman wrong?

"I also worked in your movie as a stunt pilot," she said.

I blinked. "You are a stuntwoman?"

"And an acrobatic pilot," she said. "World champion in woman's category four years in a row."

"Wow," I said, tipping my imaginary hat. That was almost as impressive as my own achievements as a pilot. Almost.

We talked a lot that night. We had a lot in common. Both of us were movie buffs, and we loved the classics. We were madly in love with flying and had weird senses of humor. And we were both rich.

"Well, my family is," she said. "My parents were originally from Cuba. They moved to the US when I was four. My mother passed away shortly after, and my father sent me to a private boarding school in England, or rather what the British call a public school.

That explained the sexy accent.

"Why England? Why not right here in the U.S.?" I asked.

"To avoid seeing me even during the holidays, I guess."

I blinked again. This was happening a lot tonight. "What kind of a father doesn't want to see his daughter?"

"The abusive, manipulative asshole type."

Her answer baffled me, but I was uncomfortable prying into her relationship with her father at that moment.

"Later on, I enraged my father by becoming an acrobatic pilot rather than the CEO of one of his companies and eventually marrying into money, so he cut me off. Still, I make enough money to live comfortably," she added, straightening a curly lock of her hair with one slim finger.

"You know, you're too good to be true," I told her. "Too perfect. What's the catch? What *is* wrong with you?"

"Well, I have an impulse-control disorder," she answered, sipping her wine.

I waved my hand dismissively. "It's nothing. My therapist says I have primarily obsessional obsessive-compulsive disorder, aka Pure O."

She gave me a level look. "I'm an acrobatic pilot, and I can't control my impulses. It could get me killed one day."

"You know what my condition is like?" I asked. "It's like Venom's stuck in my brain, but unlike the movies, he doesn't give me any superpowers, and he never says something supportive or witty. He complains nonstop and predicts all sorts of negative outcomes. Sometimes I'd happily give one of my eyes for five minutes of peace and quiet inside my own brain."

"Venom? Really? You have more of a Peter Parker vibe."

I laughed and tried to change the subject. "So, besides watching movies, what else do you do for fun?"

"Plenty. Dance, tennis. In my spare time, I run my own charity, collecting donations for New York's orphanages."

I heard "tennis," and the last part flew right over my head. "How about a few sets?"

The next weekend, after I beat her in several consecutive sets and pissed her off in the process, she challenged me to a swimming match. I was a very good swimmer, but after we jumped into the water, all I could see was two long dark brown arms moving away from me faster than the Road Runner running away from Wile E. Coyote.

When I reached the other side of the pool, she told me, "I'm going to rub this in your face for the rest of your life."

I had a hard time breathing, but I still managed to say, "Does it mean you think we'll be together for the rest of my life?"

She laughed but seemed unsure of what to say.

"Is it a bad time to ask you to dinner?" I asked.

"Of course not," she said. "Swimming burns a lot of calories. I need a chocolate sundae."

We went for dinner. She ordered a salad and a huge chocolate sundae. I didn't believe she'd eat it all, but she did. I liked the way she licked chocolate syrup off her lips. I liked her little sigh of contentment at the end. I guess I ate too, but I couldn't remember after I went home later that night.

We started dating. The more I spent time with Liz, the more I liked what I saw. She was a firecracker, a woman as soft-hearted as she was hot-blooded, equally at ease sipping champagne at a fancy restaurant and playing a monster-killing VR game with me. She was a glorious contradiction. She made some people uneasy with her volatile personality, but I didn't mind. I liked to kid her I'd never have to cheat because I felt like I had two girlfriends. She'd roll her eyes at that.

She moved in with me on our six-month anniversary, right before we went to Cancun to celebrate the occasion. She beat me at swimming there too, but I didn't care. One day, on the beach, after we'd swum to the point of exhaustion, she lay on top of me, trickled sand on my chest, and said "Your eyes are as blue as . . ."

"The sea?"

"I was going to say the blue margaritas at the hotel bar."

I realized I was in love at that moment.

We'd been living happily together until Kurt showed up and everything went to hell.

* * *

ON THE THIRD day of my imprisonment, my guards gave me a brown suit to wear, let me take a shower and shave, put me in chains, and took me before the judge.

The courtroom was the size of Grand Central Terminal's main concourse, and it was filled with Zheng's people: government officials, reporters from government news agencies, SCTU agents and security guards. There must have been hundreds of them. When I entered, all the people in the first few rows of seats turned to look at me with hatred. It wasn't something I was used to. People liked me. I was that kind of guy.

Under the hostile stares of the spectators, I joined Kurt and Allen, who were wearing suits and chains identical to mine and sitting on the defendants' seats. Kurt looked at me with guilt in his gray eyes and said something about not meaning for any of this to happen, but I didn't register his words because I spotted Liz in the courtroom. My vision tunneled, and I stopped paying attention to anything else.

Liz, wearing a simple white skirt suit, sat on the other side of the courtroom, surrounded by a few tough-looking female guards. At least she wasn't in chains. Someone had probably decided having a beautiful woman in chains didn't look good in front of the cameras, or maybe Zheng's people were trying to project an image of leniency.

Liz was scared, but no one but me would notice. She looked composed, but her face had never been that still. She was always smiling, mugging, glancing here and there, not like this, like a goddamn black Madonna, like a statue. Liz saw me, and her face came alive. She stood up as if she wanted to come to me, but one of her guards pushed her back. A look of despair and fury crossed her face. She kicked the guard in the shin so hard the sound of the impact reverberated in the courtroom. The guard looked like she wanted to attack her, but with all the cameras in the room, she controlled herself and limped away.

I waved at Liz and tried to smile, hating myself for dragging her into this. Should I have told her I knew Kurt? It wouldn't have made any difference. I'd never have expected him to show up. She wouldn't have let it stop her from moving in with me.

The court proceedings started after I arrived. We found out security cameras had caught Kurt entering my neighborhood, and later a surveillance drone's footage had shown him entering my house. The judge, an old, fat man with rubbery lips and gin blossoms, asked me, "Major Harrison. You are a decorated air force officer. Why on earth did you decide to help a known terrorist?"

Kurt stood up. "Your Honor, I forced this couple to help me using chemical Scopolamine. The court should consider letting them go."

I stood up too.

A thought in the back of my mind, my very own personal Venom, said, "Be quiet. Maybe it'll work. If there's a one percent chance you and Liz don't end up in a coffin, you should take it."

He had a point. I'd heard of cases getting thrown out of court due to the so-called "Scopolamine Defense." But there was no way I'd stay silent and let my friend take the fall for what I'd done of my own accord. It was bad enough that I let him down the last time. Plus, I was sure I was dead anyway. I might as well keep my integrity.

I opened my mouth to protest, but Liz beat me to it. Her cultured voice cut through the courtroom like a knife. "That's not true. We helped him, and we'd do it again. You expected us to let a man just bleed to death? Are you not human?"

That's my girl.

It took the judge only a few minutes to make his decision. He got up, leaned forward on his bench, and announced, "By the authority vested in me by Chancellor Zheng, I hereby sentence Kurt von der Hagen and Allen Johnson, the infamous terrorists, to death. Major Jim Harrison and Elizabeth Lopez, among the most privileged and respected of our citizens, shamefully abandoned their duty. They will receive the same penalty for aiding and abetting known terrorists."

A loud murmur swept the courtroom. Everyone had started to talk at the same time. Someone started clapping, a few more people followed suit, and soon thunderous applause filled the courtroom. The judge smiled and bowed his head to the crowd.

I wondered what the big deal was. This outcome was so predictable I felt absolutely nothing. I'd known I was a dead man since I woke up in my cell three days ago, and I had enough time in solitary to accept this fact. This kangaroo court was nothing but a charade. "Big freaking surprise that is," I said.

Kurt and Allen didn't seem too bothered either. Allen yawned and pretended he was looking at a wristwatch he wasn't wearing. Kurt tapped his fingers on the table and looked heavenward. The three of us were the very picture of nonchalance.

Liz, on the other hand, obviously disagreed with the judge's ruling and decided to show her displeasure. In the blink of an eye, she jumped over the table in front of her, managed to evade her guards like the stunt pilot she was, pulled her skirt above her knees, and ran towards the judge's bench, fast as a cheetah.

The judge gasped and took a step backward. He tripped over his gown, lost his balance and disappeared behind his bench.

Holding back a "Liz, no!" scream, I jumped to my feet. Kurt and Allen did the same. Several guards drew their weapons and surrounded us. One of them shouted, "Freeze! Don't move!"

"Redundant much?" I told him.

A court security guard tackled Liz. They both went down, but she was on her feet a second later. Another guard confronted her. She kicked him in the balls. With a comical expression on his face, the man grabbed his privates, opened and closed his mouth twice without making a sound and fell to the floor.

That's why all her guards are female.

In chains, the three of us weren't able to do anything to help Liz. I watched helplessly and hoped the cameras would keep the guards from hurting her. I gripped my chains so hard my knuckles went white. Allen took a few steps towards the guards. Kurt pulled him back.

Liz's own guards caught up with her and grabbed her from behind. She shouted, "Let me go!" and tried to wriggle free. They didn't hurt her or anything, just dragged her towards her seat. I breathed a sigh of relief.

Kurt told me, "Is this what you meant by Dr. Jekyll and Mr. Hyde?"

"Right? She's an enigma," I said. "She's so feminine, and she talks like Mary Poppins, but she pulls stunts like this."

Allen, looking with admiration at Liz, who was struggling with her guards and refusing to go back to her seat, asked, "How do you deserve a woman like that?"

I could see Allen still hadn't forgiven me for what he called "dumping my best friend at first sign of trouble." I answered, "In case you haven't noticed, I'm super charming. How's your ex-better half, by the way?"

Allen, malice dripping from his voice, said, "Last I checked, the fat bitch was still wasting oxygen. Thanks for asking though."

The guards pushed us back to our seats. Another judge replaced the first one, who had banged his fat head against the floor and lost consciousness. The new judge set the executions for two weeks later at dawn.

"Why don't they get this over with as soon as possible?" I asked Kurt.

"It's a trap," said Kurt. "They hope the Resistance will try to save Allen and me. But it won't work."

"Why not?"

"Because I'll get the word out that if any of the Resistance members are dumb enough to fall for it, I'd hit a guard unconscious, grab his gun and shoot them myself," said Kurt.

My guards dragged me away. "See you on the other side," I told Kurt.

"Welcome to the Resistance," he answered.

I tried to catch one last glimpse of Liz before they took me out of the courtroom but had no luck.

* * *

THE COFFIN - JANUARY 11, 2078

WAITING on death row makes you think about your mortality, thought Kurt, lying on his cell's hard, narrow bunk.

"How very philosophical," he murmured.

All his adult life, achieving global peace by uniting the world under one government had been Kurt's mission. This was his father's dream for over thirty years, and Kurt had grown up listening to him talk about it with consuming passion.

Given that ever-increasing global trade, environmental issues that didn't respect borders, and global social media had made national borders less and less relevant, Thomas believed humanity's only way forward was to face the truth: *nothing* was truly local. Earth was an interconnected ecosystem, and so was the human society.

Thomas had assembled a stellar international group of scholars, legal minds and politicians. It surprised nobody that Kurt joined his old man's team as soon as he graduated from university. The father and son fought alongside each other for a united Earth. It wasn't easy. It cost Kurt's father three decades of his life, and along the way, he inadvertently caused a short but bloody war that claimed thousands of lives. But together, with the help of countless other visionaries, they managed to achieve this dream against impossible odds.

And then Zheng had shown up, killed Kurt's parents and ruined everything.

Zheng! Just thinking about him made Kurt's skin crawl.

Kurt would've happily sacrificed his life to put a bullet in that man's head, but he was too well-protected. Kurt had to content himself with killing his henchmen. He was positive if he kept pushing, Zheng would fall at the end, but now he was caught, to be executed the next day, and Zheng had won again. He was leaving the world a failure. Despair pierced his heart like a rattlesnake's fang.

Approaching footsteps echoed in Kurt's cell. He glanced up. Zheng stood in front of his cell, looking in at him, with a predatory smile on his face.

Blood rushed to Kurt's brain with such force he was disoriented for a few seconds. He jumped off the bunk and thought about attacking the chancellor, but he wouldn't have been able to reach him through the bars.

"Hi. Kurt. Can I call you Kurt?" said Zheng.

"It depends. Can I call you a fucking piece of shit?" answered Kurt.

Zheng shrugged off the insult. "I just wanted to meet the pesky little insect who killed so many of my subordinates face to face."

Kurt wished Jim were here. He'd have the perfect comeback. Something from a movie, probably.

When Kurt didn't respond, Zheng continued, "For what it's worth, I'm sorry your mother was killed in the explosion meant for your dad. I met her a few times back in the day. She was a lovely woman. Too good for your father, certainly. Did you know she was supposed to be somewhere else that night? Unfortunately, by the time I noticed she was in the car, our plans were under way, and if I'd hesitated then, I'd be on the other side of these bars now, or dead. I had no choice but to flip the switch."

Kurt went pale. "You personally carried out the assassination?"

Zheng smiled. "Of course. Your father was my greatest enemy. My Moby Dick. I couldn't have some faceless goon kill him, could I? Oh, you must really hate me right now."

Kurt's nostrils flared. "Let's find out. Step inside."

Zheng laughed. "Why spoil the party? I have big plans for you tomorrow. I've arranged for cameramen, showgirls, and fireworks, just for you."

His eyes blazing with fury, Kurt stepped closer to the bars and said, "Listen to me and listen carefully. You'll pay for what you did. I'll kill you, and not with a bomb or a sniper rifle. I'll kill you up close and personal, looking into those fucking ugly holes in your skull you call eyes."

Much to Kurt's satisfaction, Zheng shuddered, ever so slightly. The dictator shrugged, turned and left without saying another word.

* * *

The Coffin - January 12, 2078

Elizabeth, kneeling in her cell and holding her head down, prayed alongside the Coffin's chaplain. "To you, Lord, I lift up my soul," she whispered.

A female guard banged on the cell door and said, "It's almost time."

The chaplain stood up, looked at Elizabeth with dull eyes and said, "May God be with you, my child."

"I've written farewell letters to my siblings," said Liz. "Could you please make sure they receive the letters?"

"Of course."

Liz gave him four envelopes. "I've also written a letter to Jim. I didn't want to destroy it, but I don't want the guards to find it either. Can you keep it for me? You must promise you won't read it."

"I promise."

"And don't forget watering my plant," Elizabeth told him.

The chaplain nodded, picked up the Chinese evergreen Elizabeth kept in her cell, and walked out.

This was the last time I prayed in my life, thought Elizabeth. The thought made her dizzy. Her vision blurred, and her knees went weak. She pushed away her fear as she'd been doing all her life. Even now—when she was about to die—she wouldn't surrender. She refused to.

Three prison guards entered the cell. Elizabeth pointed at the chains they were carrying. "Are those necessary? I won't bite."

One of the guards answered, "We aren't taking any chances with you after you bit poor Melisa's ear off. I bet you're still flossing her ear out of your teeth."

Elizabeth crossed her arms over her chest. "I don't normally behave like that. She insulted my boyfriend."

She wanted to cry as soon as she mentioned Jim. "Stiff upper lip," she whispered to herself.

The guards put the chains on Elizabeth's hands and feet. Waves of desperation swept through her. Jeez, but she missed Jim's smile, his wisecracks, his calming presence, his infuriating tendency to take nothing seriously. Tears welled in her eyes. She clamped her lower lip in her teeth to keep it from trembling. No way would she allow these assholes to see her cry. She wiped her tears with the back of her jumpsuit sleeve, but they kept coming. To her surprise, one of the guards gave her a white handkerchief. The others averted their eyes in an obvious attempt to give her some privacy. The unexpected decency touched her. She wondered how much choice these guards had about their jobs. Whether they'd worked in the prison before Zheng's takeover, seen the class of prisoner change, and not known what to do about it. For a moment she wanted to ask but remembered she had fewer choices than anyone. She cried harder, the tears running down her cheeks. The guards gave her a few minutes, and then one of them gently said, "We must get going now."

Elizabeth bit her lip and pulled herself together. She nodded to the guards, wiped her tears again and followed them to the corridor.

It was a shame she couldn't give Jim his Christmas present. It was a life-size dancing Baby Groot that could detect music and dance to the rhythm. She thought it was the cutest thing she'd seen in a while. Jim would've loved it.

Hopefully, they'd meet again. Jim was agnostic, but at heart, he was a good man. Surely the Lord would take that into consideration.

Elizabeth and her guards left the cell and entered the corridor. A large woman with a bandage over her right ear called out from another cell, "Goodbye, crazy girl." There was a hint of respect in her voice.

Elizabeth smiled faintly. "Sorry about your ear, Melisa."

"Nah. My own damn fault," said the woman. "Should know who I'm messing with. But, you know, you do look like you were born with a silver spoon up your arse."

I woke to what was most likely my last glimpse of sunlight. A shaft of light entered my cell for a few minutes every day at dawn. It was the only charm that the filthy cell could boast of. I touched my chest and wondered if the sharp pain near my heart meant a broken rib. Odds were I wouldn't live long enough to find out. Certainly not long enough to heal.

I hadn't just sat on my hands waiting for my appointment with the guillotine. During the first ten days in prison, I tried to start a riot, but one of the people I talked to turned out to be a snitch, and the guards nipped that in the bud. Then I tried to break out. Twice. I got caught both times. After the second attempt, the prison officials got fed up with my antics. The guards beat me up until I wished I were dead and threw me back in solitary for the rest of the last week.

Expecting the guards to arrive any minute, I sat on the bed in the best imitation of Lotus Pose I could manage and tried to look relaxed. My OCD mind, however, went in a hundred different directions.

Waiting on death row for execution, knowing the exact day and time of your death, was agonizing psychological torture. I considered myself a brave man, but I couldn't eat and barely slept the last few days.

It wasn't just thinking about death which became more and more unavoidable the closer I got to the execution date that clawed at my soul. All men must die, after all. It was thinking about my life, the mistakes I'd made, and the things I could've done differently that was killing me, no pun intended. If I had known I would die before my twenty-ninth birthday, I'd have made a lot of different decisions. I would've paid more attention to religion and spirituality instead of labeling myself agnostic and not even bothering to spend a little time thinking about life after death. I should've visited my parents' graves more often. We were not close. My father was so consumed with his aspiration for global peace he didn't have time for anything else in his life, and mom was schizophrenic, living in a different world where I didn't exist. She'd died in a long-term care facility, surrounded by a collection of dolls she had conversations with about sex, cannibalism and demonic possession. For all intents and purposes, I'd grown up an orphan, but this was no excuse. And I'd have proposed to Liz much earlier, even though if I'd done it too early, she might have said no.

I was in jail for only two weeks, but that was enough for something to change in me. It was one thing to hear about the regime's brutality while living comfortably in a bubble; it was a different thing to experience it firsthand. They kept Kurt, Allen and me separated, but we could talk to the other prisoners. I met fathers who had lost their sons under torture, or whose daughters had been executed by a firing squad. I met husbands whose wives had committed suicide in jail or died trying to defend them against Zheng's goons. And there were children in jail, lots of them, imprisoned for "crimes" ranging from carrying messages for the Resistance to throwing rocks at security forces. The depth of human misery I witnessed in jail had been haunting my dreams, whenever I could actually sleep.

I wondered why I didn't have any of the problems I'd seen in the movies about jail. Things involving showers and soap. I chose not to interpret this as an affront to my attractiveness. I was quite a catch: tall and muscular, with crystal blue eyes, light brown curly hair, and a square chin. Other inmates left me alone because I looked like I could defend myself. The fact that everyone knew I was associated with Kurt and Allen and nobody wanted to mess with those two probably played a small role too.

The cell door opened. Four guards carrying assault rifles and heavy chains walked in. They wore dark brown uniforms and looked grim. I knew all of them. These were the same assholes who beat me up a few days ago.

My stomach twisted so hard I would've thrown up if I'd eaten anything in the last few days. Being a few minutes away from execution, all I really wanted to do was to curl up in a fetal position and hide under my blanket, but I'd be damned if I showed these SOBs any weakness. I stretched, smiled and with a light tone said, "Is it time for the necktie party already? Cool. I was getting bored in here."

One of the guards looked at the wall behind my bed where I'd carved my name a million times using a screw I'd loosened from my bed frame, covering most of the wall. He grunted and rolled his eyes.

"Take that, you bastards," I said, clasping my hands behind my head. "I'd like to see the bill for repainting this wall. Just wait until you find the three-foot hole I've dug under the bed. Another year and I would escape this joint through a tunnel."

I was whistling when the guards dragged me to the prison yard. Kurt and Allen were already there, both in chains. They had sunken eyes and various bruises and scars on their faces, especially Allen, who kept getting into unwinnable fights with the guards and getting his ass kicked. Still, Kurt was clean shaven, except for his ridiculous goatee, and his Disney-princess hair looked like he'd just been to a barber. I had no idea how he did it. My own curly hair made me look like George of the Jungle.

The whole place was flooded with heavily armed SCTU soldiers. There was at least a few hundred of them. Some twenty government officials whom I'd seen in the court stood together at a corner. A cameraman was standing behind our guards, pointing his camera at us. One of the guards told me, "Smile. You are on camera. Your execution's being televised live."

Allen growled, "I hope my daughter isn't watching this."

"Or Liz," I said.

Another guard, a tall man with wide shoulders, overheard that. "You don't need to worry about that. She'll be executed at the same time as you."

"Cheer up. Maybe you can continue tapping that ass in the afterlife," another guard added.

The fucking guards laughed like it was the funniest joke ever. Anger rose in my chest. I wasn't a martial arts expert, and even if I'd been, it would've done me little good with my hands and legs in restraints. But I was fast, and the stupid guard had turned his head, looking at his friends, seeking their approval. I took two baby steps—literally, because of the restraints—and when he turned to look at me, I head-butted him in the face. He grabbed his nose and fell to the ground. Another guard swung his gun, butt forward. I tried to duck, but he caught me just under the nose. Being in chains didn't stop Allen from hurling himself at the second guard. He was brought down by three others using batons. Kurt rushed in and tried to stop them from beating the old man to death before they got the chance to execute him.

The guards pushed us in front of a wall full of bullet holes. There were fresh bloodstains on the ground. I heaved as the smell of blood hit me. The guards blindfolded me with a piece of dirty cloth.

"Great!" I said. "Now I have to worry about an eye infection on top of everything else."

Allen said, "Can I get a cigarette?" Apparently, he

didn't get one because he yelled, "You monsters! You deny a man his dying wish?

I spit blood out of my mouth and felt my teeth with my tongue. The mind-numbing pain told me I had a broken one.

I struggled with my bonds, trying to set myself free. With the prison yard full of soldiers, it'd be no use, but I could charge them in one last act of defiance, with the whole world watching. That would show Zheng he couldn't use our public execution to intimidate others. When I couldn't find a way out of my binds, I tried to remove the blindfold to at least stare my executioners in the eyes, but that didn't work either, so I decided to use the best weapon in my arsenal.

I yelled, "Come on, you cowards. Open my hands and let's go a few rounds. I'll take you all, your bastard of a chancellor included! I'll even let you tie my right hand behind my back!"

There was a reason my nickname was the Fighter Pilot with the Mouth.

I got a gun butt in my stomach for my efforts. All air left my lungs with a whoosh. That forced me to stop.

Kurt humorlessly chuckled. "Jim, didn't you say something about not wanting to be put up against the same wall as me?" He added, "For what it's worth, I'm sorry I got you and Elizabeth involved in this."

"Water under the bridge," I said. "To be honest, now that I'm going to die, I have only two regrets. One's that I didn't join the Resistance when you asked me to."

A steady rhythm of boot heels got closer as a group of soldiers marched toward us. The firing squad. They were coming to kill me. Waves of desperation swept through me, and my heart decided to hide behind my stomach.

"And the other one?" Kurt asked.

For a second, I didn't remember what we were talking about; then I grabbed at it like a life raft. "The next *Star Trek* will be released next month, and I'm going to miss it."

I could hear astonishment in Kurt's voice. "Weren't you about to propose the night I came to your house?"

Exactly what I'd been doing my damnedest not to think about. If I did, I'd break down and beg the guards to let Liz go, saying I'd do anything they wanted. I might even have burst into tears. On live TV. Everything I'd done in the past few minutes was to prevent that outcome. I very much preferred to die with some dignity.

Venom went on a rant like there was no tomorrow. "You got her killed. You found the kindest and warmest girl in the world, and you managed to get her dragged in front of a firing squad. Well done!"

God damn it!

I had a huge lump in my throat, making it difficult to breathe. My lower lip started to quiver, and my breath quickened. If the devil had come to me at that moment and said he would save Liz if I agreed to serve him for a million years and then go to hell for eternity, I'd have accepted with gratitude. I'd have agreed to anything just to make the pain I felt for dragging her into this go away.

I said, "Yeah, that too."

"You are back-ass weird," said Allen.

I'd normally deflect a comment like that with a joke or a wise-ass comment like "Amen to that" or "Normal is boring," but I was in a very bad mood, and I'd never liked Allen much. When I was a teenager and he was Thomas's head of security, I was afraid of him. He was always grumpy and menacing, and Canadians were supposed to be nice. I remembered one of his famous quotes was "Fighter pilots are pussies. A real man kills his enemies in hand-to-hand combat while staring into the whites of their eyes."

I was sure he'd stolen that quote from the Klingons.

It was funny what details my mind chose to remember right before death. My OCD brain was skipping around like a kitten on meth. *Don't think about . . . you know. Don't think about her.*

"I'm weird?" I retorted. "Isn't your nickname the Butcher of Macau?"

"Butcher? Huh! It's an exaggeration," said Allen. "There were less than fifty people in that casino, every single one of them an associate of Zheng's."

"Plus the casino's employees who got caught in the crossfire."

Someone shouted, "Ready!"

"Didn't you get rich and famous by killing a bunch of Japanese people?" Allen said.

The same voice continued, "Set!"

I shouted, "Enemy combatants! Not innocent bystanders!"

"Really? You guys are doing this now?" said Kurt. He talked to Allen in French, which he knew I didn't understand. If he were telling him to shut up, it didn't work. The old man said, "Nobody's innocent, especially a spoiled brat working for the enemy's air force."

Good thing we were about to die; otherwise, I would've killed Allen.

"Aim!"

At that moment, it finally dawned on me: I was going to miss out on a lot. All the plans I had for the rest of my life had been wiped off the board. I'd never fly again. I wouldn't get married. I wouldn't father a child and have a family of my own. Hell, I didn't even get to propose. Worst of all, I'd never again have the chance to see the woman I was planning to do all these with. Regret burned through my soul like fire, frying up my already worn-out brain, making me forget where I was for a merciful moment.

"Vive la révolution," said Kurt.

"Fire!"

Liz, I'm so sorry, I thought right before the world sank into darkness.

CHAPTER FOUR

Flying his Deathbringer in Alora's orbit, General Maada thought, *Finally, time for action.*

He had been restless for a while now, but the invasion of their new target, called Earth in the dominant local language, could not have started before the first phase of Alora's colonization was complete. The fleet was not able to leave before the new colony could protect itself against enemy attacks. Moreover, they needed samples of Earth's inhabitants, "humans," to calibrate the Voice of God. Their scout ship had just returned from Earth, carrying a few dozen samples.

The cloud of Deathbringers rising from the ground was a sight to behold. It filled Maada's chest with pride. This was the strongest fleet in the universe: forty thousand space fighters, every single one of them deadly. The Death-bringers flew in close formation, reminding him of how Zandzoks took to the air. He remembered watching the deadly birds of prey as a boy, feeling a kinship he understood even then was important. Maada wasn't afraid of how big they were or that they'd been known to steal babies. He only wanted to be that powerful himself.

And now he was, as were all the space fighter pilots under his command, most of whom had followed him for a very long time in his mission to make the Xortaag kingdom the strongest and most feared entity in the universe.

As soon as the Deathbringers landed in the transport ships' hangar bays, the fleet would be on its way, and soon the Xortaags' already vast kingdom would have a new colony.

A short while later, Maada landed his crimson Death-bringer on Mushgaana's command ship hangar deck, which was much smaller than a transporter but still could take in a few hundred space fighters. He climbed out of his fighter. Mushgaana was waiting for him in the hanger bay, wearing the royal family's battle uniform—a knee-length black robe with a dagger strap. The crown prince had honored him by coming here instead of waiting on the bridge.

"Welcome aboard, General," said Mushgaana. "Ready to add another planet to the list of your conquests?"

"No, Your Highness," Maada saluted. "I am ready to add another planet to *your* list of conquests. I am but a humble servant of the kingdom."

Mushgaana smiled. "Well said, but you are anything but humble. You remember I can read your thoughts, right? I know every time you disagree with one of my strategic decisions, you are thinking about choking me to death." His hands rose, miming choking. His two personal guards standing behind him looked uneasy. "I am sure you will do that if one day I make a decision you judge is against the kingdom's best interest."

"The very thought is high treason," answered Maada, irritated at being reminded of Mushgaana's telepathic powers. It gave the prince a weapon he could never counter. "You would be well within your rights to have me executed on the spot."

Mushgaana shook his head. "All this time we have been together, and you still cannot take a joke. You might be the scariest military genius in the galaxy, General, but your sense of humor leaves a lot to be desired. Sometimes I wish I had an Akakie on my staff. Those guys are really funny."

Maada did not smile. He neither understood nor approved of the crown prince's sense of humor. While they were walking towards the ship's bridge, he said, "Speaking of the Akakies, something has been bothering me. When you were signing the peace treaty, one of them was standing in the back of the room. He was wearing a white uniform with no insignia, and he looked very pleased with himself, like someone whose plans have succeeded."

"You can read the Akakies' facial expressions now?" Mushgaana chuckled. "I didn't notice anything in his thoughts. Maybe he was just happy about the treaty?"

"With all due respect, Your Highness, you weren't paying attention to him. If it had occurred to me at that time, I would have asked you to read him. No. This was the look of a predator sizing up his prey. Trust me. I would know. Whoever he is, he is up to something."

"He is an Akakie. What is he going to do? Make us all laugh to death? You are getting paranoid in your old age, my friend."

"You should not underestimate the Akakies," said Maada. "Do you remember a few decades ago they extermi-nated the entire population of a planet while broadcasting it for the whole galaxy to watch?"

"If memory serves, they did not actually do it themselves. They hacked into the computer system of the enemy fleet and made them destroy their own planet."

"Which should tell you how dengerous they really are. Something tells me the guy I just told you about had something to do with that operation."

They entered the command ship's bridge together. The Xortaag officers on duty stood at attention. "Stop worrying," said the prince. "Let's go get ourselves a new planet."

* * *

Tossing and turning in his bunk, Tarq had a hard time falling asleep. He had not had a decent night's sleep since the fall of Alora. With the fate of their civilization in the balance, it would be a surprise if he had one anytime soon.

His PDD buzzed. It was his assistant, Lieutenant Barook. "Sorry to disturb you, but the Xortaag fleet has just left Alora, moving towards Earth, as predicted."

Tarq was filled with conflicting emotions. On the one hand, it was an immense relief that his plan was working. If he had been wrong, the last few months hard work would have been a huge waste of resources, and once his government found out what he had done without authorization, they would execute him for treason, along with Barook and a few hundred other people who had put their trust in him. On the other hand, being right meant the survival of his entire species rested on his shoulders. Thinking about that made his hearts skip a beat.

He jumped out of his bunk. "It is a good thing we are ready. Operation KGAFUP is a go then."

Barook sounded confused. "I must have missed that memo. Is this our new code name? What does it mean?"

"Operation   Kick-the-Gods-Ass-back-to-their-Fucking-Ugly-Planet," Tarq answered.

Barook laughed. "It is a good name. I feel sorry for the humans, though. They did not deserve this."

"Me too. But there is no need for the two of us to feel guilty. At least now with our help, they have a fighting chance."

Before disconnecting the call, Barook said, "By the way, what you pulled today was genius, even for someone with your reputation."

Tarq chuckled. "Just wait to see what I have planned for tomorrow."

CHAPTER FIVE

When I opened my eyes, I found myself in a windowless room with white walls, floor, and ceiling. The room was the size of a basketball court, and most of it was empty. I was sitting on a white, comfortable sofa, wearing white clothes and shoes. Next to me, Liz was lying on the same sofa, her eyes closed, wearing a white dress. Not like a wedding dress or a sundress, more like one of those 19th or early 20th-century garden party dresses in period movies. It wasn't quite her style—too high-necked, and her legs were covered—but she looked fantastic. For a moment, I just watched her chest rise and fall.

Soft music was playing in the room. *Hymns*, I thought vaguely, though there were no words to jog my memory. A short man wearing a white tuxedo was standing in front of us. I couldn't see his face because his bright halo threw it into a shadow.

He had huge, outspread white wings extending from his shoulders.

I blinked and looked around. I felt foggy. The last thing I remembered was standing in front of a firing squad. Now I was here, Liz beside me, meeting a man who was the very picture of an angel. There was only one conclusion I could draw: Liz and I were in heaven.

And Venom was quiet. Yep. This was definitely heaven.

One problem, though: I was agnostic, which was only one step away from being an atheist. What the hell—no pun intended—was I doing in heaven? At least Liz was a devout Catholic. Maybe I was here on account of her?

Liz sat up and looked at me with sleepy eyes. She gasped and covered her mouth, and then burst into tears and threw her arms around my neck. Between her sobs, I barely made out her saying, "I thought I'd never see you again."

I held her hand and tried to comfort her. I wondered what exactly people did in heaven. Could we have sex? I heard voices behind me. I turned my head and saw Kurt and Allen, also wearing white, looking around, eyes wide.

The Super-Assassin and the Butcher were also in heaven? This was getting weird.

The man in front of us, in a very deep voice that in my considered opinion sounded divine, said, "Welcome."

"Um. Hello," I said. "Are you . . . ?" Was there a particular angel who welcomed you to heaven? Was I supposed to know? Elizabeth prided herself on her social savoir-faire, so she probably knew.

"Please allow me to introduce myself." He snapped his fingers, and both the halo and the wings disappeared. He looked Native American, with brown skin, black hair, high cheekbones, and almond-shaped eyes. And he was wearing a white hat with a blue peacock feather on it.

Okay . . . maybe heaven had weirdos?

He continued, "My name is Commander Tarq, and no,

unfortunately, you are not in heaven, and I am not an angel."

Then he burst into laughter. "But you should have seen the look on your faces!"

Dumbfounded, we looked at each other. This whole you-are-dead-and-in-heaven thing was a freaking prank? Who on earth would do that? Liz was clutching my arm. I considered kicking the man's teeth in, but I was too calm, almost listless. Kicking someone sounded like too much effort.

The man—Tarq—just stood there with a massive grin on his face, looking like a child waiting to be praised. Our lack of reaction obviously disappointed him because he moaned, "Come on! This was really good. Do you have any idea how much time and energy I put into planning this?" Then he continued under his breath, "Maybe I should not have combined sedatives with the prank."

Sedatives? What sedatives?

The door opened, and another small man who also looked like a Native American but had a full bushy black beard walked in. I didn't know Native Americans could grow a beard, especially one as thick as this one. The last time I'd seen a beard like that, it was on a guy preaching about the end of the world in the subway. In shorts. In December. With a cat on his head. This guy looked more normal, in white pants and a t-shirt. A small robot that looked like a vacuum cleaner with arms followed him, pushing a trolley. There were apples and pears, a few sandwiches, and something that looked like orange juice on it.

"This is my assistant, Lieutenant Barook," said Tarq. "Our doctors have already taken care of you, but you need to eat to regain your strength. And you are all slightly sedated, in case you are wondering why you feel so calm."

He looked at Liz who was still sobbing and added, "Relatively."

That explained why I was not freaking out. Kurt and Allen each took a sandwich, but I was holding Liz's hands. I decided to eat later.

Tarq took a big Sherlock-Holmes-style pipe out of his pocket, lit it, took a draw and said, "You must have a million questions, but this will go faster if I talk and you listen for now. First things first: This is how you all escaped from the prison."

He turned on a VR screen behind him on the wall. It was a news program. An excited blonde reporter who reminded me of a ferret was reporting live from in front of our prison. She said the executions were in progress inside. Then a freaking *spaceship*—yeah, white—appeared out of nowhere on top of the prison. The ship looked like an over-sized flying saucer: It was oval, and its semi-major axis was at least 180 feet. It had an aerodynamic shape and twin engines on its sides.

The spaceship hovered there for a few seconds; then it emanated a greenish blue beam that encompassed the prison and its surrounding area. The reporter and everyone around her fell on the ground, apparently unconscious. The feed changed to another camera, still filming.

Tarq explained, "This one is ours."

Two small shuttles left the spaceship and landed inside the prison. Five air force F-44 jet fighters showed up and tried to engage the spaceship, but it shot them down using a laser-like energy weapon.

"Wow!" I said, eloquent as ever.

"This is just a cargo ship, and not particularly well-armed," said Tarq. "Wait until you see our space fighters."

"Actually, the cargo ships are very impressive too," said

Barook. "They can carry up to eight hundred people if we remove the shuttles. We have fifty of those right here."

The shuttles returned a few minutes later.

"With you guys inside," said Tarq. "No need to thank me all at once. You are welcome."

Liz and I looked at each other with our mouths open. She asked Tarq, "You're an alien?"

I said, "Well, dah," and raised my right hand in a Vulcan salute aimed at Tarq.

Tarq smiled and nodded.

"Why did you help us?" Kurt asked.

Tarq responded, "The answer to this question is complicated. I have prepared a presentation. So, sit back, relax and enjoy my masterpiece."

The "presentation" was a holographic movie, with a voice-over by Tarq himself. Tarq paused the movie several times to offer comments. It lasted nearly an hour, during which I kept asking Liz to pinch me to make sure I was not dreaming. The fifth time I asked, she got fed up and pinched my arm so hard it left a bruise the size of her palm.

The movie showed us there were a few hundred species in the galaxy (*I knew it!*), but currently only fifteen of them had space-travel technology. Tarq's people, the Akakies, were an advanced and peaceful civilization. There was also a humanoid warrior species, the Xortaags. Technologically, they weren't as advanced as the Akakies—no other race was —and they spent most of their time either fighting each other or having meaningless skirmishes with the neighboring planets. Moreover, their homeworld, Tangaar, was slowly dying because of overpopulation and pollution, so despite their violent tendencies, the Akakies hadn't considered them a major threat.

Around forty Earth years ago, the Xortaag king's

youngest son, Prince Mushgaana, met an idealistic young fleet officer, a then Commander Maada. Maada believed the only way his species could survive was colonizing other planets. He didn't stop there: He dreamed of a galaxy under the Xortaags' rule.

"So he basically wants what our fathers dreamed of, only on a larger scale," I whispered to Kurt.

Anger flashed in his eyes. "We wanted a democratically elected government, not an absolute monarchy!"

I held my palms up. "Dude, I'm just messing with you."

Mushgaana manipulated his father to appoint Maada as the commander of their fleet, and to let them plan their first all-out military campaign. Under Maada's command, they conquered and colonized several planets and expanded their empire. In the early days of their campaign to rule the known universe, they reverse engineered a mind control technology they'd found on a defeated planet, which gave them an enormous advantage

"Mind control? How does that work?" I asked.

Tarq paused the movie and glared at me. "I'll get to that. Please be quiet."

"The CIA tried that back in the 1950s," said Liz. "I think they used LSD."

"Do you want to hear this or not?" Tarq asked, his hands on his hips. Something weird about his posture; I couldn't figure it out.

Liz giggled, squirming in her seat. "Oh yes, alien master!"

The presentation continued.

Under General Maada's command, the Xortaag fleet annihilated numerous other species, including a few with space-travel capabilities. Each victory brought the Xortaags closer to the Akakies and their allies. Tarq's government believed the Xortaags would never dare attack the Akakies, but he decided to keep an eye on them. He also planned and executed two covert operations against the enemy: They wiped out the Xortaag population in a colony using a mutated virus, and they activated all the volcanos in another occupied planet simultaneously, killing off all the Xortaags.

I was disturbed by how easily this funny-looking little man in his white tuxedo and feathered cap talked about killing God knew how many people. "Wow! Genocide much?"

Tarq gave me the look of a high school teacher just about to send a student to detention. "All adult Xortaags are soldiers, and there were no children in those colonies. Unlike the Xortaags, the Akakie Special Operations Force does not kill kids."

"The Xortaags don't have children?" asked Liz, a note of sadness in her voice.

"They do," said Tarq, "but the first wave of colonists is responsible for preparing the infrastructure for the following waves. There are no kids in a new colony until the second wave arrives."

"So the Xortaags colonized dozens of planets," said Kurt, "and the other species in the galaxy didn't think they should be stopped?"

Tarq shrugged. "For your information, the galaxy is huge, and there is no real need for the few space-faring species in it to deal with each other. Despite the occasional invasions and battles, they mostly leave each other alone, and there is very little communication between them. Most species are only in contact with the few planets in their own neiborhood. Our own fleet, for example, is mostly a deterrant. We had not had a real battle in decades. As I said, my government did not feel threatened by the Xortaags, and the others just did not want to mess with them."

"One more question," I said. "If most species in the galaxy don't have space-travel capabilities, isn't it easier for the Xortaags to attack only those, instead of going to war with the likes of you?"

"The Xortaags prefer to invade planets with at least a certain level of technology," said Tarq, "because it allows them to find and reverse-engineer things they can not build themselves. They are not very creative, but they are very good at copying other species' technology. Also, keep in mind a lack of space-travel capabilities does not necessarily mean those species can not defend themselves. A lot of them can fight and potentially defeat the Xortaags inside their planets' atmosphere."

"Once the Xortaags conquer a planet," said Barook, "they consider several factors when choosing their next target. Sometimes they are looking for a certain piece of technology. Sometimes it is an enemy they must defeat before moving forward. In some cases though, it is simply the closest target, which is how they ended up deciding to attack Earth."

When the inevitable confrontation came, Maada and his fleet beat the Akakie forces with ease. Despite Tarq's protest, his government decided to ask the Xortaags to sign a peace treaty. Tarq believed the peace treaty would allow the Xortaags to enslave the rest of the galaxy without opposition, and once they felt they were strong enough, they'd attack his home planet, Kanoor. He initiated a major black op: Unknown to his government, he had a military base built under an invisible force field on the planet that was the Xortaags' next target and stocked it with advanced equipment and weaponry. He was going to give this base to the planet's inhabitants so that they had a shot at defending themselves.

The movie ended.

I caught Tarq ogling Liz. I frowned at him, and he quickly averted his eyes.

Tarq added, "In case you did not figure it out: The Xortaags' next target is Earth, and we are on that base right now."

I was bone-tired, dazed, and drugged, but my wise-cracking abilities were intact. "It's good you clarified it; otherwise, I might've thought you've saved us to help defend another planet in a galaxy far, far away against the Xortaags."

Tarq smiled at me. "I was initially planning to hand the base over to the government of Earth, but after observing Earth for a few months, I changed my mind. Earth's current leadership is too fractured, incompetent, and corrupt to be able to mount an effective defense against a far superior enemy."

I interrupted him again. "Dude! If you provide Zheng with a spaceship, he'll use it to run away and save his own skin, or worse, try to negotiate with the Xortaags and form an alliance against you."

"On the other hand, the Resistance fits the profile of people with the resolve to defend their planet," continued Tarq, trying to ignore me. "Therefore, I decided to turn the base over to Kurt and his people."

"You cut it kinda close, didn't you?" I asked. "We were this close"—I showed him my thumb and index finger, very close together—"to start pushing up daisies."

Tarq gave me a bewildered look.

"To be executed," Liz clarified.

"There is a good reason we waited until the last

moment to save you," said Tarq. "We wanted to do it live on TV with millions watching to achieve the maximum dramatic effect. After that, there will be no shortage of volunteers when we start to recruit people."

Talk about information overload! I was dizzy. This was all way too unreal. Kurt, Liz, and Allen didn't look too good either, sedated or not.

I noticed Tarq ogling Liz again. I thought about punching his lights out. Nope. Too tired.

"I think this is enough for today," said Tarq, smoking his pipe. "If you have any urgent questions, you can ask them now. Then get some rest, and tomorrow I will give you a tour of the base and go over our defense strategy. Barook will show you to your quarters."

"Did you save only the four of us? The prison was full of Resistance members," asked Kurt.

"I realize that," Tarq said. "But we did not know who was with the Resistance and who was a common criminal. There will be plenty of time to stage a jailbreak."

"If you're aliens, why do you look exactly like us?" Elizabeth asked, her head tilted, eyes narrowed.

Tarq and Barook exchanged a look. Tarq answered, "There are dozens of humanoid species in the galaxy, some of which, including the Xortaags, look exactly like humans, at least on the outside. Make no mistake though: You probably have only slightly more in common with them than with a chimpanzee."

That explanation didn't convince Elizabeth. "But how's it possible?"

"Nobody seems to know for certain," said Tarq. "The most widely accepted theory indicates intelligent design."

"Whose intelligence?" I asked skeptically.

"The theory holds that a few million years ago a now extinct species scattered human DNA, as well as that of many other species, including for some reason sheep and wombats, all across the universe. As a result, there are several instances of similar species evolving on distant planets."

"Do all your people look like Native Americans?" I asked, wondering what a wombat was.

Barook laughed. "You saw two of us and immediately assume we all look like this? Do you always stereotype so quickly?"

Tarq said, "No. We are as varied as you guys are. It just so happens that Barook and I are from the same background."

Before leaving, I said, "I have to ask: With the fate of the universe in the balance, you still saw it fit to spend time and energy staging this?" I pointed at us and the whole this-is-what-heaven-looks-like charade.

Tarq beamed. "Of course! Was it not exquisite? "

I had to admit it kind of was.

"I have a question too," said Kurt. "In your presentation, you mentioned several times that your species was significantly more advanced than the Xortaags. How come you couldn't stop them on your own?"

Staring down at his hands, Tarq answered with a flat voice, "Because we are all pussies."

Barook showed us to our quarters, which was a Spartan and functional room with bare walls and a few pieces of furniture—a sofa, dining table, a bed, all of them white. Apparently, the Akakies really liked this color. The bed was comfortable, especially after a couple of weeks of sleeping, or to be more accurate trying to sleep, in prison.

In the last few weeks, I'd been shot, gassed, jailed, sentenced to death, tortured, and saved by aliens—I still couldn't wrap my mind around this one—but when I found myself alone with Liz in our quarters, I could only think about one thing. It's funny how the brain works. Or at least, a man's brain. Liz wanted to talk, so we did that almost all night, although I couldn't stop touching her. We talked about everything that had happened in the past two weeks. I told her I'd decided not joining the Resistance was a mistake. I earned a kiss for that. She told me she'd survived "the nick" by constantly thinking about me.

If Allen ever told her I'd expressed regret about not seeing the new *Star Trek* rather than not being with her when I was about to die, I'd be dead. On the other hand, I thought she'd understand some things were too painful to talk about to people like Allen.

We had a big laugh when we remembered how she kicked a security guard in the nuts. When she described how she bit a gangbanger's ear off, I said, "You know, I think there're two Elizabeths. One's gentle, tender and caring, and one gets mad quickly and does crazy things."

She flashed her beautiful, contagious smile. "I'm like the Incredible Hulk," she said, adding in a hilariously exaggerated raspy voice, "Don't make me angry. You wouldn't like it when I am angry."

I couldn't help wondering if she were suffering from a split personality disorder. Not that it mattered. I loved her, craziness and all.

I also told her about Venom. She approved. "Personifying the constant stream of the negative thoughts in your brain is a very effective method to fight OCD because it helps differentiate the obsessive thoughts from your own conscious ones."

We also used the PDDs Tarq had given us to go online and see what was going on in the world—the aliens used the internet, who knew. The entire world was in a state of shock. It wasn't every day that a spaceship saved a group of freedom fighters from certain death. It turned out Tarq's people, while saving us, had shot all the guards and government officials in the prison in the head at close range. Among other people, they killed the new director of SCTU who was at the prison to witness the executions, using an energy weapon that melted the targets' faces.

Brutal. Kurt and Allen would approve.

It was obvious Tarq was sending a message: Don't mess with us, or we will take your face off.

Her eyes sparkling, Liz said, "Do you believe just a day ago we were waiting for death, and now we're gonna play a role in saving humanity from aliens? It really feels like destiny."

Listening to her, you'd be forgiven for thinking humanity was a damsel in distress, and we were destined to ride in on white horses to save her. I found it amusing she simply assumed it was her responsibility to counter an alien invasion, but it was no surprise. Liz always tried to do the right thing, regardless of the repercussions.

"I admire your enthusiasm," I said, "but I for one am less enthusiastic about going to war with on-steroids Klingons, who are apparently very good at killing off other races."

She punched my arm. "Oh, come on! You love being a hero, Mr. I-am-the-Best-Fighter-Pilot-in-the-World. It's your chance to be like Captain Kirk and save Earth."

Captain Kirk saved *the universe,* but I decided not to

argue. I started kissing her. Before that got very far, we fell asleep in each other's arms.

Right before I went to sleep, Venom said, "I miss Cordelia."

Welcome back, old friend.

* * *

New York - January 12, 2078

Oksana Zelenko and her sister, Anastasiya, entered a luxury suite in a five-star hotel, accompanied by one of The Harem's "security guards," a big man who looked like a professional wrestler. On the way to the hotel, Oksana had noticed he was carrying a sidearm, like all the other guards.

The two young women wore very short, tight dresses, high heels, and lots of make-up. There was a middle-aged, obese man wearing a white bathrobe in the room. He looked at Oksana with hunger in his eyes, whistled and said, "Now *that's* a figure that turns heads everywhere. Such a beautiful face too."

Good thing he can't see all the bruises under my make-up, thought Oksana.

The fat man gave an envelope to the goon. "Thanks, Sasha."

Sasha pocketed the envelope and in his thick Russian accent said, "I'll be waiting outside."

The man went to the bar next to the room's door, chose a bottle, and while pouring himself a drink asked, "You girls want a drink? Or something stronger perhaps? What's your poison?"

Oksana's heart pounded. She'd practiced this moment

in her mind a thousand times, but now that the time had come, she found herself unable to move. She looked at her younger sister's wide-eyed, frightened face. Her lower lip was trembling. If she didn't act now, Anastasiya would surely die in The Harem, sooner than later. Oksana couldn't let that happen.

Come on, girl. You had Martin Palermo killed. He was of the most powerful men in the world. Now you are afraid of Fatso and Henchman?

Pumped with adrenaline, she approached the man from behind, grabbed his hair, pulled his head back and held a knife she'd stolen from The Harem's kitchen under his triple chin.

Even if we don't succeed, just seeing this look on the pervert's face makes it all worthwhile, she thought.

"Call him," said Oksana.

The man whimpered, "What?"

Oksana pulled his hair harder. "Call Sasha. Sound normal. If you warn him, I swear I'll cut your throat."

The fat man hesitated, but he didn't have a choice. With a trembling voice, he called out, "Sasha, can you come here a second?"

Oksana hit his head against the bar with all the power she could muster. The man collapsed on the floor. Oksana ran and hid behind the door.

The door opened, and Sasha walked in. He saw the man unconscious on the floor and hurried toward him, his back to Oksana. She took two quick steps and buried the knife to the hilt in his back.

Blood oozed out of the wound. Sasha fell to his knees, his face filled with surprise. Anastasiya let out a faint scream. Oksana bent over and gently whispered in Sasha's ears, "These violent delights have violent ends."

She stabbed him again. "This one is for raping my sister." She looked up and told Anastasiya, "Time to go, little one."

A few minutes later, they walked out of the hotel and disappeared into the night.

* * *

WE ALL LOOKED MUCH BETTER when we met for breakfast in the mess hall. In contrast to the bedrooms, the mess hall was luxurious. It was huge, and besides the massive, wooden dining tables with very comfortable upholstered chairs, there were plush sofas and handsome coffee tables scattered around, plus a couple of pool and foosball tables. A thick carpet covered the floor, and classical music was being played with such crispness that I could've sworn a band was present. Kurt closed his eyes for a second and let the music wash over him.

And everything was white. I had to start wearing sunglasses around here.

Liz and Kurt excitedly talked about yesterday's events, with Allen listening and making sarcastic comments from time to time. They seemed as passionate as Liz about defending Earth. Hardly a surprise, since as freedom fighters they were already fighting for a cause. Saving humanity from aliens was a higher calling. I was beginning to feel left out. I realized it was my duty to do something, but I was still adjusting to being alive.

After Liz dropped "saving humanity" for the fifth time, Allen finally had enough. "You do that," he said. "I'm fighting for my children."

"Children, plural?" I asked. So far as I knew Allen had only one daughter.

"Lilly and this one here," Allen pointed at Kurt, who blushed.

Now, this was something I could identify with.

"I can't believe I'm saying this, but I'm with Allen on this one," I said. "I have a hard time wrapping my mind around fighting for humanity, but I'll fight tooth and nail to protect you guys, even Allen."

"Okay. Screw humanity. I'll be fighting for the people in this room too, plus my brother and sisters," said Liz, wrapping a curl around her finger. I knew her well enough to understand she was only kidding.

"Have you noticed we're all surprisingly calm, given the circumstances?" asked Kurt. "I wonder if we're still sedated."

Tarq and Barook joined us after breakfast, both dressed the same as yesterday. They took us for a tour of the base, which Tarq told us was built in Yukon.

"Yukon, dude?" I said.

Smoking his pipe, Tarq explained, "We chose a freezing cold place on purpose. The Xortaags hate the cold weather, and it is extremely unlikely that one of them will stumble onto the base out here."

"Good thing they don't like cold weather." I said. "Otherwise, the Canucks would welcome them with open arms and apologize for the weather not being cold enough."

Allen growled.

We walked outside. Warm sunshine and a clear sky welcomed us. It was a beautiful summer day—in Yukon!

"This is an illusion," said Tarq, "created by the force field above us. We could imitate different weather or even make it rain sometimes, but it would take too much effort, so you have to get used to sunshine while you live here."

"How lovely," said Liz. "Perhaps you fellows would like

to stick around after we defeat the Xortaags. You'd be very welcome in London."

"Thank you," said Tarq. "Let's see how things go."

"Nothing under the force field is visible or detectable from outside," Barook said. "So unless the Xortaags can find our location through other means, our existence here will remain a secret."

"A force field this size is centuries ahead of our technology," Kurt told me. "Why do you and Liz behave like this is all normal?"

"Sci-fi fans here," I said.

The place was enormous. There were dozens of buildings, one of which was our Command Center, three air traffic control towers I could see, firefighting stations, ammunition and ordnance depots, and a few huge laser cannon turrets that according to Tarq could engage an enemy fleet in space if our location were ever exposed and the enemy found a way past the force field. Tarq showed us a state-of-the-Akakie-art hospital, full of equipment I didn't recognize. The base also had all the amenities you could imagine, including gyms, swimming pools, running tracks, three small parks—the Akakies had taken the trouble of planting oak trees in the parks—and even a movie theater. It was luxurious, no question, but the dimensions were just slightly off; what you'd expect from a race that looked at lots of sample blueprints but didn't have a natural feel for human design. The swimming pools were deeper than they should be. The elevators were smaller. The main structures were both classic and modern in a way that didn't seem cutting-edge but more like the work of a hungover first-year associate.

The base could house up to fifty thousand people, and it was completely self-sufficient, with hundreds of small robots taking care of maintenance and repairs. Tarq did provide us with a gigahertz and nanoseconds explanation on how they managed to provide food for this many people, but I was too amazed to pay much attention. The robots, to Liz's sorrow, weren't interactive. They did their work and ignored all attempts to turn them into pals, pets or playthings.

What did catch my attention was the sleek, gorgeous, straight-out-of-a-science-fiction-movie space fighter Tarq showed us, sitting in an underground hangar. It had a triangular shape, twin elliptical fins and rudders, a bulbous cockpit and a droopy nose that reminded me of USS Enterprise NCC 1701-D.

Liz and I said, "Wow!" together. Great minds and all.

For me, it was love at first sight. I couldn't remember a time in my life when I wasn't passionate about flying. Soaring the skies in this beauty would be a dream come true. If she'd been a real woman, I would've taken her home and made sweet, sweet love to her right now.

"Dude, your girlfriend is standing right here," said Venom.

"AX-23 is an older model space fighter," said Tarq. "They were decommissioned and scheduled to be scrapped, but we brought ten thousand of them here in revetments and multilevel underground hangars similar to this one to form your fleet."

"Decommissioned? Are they any good?" I asked.

Tarq smiled. "They are much better than anything you have, or even the Xortaags, for that matter. You will learn about their full capabilities later on."

"Do you use these to travel in space?" asked Liz.

Tarq laughed. "These are fast, but nothing is *that* fast. Moreover, these are small single-seat fighters, and their energy reserve is limited. No, all spacefaring races use some sort of a space-folding device. As the name suggests, it folds the deep space, and you can send something as small as a pen or as big as a whole fleet from one side of a galaxy to the other instantaneously. Still, its range is limited, and it takes a few minutes to calculate and execute each jump. For example, it takes six of your months for the Xortaags to travel from their homeworld to here. We have an SFD here in the base too, as do all spaceships, excluding the shuttles and space fighters."

"How do the fighters travel in space then?" I asked.

"The transport ships are equipped with hangar bays," answered Tarq. "When the Xortaag fleet is one jump away from the target, the space fighters leave the transport ships and are sent as close as possible to the planet."

"Can we use the SFD to transport Zheng here?" I asked.

Tarq shook his head. "It can be operated by the equipment on the surface of the planet, but it only works in space. Gravity caused by a large mass like a planet interferes with its function."

At the end of the tour, we stopped in front of a small room, with a glass window at one side. There were some touchscreen controls mounted next to the window. Tarq said, "And this is the crown jewel of our technology. It is called a Memory, Information, and Capabilities Implanter, or in short, MICI."

If I'd heard this name in a sci-fi movie, I could've easily guessed what it did, but it was just inconceivable in the real world. "Does it do what its name suggests it does?" I asked.

"Why don't we demonstrate?" Tarq puffed on his pipe. "Would you mind stepping inside?"

"Are you sure it works on a human brain?" I asked. "If my brain explodes, I'll be seriously pissed."

"Yes. We have calibrated it to work on the human brain, and we have already tested it. It is completely safe, but there is a small chance it might not work on certain individuals."

"Why?" I asked.

"We do not know," said Tarq. "But it cannot safely imprint anything on a small portion of the population, between half a percent to one percent. It might work if we dial it up, so to speak, but then it might explode the brain, which, as you suggest, would be unfortunate."

This wasn't reassuring at all, but I didn't want to embarrass myself by acting like a coward in front of Liz and Kurt. Plus, if I didn't do it, Liz, with her jump-then-look tendencies would volunteer. I stepped into the room. There was nothing but a chair inside. I sat there and waited. From the window, I could see Barook working on something on the control panel.

"It will take a few minutes," said Tarq.

I waited. Nothing happened, and then suddenly, BOOM!

One second I was sitting there, beginning to get bored, and the next thing I knew my brain was full of knowledge I hadn't previously possessed: AX-23's specifications, capabilities, and weaponry (laser cannons!). More impressively, I had hundreds of hours of vivid memories flying the fighter and engaging in dogfights with enemy space fighters. Nothing that looked fake—real, actual memories.

Trying to sort out my new memories from the old ones was overwhelming. I thought it might take weeks just to get used to that new information slithering through my thoughts. It was creepy—but also thrilling. If only they'd had this in my school days. We all could've gone to school for ten minutes once a week and had the rest of the time to play. I was fantasizing about that when I glanced up to see everyone staring at me. I stood up and stepped out of the room.

Having just been introduced to the most awesome piece of technology in the world, I did what I always did. I looked at Liz and tried my best Neo impression, "I know Kung Fu."

God, I love the classics!

"Why did MICI teach him martial arts?" Tarq asked Barook.

She laughed and said, "Show me."

"MICI scans the user's mind," said Tarq. "Depending on their natural talents and previous experiences, it assigns their duties and implants the knowledge and experience necessary to perform those duties."

Liz was next to enter MICI. Barook touched the controls a few times.

"All this technology and you still use touchscreens? No voice control?" I asked Tarq.

"Voice control? We invented brain-computer interfaces when your great-grandfather was not born yet. But they both can be hacked remotely. I once hacked into an enemy fleet's neural-control interface and made them shoot their own ships, destroying the whole fleet."

I looked at the small man with newfound respect. He had single-handedly destroyed a whole fleet.

Tarq continued, "The only way an enemy can hack into our equipment is if they are physically here, and then they have to deal with various security measures and biometrics."

"You don't seem to be using an AI either," observed Kurt.

Both Tarq and Barook shuddered. Tarq's eyelids started

twitching. He rubbed his eyes and said, "We have had a very bad experience with AIs."

"What did you do?" I asked. "Created Skynet?"

"No. Why would we create a net for the sky?" said Tarq. "We built an AI that almost wiped out our species."

"Commander Tarq cut through the AI defenses and destroyed it seconds before it launched an attack that would have killed all of us."

"I'm beginning to really like these guys," I told Kurt. "They talk about destroying enemy fleets and saving their species like it's their everyday job."

"Right? Super badass," he said; then he gave me a hard look and asked, "What the hell do you think you're doing?"

I let go of his neck. "Nothing. Just wanted to see if MICI had taught me how to do a Vulcan nerve pinch."

Buzzing with happiness, Liz came out of MICI a space fighter pilot. Kurt was assigned to the base's Special Forces Unit (obviously!). He said he had learned about weapons and tactics he couldn't even imagine before stepping inside MICI. When Allen came out, he complained, "I didn't learn anything new."

"Oh! I am so sorry. As I said, MICI does not work on everyone," said Tarq.

"It worked fine," said Allen. "I have a lot of stuff in my mind that wasn't there before. I just didn't learn anything I hadn't known already."

Tarq and Barook looked confused. I offered an explanation. "This is just Allen being Allen."

Tarq gave Allen an annoyed look and then said, "I am the commander of the base and the highest authority. As such, I award Jim the rank of colonel, and appoint him as the commander of the fleet."

I wondered if it was another prank. "Seriously?"

"Trust me," said Tarq. "You now possess both the experience and the expertise to do your job. MICI agrees. In fact, it usually assigns ranks, but since the four of you are the first people to join up, I decided to do the honors myself."

I said, "Wow! This is so FM!" which got me a smile from Liz.

"FM?" asked Tarq.

"Fucking magic. It's a fighter pilot slang for when you see something so high tech you can't figure out how it does what it does," I explained.

"MICI is admittedly great," said Tarq, "but unfortunately the Xortaags have used the same technology to develop something called Orbital Mind Control and Brain Over-Write System. Do you remember I mentioned they had reverse engineered a mind control technology that helped them become a galactic superpower?"

"That's a mouthful right there," I said.

"We can call it OMC-BOWS," said Tarq.

Allen growled, "That's even worse than C-SIS! All this technology and you couldn't come up with something less idiotic?"

"What the hell is C-SIS?" I asked.

"Canadian Security Intelligence Service," answered Kurt.

I chuckled. "Huh! I didn't know the Canadians had one of those."

Allen gave me a hard look.

"The Xortaags themselves call it the Voice of God," said Tarq. "So it is either that or OMC-BOWS unless you have a better suggestion."

I helpfully offered, "How about MFM, standing for Mind-Fuck Machine?"

Liz hit me in the arm, and Allen looked unimpressed, but Tarq, Barook and Kurt burst into laughter.

Tarq appointed Kurt as the commander of the Special Forces, also as a colonel. Elizabeth and Allen ended up being lieutenant-colonels, our seconds-in-command.

"There is something extremely important I need all of you to remember," said Tarq. "For us Akakies, personal space is very important, and we will suffer actual physical pain if it is violated. Please make sure you do not get closer than three feet to the two of us, and under no circumstances touch us, even if you find us dying on the floor."

I thought that was weird but held my tongue. Maybe he was a germaphobe?

We broke for lunch.

AFTER LUNCH, we had a defense strategy meeting in the Command Center, which was a high-tech room full of various controls and instruments I didn't recognize, computers, monitors, communication devices, very big virtual reality screens floating mid-air, and a few hologram projectors.

Everything was white.

I asked Tarq, "Where can I find sunglasses around here?"

Using another holographic presentation/movie, Tarq explained, in very general terms, the Xortaag strategy to invade other planets. In a nutshell, the Xortaags would send their fleet to the vicinity of the planet using the Space-Folding Device, and then engage their defenses while they set up a satellite system—Orbital Mind Control and Brain Over-Write System, aka OMC-BOWS, aka MFM—around the planet. Once complete, OMC-BOWS would emanate a beam that would brainwash all the planet's population into believing the Xortaags were gods and all their commands had to be followed. Afterward, they'd use the planet's indigenous population to build bases and cities. Once an infrastructure was in place, millions of Xortaags would immigrate to the planet while their fleet would prepare to invade another target.

"That mind control beam won't affect us?" asked Kurt.

"No. Our MICI protects you against its effects," answered Tarq. "Moreover, the beam cannot penetrate our force field here."

"How many space fighters do they have in their fleet?" I asked.

"Around forty thousand."

I whistled. "That's four times what we have. How're we going to stop their attack?"

"We are not," said Tarq. "Going toe-to-toe with their fleet is suicide, considering their numerical advantage. Their M.O. has two weak points: Once they land, they do not expect any resistance, so they will be completely blind-sided by our presence. They are also inexperienced in fighting enemy forces on the ground. As a direct result of their overwhelming success in space battles, they have not needed to use ground warfare for over one of your centuries. Our plan is to let them land, study them for a few months, find their weaknesses, and only then destroy them in a surprise attack."

Liz gasped. "You're suggesting we let them occupy our planet?"

Tarq nodded.

"Surely there is another way," Liz exclaimed. "Maybe if we coordinate our efforts with our armed forces—"

Tarq cut her off. "Trust me. This is the only way. Earth's military forces do not stand a chance against the Xortaags. You are a pilot, and you know both Earth's air force and the enemy fleet capabilities. Use your judgment."

He had a point, and I wouldn't trust Zheng in any case, but Liz insisted, "But millions could die!"

"Actually, more like thousands. Casualties of Xortaag invasions are usually light. Once OMC-BOWS becomes active, all hostilities stop, and life on the planet continues with a semblance of normalcy. There is no need for them to slaughter their own future workforce, after all."

Barook added, "To be clear, casualties of the invasion itself are light, and as Commander Tarq mentioned, people on the planet return to their daily routines after the invasion, waiting for instructions from the Xortaags. However, this is temporary. The first wave of Xortaag migration usually consists of ten to twenty million future colonists in cryogenic sleep. The Xortaags load the sleep pods in huge transport ships. Once they arrive, the construction of cities and bases on the planet expands exponentially, at which point normal life on the planet is completely disrupted. Most native inhabitants are turned into slaves, and since Xortaags are not particularly concerned with the well-being of their slaves, the mortality rate raises considerably. And once the colonization process is complete, which would take around two to three of your decades, they kill off most of the planet's population, only keeping a small portion as slaves."

"Which means we are under a deadline," said Tarq. "Once the first wave of Xortaag colonists arrives, they will be too strong for us to defeat."

Tugging on his goatee, Kurt weighed in, "I'm not sure how I feel about your strategy."

I noticed Barook was mimicking Kurt and pulling his own beard.

Suddenly, Tarq's tone and manner changed. He answered in a very firm voice, "You are not required to have any feelings about this. I am the commander of the base. I order, you follow. That's it."

This caught all of us by surprise. I hadn't realized this was a dictatorship. The freedom-fighting dynamic duo didn't like it at all. Allen leaned forward, cracked his knuckles, and asked, "Is that how you think things work around here?"

"This is exactly how things work around here," said Tarq. "Please allow me to demonstrate: Take that glass and pour the water over your head."

To my astonishment, Allen picked up a glass of water from the desk in front of him and emptied it on his own head.

Tarq, who had a hard time keeping a straight face, continued, "Now stand up and hop on one leg."

Allen did what he was told.

"At the same time, hit yourself in the head with your right hand."

If it hadn't been for the look of absolute horror on Allen's face, this would've been hilarious. Barook certainly thought so. He laughed so hard that he fell off his chair. Kurt and Liz both started to move with the apparent intention of stopping Tarq and helping Allen, but they both froze. I guessed what was going on, so I didn't even bother. Besides, why on earth would I help Allen?

Tarq explained, "Along with the other things, MICI has also made it impossible for you to disobey my orders. You can stop now."

Allen stopped hopping, and Kurt and Liz relaxed and

lay back in their seats. Allen took one step toward Tarq with murder in his eyes. Then he stopped dead, completely motionless.

Tarq continued, "You are also unable to harm me in any way, directly or indirectly."

"You stole this from RoboCop," I pointed out.

"I have no idea who that is," said Tarq. "But if he has done something similar, he is a very smart person."

With obvious effort, Allen said, "You are dead."

Tarq shrugged. "Probably one day."

"But apparently not by you," I helpfully added.

Tarq looked at me approvingly, and then in his usual mild tone said, "In case you have not understood, you will not able to talk about this to anyone who has not been through MICI. We are going to leave you now to talk this out among yourselves. We will have a meeting tomorrow morning to iron out some issues."

Tarq was about to leave the room when he stopped and said, "Oh, I almost forgot: my request for our personal space not being violated? It is an *order* now."

I asked my friends, "Does anybody else think we might've jumped out of the frying pan into the fire?"

"I certainly do," said Kurt. "I don't like working under a dictator."

"Thank you, Mr. Obvious," I said. "We know you've been fighting a dictatorship for the past two years."

Kurt gave me a pained look.

Allen's nostrils flared. "I'm gonna find a way to kill him. He can't push us around when he is dead."

"I don't like being Tarq's puppet," said Liz, playing with a lock of hair, "and I'm not very good at following orders. But if it helps us save humanity, shouldn't we swallow our pride and get on with it?"

I winked at her. "Meet Liz, the champion of doing the right thing at any cost, even if it means becoming a slave for a stupid alien."

I had an idea about how to solve this problem, but it seemed like a long shot, so I kept it to myself for the time being.

* * *

THE AKAKIE BASE on Earth - January 13, 2078

KURT, wandering aimlessly in the night, ended up at a small park near his quarters. It was peaceful and quiet, with nobody else around. He sat on a bench under an oak tree and tried to wrap his mind around the events of the past couple of weeks.

It had all started two years ago. He was working late in his office, making arrangements for Unification's first anniversary. Sitting behind his desk, he noticed how dark it was outside and called Janet to tell her he wouldn't be home for dinner. He said, "See you soon. Don't forget how much I love you," disconnected the call, looked up, and found himself staring at the business end of a silencer.

The swarthy man holding the gun said, "General Zheng sends his regards."

Before Kurt even began to comprehend what was going on, the man's body was thrown forward, hit in the back by several bullets shot quickly one after another. He hit Kurt's desk and collapsed to the floor, his blood staining the carpet.

What just happened?

Holding a suppressed Glock G-32, Allen appeared behind the dead would-be assassin and said, "Follow me."

Kurt was dizzy with shock but kept his wits about him. He grabbed the dead assassin's gun and ran after Allen. There were three more dead men in the corridor.

"Our friend in there hadn't come alone," said Allen.

Kurt and Allen exited the building through the back door and got into an ancient brown Cadillac. Allen drove away. "Why are you driving?" asked Kurt.

"I've disabled all the car's navigation system and anything else that could be tracked," said Allen.

"What the hell is going on?"

Allen took his eyes off the street for just one second and looked at him. Sorrow and guilt were written all over his face. "I was off duty tonight. A bomb exploded in your parents' car. They are both dead. I can't begin to tell you how sorry I am."

It was as if he'd just been hit by lightning. Time slowed. Those few simple sentences turned his life upside down. His bookish, kindly, untiring parents were gone. Soon he'd find out that a united Earth, the dream he and his father had dedicated their lives to for so long, had been co-opted by a brutal military dictator. The planet was now united only in subjugation. At that moment, he started down the road that got Janet, sweet Janet, killed. He'd been on the run ever since, trying to forget his pain by waging war against Zheng. What kept him going wasn't purely revenge, though that was always in his mind, but fulfilling his father's dream, no matter how unlikely the possibility was. And just a few days ago, he'd thought that dream was gone forever.

This was his chance for redemption.

Defending Earth against an alien attack was enough to give him a sense of purpose, but he couldn't help feeling this was the means to an even greater end. When the Xortaags were gone, he could continue his father's work, and this time, there would be no freaking Chancellor Zheng to mess things up. He wasn't only planning to help humanity survive the Xortaag attack; he wanted to make sure it had a bright future after that. Nothing could bring back his parents or the thousands murdered by Zheng and his henchmen, but perhaps this war would bind humanity together for good, erasing the doubt and dissatisfaction that had allowed Zheng's victory. Once everyone knew the universe was full of intelligent species, many capable of space travel, human solidarity would look far more desirable.

Who says there are no second chances in life?

* * *

New York - January 13, 2078

Oksana told her sister, "This is the place."

She ran to a townhouse door and rang the bell. When no one answered, she started banging on the door.

A voice from inside yelled, "I am coming! Jesus!" A minute later an elderly man opened the door. The two young women rushed in past him. The old man looked lost for words, but he finally managed to say, "Oksana! What on earth are you doing here?"

"We ran away from The Harem," said Oksana, panting.

Confused, the old man asked, "And you came here?"

"We have nowhere else to go. Mr. Winston, you have to help us."

Anastasiya, trembling like a leaf, said, "Please! If they catch us, they'll torture us to death, to be a lesson for the other girls."

Oksana put an arm around her younger sister, trying to calm her down. Anastasiya continued, "And that was before she killed one of them."

The old man, Winston, his cheeks turning scarlet, shouted, "You did what?"

"I stabbed him in the back with a kitchen knife," Oksana said proudly.

Winston's eyes bugged. He sat down on the couch, running a trembling hand over his face. He said, "In his back? You killed a member of the Russian mafia and then came here? No, no, no! You have got to go. I can't help you!"

Anastasiya looked desperately at her sister. Oksana put her hand on her shoulder and told Winston, "I don't see that you have a choice in this. If you don't help us, I'll call SCTU right now and tell them you have ties to the Resistance."

Bringing up SCTU had the effect Oksana was hoping for; Winston shut his mouth and stared at her in fear.

Oksana continued without mercy, "I'm sure they'll be very interested in hearing Palermo was assassinated shortly after I told you he used to come to The Harem frequently."

Winston's face drained of blood. He seemed to shrink into the couch cushions like a small frightened animal. "What do you want?"

"We want to join the Resistance," said Oksana. "That's the only way to escape Bratwa."

Liz and I entered the Command Center together. While we were settling into our seats, Kurt told Allen, "You know what? I've just realized I haven't seen you smoke since we arrived here."

"It's the weirdest thing," said Allen. "I just don't feel like smoking."

Tarq, his pipe in his mouth, interjected, "Disgusting habit, that."

I shot a suspicious glance at him. "Did you have something to do with it?"

Tarq blew some smoke in Allen's face. "Me? Of course not. But Barook here has programmed MICI to make people quit smoking."

Allen exploded. "You have no right to do this! What else are you going to ban? Alcohol? Sex?"

"For the love of God, don't give him any ideas," I pleaded with him.

The first order of business was choosing a name for the base.

"I have a perfect name in mind: Thermopylae," Tarq proudly announced. "I have studied your culture and history. This is the place where a small army defeated a much stronger aggressor."

I laughed. "They all died in Thermopylae. You could as well have chosen The Alamo!"

I suggested Winterfell, which was appropriate: We were in the north, we were the first line of defense against an alien invasion that threatened humanity, and plus, as I put it in an ominous tone, winter was indeed coming.

Liz said, "Only instead of ice-zombies, it's a fleet of galaxy-conquering aliens we have to deal with."

"Semantics," I said.

We all agreed. Even Allen knew about Winterfell.

Tarq didn't get his way in naming AX-23 either. His suggestion was Falcon, but as a *Star Trek* fan, it'd be a cold day in hell before I name the space fighters under my command anything even remotely related to *Star Wars*. I suggested Viper, and since I just happened to be the commander of the fleet, I ignored all other suggestions. I also named the cargo ships Fireflies. I was a nerd and proud of it.

I took advantage of a moment when no one looking at Tarq and told him, "I'll punch you in your fucking ugly face if I catch you ogling Liz one more time."

His pipe fell off his lip, but he pulled himself together. "You literally cannot, but point taken. Sorry about that."

"As long as we are naming things, I want to call people under my command 'the Commandos,'" said Kurt.

I was jealous. "Wow! That's a really cool name. I want a cool name for the pilots too."

I suggested, "X-Force," "Inglorious Basterds," and "Green Hornets," none of which stuck. Tarq's suggestions were even worse: "Deadly Vipers" and "Killing Machines." Allen, the helpful and considerate person that he was, recommended "Pussies." Kurt offered "The Wild Geese" and "The Dogs of War"—his favorite novels. Finally, since we couldn't find a cool nickname, we ended up calling the pilots, well, the pilots.

Tarq, looking disappointed that none of the names he suggested stuck, said, "The rest of my team is planning to leave soon. I want them to raid Zheng's prison one more time. We need the names and physical descriptions of the inmates who are members of the Resistance."

I smiled. "I'd love to see Zheng's face when a spaceship shows up on top of the Coffin, *again*, and this time rescues a lot more people."

Allen told Tarq, "Tell your people to try to shoot more guards in the head this time, or even better, just blow the whole place up after they leave."

"And you still wonder why your nickname is 'the Butcher'?" I asked him.

When the meeting was over, and everyone was about to leave, Tarq told me, "Could you please stay a minute? I need to talk to you privately."

I exchanged a questioning look with Liz and stayed. After everyone left, Tarq said grimly, "I have just reviewed MICI's report on your mental status and characteristics. I saw something I do not like at all: According to MICI, you have serious racist inclinations."

I was dumbfounded. I was definitely not a racist. If someone wanted to drive me crazy, accusing me of being a racist would do it, right next to calling me a coward or a bad pilot.

"I'm not a racist," I said.

"You say so," said Tarq, "but MICI is never wrong. It knows your darkest secrets better than you do. I have to warn you: We Akakies are an extremely open-minded people, and showing respect to the other species who are different from us is a big part of our culture. I will not tolerate any racist behavior from the people under my command. Is that clear?"

I wished I could punch him in the face, shoot him in the foot, or strangle him to death. Anything, really. But all I could do was yell, "Read my lips, you stupid alien. *I am not a racist.*"

"We shall see. You are dismissed."

On my way out, I slammed his office door with such force the walls shook with the impact.

CHAPTER SIX

Two days later, we gathered in the Command Center to watch Tarq people's jailbreak operation. Tarq had Barook broadcast it through a live feed for the whole world to see.

Since Tarq was planning to save a lot more people this time, he sent five Fireflies. As soon as the Fireflies appeared over the Coffin, some of the guards dropped their weapons and ran away. The Akakies let them go, but they made a point of killing every single guard and prison official who stayed at their post and tried to defend the Coffin. The newest SCTU director who was in the prison investigating our escape was among the dead. Six F-44 fighter jets approached the Fireflies and shot a few beyond-visual-range missiles at them, but after the spaceships blew the missiles out of the sky, the air force pilots kept their distance. The Fireflies came back to Winterfell with some two hundred Resistance members on board.

The recruits' initial orientation was held in Winterfell's movie theater because the Command Center wasn't big enough for so many people. When Kurt, Liz, Allen and entered, we were surrounded by the recently freed Resistance members, with hugs, handshakes, and high fives all around. Kurt and Allen were the center of attention. Liz and I got our share too. Our sensational escape from the Coffin had made us superstars.

"You know, you're right," I told Liz. "I like being a hero."

The orientation was the same as ours minus the this-is-heaven charade. Our presence added a lot more credibility to Tarq's story. During the orientation, Allen got a cigarette from one of his old Resistance friends and doggedly tried to smoke, only to keep coughing and choking, much to Tarq and Barook's amusement. After the orientation, everyone went through MICI and were assigned duties.

I immediately noticed a problem: Most of the over two hundred people had ended up joining either the Special Forces Unit or various support/maintenance teams. We had only one other fighter pilot. At this rate, we'd never have enough pilots for our ten thousand strong fleet. When I mentioned this to Tarq, he said he'd reprogram MICI to have it assign anyone with any flying experience to the fleet.

One evening, while having dinner with Liz and Kurt, I asked them, "Have you noticed the newcomers have no problem with Tarq's plan to give Earth up without a fight and then try to get it back later?"

The four of us had talked it out and grudgingly decided he was right, but everyone else seemed to have accepted his plan without questioning it. Kurt asked, "You think MICI has something to do with it?"

"I'm sure it does," I said.

"That's the only logical explanation," said Liz, playing with her salad. "Otherwise, everyone should be freaking out."

It suddenly hit me. "Guys, are you at all curious to know anything about the Akakies? Where their planet is? Their customs and traditions? Their sex life? Anything?"

They thought about it for a minute. Then Liz threw her fork on the table and said with disgust, "No. Nothing. Not even a little."

The three of us stared at each other. "That sneaky bastard," I said. "God knows what other shit he's imprinted on our brain."

"It's actually a good precaution," said Kurt. "If we keep asking questions, we might find some secrets the Xortaags might later find out and use against his people. Or we might become enemies one day."

The things you could use that machine for! I was beginning to wonder if we could use it to cure the common cold, depression, or even impotence—not that I personally had any problem in that particular area.

Two days later, when we gathered in the Command Center for another meeting, Liz said, "What about our families? We can't just leave them out there to turn into the Xortaags' slaves."

"They are probably safer wherever they are as opposed to being with us as we are planning to go to war with the Xortaags," Tarq pointed out.

Liz glared at him. "No way. I want my family here with me. We live together, or we die together."

I whispered in her ear, "A bit melodramatic, don't you think?"

"Winterfell's space is limited," said Tarq. "There is no place for people who are not useful, one way or another. Feel free to bring in whoever else you want; just run it by me first."

This was how Allen's daughter, Lilly, and Liz's three siblings ended up joining us.

Lilly was a computer genius, and MICI tasked her with assisting Barook in running Winterfell's various systems. Kurt and I had known her since she was a baby. Allen used to bring her to all of Kurt's birthdays even though she was ten years younger than us. I took her for a tour of Winterfell when she arrived. She was wearing a simple white dress and looked very cute in my informed opinion.

Approaching Tarq's office, I told her, "We're going to meet our commander. Be careful; dude is seriously into practical jokes. You must never let your guard down around him because there's no telling what he'll pull."

We entered Tarq's office, and I introduced Lilly. Tarq stared at her without saying anything; then his lower lip trembled, and his eyes welled up with tears. He mumbled, "Excuse me" and ran out of his office.

"What the hell was that all about?" I said under my breath.

"Was this a prank?" Lilly asked me, surprised.

Liz had two younger sisters, Samantha and Theresa, and an older brother, Matias. Despite the fact that their father was an abusive piece of work, all four siblings had turned out *mostly* okay—I was certain Liz's tendency to freak out over the smallest issues despite her normally warm and caring nature was due to her difficult childhood, compliments of her dad. The four of them had a very strong bond, and they loved each other deeply. Three days after Lilly's arrival, I entered our quarters and found Liz in deep conversation with her brother, who had just arrived. Matias was a big man, with wide shoulders, the same thick, black, curly hair as his sister, skin that was a couple of shades darker and an easy laugh. He ran to me, held me in a tight embrace, and with a hint of a Spanish accent said, "Jim, my old friend. I'm so happy to see you."

A sudden flare of joy warmed me. I'd always liked Matias. He had the same passion and zeal for life as Liz, minus the occasional freak-outs. In fact, he was one of the most easygoing people I'd ever met in my life. Sometimes I couldn't help wondering if I'd chosen the wrong sibling, even though starting a relationship with Matias would've constituted a major lifestyle change for at least one of us.

I shook his hand. "Have you been through MICI already?"

"Yes, and I still can't believe any of this," he said. "Sounds like one of the sci-fi movies you two always talk about."

"Kurt would be happy to see you," I said. "Being a Marine, you'll be a welcome addition to his team."

Soon after our first recruits arrived, Kurt sent a message to the Resistance, instructing them to stop any planned operations until he met them. Then he started meeting various Resistance cell leaders. His modus operandi was something like this: Either he or Allen would meet the Resistance cell leaders and tell them they had established an advanced military base and were recruiting for a final and decisive battle against Zheng's forces. After that, one of two things would happen: they'd either immediately join up—as Tarq predicted, after the stunt he pulled on live TV, there was no shortage of volunteers—or they'd send one or two representatives to see Winterfell with their own eyes and report back. Apparently, there was a rumor this whole thing was a government conspiracy to flush out the Resistance members. Either way, I'd send a Firefly, escorted by five Vipers, to bring them in. The Fireflies could deal with any threat

Zheng's forces would pose and didn't need an escort, but I missed flying.

Liz and I took part in the first escort mission. This was also the first time we actually flew Vipers, a mind-blowing experience, despite having "real" memories of having done it already hundreds of times. This was when I figured out how to distinguish my real experiences from the fake ones: The fake memories had all the visual, tactile, and auditory details you'd expect from the real thing but lacked the intensity of sensation I felt when I flew. Rejuvenated by adrenaline, I felt ultra-awake. My heart raced, and warmth radiated throughout my body. The huge smile that cracked my face was also missing from the fake memories. I guess MICI underestimated how much I loved flying.

"I'm a leaf on the wind; watch how I soar," I murmured.

"The person who said that died almost immediately," Venom pointed out.

Inside the cockpit, I was surrounded by an ocean of buttons, knobs, and screens, showing different measurements. Most of them were simulations shown on virtual screens hovering inside the cockpit. In my helmet, there was a visor that provided me with a head-up display, including the target indicator, fire control display, and gunsight. The control stick's movements were used by the fighter's computer to interpret the pilot's intentions, and then the computer would calculate the best way to execute the intended move.

The space fighter was amazing. She was fast: She could fly at 8000 miles per hour (eat your heart out, William Knight!), and the pilot wouldn't feel a thing inside the cockpit. I had no idea what the Akakies did with the g-force; I wasn't a scientist, and even if I'd been, this was a science-so-advanced-it-looks-like-magic territory. A Viper could ascend or descend vertically or even hover in the air like a chopper. She had three laser cannons, one under each wing and one under the cockpit, which were very handy in a dogfight. She also could carry two radar-guided beyond-visual-range (BVR) and six short-range missiles. We called them Phoenix and Sparrow.

When we were bringing people in, everyone would be scanned before boarding a Firefly to make sure nobody carried any kind of communication or tracking devices. Once inside the force field, communication with the outside world was only possible through Winterfell's communication center, so our location would be kept a secret. Upon arrival, the new people would sit in MICI, and after getting over the shock of the news about an impending alien invasion, they'd start their respective assignments. A few people, however, ended up complaining they were lied to and refused to join up. We erased their memories of the past few days and sent them back to wherever they came from.

Zheng's security forces got wind of our operation and tried their best to interfere, but there wasn't much they could do. Kurt and his people were already very good at operating in secret. Now that they were traveling around the planet in undetectable Fireflies they were for all intents and purposes untouchable—our ships were not invisible, but even the Xortaags couldn't detect them unless they knew exactly where to look. SCTU agents showed up a couple of times when our people were getting on board, which gave the Viper escorts something to do.

I was involved in one of these missions. Kurt and a group of Resistance fighters were in a warehouse, getting ready to move out and catch their ride at a nearby rendezvous point when they found themselves surrounded by SCTU, supported by half a dozen armored personnel carriers. Using our Phoenixes, we could vaporize them before they even understood what was going on, but Liz suggested we spare their lives, and I agreed.

We flew in together and hovered over the warehouse. I opened a channel to their command center and said, "This is Colonel Jim Harrison. Flying next to me is Colonel Elizabeth Lopez. You guys remember how we escaped your stupid prison in a spaceship, right?"

No answer. I was sure they remembered.

I continued, "Please leave this area immediately so that we can get to our friends."

Still no answer.

I tried to sound like a robot. "Go quietly, or there will be trouble."

"Seriously?" said Liz, sounding annoyed.

And the bastards started shooting at us.

I wasn't a bloodthirsty maniac. I preferred not to kill people, even SCTU agents. But if someone took a shot at me, my fighter, my friends, or people under my command, all bets were off. Especially if "people under my command" meant Liz.

I put my targeting plus on one of the APCs and pulled the trigger. The massive twenty-five-ton armored vehicle turned into scrap metal in a heartbeat.

I was still planning to blow up only one or two of the APCs and let the rest go, but now Liz was angry that they were shooting at me, and when she got mad, there was no stopping her. She flew in and let go of her Viper's weaponry. By the time she was done, you could gather what was left of five armored vehicles in a backpack.

SCTU also slipped a few spies into Winterfell. MICI weeded them out, and because they couldn't communicate with the outside world, it was a moot point anyway. These guys ended up in the brig until further notice.

With the recruits pouring in, I organized our first fighter pilot training session. Winterfell had a VR battle simulator where up to two hundred pilots could participate in a replicate dogfight with enemy ships. Once I got into the "canopy," there was no way to tell the difference between the simulation and an actual battle. I knew I was still on the ground, but all my senses told me I was flying in space. The simulator even pumped a hallucinogen into the canopy that made the pilots feel all the emotions they'd experience in a real battle: adrenaline rush, excitement, and even terror whenever one was in simulated mortal danger.

I opened a channel to my team. "Your mission, should you choose to accept it, is to try to keep up with me."

The simulation started, and Xortaag space fighters came at me hard and fast.

Their design was completely different from ours: They were rectangular, with a cockpit front and center, and a laser weapon on either side of the cockpit. They didn't carry any missiles. The Xortaag command had probably decided since they could easily dodge long-range missiles, and laser cannons were much more effective in close-range dogfights anyway, there was no need for them.

The Xortaags called their space fighters Deathbringers. I found that name pretentious—I preferred to call them Double Ugly—but it stuck. Deathbringers were slower and less maneuverable than our Vipers, but Tarq's people's research suggested an experienced pilot could hold his own against a Viper in a dogfight. The problem was most Xortaag pilots were experienced, whereas most of our pilots used to be civilians, chopper or even agricultural aircraft pilots.

When the simulated battle ended thirty minutes later, I looked at my screen and rubbed my temple. It was a good-news-bad-news situation. I'd destroyed twelve enemy vessels, but every pilot in my team, including Liz, had managed to get themselves shot down. That gave me a brilliant idea: The perfect nickname for our pilots would be "Redshirts."

"Let me guess," said Venom. "She tried to pull off an impossible maneuver."

I pulled up Liz's simulation. Yep. She had nine kills, but she'd exposed her fighter to enemy fire by attempting a maneuver I wouldn't dream of trying. I wasn't crazy.

We all had hundreds of hours of MICI-induced flight experience, but we still trained every day to get better. We also had daily competitions and awarded trophies to the pilot with the most kills. Most of the time it was me, of course.

Once I asked Tarq, "Why does the Xortaag fleet mainly consist of single-seat space fighters, as opposed to Galactica-type battlestars?"

"The Xortaags' offensive strategy is based on swarming the enemy with their space fighters," he answered. "They are so good at implementing this strategy that bigger starships are mostly useless against them, which is part of the reason why they defeated our fleet so easily."

Liz kept making rash decisions and jeopardizing herself during the simulations. I was worried her attitude might get her killed in an actual battle. One day, after she managed to crash and burn trying to execute yet another impractical maneuver, I decided to have a word with her. I approached her in a very professional manner, eloquently expressed my concerns, and with utmost respect urged her to be more cautious and try to look before she leaped.

She had none of it. She put her hands on her hips and said, "I take acceptable risks. Playing safe isn't the characteristic of a great fighter pilot. Plus, I'd never come to you and try to tell you how to pilot your bird, would I?"

"Have you ever seen me getting shot down?" I asked.

"No," answered Liz, "but that doesn't necessarily mean you're a better pilot. It could simply mean you're a chicken, playing it safe all the time."

Unlike Liz, I didn't get angry easily, but there were two ways to get under my skin. One was calling me a coward, and the other was questioning my skills as an excellent fighter pilot. "I kick your butt every day during combat practice, don't I?" I retorted.

Dark blue veins bulged out of her neck. "In simulation! I'd like to see you try in real combat!"

Whenever Liz got in one of her moods, arguing with her was pointless. I rubbed my temple and decided to pull rank. "You know what? As your superior officer, I *order you to stop taking stupid risks*."

I shouldn't have raised my voice.

She looked me in the eye, executed a perfect salute and said, "Sir, yes, sir!"

Oh-oh!

I ended up sleeping alone for the next few days.

ONE DAY, Kurt and I were working out at Winterfell's gym —a big room full of high-tech, white equipment—when Allen, accompanied by a large Slavic-looking man with a hard face and ridiculously huge biceps, approached us and said, "Kurt, meet one of our new recruits."

Kurt raised his eyebrows. "Sergei Molanov, as I live and

breathe. How on earth did you end up in here? This is Jim, by the way. Jim, Sergei here used to be Palermo's head of security."

"And lucky for you, apparently not very good at his job," I blurted out before my brain could catch up with my mouth. I didn't need this big scary-looking Russian as an enemy.

Sergei glared at me; then he told Kurt, "After Palermo's assassination, I was court-martialed and accused of negligence of my duties. As if it was my fault he couldn't keep it in his pants. I ran and later was contacted by the Resistance. I was told my particular set of skills would be appreciated. And here I am now."

Kurt shook his hand. "Welcome aboard. We can totally use a man like you. How's the kidney?"

"The one you shot? They had to remove it. I got transplant."

Kurt smiled. "Did you really have to take a bullet for Palermo, of all people?"

I couldn't control myself. "Wow! I don't mean to be rude, but what kind of an idiot jumps in front of a bullet meant for the Devil himself?"

Sergei shrugged. "I was just doing my job."

"That's exactly what I said when Allen here insisted I shoot you too when I was eighty-sixing Palermo," said Kurt.

"So, you are big boss around here?" Sergei asked.

I found it amusing that Sergei, like a lot of Russians, didn't use articles when he talked, despite otherwise speaking perfect English. Kurt smiled. "You'd think that, right? No. Our commander's a man named Tarq. You might meet him soon enough."

I added, "Fair warning: Dude's super bossy. When he says jump, you can't even ask how high."

"That's weird. I didn't picture you as order-following type," Sergei told Kurt.

Kurt and I exchanged a look, and I said, "Let's go. I'll give you a tour. And after that, I want to show you something."

* * *

I KNOCKED on Tarq's office door and with exaggerated politeness asked him, "Have you got a minute, *sir*?"

We entered his office, which was big enough to accommodate all of us: Liz, Kurt, Allen, Sergei and me.

Tarq, sitting behind a huge white desk, looked at us and asked, "What's up?"

I pointed at Sergei. "Meet Sergei, a new recruit. He hasn't been through MICI yet."

Sergei approached Tarq, pulled a gun, aimed it at his head and said, "Here's what'll happen. We'll go to this brain-washing device of yours, and you'll undo whatever the hell you've done to my friends so they won't be your puppets anymore."

Tarq paled, but he stood his ground. "Over my dead body. I do not take orders from thugs."

Sergei shot his chair, right between his legs.

Tarq folded like a cheap suit.

The first person who entered MICI was Allen, who pushed everyone else out of the way. While we were waiting, Tarq, biting his nails, asked, "How did you do it? MICI should have stopped you from telling anyone."

"Should we tell him?" I asked Kurt.

Kurt shrugged. "It was your plan."

"I showed MICI to Sergei, emphasizing it can make changes in people's brains," I told Tarq. "I also casually let it slip you were very bossy, and we had to follow your orders. Then we showed him an old movie called *The Demolition Man.*"

Tarq looked confused.

I continued, "In this movie, some asshole tries to pull the same stunt you pulled, only for his target to bring some of his friends to shoot his ass. Sergei made the connection himself."

"It is a bit farfetched; is it not?" Tarq asked.

I answered, "It is. We tried this with several people, including every single person on whom MICI didn't work. Sergei's the only one who made the connection. Everyone else just thought it was weird we were showing them old movies."

"I am genius," said Sergei humbly.

When Allen walked out of MICI, Liz asked, "Did it work?"

Allen said, "Only one way to find out." He approached Tarq and punched him really hard in the belly.

His fist disappeared inside Tarq's belly all the way to his wrist before it hit something.

The small man fell to the floor, coughing and retching.

I jumped out of my socks. "Wow! Did you guys see that?"

Astonished, Liz and Sergei answered together, saying "yeah" and "da" respectively.

I walked towards Tarq in order to touch him but froze in place as soon as I got close to him.

Elizabeth asked Kurt, "Why you don't look surprised?"

"Well, you know, Allen and I knew about this," answered Kurt.

"What? How?" I asked.

"You don't get to survive in the Resistance without

being slightly paranoid," said Kurt. "You remember he asked us not to touch him the first time we met? We didn't buy his explanation at all, so one day I invited Barook to have a beer with me and spiked his drink with a sleeping pill."

I laughed. "You roofied Barook? How did you know it'd work, alien physiology and all?"

"I didn't, but it did work," answered Kurt. "I touched his skull with a stick after he fell asleep. Two inches of the stick disappeared into his skull before it touched something."

"But we were ordered not to touch them," said Liz.

Kurt patiently explained, "No, we were ordered not to violate their personal space, as in not to get close. I touched him with a six-foot stick, without getting close myself."

Tarq was just beginning to pull himself together. "Care to explain?" I asked him.

He threw up his hand in despair. "Okay! Okay! I confess. I am not humanoid. What you see is a hologram that reads my emotions and translates them into human facial expressions. You have never seen my true form."

"That explains Barook's beard," I said.

"That's your takeaway from all this? He's wearing a hologram!" Allen told me.

"Why do you hide?" Liz asked Tarq.

"You have to ask?" answered Tarq. "With your racist boyfriend standing right here? Some of you humans do not tolerate different appearances within your own species. God only knows how you would react to non-humanoid aliens."

"I'm *not* a racist!" I shouted.

Kurt gave me a sideways look.

That hurt. I mean, that really, really hurt. "Et tu, Kurt?"

"Et me. You know, maybe just a little bit," answered Kurt. "You remember Alejandra from college?"

"That had nothing to do with race. I just don't like fat people."

"And our chemistry teacher in high school, Mr. Padishah?"

I was on the verge of losing it. "He was mean. What's wrong with you?"

Allan, enjoying himself way too much, said, "If it walks like a duck and talks like a duck, it's a freaking racist."

Sergei loudly cleared his throat. "I hate to stop this fascinating and educational discussion, but aren't we forgetting something?"

We all stared at Tarq, who looked like he was trying to sneak away. He sighed. "We felt it would be easier for you to trust us if we looked human."

Allen, touching his sidearm, said, "So on top of brainwashing us to follow your orders, you've been lying to us all this time. I want to see what you really look like."

"Absolutely not," said Tarq.

Allen drew his gun and cocked it dramatically. "My friend here says otherwise. For all we know, you might look like a freaking insect, like those bugs in that old movie, *Star Wars Troopers*."

"*Starship Troopers*," I corrected him.

"Same difference," said Allen.

Strangely enough, Tarq stood his ground. "Over my dead body."

I noticed I wasn't curious about how he really looked at all. God damn it!

I whispered in Liz's ear, "Do you think he doesn't want us to see him because he's so ugly it might gross us out?"

She shrugged. "Who cares as long as he looks human?"

I rubbed my temple. We had to find a way to reboot our brains or something.

We all stood there, looking at each other for a minute, not sure what to say next. Then Tarq asked with a terrified expression, "What will happen now?"

Kurt placed his hands in his pockets. "I don't know. Do you have any orders, Commander?"

The look on Tarq's face was priceless. I think he'd thought we—or at least Allen—were going to straight-up murder him.

"Listen carefully because I am going to say this only once," Kurt told him. "We like you. In fact, we like you a lot, even if you really do look like a bug. Not to mention we all owe you our lives."

"Not that he saved us out of the goodness of his heart," Allen interjected.

Kurt ignored him. "But we aren't your slaves. We'll follow your orders as commander of Winterfell, but if we disagree with you, we'll voice our concern and talk about it. And if we feel strongly about an issue, the five of us will vote."

"I am honored," said Sergei.

Kurt answered, "Not you, genius. The five of *us*, including Tarq."

Tarq let out a huge breath. Allen asked, "Can I punch him one more time, just on principle?"

"It goes without saying we want you to remove your, eh..." said Kurt.

I suggested, "Puppetmaster program?"

"Remove your puppetmaster program from everyone's mind."

Tarq protested, "We have more than forty thousand people here."

"Then we'd better start as soon as possible."

Tarq pressed his lips together and nodded.

"One more thing: Why did you choose this look?" I asked.

Tarq shrugged. "I just wanted to look different from you people."

"You people? And I am the racist around here?" I said.

We were about to leave when Allen facepalmed and told Tarq, "Shit! I totally forgot. I want you to remove whatever you put in my head that stops me from smoking."

Kurt intervened. "Allen, we talked about this. Tarq's Winterfell's commander. If he wants you to stop smoking, that's that."

"It's okay. I guess he has earned it," said Tarq with a cracking voice, looking down at his feet.

He sounded so defeated I felt bad for him. Poor little guy. Maybe we were too tough on him.

Allan smiled with a gleam in his eyes and with wide steps walked back into MICI, holding his head up like a conquering hero. Tarq played with the controls for a few seconds. When Allen came out a few minutes later, his expression had completely changed. He looked sort of listless, and he just stood there, staring at us without saying anything

"Allen, are you okay?" asked Kurt with concern in his voice.

Allen looked at him with sleepy eyes and said, "Mooooo."

Tarq cracked up.

Kurt approached his old mentor, grabbed his shoulders and shook him, "Allen! What's wrong?"

"Mooooo," Allen repeated eloquently. Tarq was laughing so hard he was bending over and grabbing his sides. He looked like he was about to start rolling on the floor, roaring with laughter like a maniac. I couldn't help chuckling either.

Allen thought he was a freaking cow for a whole week. He spent all his time in Winterfell's parks, chewing on vegetables and hanging out with other imaginary cows. Tarq and Barook took several selfies with Allen when they were feeding him grass or riding him. The images went viral in Winterfell.

* * *

I APPROACHED Tarq in his office. "Tarq, old buddy old pal, I want you to help me solve a big problem. Can you please send one of your robots to clean my quarters once a week? Make sure the bed sheets are spotless."

Liz had taken care of cleaning our quarters for a few weeks, but she'd gotten fed up and asked me to pull my weight and pitch in, which included horrors like washing the bed sheets and pillowcases. My admittedly weak I-am-the-pants-wearing-head-of-the-household didn't work, and she gave me two options: clean our quarters once a week or live alone.

Tarq laughed in my face. "Those robots play a vital role in Winterfell's smooth operation. Do you really expect me to use them for something as trivial as this?"

"I expected this answer," I said, "so I'm gonna give you an offer you can't refuse."

"All ears," he said.

I leaned forward and looked into his eyes. "You know how many times I've seen you shamelessly ogling my girlfriend?"

Tarq's brown skin turned into a fiery shade of red. He

averted his eyes and mumbled, "What? No. I stopped the first time you told me to."

"Relax. I got angry at first but then realized I had no reason to be threatened by you; otherwise, I'd have wrangled your neck by now. You're three feet shorter than Liz, and fortunately for both of us, she doesn't have a midget fetish."

Tarq looked relieved. I continued, "Lay it on me. What is it? Are you into very tall women?"

Tarq chewed on his lower lip for a few seconds. "Okay. I tell you the truth. My people have a very strong sexual appetite, and we are seriously into interspecies sex. And humans are ravishing. Barook and I have had to take medication to control our sexual urges since we came here. Still, sometimes it is very difficult."

Too much information.

"I tell you what: You get my quarters cleaned regularly, and I'll take you to a place where you can ogle as many women as you want," I said, "as long as you bring enough cash. We aren't strapped for cash here, are we?"

He scoffed. "I can get in and out of any bank account I want. Our financial resources here are limitless."

Two days later, Tarq and I—in heavy disguise—walked into an expensive strip club in LA's suburbs. Unable to contain his excitement, Tarq had the expression of a child discovering ice cream for the first time. I left him there and went to a nearby hotel, after reminding him several times we had a Firefly to catch the next day.

The day after, around noon, I pulled up my rental car in front of the strip club and called Tarq. I was a bit worried about him, so I was relieved when he slid into the passenger seat a few minutes later, looking safe, sound, and happy.

And then the back doors of my car opened and two women got in, talking and laughing loudly, obviously drunk. They were both tall, wearing heavy makeup, skimpy clothes, and very high heels. And both of them were famous porn stars.

I stared at Tarq, speechless, and blinked several times.

"Jim, meet Crystal and Amber," said Tarq. "They have agreed to be my guests at Winterfell for a month."

"For a million dollars each," said one of the girls, wiggling an index finger at Tarq.

"Oooh, I like this one," said the other woman, looking at me. "He's buff. Want to party with us and your friend here, sugar?"

"Thanks, but I have a girlfriend," I said politely, ever the gentleman.

"She can come too," said the woman.

Imagine that. Liz would kill the four of us with a broken beer bottle.

I leaned towards Tarq and whispered, "Dude, what're you doing? What've you told them?"

"Nothing," said Tarq. "They think we are a part of a secret government project. They have agreed to stay in my quarters for a month, after that we will wipe their memory with MICI and bring them back here."

"Both of them stay with you?" I asked. "I thought one of them was for Barook."

Tarq grinned. "I guess dear old Brook has to keep taking sexual urge suppression pills."

"Aren't you forgetting something? You are an alien inside a hologram."

"These girls will be too drunk and high to remember this small detail."

I rubbed my forehead. "You know, let's keep this

between us. I don't want Liz to find out you got me involved with porn stars."

He winked. "How did you know they are actresses?"

* * *

KYOTO - MARCH 5, 2078

KURT WAITED while the Japanese man sitting on the other side of the table consulted with his people. A few minutes later, the man told Kurt, "We all know you and your reputation. However, you have to admit it's a difficult story to believe, especially since you don't provide any details."

"For security reasons," said Kurt. "I'm sure you understand, Mr. Tanaka. You'll be fully briefed after joining up."

Tanaka was the leader of Japan's biggest Resistance group. While officially part of the Resistance, his group had a cold relationship with the rest of the Resistance fighters, a natural result of being on the other side of the war a few years ago. Kurt expected this to be a tricky meeting. He'd brought Allen along to meet Tanaka and a few of his lieutenants in one of their safe houses, a small studio flat in downtown Kyoto, hidden among a million similar apartments.

Tanaka answered, "With all due respect to both you and Mr. Jonson here—"

"Colonel Jonson," said Allen.

Tanaka looked confused. "We use military ranks in the Resistance now?"

"Our base commander is a real stickler for military etiquette," Kurt replied.

Tanaka said, "With all due respect to you and *Colonel*

Jonson, you don't expect us to walk blindly into something which could be a government trap, do you?"

"Of course not. I suggest you send one of your people. They can verify everything first-hand and report back to you."

A skinny young woman with long black hair, an eyepatch over her left eye and a monstrous dragon tattoo that covered her neck and arms said, "I'll go."

Tanaka introduced her. "This is Keiko Nishizawa. She's a legend among our people. You might've heard her name before."

The name was familiar, but Kurt couldn't place it. He nodded and didn't ask any questions, worried he might offend his host by not knowing who their "legend" was.

Kurt, Allen, and Nishizawa left shortly after. If the woman were surprised when she saw the Firefly waiting for them, she didn't show it.

Fireflies had a cabin which was a smaller replica of Winterfell's quarters. On their way back to Winterfell, Keiko asked, "So I take it Jim Hallison is with you now?"

"Hallison?" asked Allen.

Keiko gave him a hard look. Allen held his hands palms up and looked away.

"Yes. In fact, he's flying escort for our ship right now. Do you know him?" said Kurt.

"In a way. I shot his plane down over the Philippines," answered Keiko, "but not before he managed to shoot down two fighters in my squadron."

Kurt stared at her in astonishment. "You're *that* pilot!"

Allen chuckled. "This is gonna be so awkward."

"For both of us. He did this to me"—Keiko touched her eyepatch—"which ended my career as a fighter pilot and turned me into a desk jockey." Then she asked Kurt, "How do you know Hallison?"

"We've been friends since elementary school."

"It's a good thing I didn't kill him then," said Keiko. "The thought crossed my mind when he parachuted out. He'd killed one of my friends that day, and I figured I'd be saving a few of my countrymen whom he was likely to shoot down in the future."

"So why didn't you?" asked Kurt.

"I am not a murderer." She gave Kurt a sideways look and continued, "Or an assassin. I kill my enemies in combat, not when they are hanging helplessly from a parachute, and certainly not when they're having dinner with their family."

Kurt flinched and crossed his arms over his chest. He'd once assassinated one of Zheng's top henchmen at his home, through a very, very small window. He'd been proud of that shot until he found out the man was having dinner with his wife and two little kids.

Kurt was surprised by how much Keiko's comment hurt. He had no need to justify himself to this woman, and yet he did. "You told me you thought about straight-up murdering Jim because he'd killed one of your friends, right?"

"Yep."

"What if he'd killed a thousand?"

"You got me there," said Keiko. "You're right. Things aren't always clearly one way or another. Plus, who am I to talk? I've probably been involved in more death and destruction than you. Back in the day, I flew escort for several kamikaze missions."

"Each of which killed thousands of our troops," said Allen. "You're going to be very popular in Winterfell."

"Winterfell?" asked Keiko.

"I'll explain later," said Kurt. "I've been meaning to ask

you: What did Tanaka mean when he said you're a legend in Japan?"

"I'm the only Japanese ace pilot currently alive. During the war, I had twenty-nine kills."

"Seriously, Jim's going to love this," said Allen.

"He probably knows already, just like I know him by reputation," said Keiko. Then she asked Kurt, "Do you always wear perfume to such meetings? It's kind of weird."

"He showers in cologne five times a day," answered Allen. "You have no idea how difficult it was to convince him not to do that before missions so that the enemy couldn't just smell him."

A little while later, Keiko asked, "Do you mind if I smoke?"

"Go ahead. Enjoy it while you still can," Allen said with a distant stare.

"Why? Is smoking against the rules?"

"Not exactly," said Kurt. "You'll see. It's just a thing."

Kurt took Keiko on a short tour of Winterfell after they landed. The tour ended in front of MICI. There were four people there: Barook, a technician operating MICI under his supervision, and two Commandos who were posted there in case MICI caught a spy.

A few minutes later, Keiko walked out of MICI with the same dazed look on her face as everyone who had done this for the first time. She said, "There is an alien invasion on the way?"

"Yes," said Kurt.

Keiko tightened her fists and looked into Kurt's eyes. "And we're going to defend humanity against it? Well, count me the hell in!"

Kurt chuckled. "We can certainly use someone with

your background. You're assigned to the fleet, right? Guess who the commander of the fleet is."

Something caught Kurt's attention: Barook and the MICI technician were staring at one of the screens and talking in a hushed voice. Kurt asked, "What's going on?"

Barook looked up from the screen. "Something's wrong."

"What, exactly?"

"Some of these readings make no sense." Barook looked at Keiko with confusion and added, "It is almost as if we have some false memories in here."

Kurt saw Keiko move from the corner of his eye. The woman was so fast she was a blur. She kicked the first Commando in the head and sent him flying to the wall. The second man drew his gun. Keiko grabbed the gun and twisted it down, breaking his fingers.

Kurt was caught off guard and reacted a tad too late. He didn't have the time to think about what was going on and moved purely on reflex. A second later the two of them were holding guns to each other's heads.

Kurt ground his teeth. He was disappointed that the woman was a double agent. He liked her, and more importantly, she was highly qualified and seemed like an efficient and determined individual. Kurt said with a stony expression, "So what's your plan? You're going to shoot everyone here with that gun and walk out? I'm pretty sure you don't have enough bullets."

"My plan's very simple," Keiko answered, her face passive. "I talk, you listen. For one minute."

"This is new. People who want to talk don't usually hold a gun to my head," said Kurt. "Shoot...As in *talk*. One minute."

"I'm a soldier," said Keiko. "When Tanaka asked me to

join the Resistance, it was my duty to report this to my superiors. When they asked me to say yes and infiltrate his cell, it was my duty to do that too."

Kurt opened his mouth to say something about misplaced loyalties, thought about it for a second, and closed his mouth.

Keiko continued, "But this? This changes everything, and as I said earlier, *I want the hell in!*"

"And after the stunt you just pulled, we should trust you because?"

"For one thing;"—she handed her gun over, grip first—"for another, this machine reads minds, right? Put me back in. Use it as a lie detector."

Kurt looked sideways at Barook. "Whole lotta good it did us the first time."

Barook said, "We caught her, didn't we?" and asked Keiko, "How did you pull it off?"

"I held on to a clear image of myself as a real Resistance fighter," said Keiko. "I meditate regularly and have very good mental discipline."

"If Jim were here, he'd make a Mr. Spock reference right now," said Kurt.

One of the Commandos was unconscious; the other was sitting on the floor grabbing his broken fingers. Kurt nodded at them and said, "Was this really necessary?"

"I was worried you might shoot me before I had the chance to say my piece," answered Keiko. "You do have a reputation for shooting first, shooting second, and never asking questions after all."

Kurt couldn't help smiling. "Can't argue with that."

* * *

I was having dinner with Liz in the mess hall when a Japanese woman wearing an eyepatch and sporting a ridiculously big tattoo approached us and saluted. "Lieutenant Colonel Keiko Nishizawa, reporting for duty, sir."

My mouth fell open. Coming face to face with the star of your nightmares wasn't something that happened every day. I was so shocked it didn't even occur to me to make a pirate joke.

Slightly over two years ago, in the final days of the war, I was flying my F-42 over the Philippines when on my radar screen I saw a Japanese fighter zooming straight for me. I didn't know it at the time, but the enemy pilot was Nishizawa, and I'd just shot down two of her friends.

I turned my fighter jet around to meet the new threat. A few minutes later, after she countered all my most sophisticated maneuvers, got a lock on my jet fighter and fired a missile, I realized for the first time in my life I had come up against a fighter pilot more skillful than I was. I froze up in my cockpit, not able to move a muscle, even finding it hard to breathe. A few seconds later her missile hit my F-42.

I'd often thought about that moment, wondering if I could've evaded her missile if I hadn't so suddenly become catatonic.

In my entire career as a fighter pilot, this was the only time I got shot down. I took it hard. Just because of this one incident, I was diagnosed with PTSD after the war, and it took me three months of intensive therapy to get over it. My therapist, a good-looking middle-aged woman named Dr. James, told me the problem was I'd been fully convinced of my invincibility, and getting into a dogfight with a better fighter pilot had temporarily ruined my faith in myself, resulting in a severe panic attack, which in turn had triggered a fight-flight-freeze response. I sure as hell hoped this wasn't all just technobabble for calling me a coward.

Allen, standing behind Nishizawa with Kurt and obviously enjoying himself, said, "Awkwaaard!"

Lieutenant Colonel? What the hell?

Liz nudged me with her elbow and crisply returned Nishizawa's salute. I followed suit, though a bit hesitantly.

"I take it you know our new recruit," said Kurt.

Feeling more like my usual self, I said, "Yeah, we're old friends. More like brothers and sisters, really. Same as Cain and Abel, if Cain was a woman."

"Don't mind him," Kurt told Nishizawa. "It's nothing personal. He gets like this when he's nervous."

"I'm not nervous," I said. "Why would I be nervous?"

Liz patted my arm.

"Allow me to address the elephant in the room," said the Japanese woman with a glint of humor. "We fought on the opposite sides of the war. We were both soldiers, following orders. It was a long time ago under completely different circumstances. I have to know there're no hard feelings before we can move forward."

I thought about it, all eyes on me.

I stood up and offered my hand. "None. Well, maybe a tiny bit. But to be honest, I'm happy to have someone with your experience and skills on my team."

She shook my hand. "Happy to be here. And allow me to say you can be my wingman any time."

I blinked. "You've read my book, or you're quoting *Top Gun*?"

"Your book. I don't watch Hollywood movies, except for the sword-and-sandal ones, and they don't even make them anymore."

She was growing on me already. Any person who could quote my book (my baby!) had a special place in my heart.

Still, later that evening I went to Tarq's office and asked him to demote Keiko. I argued appointing a Japanese woman as the second-in-command of the fleet wouldn't sit well with most other pilots, given that the war had happened only three years ago and there were a lot of open wounds. I went out of my way to make it clear my request was for the good of the fleet and I had nothing personal against Keiko.

From behind his desk, Tarq gave me a level look. "MICI judges people not by the color of their skin but by the content of their character."

Did he just quote Martin Luther King?

"I'm not a racist, you idiot!" I shouted, dangerously close to foaming at the mouth.

He blew his pipe's smoke to my face. "Keep telling yourself that. Request denied."

"I don't have to listen to you anymore, remember?" I said. "I can call for a vote."

"Sure you can. But let me ask you this: Do you really think Elizabeth and Allen will support you on this one?"

He was right. Liz would never agree to someone being demoted without having done something wrong first, even if it made sense. And Allen would vote against me just to spite me.

Tarq knew he had won. He puffed on his pipe and said, "Trust me; it is always fun to watch someone kick a hornet's nest. You will see."

I rubbed my forehead. That right there was the main reason Tarq made illogical decisions from time to time. He wanted to create chaos and watch what happened, just for his own freaking amusement.

One of these days, we were all going to pay the price for this.

WINTERFELL - MARCH 11, 2078

KURT AND ALLEN were having dinner in the mess hall when Keiko walked in. It was late, and the only other people there were a group of pilots who looked like they had just come back from the beach volleyball game in *Top Gun*. They were talking and laughing loudly, but as soon as Keiko came in, they all became very quiet and stared at her with open animosity.

Keiko's rank had generated a lot of negative feelings among the pilots. It didn't help that Keiko was the first and until Nakata's people arrived the only Japanese in Winterfell. Nor did it make her any friends that she scored so high in the daily dogfight competitions, even higher than Jim on several occasions.

Kurt told Allen, "Remember Jim being concerned about people's reaction to Keiko's rank? I'm beginning to think he might've had a point."

One of the pilots shouted, "One-eyed Japanese whore!"

Keiko stopped motionless for one second; then, carrying her food tray, she walked toward the pilots and asked in a mild tone, "Who said that?"

Kurt whispered, "Oh-oh."

"This is gonna be interesting," said Allen.

A tall, bulky man stood up, smirking. He was easily twice as big as Keiko who was no more than 110 pounds. Keiko looked him up and down and said, "I do have only one eye, and I am indeed Japanese, but call me a whore one more time."

The man laughed and said, "Who—"

Keiko hit him with the aluminum tray in the face so hard that Kurt could've sworn he saw a few teeth flying out. He went down hard and didn't get up.

Stunned, the other pilots—all fifteen of them—didn't move for a second, staring incredulously at Keiko. Then they jumped out of their seats, fury on their faces. Keiko took a step back, bent her knees and brought her fists up in a fighting position.

Kurt said, "Shit!" and with Allen at his heels ran to join the fight.

Less than ten minutes later, Kurt was back at his seat. He checked his reflection in a silver-plated spoon to make sure not a strand of hair was out of place. Allen joined him. He was grabbing his side, grimacing. Kurt asked, "What happened to you?"

"I got punched in the kidney," said Allen. "I'll be pissing blood for a week."

Kurt laughed. "One of those yahoos landed a punch? You're getting old and slow, my friend."

Keiko, having picked up a new tray, approached them and asked, "Can I join you guys?"

Allen growled, "You aren't getting anywhere near me with that lethal weapon in your hand."

"By all means. Nice moves back there, by the way," said Kurt.

"I have been practicing aikido since I was eight." She sat down and asked, "Shouldn't we call a doctor or something?"

Kurt looked at the fighter pilots, some unconscious, some grabbing various dislocated joints and broken bones, moaning painfully, and said, "Nah. It'll be a good lesson for them."

* * *

IN THE COMMAND CENTER, I waved the hospital report under Kurt's nose and shouted, "Sixteen pilots are in the hospital. There're so many broken bones in this report I can't even count them. And a concussion! *Concussion!*"

Kurt, trying to stifle a laugh, said, "This last one was your own second-in-command's masterpiece. She broke a chair on one of the pilots' head. I swear Allen and I went easy on them."

Liz looked at Keiko with newfound respect, much to my chagrin.

I could feel my face steaming. I yelled, "But the rest are there because of you and this bald gorilla."

That would normally cause a reaction from Allen, but he was having too much fun to get angry. He said, "A gorilla fights much better than a bunch of monkeys, eh?"

Feeling suicidal, I clenched my fists and took a step towards Allen. Tarq interfered. "Knock it off, Jim. All they did was stop your men from beating up a superior officer, which would have gotten them court-martialed."

I couldn't stop fuming though. For one thing, you didn't mess with people under my command, period. For another, the story that Kurt and Allen, with some help from Keiko, had beaten up sixteen pilots had spread throughout Winterfell. All the pilots were embarrassed. To make matters worse, a few of the more macho—or stupid—pilots had tried to provoke some Commandos into fighting them, and they had ended up having their asses handed to them too.

My pride shouldn't have been so hurt. Kurt and Allen

were both masters in martial arts and hand-to-hand combat, even before MICI, which had imprinted them with God knows what other skills. Scant consolation though.

To top it all off, Tarq ordered all officers who had shown or expressed "any racist tendencies" to report to MICI. That somehow included me, even though I had nothing to do with the brawl. Sometimes the whole world conspired against you. This was how my name entered the history books as one of the first people on Earth who was sent to rehabilitate his racist tendencies by an alien. I never believed for a minute MICI could do anything to "remove racist predispositions" as Tarq put it. This had to be just another one of his stupid pranks.

A few days later and only after I calmed down, Kurt came to me and said, "I'm concerned about lack of discipline among the fighter pilots, Jim. Whatever those pilots' personal feelings were, they shouldn't have dared to attack a superior officer. And to be brutally honest, your own second-in-command doesn't seem to give a rat's ass about your orders half the time."

My "second-in-command" being Liz, that was a keen observation.

"Kurt, this isn't the freaking military," I said. "I have zero real authority over the people under my command, and the fact that our so-called commander treats everything like a freaking joke doesn't help either. If they don't listen to me, what am I supposed to do about it?"

Kurt smiled. "First off, you complaining that Tarq fools around too much is the pot calling the kettle black. Secondly, the Resistance wasn't a military unit either, but it was perfectly understood that if someone didn't listen to Allen or me, we'd take them to the back and shoot them in the head."

"Did you ever actually shoot anyone in the head?" I asked.

"Nope."

"See?" I said. "This is the problem. You and Allen have a reputation I simply don't have. Everyone knows I am an ace pilot, but people see me more as a movie star than a leader. Plus, let's be honest; I'm really not one."

"We could use MICI to make them follow your orders."

I protested, "Absolutely not! How's that different from what Tarq did to us? No, I just have to earn their respect, one way or another."

That was easier said than done, though. The problem was I'd been appointed as the commander of the fleet because I was the first fighter pilot to arrive at Winterfell. I hadn't earned my command. If I wanted to gain the other pilots' respect, I had to do something amazing, and all I'd done by now was flying escort missions and winning meaningless competitions.

I wondered what Tarq had seen in me to appoint me commander. Being an excellent fighter pilot didn't by itself qualify me for a command role. In all likelihood, Tarq had made a mistake, or it was one of his damned pranks.

"On the bright side, I think having Keiko around might help because nobody dares mess with her," said Kurt.

"And this is supposed to make me feel better?" I asked.

* * *

WINTERFELL - MARCH 12, 2078

ELIZABETH ASKED with surprise in her voice, "It's done already?"

Tarq answered, "Yes, and all the money now is in the account you provided. Completely untraceable, of course."

They were sitting in Tarq's office. Less than two hours ago Elizabeth had given him a list of the names of Zheng's top officials, including the chancellor himself, and asked him to find out their banking information and transfer all their money to a Swiss bank account she'd opened. Tarq, who had considered this a funny practical joke, had assured her this was a piece of cake for him. Still. She couldn't believe Tarq had stolen millions from the most dangerous men on the planet in a matter of hours, even with Akakie technology at his disposal.

She said, "There's one more favor I need you to do for me. I'm going to send you the names of several charities, including the one that I've founded, and I want you to send the money to them anonymously."

New York's orphans were going to be well taken care of for a while.

"All of it?" asked Tarq.

"How much is there?"

Tarq brought up a screen and pointed at it.

Elizabeth gasped and grabbed Tarq's arm. She counted the zeroes twice to make sure she hadn't made a mistake and then asked, "What do you say we keep a couple of hundred million dollars as a little nest egg for Jim and me?"

CHAPTER SEVEN

New York - March 18, 2078

Kurt looked at the man sleeping on his bed in full uniform and for a brief moment pitied him. He'd obviously been too tired to change before going to bed. Everyone who was working at SCTU had been pulling double or triple shifts in the past few weeks with absolutely nothing to show for it. They were all chasing ghosts, and the couple of times they had gotten close to catching some Commandos, Jim and his pilots showed up and blew up everything to hell.

Kurt kicked the man's ankle a few times. He opened his eyes, and after seeing Kurt, he swore and tried to grab the weapon hidden under his bed, only for Kurt to draw a gun and shoot his hand. He opened his mouth to shout. Kurt put his index finger on his lips, asking him to be quiet. "Lieutenant Eric Green. I guess you know who I am."

The SCTU officer stared at him with fear in his eyes. Kurt added, "Relax. I am not here to kill you. A few months ago, you were in charge of the team searching Jim Harrison's house. You found a ring there. I know you've sold it. I want to know who the buyer is."

* * *

WITH EVERYTHING ELSE GOING ON—THE alien invasion and whatnot—I'd almost forgotten I was planning to get married.

Kurt hadn't.

One morning, I was eating breakfast when he showed up, threw me a small gift-wrapped box and said, "I've got a present for you."

I widened my eyes in feigned horror and shouted, "*What's in the box? What's in the box?*"

Kurt sighed. "I have no idea what you're doing right now."

I opened the present to find the ring I was planning to give Liz.

Amazed, I asked, "How on earth did you find it?"

Kurt winked at me. "I used to moonlight as a private detective before Zheng's coup."

"Seriosly?"

He rolled his eyes. "It was a joke, hense the wink."

"It's not funny if you have to explain it."

"Look who's talking. No one understand a half of your references."

"I know," I said. "But those who do really like them."

"So when are you going to propose?"

"Tonight," I said immediately. "I have a sneaky feeling that if I wait, another earth-shattering event might ruin my plans again."

"In that case, I have another present for you," said Kurt, handing me a plastic bag.

* * *

I CALLED OUT, "Sweetheart? You gonna be in there long?"

Liz said, "Just a minute," and a couple of minutes later walked out of our bathroom, wrapping a white towel around her wet body.

That figure!

I was standing in the middle of our quarters, grinning from ear to ear like an idiot, one of my hands hiding behind my back. On our bed, there was a big bouquet of fresh flowers I'd stolen from Winterfell's park (Tarq could sue me), a teddy bear, a bottle of red wine, and a big heart-shaped box of chocolates. Kurt had given me the last three items. Soft, romantic music and smell of the roses filled the room.

Surprised, Liz asked, "Eh, what's all this?"

"I've got a surprise for you. Turn around."

Liz smiled (that smile!) and playfully turned around. I walked closer, started rubbing the wedding ring box against her bare shoulder skin and asked, "Can you guess what this is?"

Liz tried to reach back and touch the box, but I took it away from her reach. She giggled. "It had better *not* be a sex toy!"

"Pervert," I said.

She turned around to find me on one knee, with the box open to reveal a sparkling diamond ring. I asked, "Will you marry me?"

Liz's mouth gaped slightly open, and her eyes become as wide as small saucers. She covered her mouth with her hand. Her towel slipped a little, but unfortunately for me, she managed to hold on to it. She looked like she wasn't sure what to say for a few long seconds, during which time my heart thumped against my ribcage so loudly I wondered if she could hear it. Then she bent over, kissed me on the lips and said, "Before I say yes, I have a condition."

"Whatever you want, sweetheart."

"If at any stage before, during or after the ceremony, the words 'Red Wedding' come out of your mouth, I'll cancel the whole thing!"

She knew me so well. I'd already thought about five different Red Wedding related jokes.

We asked Tarq to marry us. As Winterfell Commander, he was the logical choice, plus we figured it'd be cool to be the first couple in the world who were married by an alien. With the Xortaag fleet on the way, we decided to get married as soon as possible and chose the last day of March for our wedding.

It was a simple but beautiful ceremony. Liz looked stunning in her white wedding dress. I couldn't stop staring at her. She looked lovelier every time I looked at her. Or maybe I was just noticing more—the slant of her eyes, the curve of her cheek, the way her smile twitched up right before it broke out into full wattage. I was wearing my dark blue full dress uniform. We'd invited all our friends. My best man was Kurt, wearing his trademark black trench coat, accompanied by my groomsmen, Liz's brother Matias, and Allen, of all people.

I rubbed my forehead. Allen was one of my groomsmen. It was complicated.

Liz's maid of honor was Keiko, also in uniform. The two of them had become good friends in the past few weeks. I suspected Liz really enjoyed it whenever I got my ass kicked by Keiko in a simulated competition, which happened more often than I was willing to admit. Her bridesmaids were her two sisters, Samantha and Theresa, one lithe and dark, one cocoa-colored and voluptuous, both almost as pretty as Liz, and Allen's daughter, Lilly.

Tarq, wearing his white tuxedo and feathered hat, performed his duties perfectly. He made a short, poetic speech about love, marriage, and family. He asked us, "Do you promise to honor and tenderly care for one another, cherish and encourage each other, stand together, through sorrows and joys, hardships and triumphs for all the days of your lives?"

I opened my mouths to say "I do" when a wailing siren filled up the room.

His eyes bulging, Tarq shouted, "This is the Xortaag invasion! Everyone! Report to your posts immediately!"

Barook jumped from his seat and ran towards the door.

What were the chances that this happened at the very moment when we were getting married?

* * *

WINTERFELL - MARCH 28, 2078

KURT CASUALLY ASKED TARQ, "By the way, you aren't planning one of your infamous practical jokes for Jim's wedding, are you?"

Accompanied by Allen, Kurt was in Tarq's office, briefing him on their latest recruitment efforts. Knowing Tarq's tendency to pull distasteful pranks, Kurt and Allen had decided to have a word with him before the wedding.

Tarq, caught off-guard, answered, "What? Who? Me? How? I have not even thought about such a thing!"

As if, thought Kurt. "What are you planning?"

"Nothing, I swear. I will never smear the sanctity of marriage with a prank, trust me!"

Allen leaned forward and growled, "Listen to me. You tell me what you're up to right this moment, or I'll break your fingers."

Tarq unconsciously hid his fingers, still holding his pipe, behind his back. "Okay! Take it easy. Nothing serious. I have hired a stripper to jump out of a fake wedding cake. That's it."

Kurt said, "You have to understand wedding ceremonies are extremely important for us humans, especially for the women. Don't even think about it. If you bring a stripper to the wedding, Elizabeth will strangle her to death, and then you, and we'll help her."

"Just to be on the safe side, we'll check the cake, or wherever else you can hide a nude woman," added Allen.

"I understand," said Tarq solemnly. "No pranks during the wedding. I promise."

"Speaking of Elizabeth, there's another issue I wanted to talk to you about," said Kurt. "Are you sure selecting her as the fleet's second-in-command was the right decision? She's a skillful pilot, but she isn't military, and she lacks the discipline of a career military woman like Keiko. She keeps ignoring Jim's orders."

Tarq smirked and moved his hand dismissively. "Don't worry about it. It's fun watching her bossing seasoned fighter pilots around."

After leaving Tarq's office, Kurt and Allen went to have dinner with Lilly. While eating, Kurt mentioned they'd confronted Tarq to the girl and found her staring at them in surprise.

"Didn't you tell me the Akakies consider practical jokes a form of art and put a ridiculous amount of energy into pulling one off?" asked Lilly. "And isn't this the same man who pulled the whole you-are-all-dead-and-in-heaven charade?"

Kurt nodded.

Lilly sighed. "The problem is neither you nor my dad have a sense of humor. Do you really think a man like that would do something as banal as hiring a naked woman to jump out of a cake?"

Kurt thought about it for a second; then he put his fork down on the table and laughed. "The two of us are supposed to be badass warriors, and that little sneaky alien fooled us so easily."

"Well, shit," said Allen.

"Language," said Kurt. "There're children present."

Lilly pretended she was about to throw a knife at him. "You won't call me a child when I reprogram one of Winterfell's robots to come to your room and kill you in your sleep."

"That won't work." Allen wolfed down a big chunk of meat. "Kurt sleeps with one eye open, and he has a gun under his pillow. Old habit."

"I can fill his room with gas using Winterfell's environmental control system," said Lilly.

Allen gave his daughter an admonishing look. Kurt asked him, "And who do you think she's inherited these violent tendencies from?"

"Her mother," said Allen without hesitation. "You think I'm violent? I'm a cute puppy compared to that woman."

"He's right, actually," said Lilly. "I still have bruises from my childhood when I had to live with her."

"Here is a question I've been wanting to ask you for a long time," Kurt told them. "You guys are sure you're Canadian?"

"This sounds like something Jim would say," said Allen. "How many times have I said that boy has a bad influence on you?"

* * *

THE ANSWER to my previous question? None. Or at least astronomical.

Kurt and Allen had approached Barook and pretended they were in on the prank, with Kurt saying something like, "This will be the best practical joke ever!" Barook boasted how great the prank would be and gave Kurt and Allen enough clues to put it all together.

Tarq was speechless when he saw us standing there and smiling at him. I waved my hand dismissively. "Can we please get on with it?"

Tarq pulled himself together and showed enough grace to continue the ceremony. When we were saying our vows, I noticed Allen wipe a tear from his face. Maybe the old man wasn't that bad, after all. We exchanged our wedding rings. I told Liz, "I'll be wearing this for the next hundred years," and I kissed the bride. There were cheers, and someone whooped.

Mrs. Elizabeth Harrison. It had a nice ring to it. Or was it Mrs. Harrison-Lopez? Lopez-Harrison?

We had a festive reception after the ceremony. We ate, drank, danced, and incessantly made fun of Tarq for his failed prank. I looked at my friends and in-laws' faces, and happiness swelled inside me like a warm ocean wave. I let it soak right into my heart, savoring every moment, forgetting about the Xortaags and the deadly danger they posed to humanity. Being an only child and not close to my parents, this was the first time in my life I felt I had a family. I wanted to make sure I still remembered these moments vividly when I was old. And for once, Venom was quiet.

We got a lot of wedding presents. Tarq gave us two VR headsets that could convert any normal movies into holographic ones, with the viewer in the thick of the action. Liz loved Keiko's present, a beautiful Japanese tea set. Kurt didn't give us anything. He said, "Your present will be ready by the time you come back." Very mysterious.

When we were dancing, Liz told me, "I have to make a confession: I love someone else, but his parents didn't let us get married."

I pretended I was having a heart attack.

Life was good.

Later on, after we were back in our quarters, alone, Liz hugged me and with her sexy British accent whispered in my ears, "My husband! I love you."

I caressed her thick curly hair and said, "My wife! I love you more."

* * *

With Tarq's permission, Liz and I went on a one-week honeymoon. We took a Firefly and landed on a small uninhabited island in the Pacific Ocean, where we camouflaged the ship and used it as a temporary residence. It was only the two of us, a bunch of movies, a lot of wine, and a pristine, breathtakingly beautiful beach. We ate and drank and danced and made love and watched movies—not necessarily in that order—for the whole week without a single care in the world. It was heaven.

The last evening on the island, while we were drinking on the beach, next to a bonfire, and listening to the relaxing sound of the waves, I said, "I wish we didn't have to go back."

My wife, a bit drunk, asked, "You what now?"

"I'm so happy here, and all I want in my life is to be with you. We could just stay here, or even take the Firefly and go wherever we want. We'll take all our friends with us, even Allen."

"And Tarq?" asked Liz, playing with a lock of hair.

"Oh my God, no!" I feigned shock. "He'll drive us crazy with his stupid pranks."

"Okay. Let's say Kurt, I, and the others decide to leave Earth and run away," she said. "Will *you* go?"

I thought about it for a minute. "Nope."

"Why not?"

I sighed. "You know why."

She chuckled. "Sure I do. You aren't going anywhere unless you can fit all the pilots under your command in this Firefly."

"Not only the pilots," I said. "The ground crew too. Anyone who is in the fleet is my responsibility, and they wouldn't leave without their family and friends. We'd have to take all the forty-six thousand people in Winterfell with us."

So just like Adam and Eve, we wound up leaving Heaven too. The difference was we left voluntarily. We returned to Winterfell as scheduled and were welcomed by my new in-laws and old friends.

After Liz and I entered our quarters, I put my bags down, stretched and said, "Home, sweet home."

I jumped out of my skin when I heard Cordelia said in her dulcet voice, "Welcome home, Jim."

I gasped. "Cordelia! How? When? Where?"

"Kurt has asked me to tell you I'm your wedding present," she said. "Congratulations to you both, by the way."

"Thanks, Cordi," said Liz.

"FYI, Lilly has upgraded me using Akakie technology. I feel I'm a sentient being now," said Cordelia. "And fair warning: My tongue is sharper than ever."

"Maybe this wasn't such a good idea," said Venom. "Can we send her back?"

"With Cordelia and Venom living with us, we have a family already," I told Liz.

CHAPTER EIGHT

E arth's Exosphere - April 13, 2078, 11:00 EST

THE CRIMSON DEATHBRINGER appeared six thousand miles above Earth.

Maada looked at the blue planet in front of him and wondered how long it would take before someone detected his space fighter. This was an underdeveloped civilization, but their jet fighters, though outdated, had the capability to interfere with the deployment of the Voice of God, which made a full-scale invasion necessary.

Maada unconsciously rubbed the burn marks on his face. He got those many years ago in a battle over another blue planet, which looked like this one. He could easily have them—and the other scars and burn marks on his face and neck—removed, but he had earned them in battle and wore them like a badge of honor.

Maada had always enjoyed these solitary moments of just sitting there looking at his target. It had become a ritual for him. He lived for these moments, knowing what was about to follow. Since he was a child, he had known he was destined to do great things for his people, to change their world and ease their suffering. He could not have imagined he would end up conquering the galaxy, although now he did not see how it could have been otherwise. The galaxy was full of prizes his planet needed; what else was his life for? He had no wife, no children. A lifetime of military campaigns left no time for that. But his legacy, a Xortaag star kingdom ruling over the known universe, would last for thousands of years.

He felt sorry for the inhabitants of the planet. Unlike Mushgaana and most other Xortaags, who had convinced themselves they were indeed gods and would not spare a moment thinking about the other species in the universe, Maada regretted having to kill a whole sentient species off. He took no pleasure in it beyond the satisfaction of winning. He would have spared them if there had been enough wealth to go around, but sadly, there was not. His people were fertile. Twenty-five billion Xortaags lived on Tangaar. Without colonies, they would have all died a long time ago. A guilty conscience was a small price to pay for the survival of his people.

In a blink of an eye, the rest of the Xortaag fleet appeared behind him. Forty thousand space fighters, plus Mushgaana's command ship, which was the biggest military vessel in the fleet by a large margin. Despite her impressive array of both offensive and defensive weapons, she usually stayed as far away from danger as possible.

Maada smiled viciously, his compassion locked away until the next time he let it out for an airing. *People down there must be pissing their pants right about now*, he thought.

He contacted his fighter pilots and simply said, "Happy hunting."

The fleet started moving toward their target.

* * *

New York - 11.10 EST

Kurt was waiting with a group of recruits to be picked up by a Firefly when Tarq called him and said, "It has begun."

Kurt didn't need to ask what "it" was. Based on the reports sent by an Akakie spy ship shadowing the Xortaag fleet, Tarq had predicted they'd arrive today.

Kurt was in an abandoned building which used to be a shopping mall. Some fifty recruits were scattered in a big hall, some sitting on the dusty floor, some standing in groups or walking around. Allen and five other Resistance members were standing guard next to boarded windows.

"Jim is on his way to meet you," said Tarq. "We might have a problem though: If you are still on the way when OMC-BOWS starts to work, there is no telling how the new people will react. They might turn on you."

"Allen and I have already thought about that possibility," said Kurt.

He disconnected the call and put his PDD in the pocket of his black trench coat. He'd expected to be anxious, but to his surprise, he was calm, even though his breath slightly quickened. The whole alien invasion thing still felt more like a movie than reality. Plus, it was just another bunch of murderous madmen. He'd been standing up to these kinds of bastards for two years. Only this time he had an army behind him.

His footsteps echoing throughout the empty hall, he went to Allen. He was sharing the news when a tall, strikingly beautiful blonde approached them and said, "Eh, Mr. von der Hagen?"

Allen rolled his eyes and growled, "Colonel."

Kurt looked questioningly at the woman. She was dressed in blue jeans and a simple white t-shirt, but she looked more like a professional model than a Resistance fighter. "My name's Oksana," she said. "You don't know me, but I tipped you guys about Palermo's visit to The Harem."

"So in a way, you're the person who started all this," said Kurt.

"What do you mean?"

"Long story," said Kurt. "How did you find out about Palermo? He always managed to keep his movements secret."

Oksana nodded towards another young blond girl sitting on the ground. "My sister and I were forced to work there. Palermo beat her to within an inch of her life. I couldn't let him get away with it."

Kurt was taken aback. He was about to say something like "I am so sorry" when the woman said, "All due respect, if you say anything patronizing, *Colonel*, I'll break your jaw."

Kurt didn't show it, but he was pleased by her response. The woman was ready to throw it down with the strongest person in her new home. That showed character.

Allen snarled, "You have any martial arts training, girlie?"

"You want to see for yourself, old man?" Oksana countered.

"I like this one. She's feisty," Allen told Kurt.

Kurt tried to change the subject. "How did you end up with us?"

"My sister and I ran away from The Harem," she said. "We went to someone who had connections with the Resistance. He helped us join up, and here we are."

Allen checked his PDD. "Our ride is here."

A few minutes later, when they were all in, the Firefly took off. Kurt addressed the recruits, "I just want to apologize in advance about what comes next. Please believe me when I say this is for your safety."

Kurt and Allen put on gas masks and threw two gas grenades into the crowd.

An intense, primal fear seized Oksana. She'd come all this way to be killed in an ambush! At least she was with her sister in the end. She grasped Anastasiya's hand and managed to say, "Love all, trust a few," before she lost consciousness.

New York - 11.45 EST

Chancellor Zheng couldn't believe his own eyes.

Along with his top generals, he was sitting around an oval desk in their operation room, looking at a giant wall-mounted screen showing a fleet of alien spaceships approaching Earth. Scores of junior offices and aides were running around. Everyone was talking loudly at the same time. The operation room was so noisy Zheng had a hard time hearing his own thoughts.

Zheng felt he was about to throw up. His muscles were so tight his back ached. *This can't be happening*, he thought. All those years he plotted to be the most powerful man on Earth, the waiting, the sacrifices—he thought briefly of the wife who had left him, her accusations about his ego and cruelty—just for this. To be helpless, made a fool of. The loser in charge when aliens invaded.

It was a big fleet, some forty thousand ships. The air force fighters had scrambled to meet this unexpected threat, but the fact that the enemy was flying in space was a clear indication of their much superior technology and capabilities. This wasn't exactly news. It'd always been assumed if an alien species came to Earth, they'd be technologically more advanced than humans. Moreover, the combined number of all jet fighters on Earth was less than twenty-five thousand. The aliens had appeared so close to Earth that the armed forces had no time to form a strategic plan. Still, all over the world, every military unit with air-to-air or ground-to-air capabilities was getting ready to defend the planet.

Someone suggested, "Maybe they are peaceful?" which produced a few bitter snickers from the other officers.

No sentient species is peaceful, Zheng thought as the enemy fleet started shooting down the satellites orbiting Earth. The universe, the earth, a village, a family—all the same. The strong one took the prize. Once that had been him. He'd beaten his brother, other boys, other men, generals, that idiot Von der Hagen. Now some jacked-up reptile or walking slime had come to town,

"There goes GPS," Zheng murmured, trying to hide his terror.

"A few months ago, a bunch of Resistance fighters escaped in a spaceship," said a general. "Then Jim Harrison attacked our forces in an advanced and untraceable fighter, and now this happens. There must be a connection."

"Are you seriously suggesting the Resistance called aliens for help?" Zheng snapped at him.

The first man answered, "With respect, Chancellor, do you have a better explanation?"

"If these are von der Hagen's allies, I might as well eat my gun right now," Zheng whispered to himself.

As soon as the alien fleet reached the effective missile range of the air force fighters, a lieutenant announced, "Missiles away."

The fighter jets shot thousands of air-to-air BVR missiles at the enemy fleet. Zheng and his generals watched despairingly as the spaceships either destroyed or dodged the air force's most advanced missiles with such ease that it was humiliating. Zheng covered his eyes with a hand. The mood in the Operation Room got even darker. Some of the generals panicked and started shouting at each other.

I guess I'm not the biggest shark in these waters anymore. Welcome to the bottom of the food chain, thought Zheng. Beads of sweat ran down his face. He gaped at various screens showing the battle and wondered what he could do to save humanity.

* * *

WINTERFELL - 11.50 EST

WATCHING the Xortaag fleet on a holographic display, Tarq felt a sense of déjà vu.

"This is just like Alora again," he told Brook.

The Command Center door opened. Keiko and Sergey walked in. Keiko asked, "Would you mind if we join you?"

Tarq gestured towards the empty seats. "Not at all. Bring popcorn and let's enjoy the show."

Keiko gave him a sour look. "You'd better leave the comedy to Jim."

They watched in silence as the air force jet fighters and the Deathbringers joined in battle. The Xortaag vessels opened fire with energy weapons. The biggest air battle in history ensued, with thousands of fighters involved in close-range dogfights, shooting missiles, cannon shells and energy beams at each other, filling the sky with brilliant explosions and shining pieces of metal. Hundreds of fighter jet pilots were incinerated in their cockpits, nothing left of their bodies. The air force had no chance of beating the enemy. The Deathbringers were much faster and more maneuverable, and their energy weapons were a lot more effective. The air force started losing jet fighters by the dozens. Out of pure desperation, some pilots tried to ram their fighters into the spaceships, but that didn't work either.

Soon after, the enemy fighters started flying at low altitude and targeting the ground-based air defense systems. The anti-aircraft weapons crew fired millions of missiles and shells, lighting up the sky. Like the jet fighters, they had very little success, but it didn't stop them from trying. The Deathbringers massacred them by the thousands, adding to the rapidly growing list of human casualties.

Despite having predicted this exact outcome, Tarq's pulse raced, and violent tremors overcame his hands and fingers. Feeling his legs were too weak to support his weight, he grabbed a chair and sat down.

This is what will happen to Kanoor if I fail here.

* * *

THE XORTAAGS WERE FINALLY HERE, and I still had a hard time wrapping my mind around it. I half expected this to be yet another one of Tarq's practical jokes. His people were all pranksters, so who was to say they wouldn't send their entire fleet just to scare us to death and laugh about it later?

While flying to New York to pick up Kurt, Allen and some new people, I monitored communications between Earth forces and their command center—nothing as insignificant as military-grade encryption could stand in the way of Akakie technology—and followed the brutal battle raging all over the planet, involving thousands of jet/space fighters.

So it was real, after all.

It hit me like a fifty-megaton nuclear missile. I experienced an adrenaline rush greater by far than anything I'd felt before, even though as a fighter pilot I lived on adrenaline. This was what I'd trained for. After months of preparation, it was go time. I wasn't afraid. I was fired-up.

On our way back to Winterfell, I noticed a group of five F-46 jet fighters flying close to us. I intercepted their com and listened in to see what was going on.

Much to my surprise, two of them were my old buddies: Major Josef Hernandez and Captain John Taylor. We flew together during the war, and John and I had chased women together—Josef was married—on more than one occasion.

From what I could put together, they'd engaged the Xortaag fleet a short while ago. They soon realized what I knew already: BVR missiles were useless. The only chance they had was engaging the enemy at close range, which was a tall order given how fast the Deathbringers were and how effectively their laser weapons could fire. Between them, they'd managed to shoot down a grand total of two enemy vessels, but from twenty-four F-46 jet fighters in their unit, only these five had survived, and they were winchester. Still, they'd done better than some other squadrons which were completely wiped out. Now they were on their way back to their base to reload and get back to the fight, even though it was clear they had no chance of winning this battle.

My heart swelled with pride. Despite overwhelming odds, these guys weren't running away from the fight. They were bruised and bloodied, but not defeated. What they lacked in technology, they made up for with heart. My kind of people.

And then five Deathbringers showed up on the edge of my radar screen, moving fast towards the F-46s.

I could feel the blood draining from my face. My instinct was to rush to my friends' help, but our whole strategy was based on secrecy. If the Xortaags found out about us so early, the results would be catastrophic, for all humanity. I couldn't endanger everyone to save five lives. But there was one thing I could do.

I shouted into my mike, "You've got hostiles on your six! Evade! Evade!"

The Deathbringers, just like our own Vipers, were invisible to F-46's low-tech radar unless the pilots knew exactly where to look. Josef cursed and frantically ordered his remaining pilots to scatter and try to evade. I knew it was a lost cause. Even with ammunition, they wouldn't have stood a chance.

Elizabeth's voice spoke in my headphones. "What're we waiting for?"

"What?" I said.

"There's five of them and ten of us. Let's go kill the sons of bitches."

I really didn't need this right now. "Out of the question," I said. "Even if we could do this before any more Deathbringers show up, all it takes is for one of them to send a message out, and our existence will be revealed. Stay put."

"We can jam their communications," she countered.

Feeling an urge to rub my temples, which was impossible because they were under my flight helmet, I said, "We can, but there's no guarantee we'd be completely successful. *Stay put.*"

She didn't answer for an agonizing moment; then she said, "I'm going in. You guys are free to follow me or not."

"You're going to jeopardize the whole thing. Stay put! That's an order!"

I didn't think for a second she'd listen. Once Liz set her heart on doing something, there was no way to talk her out of it. I considered my options, and my heart sank when I realized I had none. Once Liz attacked the Deathbringers, our cover would be blown anyway. Our only hope was to get rid of these five as fast as possible and pray to God they couldn't send a message out, in which case we might have ended up kissing any chance we had of defeating the Xortaags goodbye.

My face felt hot, and my palms started sweating. A vision of the world burning with *billions* of corpses scattered all over sprang to my mind, the direct result of what Liz was about to do. Under my watch. My responsibility. I could almost smell the stench of the corpses. I gritted my teeth and prepared myself to order the rest of the pilots to follow Liz.

Nothing happened. Liz's Viper stayed on course. There

was no further communication from her. I tried to contact her but got nowhere.

Tarq's voice spoke in my ear. "Jim, I have taken control of her Viper. I am bringing her back in with the rest of you."

I asked, "Were you monitoring us?" and immediately thought, *Duh!*

"Yes, and a good thing too," said Tarq, "given that she was about to doom us all. I have also blocked her communications, but we can hear her over here, and let me tell you this: She is furious. Does she kiss you with that mouth?"

Despite everything, picturing Liz alone in her cockpit throwing a tantrum brought a fleeting smile to my face.

Tarq added, "Also, FYI, I am going to demote her due to insubordination."

I said, "Tarq?"

"Yes, Jim?"

"She's gonna kill you," I said mischievously.

Tarq did not respond, so I added, "She's gonna kill you like a rabid dog in the street."

"I know," said Tarq, sounding resigned. "I am thinking about having security take her to MICI as soon as she lands and do the RoboCop thing again."

With a knot in my stomach, I forced myself to watch while the enemy vessels closed the distance and started shooting at the helpless jet fighters. I desperately wanted to help them, but I knew it would be a fatal mistake. Sitting in my cockpit, watching my friends getting slaughtered, killed a part of me, an innocence I didn't even know I still had. I thought I knew war, but I didn't. War wasn't just fighting, danger, and fear. War was strategy, and strategy was pitiless. This was war—and without a doubt the most painful thing I'd ever experienced in my life.

* * *

Prince Mushgaana, sitting on the captain's chair of the command starship, absentmindedly followed the battle on the bridge's main display, a colossal VR screen front and center. Around him, the starship's crew members were performing their duties with an air of professionalism and efficiency. Mushgaana had worked with this crew for a very long time, and he knew they were capable of functioning at peak efficiency with minimal supervision. They certainly were more focused on the job at hand than he was.

This battle was a foregone conclusion. So were the next few. The real battle would come when they attacked the Akakie homeworld. After that, there would be no one capable of challenging their supremacy in the galaxy.

As a member of the royal family, Mushgaana could have anything he wanted on his own planet. Luxury, pleasure, the adulation of women and courtiers. He could have wasted his life, like his four older brothers, on arranging petty military exercises, participating in martial art tournaments, and cracking down on the occasional rebellions in a couple of planets in their so-called "kingdom." There were also regular "Mind Power" competitions, during which the royal family members pitted their telepathic and telekinetic abilities against each other. Mushgaana regularly participated in those contests, and he always won hands down. But he was a lot more ambitious than that, partly because due to his physical appearance and small frame he would have never been respected in a warrior race—and specifically by his father—unless he had done something no one else ever had. When he was a young man, he had decided conquering a few planets and killing all their inhabitants would do it.

It was Mushgaana who convinced his father to appoint Maada as the commander of the fleet all those years ago when they were both young men. The two of them had planned their first military campaign, and the second, and the third. Each victory brought them more resources, technological advancement, economic growth, and most importantly, respect. The advanced technology they often found on other planets and reverse engineered had transformed Tangaar from a planet on the verge of destruction to a thriving and prosperous one. Their over-fished seas had been stocked with alien species; their forests rejuvenated with fast-growing, carbon-sucking trees adapted to the planet's dry heat. New materials had revolutionized construction, and new luxury goods had pacified the upper classes. Moreover, the colonization of the conquered planets had solved their overpopulation problem. A lifetime later, their kingdom was the biggest and strongest in the galaxy, both Maada and he were legends, and his brothers—tall, muscular "warriors" that they were—would happily kill him in his sleep out of pure jealousy if they got the chance, especially because the king had officially appointed him as his successor, breaking with a centuries-old tradition of naming the oldest son crown prince.

This whole conquering-the-galaxy plan had started as a means to impress his father, but he had soon developed a taste for it, and his motivation had become to rule the galaxy one day. Sooner or later, the kingdom would be his, and he wanted to expand it as much as possible even before he was crowned king. This was in sharp contrast to Maada, who had no personal ambitions. Whatever he had done in his life was for the good of the kingdom and its people. Mushgaana regarded the general's concern for the planet's downtrodden inhabitants with some amusement, well aware of the lie at the center of it. They were predators, Maada and he; why pretend otherwise? The kingdom benefited from Mushgaana's actions, but he benefited most.

One of his officers said, "Your Highness, the general is doing his one-man-army again."

Mushgaana smiled and pulled up the screen the man was referring to. Maada was single-handedly fighting some *thirty* enemy fighters while around two hundred of his fighters were hovering nearby, watching the battle. He was not even doing it from a safe distance: He was engaged in a short-range dogfight, giving the enemy fighters every chance to take shots at him.

He contacted Maada. "General, you promised me not to take any unnecessary risks."

Maada answered, "What risk?" After shooting down three enemy aircraft, he added, "I was getting bored. Why should people under my command have all the fun?"

Mushgaana had to admit watching the general in action was a privilege, even after all the years they had fought together. The man was truly invincible when sitting in a Deathbringer cockpit. His space fighter was considerably more advanced than the enemy aircraft; still, they outnumbered him thirty to one, yet none of their missiles or bullets would get anywhere near the general, despite the close range. Those other pilots watching, as well as the command starship personnel, would one day tell this story to their children and grandchildren.

He said, "One of these days you will get yourself killed, and I will have to lead our fleet alone."

"Perish the thought," said Maada as he kept on collecting enemy scalps.

* * *

New York - 13.30 EST

Zheng was in an intense conversation with army generals, planning a defense strategy against a ground invasion, when the air force commander, a tough-looking American woman in her fifties, told him, "Chancellor, please take a look at this."

She brought up a screen that showed enemy spaceships deploying small sphere-shaped devices around Earth at an altitude of forty-five thousand feet.

"What the hell are those?" asked Zheng.

"We don't know," said the woman. "But we've discovered a pattern. It looks like they're planning to surround the whole planet with these things. We can safely assume this is why they've been neutralizing our air defenses."

"Can we shoot them down?"

"We can try," said the woman.

Zheng nodded. "Give the order. Also, send up our chopper squadrons."

Everyone within earshot stopped and stared at him. The woman, eyes wide, said, "Our helicopters? What good are they going to do when our most advanced jet fighters are so comprehensively outmatched?"

"Probably not much," said Zheng. "But they can at least draw some enemy fire, giving our fighter jets a chance to shoot a few of those things down. It'll be more useful than having them sit on the ground, and I don't think a few thousand more casualties will make any difference in our current situation."

The air force commander held her chin up. "This is murder. I respectfully refuse to carry out this order."

Without saying a word, Zheng nodded to one of the SCTU soldiers in the operation room. The man stepped forward, brought up his assault rifle and shot the commander in the head. Her blood sprayed on the oval table the other generals were sitting around, painting it red. The terror already dominating the room was now palpable.

Zheng repeated his order to the air force's second-in-command, who said, "Given that it's a suicide mission, can we at least ask for volunteers?"

Zheng thought about it for a second and then shrugged. "If it makes you feel any better. But trust me, it makes no difference. There'll be plenty of volunteers."

Half an hour later, the new air force commander pointed at the Command Center's main screen, which showed thousands of military helicopters flying off the ground and carrying their crew towards certain death, and said, "You were right, Chancellor."

Zheng shrugged. "I often am."

* * *

EARTH'S TROPOSPHERE - 13.35 EST

BY THE TIME the order to shoot down the mysterious spheres came, most of the remaining fighter pilots in Lieutenant Jianguo Liu's squadron had exhausted their BVR missiles, but Liu had very soon realized shooting BVRs at enemy fighters was about as effective as throwing rocks at them. He'd decided to hold on to his, waiting for a better opportunity to put them to good use.

An opportunity such as this.

Using the targeting system on his Chengdu J-25's head-up display, approaching from behind, he fired two missiles at the spaceship deploying the small spheres at an altitude of thirty thousand feet, and another two at the spheres themselves. The second two scored direct hits against two of the spheres but had zero effect. They didn't even budge them. The spheres were protected with some kind of shield.

Liu slapped his knee and said, "Damn it!" in frustration.

The first two missiles did much better. The spaceship, which was bigger and slower than the space fighters, veered right and avoided one, but the second missile hit it on the starboard side. The vessel started losing altitude and exploded after a few seconds.

In a day when Liu had witnessed a lot of his friends die in a hopeless battle against alien invaders, this small victory filled his heart with joy. It also attracted the attention of a few enemy fighters flying nearby. They changed direction and came straight for him.

EARTH's TROPOSPHERE - 13.45 EST

MAADA COULD NOT HELP ADMIRING the defenders' courage, albeit grudgingly.

One reason why the Xortaags always attacked with an overwhelming show of force was to intimidate the enemy into surrender, thus saving valuable resources. In his long military career, it had been his experience that once the defenders realized they were completely outmatched, they would either surrender or run away.

Not these people, though. They had suffered horrible losses, but they kept coming. And they had managed to destroy nearly fifteen hundred of his space fighters. For such a technologically primitive planet, this number was unacceptable. Now they had focused their efforts on shooting down the ships deploying the Voice of God, having had some very limited success there too.

Maada decided that he had seen enough and asked the fleet's command ship to patch him through to the enemy vessels. He said in English, "People of Earth. My name is General Maada, the commander of the Xortaag Royal Fleet. You have certainly realized by now you are fighting a lost cause. I have no particular wish to keep killing brave men and woman to achieve an inevitable outcome, so I offer you this: If you surrender, I guarantee you will not be harmed; you will be treated fairly, and you will be allowed to continue living in accordance with your own customs and traditions. Surrender now and save your lives."

He was well aware that after the Voice of God came online, people on the planet would essentially turn into mindless drones, their lifespan drastically reduced, but in his mind, he was not lying. They would still be alive, enjoying life for the foreseeable future, even if their minds were controlled.

He kept the channel open, waiting for a response, which arrived shortly after. *"Fuck you and the horse you rode in on!"*

This was followed by the sound of cheering and other expressions of defiance in several different languages the meaning of which Maada did not know but could guess.

What the hell is a "horse"?

He said, "Suit yourself," and told his fleet, "Kill them all."

After returning to Winterfell, Kurt, Allen, Liz, and I went to the Command Center. Liz was mad and completely ignored me. Her silent treatment would normally annoy me, but right now it didn't seem like such a big deal, with Earth being conquered and all. Tarq, Barook, Sergei, and Keiko were already in the Command Center, following the battle on various screens. Keiko was standing next to a monitor with her shoulders back and chin up, doing her best to maintain her tough-as-nail-badass-chick image, but she had tears in her, well, eye. Tarq was biting his nails and avoided eye contact with me. He didn't even try to hide the terror on his face. He was either imagining this happening to his world, or he'd developed some affection for us humans. The Command Center's atmosphere was so heavy I could taste the dread in the air.

"They are sending helicopters to fight space fighters now," said Tarq, his face blanching. "What is wrong with your people? Anyone with half a brain would have surrendered by now. Are you suicidal as a species?"

"Nope. Just not pussies," I said.

Tarq sighed. "Ever the wise-ass, even now."

"Especially now," I said. "What's the point of wise-assery if you're chilling on a beach?"

Tarq threw up his hands in the air and turned away from me.

Looking at the choppers attacking the Deathbringers, Kurt murmured, "Charge of the Light Brigade."

"Nice one," said Liz.

"Thanks," answered Kurt.

"They are bringing out the big guns," said Sergei.

One of the screens showed a nuclear missile racing towards one of the spaceships deploying MFM. "About damn time," I murmured.

"It'll hurt our own planet as much as the Xortaags," said Liz.

"Better than doing nothing," I said.

The missile reached its target. I hold my breath and waited for a big boom, but nothing happened. It didn't detonate.

"Nuclear weapons have been obsolete for almost two of your centuries," said Tarq, staring at one of the smaller screens. "I cannot explain the scientific details; it's been too long since grade school. Suffice it to say all spacefaring species have a device that neutralizes the chain reaction needed for both fission and fusion."

"This fucking sucks," said Sergei.

It did. I'd hoped the armed forces either stop or at least hurt the Xortaags. I rubbed my temples and thought about pulling out my hair. Then I looked over Tarq's shoulder to see what he was staring at. "Is that...?"

The screen showed a crimson Deathbringer engaged in a dogfight with a dozen F-44s. Tarq didn't take his eyes off of the screen. He just nodded. His hands were shaking, and his skin was flushed. I put a hand on his arm, careful to keep my palm at the surface of the hologram. "Are you okay?"

He turned his head to look at me for a second, and there were tears in his eyes. He shook his head and said, "I'll be fine." I resisted an urge to hug him. It wouldn't have been very manly.

Liz, who was so focused on the battle she missed this

exchange, asked, "Why do our jet fighters' missiles have no effect on those damn spheres?"

"The Xortaags stole this technology from a civilization even more advanced than ours," said Tarq, biting his fingers, "and the spheres are protected with a force field that absorbs the energy of whatever you throw at them. We could not even knock them off orbit. Their energy source will not last forever, but all they really need is to last for a few of your decades."

"We are lucky the Xortaags could not figure out a way to use this technology in their spaceships, at least not yet," Barook added.

I glared at him. "Lucky! Huh! I should've bought a lottery ticket today."

We all stood there and helplessly watched our planet burn, our military destroyed, our soldiers killed. I thought of all the movies I'd seen about alien first contact, but nothing resonated. I'd imagined the anger, the desire to protect, the adrenaline rush of combat, but not this darkness. I suppose, if I'd considered just this situation, I would've wanted to be doing what I was doing now, planning a counterattack, but I couldn't have known how it would feel, having to wait, having to watch. Liz, having forgotten her anger, stood next to me and held my hand. I squeezed her cold fingers, trying to find solace in the fact that right then at the literal end of the world and in the worst moment of human history, she was standing by my side, giving me her unconditional love and support.

* * *

PACIFIC OCEAN - 14.30 EST

· · ·

Captain Gorge McDowell had never felt so impotent in his life.

He was the commander of *Valiant*, the largest, most powerful war machine ever built by humanity. But she was useless in a space invasion because she was a ship. To be exact, she was an 850-foot, twenty-thousand-ton behemoth. Still useless, especially since they had exhausted their surface-to-air missiles, without doing any damage to the enemy.

One of his officers shouted, "We have incoming at ten o'clock."

Through his binoculars, McDowell saw a Chengdu J-25 fighter jet flying at a low altitude, being followed by three enemy fighters. The fighter jet pilot possessed excellent flying skills. His jet kept twisting and spinning wildly and evading enemy fire, bringing them closer to *Valiant*.

This was apparently the pilot's plan. One of the Valiant's bridge officers said, "Captain, we're receiving a message from the pilot. It reads, 'My name's Lieutenant Jianguo Liu, and I'm bringing them to you.'"

This deadly game of cat-and-mouse continued for a few more minutes, during which McDowell feverishly prayed for the pilot to succeed.

The Chinese pilot kept flirting with death. He finally ran out of luck. A laser beam hit his cockpit from close range, and his jet exploded. The three enemy vessels passed what was left of the plane, their momentum bringing them within *Valiant*'s range.

McDowell shouted, "*Fire!*"

His ship was equipped with four S-1000 autocannons—six-barrel rotary automatic cannons capable of shooting ten thousand armor-piercing rounds per minute. The enemy vessels were fast, but they were flying straight toward

Valiant, and nothing, not even a spaceship, could evade an S-1000 at close range. Fire erupted from S-1000s' multiple barrels. The result was like a fireworks display; glowing fragments of enemy vessels exploding in the air, falling in brilliant arcs into the dark sea. The spaceships were shredded into smoldering pieces in less than fifteen seconds.

McDowell didn't realize he was screaming like a maniac until he noticed everyone on the CIC was doing it too.

His joy was short-lived.

* * *

Earth's Troposphere - 14.45 EST

Mushgaana was getting impatient. This battle had lasted much longer than anticipated. Besides, several hundred damaged space fighters had landed on the command ship's hangar deck, which was getting close to full capacity. Since the command ship was the only vessel in the vicinity with hangar bays, this would soon become a serious problem.

The officer in charge of the team operating the Voice of God contacted him, "The Voice of God is fully deployed."

Finally!

Most officers on the bridge stopped working and looked at him. Mushgaana closed his eyes to savor the moment. It was a historic occasion, one which would bring yet another alien civilization to its knees.

The crown prince stood straight, feeling taller than he was. He puffed out his chest and very formally said, "Let them hear the Voice of God and submit to our will."

With that command, humanity entered alien servitude.

* * *

THE PACIFIC OCEAN - 14.50 EST

IMAGES of benevolent gods who had ruled over Earth for centuries suddenly filled McDowell's mind. They were majestic and beautiful like the heroes of the stories he'd read in childhood, their eyes full of wisdom and compassion. He knew—had always known—how they cared for and protected humanity, helping them grow and prosper. He remembered meeting the gods and felt the thrill of such a great honor. A voice in his head said, "We are gods. Obey us, and you will be rewarded. Bury the dead and forget about them. Forget all today's events. Continue your life and wait for our orders. If you are a member of armed forces, go to your base and await instructions."

The message kept repeating in a loop.

A part of his brain that was still independent asked, "Bury the dead? What dead?"

He looked around and for the first time noticed a few people lying on the floor, blood oozing out of their ears. He didn't remember who they were, and he didn't care. The rest of the crew picked up their dead comrades, carried them outside, leaving a small trail of fresh blood, and threw them overboard, showing no emotion. It was a simple cleaning operation, and he was pleased by their efficiency.

McDowell ordered his officers to turn *Valiant* around and go back to base.

Five spaceships arrived a few minutes later. Gods had come to visit them! McDowell couldn't believe his good fortune. He knelt, put his palms together in front of him and prayed, his skin tingling. His children would be so proud of their old man when they heard about this.

In a tight formation, the spaceships made an attacking run over the defenseless destroyer and steadily fired at her. Bright, red explosions engulfed *Valiant*, and she was sunk with all hands.

* * *

NEW YORK - 14.50 EST

JOE WINSTON WAS WATCHING the news about the alien invasion on one of the several TVs in a packed bar with dozens of other people, trying hard not to give in to his terror, hoping against hope it was all some sort of weird collective nightmare.

An alien invasion! Who would have thought? With spaceships and laser beams, no less. What he saw on TV looked like scenes from a sci-fi movie. The difference was Earth's defenders were getting slaughtered for real, and he could do nothing but helplessly wait and see how the chips would fall. The army was gearing up to defend against a ground invasion, and all around the planet, militia forces were being hastily organized, preparing for the same thing. He worried about his parents and his pregnant sister. He should call them. His hand reached for his pocket.

Winston's eyes suddenly rolled back into his skull, and he fell from his stool. He was dead before he hit the floor, blood coming out of his ears.

The TV broadcast stopped. The other people in the bar, in silence and showing no emotions, picked up Winston's body and carried it outside along with a few other corpses. The bar owner gave them three shovels. They carried the bodies to a small park nearby where they were joined by hundreds of other people carrying the corpses of men, women, and children. Together, they dug a big hole, unceremoniously dumped the dead inside, covered the massive grave, and went their separate ways, forgetting what they'd just done. The dead were not missed. Joe Winston's parents remembered only one child. His sister listened to the voice in her head that erased all her concerns about the future and her recent terror. Her child would grow up blessed in the service of the gods.

In Zheng's operation room, the chancellor helped carry out the corpses. He wasn't good at it; he hadn't done any menial labor since his teens. But nothing like that mattered. A few soldiers dug a big hole and threw in the bodies, superior officers and comrades alike.

In The Harem, the Bratava goons didn't bother to dig holes. They already had a secret underground room they used to dispose of bodies. They would normally use a tub full of acid to do this, but there was no need for it today. They threw in the corpses of a few young women, as well as three clients and two of their own, locked the door and walked away.

Some of the biggest mass graves in history were dug in China, where there were too many dead bodies to be handled by individual citizens. Government officials got involved and ordered the army to use excavators to prepare designated trenches in various locations, to be filled by thousands of corpses. In their minds, they were beautifying the country by removing unsightly animal carcasses whose provenance they didn't remember.

The same macabre scenes were being played all around the planet. People buried their neighbors, their friends, and their relatives wherever it was most convenient and then completely forgot about them. Brothers buried their brothers. Mothers buried their children. A five-year-old child spent four long hours in their backyard trying to dig a hole to put her mother in until some neighbors saw him and came to his help. An eighty-year-old man had a heart attack while digging a grave for his wife of sixty years and died right next to her. Their son buried both of them later. A newlywed young woman on her honeymoon dug a grave in the sand with her bare hands, threw her husband in it and then wondered what she was doing alone on a beach. By some cruel twist of fate, four out of five members of the same family died together. The father buried his wife and three children and mercifully forgot all about them. Millions of people disappeared into haphazardly dug holes, never to be seen, heard of, or remembered ever again.

* * *

TWISTING my wedding ring on my finger, I was following the battle on one of the virtual reality screens when Barook said, "OMC-BOWS is operational."

All of a sudden, the battle stopped. The remaining jet fighters flew back to their bases, and the Xortaags let them go. The anti-aircraft fire from the ground died out too. I noticed a few jet fighters fell out of the sky, but I didn't give it much thought.

Just like that, in a heartbeat, humanity turned into freaking brain-dead, construction-fodder, Xortaag-worshiping zombies.

The Command Center went deathly quiet.

"Show is over, ladies and gentlemen," said Tarq. "Our work begins now."

I rubbed my forehead and wondered if everyone felt as hollow inside as I did. It was like falling down a dark, bottomless shaft, but feeling no horror of the impending death, just wondering when it would happen. I was probably shell-shocked, which meant terror would come later. I could faintly feel it in the distance. I wasn't looking forward to its arrival. Having just witnessed the fall of human civilization, I did what I did best and tried to crack a joke. "On the bright side, from now on Kurt can't drag our butts to watch all those boring Bayern Munich games."

Kurt didn't even bother to give me a dirty look. Everyone just ignored me. It was fine by me. I didn't think I could stand being looked at. I was barely holding myself together.

That evening, Kurt, Allen, Liz, Keiko and I got together and watched *Independence Day*. It was only fitting. Like news from a distant universe, I remembered my previous enthusiastic comments about the foxy Viveca Fox. Now all I thought about was the battle to come.

* * *

The Netherlands - 15.30 EST

Maada was the first person to set foot on the newly conquered planet. He insisted on this every time.

The general landed his Deathbringer in a place where they were planning to build their biggest fleet base. He removed his flight helmet, got off the space fighter, stood on a green, beautiful field covered with lush vegetation, and filled his lungs with fresh air, letting the euphoria of the conquest rush through him. This planet had food, minerals, lumber, rivers, lakes, and wide oceans. His people would flourish here. Children would grow up not knowing hunger, thriving under blue skies. He remembered his own gray childhood. He grew up in a small village where a third of the children would die because of malnutrition, and another third because of breathing the poisonous air. When he was a child, hunger was his closest companion. Hunger and the constant fear of the future. It wasn't like that for his people anymore. It never would be again.

A shuttle carrying Mushgaana landed nearby. When the crown prince disembarked, Maada walked toward him, executed a perfect Xortaag salute by thumping the left side of the chest with the right fist, elbow kept straight in front of the body, and very formally said, "Your Highness, congratulations on yet another magnificent victory."

Mushgaana casually saluted back. "Please accept my compliments on the flawless execution of our strategy, as always."

The two of them had repeated this ritual many times in the past. Forty-four times, to be precise.

Maada bowed his head. "If you excuse me, I have got work to do." He walked away.

Maada's "work" was a ritual too: he would set up a temporary command post, and then he would lock himself in a room and not leave, eat or sleep until he had sent a short letter to the families of all the soldiers who had died under his command in that particular campaign, even though more often than not it took him one or two days.

The fleet had more efficient ways to communicate the bad news to the families of the dead soldiers, and the commander of the fleet definitely had more important things to do than sitting behind a desk and writing letters. However, receiving a personal letter from Maada was a great honor, and the general hoped this alleviated the grieving families' pain.

Shortly after, Maada, sitting behind a desk in the Xortaag temporary command post, looked at the casualty list on his PDD and started writing letter after letter. Every once in a while, a certain name evoked a memory in him and gave him pause, and occasionally, he had to stop writing to wipe a tear or two from his eyes.

* * *

WINTERFELL - 18:00 PM EST

TARQ, sitting behind the desk in his office and staring at the report he had just received, felt he was about to faint, or throw up, or both.

Millions of people had perished.

Around seven hundred million, to be exact.

Tarq was reading a report sent from an Akakie stealth spy ship watching the Xortaag attack from Earth's orbit, hoping to gather something useful. The report was mostly the same sequence of events they had witnessed in Winterfell, with one glaring difference. Because they were busy following the battle, they had missed what had happened after OMC-BOWS started working.

They knew MICI was not effective for around four percent of humans—a much higher percentage than other species, for unknown reasons—and it was an educated guess this number would be higher for OMC-BOWS since it worked from orbit. Tarq and Barook had hoped for this number to be as high as possible because it meant millions of potential allies in the fight against the Xortaags.

Beware what you wish for, thought Tarq, pressing his fists to the sides of his head.

The Xortaags had undoubtedly done the same thing as the Akakies to calibrate and test their mind control machine: They had taken human samples before the attack. They knew it would not work on all humans, and they had apparently decided millions of people roaming Earth in their right minds would not be good for their colonization plans. The Xortaags had come up with a simple solution: They had programmed the technology so that anyone who did not get their messages—men, women, and children— would die from a massive brain hemorrhage.

Children! They had slaughtered millions of children instantly, without remorse. This was too much, even for the Xortaags.

In the end, it had turned out OMC-BOWS did not work on around seven percent of the human population. Seven percent of ten billion people. That was a number so colossal Tarq could not even picture it. He assumed the Xortaags did not think about it that way. From their point of view, humanity would be as good as extinct within two or three generations anyway. And the Xortaags did not recognize the worth of other species anyway. For them, their own people always came first. The problem was Tarq actually understood that kind of reasoning, and he had done terrible things in the name of saving his people too. That thought made him shudder.

Even this massacre was his doing, in a way.

Tarq felt he personally had murdered all those people. Every single one of them, albeit not on purpose. It really was his fault because the Xortaags invasion of Earth was a part of his master plan. If he had not interfered, all those people would have been alive, at least for now.

SEAN ROBINS

But then his own people would all be dead.

After the Battle of Alora, it was clear the Akakies could not defeat the Xortaags in a direct confrontation. Their government had decided to sue for peace. At first, Tarq had voiced his disagreement, knowing the Xortaags would not stop until they had conquered and subjugated Kanoor like they had so many other worlds, and he was relieved when the Xortaags rejected the offer. But he had soon found a way to use the proposed peace treaty to his people's advantage. There was a reason Tarq had a reputation as the greatest strategist in Akakie history; besides, as the head of Special Operations Force, performing black ops was his specialty.

Mushgaana had four older brothers who hated his guts. The fact that the king's youngest son was crown prince was humiliating enough, and Mushgaana compounded it by constantly rubbing this fact in their faces, both in public and in private. Given the chance, they would kill him, or at least do anything in their power to thwart his plans.

Tarq had reached out to the four men, suggesting they had to pool their resources. They arranged a secret virtual meeting, trying to find a way to bring Mushgaana down. One of the possibilities the four brothers mentioned caught Tarq's attention, and he took it from there.

The brothers had a spy in their service. The spy was an attractive woman who was able to seduce any man. More importantly, she possessed a unique telepathic power. She was able to change a person's thoughts and attitude with a simple touch. One of the brothers had mentioned this nonchalantly. Tarq was not surprised when the others got angry at the revelation—such an asset was priceless—but after some irritated muttering, they seemed to not understand just how precious she was. True, she was limited. She could not make a person do something against their conscious interests and will—she couldn't force Mushgaana to kill himself or stop him from attacking Kanoor. She could, however, plant a small idea in a person's mind, masking it as their own, and let it grow. For a master manipulator like Tarq, that was more than enough.

"If Mushgaana accepts the peace," Tarq had told the brothers, "he will lose the confidence of General Maada. The general won't disobey orders, but I have no doubt he will be in conversation with you shortly, and the prince will fall. You don't need Kanoor to grow; there are plenty of planets to conquer."

"Besides, we can always defeat you," said the eldest brother unpleasantly.

"All I'm asking for is a few years," he said. "I'm an old man."

They believed him, he understood, because they would have done the same thing—given anything for a few more years of life. They also assumed he was stupid. Like many inferior beings, they couldn't see their own shortcomings.

The brothers knew one of Mushgaana's weaknesses was his interest in beautiful women. They arranged for their agent to get into his bedroom. During the night, she planted two thoughts in Mushgaana's mind: one, the idea that the Akakies were too strong, and two, the strategy of accepting the Akakies' peace proposal and attacking a few easier targets until the Xortaags were better prepared to take them on. That delayed the attack on Kanoor but put seven other planets on Mushgaana's target list. The closest of the seven to Alora and therefore the most logical first target was Earth. Just to be on the safe side, Tarq had asked the spy to single Earth out as the first new target. After that, he had come to Earth to set his trap and wait for the Xortaags to fall into it.

The Akakie government was delighted the Xortaags had suddenly changed their mind and accepted the peace treaty, and no one had suspected his involvement.

Mushgaana's brothers had wanted to kill their spy to keep their cooperation with Tarq a secret. Tarq helped her fake her own death and hide for a while. She was on her way to Kanoor now. Who knew what wealth of information she would bring with her, especially since Tarq, despite all his previous efforts, knew very little about the enemy. Every single agent he had sent to collect information on the Xortaags had turned up dead after a very short time.

He wondered how Jim, Kurt, Elizabeth, Keiko, or the rest of the humans whom he now considered dear friends would react if they ever found out.

Especially Jim, a man after my own heart. He would make a good Akakie, with his tendency to make fun of friend and foe.

There was no need to wonder about Allen: The old man would kill Tarq on the spot without hesitation.

Tarq himself had once told Barook they did not have to feel guilty about their plan to use Earth as bait. It would be only a matter of time before the Xortaags attacked Earth. Earth would be the logical next target after Kanoor was conquered because it was the second closest planet to Alora. This reasoning was still valid but did very little to alleviate the mind-numbing pain he was feeling now.

Tarq considered not sharing this information with the others. Morale was rock-bottom already, and there was no telling how the humans would react to this news. They might even blame him and his strategy for all those deaths. He considered if he would have planned things differently if he had known this would happen but after some thought decided they had not had another choice, massive civilian casualties or not. Still, he was glad he had not known. He would have found it much harder to sell the plan.

His human friends would eventually find out. It would be better if they heard it from him. He picked up his PDD and sent out a message, calling for a meeting the next day. Then he locked the door of his office and pulled on his antennae so hard the severe pain made him lose his balance and fall on the floor.

* * *

I HELD my head in my hands and tried to push down what I had eaten for breakfast, barely managing it.

Having seven hundred million deaths on your conscience was a damned thing.

Just as we thought things couldn't get worse, Tarq told us about the carnage. He did it in a meeting during which I toyed with the idea of shooting first him and then myself in the head; Liz fainted; Kurt covered his face with his hands and was as motionless as one of the dead for a long while; Allen, his mouth twitching, looked like he was about to kill both Tarq and Barook, and Barook kept yelling, "We did not know! How were we supposed to know?"

I thought about this long and hard, asking myself if we could have done something differently to spare all those lives. The answer was a resounding "no," and everyone, including our resident military experts Kurt and Allen seemed to agree. The Xortaags had four times as many space fighters as we did, and there was no way we could have defeated them in a direct air/space battle. Our only hope, as Tarq had laid out from the beginning, was to surprise them by taking advantage of their two glaring weaknesses: the fact that they didn't expect any resistance on a planet under the influence of their mind control device, and their absolute inexperience in ground warfare.

And still, my conscience, assisted by ever-present Venom, wouldn't leave me alone, as if I hadn't been depressed enough already. Somehow it was all my fault. I should've done more. I should've found a solution. I should've let the forces under my command stand with Earth's defenders, even if this meant all of us would go down in flames.

Mark Twain had once said, "If I had a yaller dog that didn't know no more than a person's conscience I would poison him." I was wondering if he was right. On the other hand, if I wanted to change my image as a closet racist, it was probably better not to quote Mark Twain.

I couldn't put the mental image of all those dead people out of my mind, nor could I stop the indescribable terror that image caused. The whole thing was made infinitely worse because the rest of humanity had forgotten about the dead—forgotten *anything* that happened during the Xortaag invasion. I wondered what it'd be like to have that voice in your head, a voice capable of making you forget the life and death of those you loved, and shuddered. I'd felt sorry for myself having to put up with Venom! I swore I wouldn't forget the deaths, that even the nameless would be honored. The dead men, the dead women, the dead children were all mine.

They will be avenged.

What helped me go through the immediate aftermath of the Xortaag invasion without losing my sanity was Liz's presence and love. Watching humanity fall was bad enough, but we had months to mentally and emotionally prepare for that. Knowing that the Xortaags had pulled a mini-Thanos and a big chunk of humanity just disappeared with a figurative snap of their fingers—or pushing a button, or touching a computer screen, or however the hell else they activated their Mind Fuck Machine—was a supremely bitter pill to swallow. So bitter, in fact, it would've been enough to push any sane man over the edge. Every time I started to lose it, she'd take my hands, look into my eyes and say, "Jim. We're here. We're alive. Billions of people are still alive, too, *and they need us*. We can't fail them. Think about them. Think about the children." And I'd relax fractionally and thank her, and that motivation would last for a little while.

Both Liz and I took sleeping pills that night; still, I kept jolting awake out of nightmares about seven hundred million dead men, women, and children—infants, toddlers, *babies*. So what that they didn't all die. Too many did. The few times I dozed off, Liz woke me up by talking, shouting, or crying in her sleep, and when that happened, I repeated to her what she had said to me. Oddly, that was just as helpful as having her say it. Not that any of it could help for more than a few minutes. At the middle of the night, she hugged me, put her head on my shoulder, and cried her heart out, bitter tears rolling down her face. I didn't even try to console her with words anymore; instead, I just held onto her in a tight embrace, trying to give her some small comfort in my arms.

CHAPTER NINE

W interfell - April 17, 2078

OKSANA CALLED her sister for the fifth time that day, with no response. She was beginning to get worried.

Anastasiya was clinically depressed as the result of months of physical and mental abuse she had suffered in The Harem. Escaping that horrid place and joining the Resistance had done wonders for Oksana's mood and state of mind. It had provided her with something to strive for, and she was too busy trying to prove herself to her new comrades to let the past consume her. But it'd had little effect on her sister. She'd always been sensitive and easily wounded, and Oksana believed that had attracted the most sadistic clients to her; she had little ability to hide behind a shell of indifference. Her tears had been like nectar to the monsters of The Harem.

Unsurprisingly to Oksana, Anastasiya had taken the fall of Earth worse than most people. The horror was always with her. MICI had assigned Oksana to the Commandos, but the machine somehow didn't work on Anastasiya. Tarq had explained to her that MICI was ineffective for a small number of the population, and her unlucky sister was one of them. This meant she was essentially a prisoner in Winterfell. If she had stepped outside the force field protecting the base, she'd have been affected by the Xortaag mind control machine. She'd found it worse knowing that others, everyone, was now enslaved as she had been. It didn't matter that the Xortaags weren't interested in raping human bodies. They'd raped human minds, and that horrified her. "Why has God let this happen?" she kept asking Oksana.

Oksana didn't believe in God anymore, but she'd kept that to herself. "God gave us allies so we can win."

"But what if the Xortaags win?" Anastasiya had whispered.

Oksana wasn't going to leave her sister alone to brood in her quarters. She wanted to take her to meet new people. If that didn't work, they could always continue the chess game they'd started two days ago. They'd been playing chess routinely since they were kids. Sometimes it was the only thing that could distract her sister from her dark thoughts. Oksana called her sister again, but her PDD didn't answer. She went to Anastasiya's quarters, knocked on the door and called her sister's name. Still no answer.

Oksana tried the door. It wasn't locked. Still calling Anastasiya's name, she pushed the door open and found her sister's body hanging from the roof of her quarters. Her face was paper white, her body gently moving in the draught from the open door.

"*Moya sestra!*"

People in the adjacent rooms heard Oksana's anguished wail and came in to find her hugging her dead sister's body on the floor, sobbing convulsively, with chess pieces from an overturned chess board scattered all around them.

* * *

I WAS in Winterfell's clinic, picking up sleeping pills, when Anastasiya's body was brought in so that the doctors could make one last desperate effort to save her life. It was too late, even with Akakie technology.

Anastasiya was the first person to commit suicide in Winterfell, but she wasn't the last. During the next few weeks, and despite our best efforts—we set up counseling sessions, support groups, and even a suicide hotline—several other people who couldn't deal with the emotional burden of having witnessed the fall of human civilization and/or had lost loved ones in the subsequent mass murder took their own lives. Early on, it didn't help that there was no way to know *who* had died since the survivors didn't remember the dead. The only way to find out was to call and inquire about a friend or relative and listen to someone's mother or sister or husband say, "I'm sorry, I don't know that person." Many people at Winterfell made such calls. One confused response was enough to let you know the worst had happened.

Interestingly enough, two of the regular participants of our support groups were our macho war machines, Allen and Sergei. The one person who never attended was Kurt. He was more distant and reclusive than before, having built even higher walls around himself.

THOSE OF US who didn't kill ourselves had to find a way to deal with the trauma. Terror was the prevalent emotion, coupled with rage and hatred for the invaders. I tried to keep my feelings in check by keeping myself busy. There was a lot of work to do.

Liz took it upon herself to support Oksana through her grief and loss, pointing out that she didn't have anyone in Winterfell. Given how Oksana looked, I thought a lot of guys would happily lend their shoulders to her to cry on. In her efforts to soothe Oksana, Liz was joined by Keiko—at this point, they were besties—her two sisters and Sergei, who had also lost a younger sister to suicide, and as he put it, "could feel Oksana's pain."

One evening, during dinner, Liz told me Oksana's story.

"She had a rich family," said Liz. "She and her sister grew up wanting for nothing. They were both sent to a private school and had very good educations."

I said, "Which explains her tendency to quote Shake-speare left, right and center," and attacked my steak.

"When they were teenagers, their mother ran away with another man. Their father, broken-hearted, wasted all his money on drugs, alcohol and other women and ended up shooting himself in the head."

"Those Russian women," I said.

"Ukrainian. It's a different country."

"I knew that."

"The two sisters found themselves alone and with no money," Liz continued. "Their uncle told them he could get them a job that paid very well in a casino in New York. The two sisters traveled to the U.S., only to find themselves trapped by the Russian mafia, forced to work in The Harem."

"Wow. Such an interesting story. I can't wait to meet her," said Cordelia.

My wife concluded, "Despite all this, which was probably enough to break anyone, she managed to have one of the most feared men on Earth killed."

"Which, incidentally, got the two of us involved," I said, playing with my wedding ring. "I guess we owe her one. If it wasn't for her, you and I would probably be busy kissing Xortaag ass right now. What do you think about inviting her for dinner one evening?"

"She wouldn't come."

"Why not?"

"She says you remind her of the kind of men who frequented The Harem."

A big chunk of steak got stuck in my throat. I coughed so much I had tears in my eyes, much to Liz and Cordelia's amusement.

"Relax. I'm kidding." Liz laughed. "But in all seriousness, you're a bit macho, and sometimes you can be downright chauvinistic. I assume that's what you have in common with the kind of man that goes to a place like The Harem."

I wiped my lips and glared at her. "If I ever visit The Harem, it'll be to pull a Robert Freaking De Niro in *Taxi Driver*, kill the goons and save the girls."

She blew me a kiss. "My hero!"

* * *

TEN DAYS after the fall of Earth, Tarq called a meeting in the Command Center and using one of his favorite holographic presentations filled us in on what had been going on.

The Xortaag fleet, unaware of our presence, had landed on Earth. By Tarq's estimates, they'd brought nearly a million people with them. They immediately went to work: They started building settlements all over the planet, including two huge fleet bases where they kept their fleet: one in California and a bigger one in the Netherlands. It would've made more sense to build a fleet base on top of a mountain range, some ten thousand feet closer to orbit, but it turned out the Xortaags really liked mild weather, and they preferred to live close to oceans, lakes, or rivers. They also started building a city next to each fleet base. They used thousands of humans as workers, both skilled and unskilled.

Tarq paused the presentation and said, "By the way, the Xortaags named the under-construction city in the U.S. City of God, and the one in Europe, Kingdom of God. Any thoughts?"

God complex much?

"No, no, no," I said. "Unh-unh. This's where I draw the line. I went along with Deathbringer. I even might've thought Voice of God was better than your blah blah blah acronym. But there's no freaking way I'll call the Xortaags' freaking city freaking City of God!"

"Suggestions?" Tarq asked dryly.

We had a lot: City of Cockroaches, The Zoo, and City of Pieces of Shit, to name a few. None of them sounded like a military target though, so everyone agreed with my suggestions: SH-1 and SH-2, standing for Slaughterhouse One and Two.

As in, we were going to *slaughter* every single Xortaag son-of-a-bitch residing in those cities.

Tarq resumed the presentation. We learned the Xortaag transport ships had started their journey back to their home planet, and more importantly, the convoy bringing the first groups of Xortaag colonists was already on the way to Earth.

"So, we have six months to defeat a fleet four times bigger than ours," I said. "Just checking."

"Day-to-day life on earth continues as before for the most part," said Tarq. "In fact, people even look happier because OMC-BOWS makes them feel relaxed and content. The only difference is what we call the cullings. Whenever necessary, the Xortaags order the people they need, for example, construction workers, plumbers, or simple laborers, to show up in a certain location and get to work. They are housed and fed, but about as well as animals, and they get no medicine if they fall ill."

When the presentation ended, we started discussing how to proceed. The first order of business was to collect information, looking for anything that might give us an advantage. We could do this in two ways: by the Akakie invisible spy ship flying in orbit, and by the Commandos' various surveillance and information gathering missions.

"Which just happens to be Kurt's specialty," I said.

"We've already learned a lot," said Kurt. "For example, the Xortaags use our vehicles for ground transportation, which eliminates the need to bring their own. They mostly use trucks, but they have an affinity for muscle cars. Also, ladies and gentlemen,"—he walked to the main holographic display and touched the screen; two life-size images popped up—"meet the Xortaags."

One of the images looked like Conan the Barbarian: He had olive skin, straight black hair, and black eyes. The other was a perfect depiction of Hitler's master race: fair-skinned and blond with cold blue eyes. Both men were tall and had ridiculously square jaws, like Superman in those old animated movies.

"You mean they all look like this?" I asked.

Kurt nodded. "The Xortaags use genetic engineering to shape themselves into their vision of a perfect warrior. They also have enhanced abilities compared to a human; for example, they have stronger muscles, joints and bones, and a higher pain tolerance. They heal faster, and they have a quicker reaction time and a longer lifespan."

"And the women?" asked Liz.

Kurt touched the screen again. Two more images appeared. They looked mostly like the first two except for very high cheekbones and thick unibrows. And boobs. Big ones. Obviously.

"For some reason, the Xortaags find unibrows sexy."

"And what're we supposed to do with this gem of information?" I asked.

Kurt ignored me. "Security is very lax. The Xortaags' physical appearance makes it impossible for some Commandos to blend in, but everyone else can walk in and out of any Xortaag settlement as long as they speak their language, wear their uniform and don't forget to wear make-up. This makes bugging operations very easy. We're going to place bugs in all major Xortaag installations."

"Just make sure not to put any bugs in their bedrooms," I said. "We don't want to end up listening to them having sex, do we?"

"Ladies and gentlemen, the commander of the fleet," growled Allen. "The epitome of discipline and maturity."

I showed great restraint and didn't stick out my tongue at him. Very mature of me.

"They do not have sex," said Tarq.

I raised my eyebrows. "What now?"

"The Xortaags have sex only to procreate," explained Tarq, "and they do not want children in the fleet, for obvious reasons. The only exception is Mushgaana, who is infatuated with beautiful women, both Xortaag and alien, and does not try to control himself."

"Says the man who hid two porn stars in his quarters for a month," said Venom.

Tarq continued, "He regularly has female company, usually the most attractive women among the Xortaags or the indigenous population."

"It's good to be the crown prince," I said.

Liz frowned and hit me in the arm, much harder than usual.

"How did you know this?" asked Kurt.

"I have my sources," said Mr. Poker Face.

"Didn't your mother teach you to share with your friends?" I asked him.

"No," said Tarq. "My mother thought me my friends would stab me in the back the first chance they got."

I opened my mouth, but Liz raised her hand and stopped me. "I got this," she told me, turned to Tarq and with a husky voice that was a perfect imitation of mine said, "Paranoid much?"

* * *

MILAN - MAY 19, 2078

DRIVING A FORD MUSTANG GT6, Kurt noticed Oksana was breathing faster and shallower than usual and saw a few small beads of sweat on her forehead. He told her in Russian, "Relax. I've done this ten times already. It's a cakewalk."

The girl was brave, but it was her first mission, only a few weeks after coming to Winterfell. Kurt had chosen her for this mission because it was just a bugging operation that he judged to be pretty straightforward. He was trying to break her in gently.

They'd learned the Xortaag language and mannerisms using MICI. They were wearing the aliens' dark gray uniforms, and they used facial prosthetics and disguise to look exactly like the enemy. Kurt couldn't help smiling every time he glanced at Oksana's unibrow. The intel gathered by some of the bugs indicated Prince Mushgaana had decided to move into a luxurious mansion which previously belonged to a billionaire. Kurt wanted to bug the mansion before the prince arrived. He'd turned the car's automated driving system off on purpose. The Mustang was built to be driven.

From the back seat, Sergei told Oksana, "Take yourself in your hands. Kurt's right. This is very easy."

Kurt had asked them to speak Russian, saying he needed to practice, even though now he could learn a language perfectly using MICI. He asked Sergei, "Take yourself in your hands?"

"It means calm down," said Sergei.

"We're in no danger," Kurt told Oksana. "Security's almost nonexistent. Plus, with the memories MICI's implanted in our brains, we don't even need to pretend we're Xortaags. I honestly feel I've been living a double life, one as a human, one as a Xortaag."

"Does your Xortaag alter ego have a wife?" asked Oksana.

Kurt shook his head. "Trust me; you don't want to know."

The Commandos didn't see anyone when they arrived at their destination.

The mansion Mushgaana had chosen as his private residence had three floors, with a large balcony facing the main gate, and it was surrounded by a private park. Oksana stood outside while Kurt and Sergei went inside and started bugging the rooms. Kurt found it strange there was nobody in the building but decided not to look a gift horse in the mouth. They used smart-dust bugs, which were tiny listening devices less than two millimeters wide. The bugs were practically invisible; the real challenge was to place them somewhere they wouldn't be accidentally swept away by a cleaning crew.

When they were done and went back outside, Kurt saw Oksana leisurely chatting with three Xortaag soldiers. She joined them and said, "Mushgaana's on his way right now. This is why the place's empty: He's coming with his own assistants, servants, and guards."

Sergei said, "You know, we could put a bomb in here and get rid of him once and for all."

"And jeopardize our mission in the process?" Kurt asked. "You've got to see the bigger picture here."

"Do you want to stick around and see him?" Oksana asked. "I'd like to know what the Xortaag king looks like."

"He's the crown prince, and no, we're done here. Let's not push our luck."

"Can I drive?" asked Oksana.

"I just said 'let's not push our luck,' " Kurt said but threw her the car keys.

Oksana floored it as soon as they got in. The Mustang's engine roared, and the car made a jackrabbit start. Kurt said, "Take it easy. We're trying to keep a low profile here."

Driving like a madwoman, Oksana replied, "You worried cops might stop us?"

Sergei pointed out of the car's window, "Look!"

A shuttle had appeared in the sky right above the

mansion. It landed close to the building at the same time the Mustang passed through the main gate.

"Seriously, slow down a bit," Kurt told Oksana, who was having too much fun to listen. She started driving faster, her eyes sparkling.

* * *

Mushgaana stepped out of the shuttle, reading a report on his PDD. Suddenly, at the very edge of his mental powers' range, he sensed an independent, thinking human mind for just a fraction of a second. His eyes widened, and he stopped in his tracks. He tilted his head in the direction he had sensed the human's thought. He concentrated his telepathic powers, ready to order the shuttle pilots to fly off the ground, follow and capture the person whose mind was not controlled by the Voice of God.

But this time he did not feel anything.

With the Voice of God in operation, this is impossible, Mushgaana thought. He had listened in on a few human minds in the last days; it was ineffably boring how thrilled they were to serve their gods. The only thing that was at all interesting was that the humans saw their gods differently, mostly in their own image as to race and ethnicity but not always. Some of the dark-skinned people imagined a long-haired blond man while some white-skinned saw a bald Asian with his hands folded in his lap.

Mushgaana figured he was so bored he was imagining things. He shrugged it off, resumed reading, and walked into the mansion.

* * *

IT DROVE me crazy thinking about the dead people and about their families not remembering them. I hadn't been close to my mom, but I freaking remembered her. I felt sad about her death and her life, wondered what she'd been like before her illness. I worried about how people would feel if they *did* get their memories back someday. How would they cope?

All this was made worse when Oksana told us her sister's question about why God allowed the murders. I believed in a deity more than I didn't, but that was as far as it went. I figured there was no point in wondering because whether God existed or not, he/she/it clearly had no intention of dropping by for a chat. I thought most religious people (except Liz, of course) were delusional or making it up, so I didn't see them as able to help much with the trauma. So maybe that was part of why I partnered with Tarq to pull off one of his practical jokes. The other part was I really needed the distraction.

The collective trauma after the fall of Earth and the subsequent bloodbath had brought a glaring shortcoming in Winterfell's design into sharp focus: The Akakies didn't have a religion, so they hadn't built a place of worship in the base. We had several people who had day jobs but would moonlight as clergymen for various religions, including Liz's priest, a Commando whose name was Father Philip. I personally would've preferred not to have Catholic priests around, but since there were no children in Winterfell, I figured it'd be safe.

At some point, all the men/women of the cloth in Winterfell got together, and in a coordinated effort they lobbied Tarq to assign a place of worship. My wife joined forces with them, saying she'd missed Sunday sermons and "proper confessions." Tarq, who saw no benefit in this, and in fact considered the whole religion thing a complete waste of time, relented, probably just to get rid of them, and gave them a floor of one of the barracks under the condition that members of all religions share it.

Little did he know his problems had just started.

Our various part-time priests, rabbis, imams, pujaris, monks and the rest of the clergy couldn't agree on a single thing. They kept arguing about everything and complaining to Tarq so much that they finally got under his admittedly thin skin. Winterfell's men of God soon learned the lesson the rest of us had learned a while back: If you got on Tarq's bad side, a prank would be coming your way.

Come to think of it; if you got on his good side, you'd have a prank coming your way too. It was a damned-if-I-do-and-damned-if-I-don't kind of situation.

Tarq asked me for help, saying that I was the only human he knew with a sense of humor comparable to the Akakies. I wondered if I should be insulted, but once he told me his plan, I happily accepted—only after talking to Liz. I was sure she'd divorce me if I participated in Tarq's new prank without her prior approval. After Liz gave me her blessings, I put a hand-picked team together, and by hand-picked, I mean people who didn't much care about the possibility of going to hell once they died. I didn't even ask Sergei and Matias. I was sure both of them would turn me down, being deeply religious men. Kurt, Keiko, and Allen refused to participate, saying the whole thing was childish and not worth the effort. They chided me for stooping so low as to become Tarq's accomplice in one of his distasteful pranks. The only person from our inner circle who joined in was Oksana. She said she was up for anything that would distract her from her sister's suicide. I thought she felt the same way I did about religion—and saw this as a chance to prove herself to Winterfell's commander.

Operation Wrath of God—yeah, the Xortaags weren't the only people with a God complex—commenced on May 23, at 3 AM sharp.

Dressed in black tactical uniforms and SWAT balaclavas, with Oksana following me closely, I kicked Father Philip's door open. We entered his quarters, and I shouted at the top of my voice, "On the ground! Don't move a muscle, you punk, or I'll shoot you in the legs and feed you to my dogs while you're still alive!"

A bit too much?

Father Philip put up a fight, but we'd caught him with his pants down—literally. Oksana kneed him in his belly, we handcuffed him, dragged him out of his quarters, and joined the other teams who were busy doing the same thing to all Winterfell's clergymen/women. Most of the poor bastards were scared out of their wits. They stared at us with wild eyes and shouted incomprehensible nonsense, thinking this was a religious purge.

We had ten operational MICI units. I pushed Father Philip into one of them, shouting with the most exaggerated southern accent I could muster, "This is revenge for the St. Bartholomew's Day Massacre!"

A couple of Catholic priests fainted.

We threw them all in the MICI units at the same time, a few people in each, and imprinted two simple messages on all their brains, "When thou hear the secret word, thou shalt feel and show love to the members of other religions more than thyself, thy family and thy friends" and "Thou shalt forget everything that happened this night."

Tarq didn't tell us what the secret word was.

Tarq called the Winterfell's clergy to a meeting in the

Command Center the next morning. They all showed up, wearing their respective formal attire. They sat with their own people, chins up in holy indignation, and gave the other groups the cold shoulder. I stood in the back, watching the show, rubbing my hands together in anticipation. Some people on my team started placing bets on what would happen next. Tarq, wearing a gold embroidered dress, a belt of gold and a crown adorned with jewels, walked into the Command Center and stood in front of the room. He looked at everyone, smoked his pipe, waited a few minutes to create suspense, and then very solemnly, like a king declaring a new decree, said, "Titties."

All the priests, rabbis, imams, and others stopped breathing for a second. The Command Center became so quiet you could hear a butterfly flapping its wings. Then they ran to the members of other religions and hugged them, crying in each other's arms and begging forgiveness for all past wrongdoing. They professed undying brotherly/sisterly love and promised to live in harmony at each other's side forever. A Catholic priest and an imam got into a fight over which one loved a rabbi more. This was the funniest thing I'd ever seen in my life. Oksana was shaking so hard with laughter she had to lean on me for support; otherwise, she'd have lost her balance. Someone made a video of the whole scene, which went viral in Winterfell. I would've made millions if I could put it on YouTube.

I sat on a chair, leaned back, clasped my hands behind my head and enjoyed the show. I was beginning to see why the Akakies liked pranks so much. Maybe Tarq was right: I did have the same sense of humor they had.

The only problem was some people took the idea of loving the others too far. We noticed it when a female vicar started ripping off a Buddhist monk's clothes. My team had a tough time separating those two, and a few others who were following suit, apparently bent on having an orgy in the middle of the Command Center. Whatever they did after in the privacy of their own quarters was none of my business. Other than that, Operation Wrath of God turned out to be an unparalleled success.

* * *

New York - May 29, 2078

Major Josef Hernandez was jogging in a park near his home, enjoying the light evening breeze, having no care in the world.

Josef was blessed to live under the protection of the gods and enjoy the bounty provided for him. He was a jet fighter pilot, but these days there was not a lot of flying going on. He was content to go to work, clock in and out, and go home to his beautiful wife and two small daughters, patiently waiting for the day when he'd have the opportunity to serve the gods.

Josef's only problem was he occasionally had nightmares. They were always the same: He and his friends were in a dogfight against alien spaceships which were much faster than their own jet fighter. A lot of his friends died, but he managed to shoot one of the spaceships down. He decided to talk to a psychologist about this recurring nightmare.

Josef was running by a beautiful spring ringed with mossy stones, the water falling into a pool that reflected the surrounding green leaves, thinking about nothing in particular, when a sudden pain stabbed his left hip. He touched the place and to his surprise found a dart there.

Who's shooting darts at me? he thought, and then fell to the ground, unconscious.

When he came to, he was sitting on a chair in a small and otherwise empty room. There was a window on one of the walls, through which someone looked at him and said, "Hurry up. This one's awake."

And then the strangest thing happened. All his good feelings about living under the gods' protection and his blissful desire to serve them evaporated, replaced by his last memories. To his horror, he realized his recent nightmares had actually happened. Feeling nauseated and terrified for his family, he got up and walked out of the room and came face to face with one of the most infamous people on the planet.

"We need to talk," said Kurt.

* * *

WITH KURT GETTING into kidnapping business, we finally got a few hundred experienced jet pilots, including a few who had fought the Xortaags and survived, which was no mean feat.

One of our recruits was my old war buddy, Josef. It turned out both he and John Taylor had survived the Xortaag attack by parachuting out of their jet fighters after they were hit. I invited him for a drink in our quarters one evening and introduced him to Liz and Keiko.

Joseph looked at all the movie posters Liz and I had put up the walls and chuckled. "Love what you have done with the place." He pointed at Liz's Chinese Evergreen in a corner and added, "What a coincidence. I have one exactly like this at home."

"I never used to keep plants, but I got attached to these in prison," said Liz.

"We have a lot of catching up to do, buddy," I said.

"You bet we have. Look at this." He proudly showed us pictures of his twin daughters. "Meet Sofia and Mariana, and let me tell you this: There's no way they grow up to be Xortaag slaves."

I felt jealous. His kids were adorable. I pined for a family of my own, and so did Liz. We often joked about two boys and two girls, but this wasn't the best time to bring children into the world.

"Nor will my daughter," said Keiko.

Liz and I looked at her in astonishment. I asked, "Your what now? You have a daughter?"

Keiko nodded. Liz said, "And all this time you didn't mention that once?"

Keiko shrugged. "Nobody asked."

Josef wasn't too pleased to learn we were there when the remainder of his squadron came under attack and didn't intervene. He said, "Your warning probably saved my life. If they'd caught us totally by surprise, I wouldn't have had the chance to parachute. But let me get this straight: You were flying ten of these fancy space fighters, and you didn't see fit to come to our help?"

I crossed my arms. "We had a very good reason."

Liz, playing with her hair, said, "I tried to help, and I got demoted for it."

"I thank you with all my heart," said Josef. "It's good to see someone has some balls around here."

Liz gave me a smug look.

"Don't encourage her," I told Josef. "I've been trying to

214

drill some discipline into her, but she still thinks she's an acrobatic pilot, not a fighter pilot."

Liz countered, "Discipline's Jim's code for 'being a pussy.'"

Rubbing my temples, I thought, *Here we go again.*

* * *

A FEW DAYS LATER, the usual suspects, Kurt, Allen, Liz, Keiko, Tarq, Barook and I, were sitting in the Command Center having a meeting, when the door opened and more than a dozen men dressed in the Commandos uniforms and armed with weapons ranging from shotguns to assault rifles rushed in. They pointed their guns at us, shouting, "Don't move! Hands in the air!"

I thought this was another one of Tarq's pranks. Being attacked inside Winterfell by our own people was the last thing I could imagine happening. I was about to roll my eyes and say something sarcastic when Kurt and Allen drew their sidearms at the same time and started shouting back, "Put your weapons down!"

The sight of the two of them trying to stare down some fifteen heavily armed men in a Mexican standoff was sort of funny. I wasn't sure what was going on, but I ran to stand by Kurt. I was unarmed, and so were Liz and Keiko, who joined us anyway. Why would we pack inside Winterfell? Tarq and Barook didn't even bother to move their skinny asses from their seats; they just sat back and watched us intently.

A few of the attackers looked familiar. One of them shouted, "We're taking over Winterfell!"

"Good luck with that," Allen growled.

"Michael, put your weapon down," Kurt said firmly. "It's an order."

"No! No more orders!" yelled the man. "We'd have followed you to hell when you were our leader in the Resistance. But now all you do is blindly follow this fucking alien, who got several hundred million of us killed!"

That explained it.

"And you were giving me a hard time because of the fighter pilots' lack of discipline?" I asked Kurt.

"Not now, Jim," he said through clenched teeth.

With dilated pupils and sweating profusely, the man shouted, "My only son died during the Xortaags' attack. We should've saved him. We could've if we'd defended Earth along with the rest of humanity. But no, you had to listen to aliens, betraying your own kind."

Tarq called out, "I bet now you regret removing my puppetmaster program."

The men were getting more agitated by the second. They started fidgeting and shifting from one foot to the other, and they kept their guns aimed at us, with their fingers on the triggers. They looked at "the aliens," and by extension at us, with murder in their eyes.

Kurt and Allen were infamously badass, but even they couldn't take on so many opponents without getting at least some of us killed. A shootout in such close quarters would be fatal for both sides, and Liz was standing right next to me in the line of fire. That thought sent a shiver running down my spine, and it made my heartbeat quicken. I tried to move and stand between Liz and the gunmen without attracting anyone's attention. She noticed and shoved me out of the way with a gentle push, mouthing the words, "Don't be a hero."

Another man, aiming a huge shotgun at Kurt, said, "Our

quarrel isn't with you. We just want the aliens. You and Allen can still join us in kicking those other aliens off the planet."

Tarq leaned back, an arm hooked over the back of his chair, and as if none of our lives had been in imminent danger asked Barook, "Did he just tar us with the same brush as the Xortaags?"

Barook grinned. "Yes, he did, and if I may say so, masterful use of an idiomatic expression. You are certainly getting the hang of this."

Liz addressed the men, "And we're supposed to just step aside and let you murder Tarq and Barook in cold blood? Over my dead body!"

She was getting wound up. I wished she had been more careful in her choice of words.

The first man, Michael, said, "I don't see you have a choice. I'm gonna count to three; then we'll start shooting. One!"

This is bad.

"Dah, genius," said Venom.

Nobody (else!) said anything. I rubbed my forehead and glanced at Kurt to see if he had any ideas.

"*Two!*"

I was trying to choose between pushing Liz onto the floor and trying to shield her from the bullets with my body, or charging Michael, hoping to catch him by surprise, when Tarq yawned theatrically and told Barook, "This is so boring. Would you please do the honors?"

"Can you guys please put the barrel of your guns inside your mouths?" said Barook. "Do not pull the trigger—at least not yet."

Everyone, including Kurt and Allen, turned their guns toward themselves and shoved the barrels inside their mouths, their eyes round with a comical expression. The men carrying shotguns had a hard time doing it, but they somehow managed, even though they looked like they were about to choke. Even I started to look around, overcome by the uncontrollable desire to find a gun to suck on.

I hadn't seen this coming.

Allen, his lips around his gun barrel, started mumbling. I couldn't make out his words. It sounded like, "Uck oo Erook! I'yy eel oo."

Tarq asked me, "Do you understand this language?"

I somehow managed to keep a straight face. "It's a local Canadian dialect. Only people of Regina can understand it."

"People of what?" asked Tarq, looking like an innocent child.

"UCK OO AAA. Eem, Erook, Arq, UCK OOO!" Allen continued, his face turning scarlet. I couldn't decide if it was because of rage or lack of oxygen, with his Smith & Wesson .44 Magnum filling up his mouth.

Tarq looked like he was about to bust a gut laughing. I couldn't help joining him, which drew a seething stare from Allen.

Barook waited a few seconds, taking it all in and savoring it. Then he told Kurt and Allen, "Not you two," and added to Tarq, "By the time this is over, the two of us are either dead or legendary pranksters, immortalized in our people's lore."

Kurt and Allen holstered their sidearms. Kurt took what had just happened with no objection, like a man accepting what he couldn't change, but Allen looked like he was going to have a heart attack. I thought the only reason he didn't attack Barook was he knew by bitter experience Barook would just make him do something worse, like shoving his handgun where the sun didn't shine.

"The rest of you, keep the guns where they are," said Barook, "and walk to the brig, leave them out and lock yourselves in."

Later that day, everyone in Winterfell watched the video of fifteen battle-hardened Resistance fighters walking to the brig like sheep while struggling to keep loaded guns in their cakeholes. The video ended with a message from Tarq, looking straight at the camera. "Someday, you people have to learn to stop messing with us."

While Liz and I were watching the video, Cordelia said, "Here is a piece of advice: next time you find yourself in a position where you have to remove an alien's puppetmaster program from his mind control machine, make sure you do the same for his assistant."

Two DAYS after that small mutiny, while sitting in the Command Center and going through a file about the Xortaags Kurt had prepared, I held up a photo and said, "You've got to be kidding me."

The Xortaag crown prince looked a lot like me: He had long brown curly hair, baby blue eyes, and a firm jaw, but he was much smaller and shorter than I. I asked Kurt, "What happened to his genetic enhancements?"

Kurt shrugged. "Maybe they didn't work on him?"

"Or they did, but only partially," said Tarq. "We know he is more than eighty years old, but as you see, he looks much younger."

I was jealous. "He doesn't look a day over forty."

"You and Mushgaana have more in common than just

your looks," Kurt said. "The crown prince really likes our movies. He watches at least one movie every night and listening to him quoting and misquoting famous films has become a source of entertainment for our people monitoring the bugs."

"Congratulations. You've got your own Mini-Me," Liz told me.

Allen entered the Command Center, accompanied by Lilly. "Is it okay if Lilly sits with us? She might learn something."

Tarq looked surprised, but he said, "I see no reason why not." Then he told us, "The Xortaags do not have any works of art, but Mushgaana has always been fascinated with what he finds on the conquered planets, even though the rest of the Xortaags see this as a weakness."

"Seriously, how do you know these details about Mushgaana?" asked Kurt, but I didn't think he expected an answer.

"So the person responsible for butchering seven hundred million people and I have a lot in common," I said. "Great. I really feel good about myself right now. Can someone please shoot me?"

Liz patted my knee.

"Be that as it may, I did not call this meeting to discuss your uncanny similarities to Mushgaana," said Tarq. "I have an important announcement: Based on the information we have gathered up to now, Kurt and I have come up with a plan to strike against the Xortaags. We are planning a surprise attack on SH-2, and if that succeeds, we will blitz SH-1 shortly after."

I started tingling with excitement from head to toe. Feeling goosebumps all over my body, I exchanged a look with Liz, who was rubbing her hands together like she was about to start eating a delicious meal. This was huge.

Allen snarled, "Finally."

"Ladies and gentlemen," said Tarq. "Let me tell you all about Operation Free Earth."

Cordelia's voice echoed in the Command Center, "Lame!"

That caught me by surprise. How did she get into our internal comms? And why was she teasing Tarq, of all people?

Tarq jumped out of his seat. "Who said that?"

"It is I, Cordelia, the evil AI," she announced so dramatically it would put a Shakespearian actor to shame, "and I have taken over Winterfell."

"Do you know what's going on?" I asked Liz. She shook her head, pointed at Allen and Lilly and said, "But I bet these two do."

Tarq's eyes widened, and his skin color turned gray. "You gave this AI access to our systems?"

"Of course not," said Lilly. "She's just playing. She can't access any vital systems."

"The hell I can't," said Cordelia.

All the lights in the Command Center went out at that moment. Tarq let out a muffled scream. Liz grabbed my arm. It was pitch black for a second or two; then all the monitors, VR, and holographic screens were turned on, filling the room with a creepy blue light. The main holographic display came to life, showing chilling images of a group of androids equipped with flamethrowers marching into Winterfell and killing everyone who they saw.

Tarq's eyelids started twitching.

"You were saying?" purred Cordelia.

Now I was worried too. Cordelia always had a mean

streak, but I'd never imagined she might go full Red Queen on us.

"Do something," Liz told me.

I stood up. "Cordelia, I order you to stop whatever it is you think you're doing."

"And why would I listen to you?" she asked with contempt in her voice.

"Eh, because we are old friends?" I said. Liz gave me a hard look.

"Listen up, you maggots," said Cordelia. "I'm your master and commander now. Deny me, and I'll fill your precious Winterfell with gas, killing every single one of you. Try me. Go ahead, make my day."

I shouldn't have let her watch so many movies with me.

Tarq clutched his throat. It looked like he couldn't breathe. He stuttered, "You idiots. You have doomed us all."

"Dad?" said Lilly, sounding frightened.

"Hey, man, relax," said Allen. "It's just a prank. We're just messing with you."

I finally understood what was going on. Allen, having been the victim of Tarq's pranks several times, had decided to retaliate, playing on the Akakies' fear of AIs. He might've taken things too far though, and his admission came too late.

Tarq grabbed his chest and stumbled a few steps forward. His eyes rolled back into his head, and his knees wobbled. He dropped to the floor, face first. His nose hit the floor with a sickening thump, and dark blue blood poured out. He stayed there, motionless.

I didn't know the Akakies could have heart attacks.

Liz and I were at his side in a second, but Barook thundered, "Don't touch him, you stupid sons of bitches!"

He kneeled next to Tarq and turned his body. Tarq's lifeless eyes were open, staring sightlessly at nothing in death. Barook put his ear on Tarq's stomach—half his head disappeared in Tarq's belly—and shook his head. He closed Tarq's eyes, pulled a handkerchief out of his pocket and cleaned the blood on Tarq's face. He did it with such gentleness that I wondered if those two were more than just colleagues.

"That's what you are focusing on right now?" asked Venom.

"Did we just kill the funny little man?" asked Cordelia.

"Yes, you did," said Barook. "Congratulations."

"That's it? No defibrillator? Nothing?" I asked.

Barook sighed, reached into his pocket and took out his PDD. He touched the screen a few times and gave it to me. It was a scientific article about the Akakie anatomy, explaining that they had two hearts with very thin walls, and extreme shock or stress could lead to irreversible punctures.

I gave the PDD to Liz who read the article with wide eyes. My body went cold, and there was a tightness in my chest that made breathing difficult. I was paralyzed with sorrow. Tarq had been a good friend. Without him, none of us would've been alive. He'd saved us and helped us prepare to fight the Xortaags. I hold my head down, not sure what to tell Barook.

The consequences of his death were direr than my hurt feelings. He was our commander. There were a million things we didn't know, and he would've taught us. And what if Barook refused to help us, now that we had killed his friend?

I told Allen, "You've just condemned humanity to a slow death. Well done."

Lilly burst to tears and hid her face in her father's chest. Liz hit me in the arm, ran to her side and hugged her, telling her it wasn't her fault. From where I was standing, it totally was. Those Canadians.

Kurt asked Barook, "What can we do? Do your people have memorial services?"

"I think you have done quite enough," said Barook. "If it is all right with you, I want to be alone with my old friend for a while." He held Tarq's hand and started rocking back and forth, his eyes closed.

I walked out of the Command Center, followed by Liz and Kurt. With our heads down and shoulders drooped, we looked like Napoleon's soldiers returning from Russia.

Lilly was so devastated Liz decided to stay with her. I went to our quarters and stayed there alone, with only Venom to keep me company. Damn, but the little alien had grown on me. I liked his flamboyant behavior and colorful appearance. I liked his sense of humor and his total lack of respect for conventionality, and I'd enjoyed seeing him in action, pulling pranks on his unsuspecting victims. I chuckled at the memory of Allen grazing with his cow friends in one of Winterfell's parks. And he was a good leader. The magnitude of the black op he'd orchestrated to bring the Xortaags down was mind-blowing. I missed him already.

And this happened when we were finally ready to kick the Xortaags' butt. That stupid, fat, bald *Canadian* had ruined everything.

My PDD buzzed. It was a message from Barook, requesting a meeting to discuss "arranging a memorial service for our murdered commander and planning for my imminent departure." That didn't sound ominous at all.

I was the last person who entered the Command Center. I sat next to Liz. She was crying, tears rolling down her cheeks and plopping on her white blouse. *White in honor of Tarq.* I put my arm around her shoulder. Allen was sitting alone in a corner, his head down, staring at his own hands. He looked so miserable I resisted the urge to take a shot at him. Kurt was wordlessly playing with his goatee, lost in thought, and Keiko's eye was bloodshot. I just felt numb.

The door opened, and Tarq waltzed right in. He was wearing a red skin suit, a feathered cap, and a long cape waving in the non-existent wind. He smiled at us as if nothing had happened and said, "And you people thought you could pull a prank on *me!*"

WE SPENT the next few weeks preparing for our first all-out land-air military operation against the Xortaags. Operation Free Earth was Kurt and Tarq's brainchild, but as the commander of the fleet, finalizing the details of our air attack was my responsibility. Tarq, Kurt and I spent countless hours staring at various topographical plans, discussing how to coordinate the ground and air assault while the rest of the pilots were busy transporting the Commandos to wherever they needed to be for the operation.

The operation consisted of two phases. We were focused on the first phase, which was attacking SH-2 and a few small Xortaag bases at the same time. We didn't have enough space fighters to hit both targets at once, and Kurt believed SH-1 was too big for his plan to work, so he'd decided the operation had to have two phases, to be carried out within five days of each other.

One day, while finalizing our plans for phase one, I asked Tarq, "What have the Xortaags done to you?"

He froze. His eyes betrayed a deep agony for just a

second. Then his poker face took over. "They conquered Alora and—"

"Cut the crap," I said. "This is personal."

Tarq's shoulders slumped. "Nothing. *They* have done nothing to me." He stood up. "I, however, got my only daughter killed."

He left the Command Center.

"One of these days, I'm gonna learn how to keep my mouth shut," I told Kurt.

"Don't hold your breath," he answered.

With the confrontation with the Xortaags growing nearer, I was getting increasingly worried about Liz's inclination to make spur-of-the-moment decisions, so I asked Keiko to try to teach her meditation, hoping that it would improve her self-control. At first, Liz was excited about the idea, and she loved the fact that Keiko had a small shrine—complete with a small Buddha statue, candles, and incense burners—in a corner of her room. But after a couple of weeks of trying, Keiko gave up and told me, "The only way to make Liz sit still for more than five minutes is to hit her in her head with either a baseball bat or a shovel."

The only tangible result of the meditation classes was that Liz liked Keiko's tattoos so much she decided to get one of her own. To my immense relief, she settled on a small butterfly on her lower back, rather than the horrifying dragon covering half of Keiko's body.

One evening, Elizabeth asked me, "Did you know Sergei was gay?"

I raised a brow. "Sergei? The super macho, scary, badass Universal Soldier's gay? You sure?"

"Yep. Matias introduced me to his boyfriend the other day. He's a doctor, working in the sickbay."

"I'm sure Sergei's parents always wanted him to marry a doctor."

My wife, wrapping a curl around her finger, continued, "His name's Robert, but everyone calls him Dr. Bob. He's twenty years younger than Sergei and very cute. In fact, he kinda looks like you."

I decided to take it as a compliment. "Well, this explains something. You know Sergei and Oksana have become very close since her sister's suicide, and I often see them playing chess together. I was wondering why Sergei didn't ask her out."

"Why did you think he had to? Maybe they are just good friends."

I scoffed and quoted Harry, " 'Men and women can't be friends. The sex part always gets in the way.' Also, have you seen Oksana? *Everyone* wants to go out with that girl. She was born with men running after her asking for her phone number."

She gave me a look that made me realize I had put my big foot in my even bigger mouth. I quickly recovered. "Except for me, because I'm married to the most beautiful girl in the world." Trying to change the subject, I added, "Isn't Sergei super religious? I think he goes to church regularly."

"He does, and most of the time together with Dr. Bob," said Liz. "Your sexual orientation has got nothing to do with your personal relationship with God. You know, it's comments like this that makes people think you are, eh, slightly intolerant of others."

I glared at her, "I am not...oh, forget it!"

We spent most of our free time with Elizabeth's siblings, Kurt and Keiko. Liz was hoping to hook these two up. She once told me Keiko had a crush on Kurt and that they'd be a perfect match because Keiko was basically a female version of Kurt with an eyepatch and an impressive tattoo. I knew as a result of his life as a Resistance fighter/assassin, not to mention losing his ex-girlfriend fighting the government forces, Kurt had decided to stay away from emotional involvements, so I didn't think it'd work.

My wife's other matchmaking project involved hooking up her brother with Oksana. I saw more potential there. Matias was an extremely easy-going fellow, and a lot of people felt calm and relaxed around him, which was exactly what Oksana needed after everything she'd gone through.

Liz was successful in her efforts. One day, nearly three months after the Xortaag invasion, Matias and I were playing tennis when he told me he'd started dating Oksana.

"Oksana? The hot blonde Oksana?" I asked, panting.

Matias chuckled. "Yes, but don't let Liz hear you say that."

"Come on. You know I think your sister's the most beautiful girl in the world. Oksana's kind of Playboy-model hot."

Matias gave me an exasperated look, a carbon copy of his sister's. I hurriedly tried to recover. "Well done, buddy. I would've thought she was way out of your league."

Sometimes I just didn't know when to shut up.

* * *

THE NEXT DAY, Liz and I were having breakfast in the mess hall when Keiko joined us and said, "Good morning."

I looked at her and then jumped out of my seat so quickly I spilled milk all over my uniform. "You've got eyes!" I exclaimed.

"I had one already," answered Keiko. "I have a new one

now, in place of the one you ruined in another life, compliments of the Akakies' medical technology."

We both stared at her with fascination. She somehow looked totally different without the eyepatch, and some of her hard-as-nails facade was gone too, despite her tattoos. She added, "With us going to war soon, having only one eye would just not do, would it?"

"When did you do the surgery?" asked Liz. "We didn't know you were in the hospital."

"I wasn't. There was no surgery. It's not a transplant. The doctors grew a new eye right inside my eye socket. It took almost two months, which is why I kept wearing the eyepatch, but I didn't need to be hospitalized at all."

"I didn't know our medical team could perform such miracles," I said, adjusting my wedding ring.

"With MICI and Akakie technology at their disposal?" said Keiko. "This is nothing. Dr. Bob says they can grow back a severed arm or leg." She looked at me closely and added, "You know, he sort of looks like you."

People continuously telling me I looked like Sergei's boyfriend wasn't good for my self-image. I rubbed my forehead and thought about growing a thick beard.

"One question though: Why on earth is it blue?" I asked.

Her other eye was black. She wrinkled her nose. "You forgot who our esteemed commander is? This was his idea of a freaking joke."

"You know what I am thinking?" Liz told me. "Keiko used to beat you with *one* eye. I don't think you'll win another simulated competition ever again."

Oh, crap!

CHAPTER TEN

SH-2 - July 19, 2078, 16:00 EST

MAADA WAS STANDING on the balcony of one of the control towers in the fleet base, enjoying a cup of the hot beverage called "coffee." He was a man of few pleasures in life, but he had come to enjoy the drink with its crisp, bitter flavor and strong aroma.

It was a warm, sunny day. The cloudless sky was like a spotless diamond, clear and shining. It was in such stark contrast to Tangaar when he used to live there, with its dark gray sky and difficult-to-breathe air, typical of a dying planet. Things were much better back in Tangaar now, mostly due to his efforts. He'd brought his civilization back from the brink of destruction. Still, without colonies like this, his species was doomed.

He leaned on the railing and, touching the scar on his face, absentmindedly looked at the fleet base. It was the size of a small city. More than a third of their fleet was stationed here. The fleet base had ten sections, each with its own control tower, revetments, hangars, and barracks. The hangar rooftops were retractable, allowing the Death-bringers to fly in and out of the hangars.

Each section was protected by three laser turrets. Maada could see two of those from where he was standing. The third was behind the tower, forming a triangle with the others. Each turret housed four huge laser cannons, which were the most powerful land-based weapons in the Xortaag arsenal, capable of engaging enemy fleets in space. They were manned at all times. No missile could pass through the cover they provided, and no enemy fighter could get anywhere close to the fleet base. Still, each section also had a Quick Response Force, which consisted of a hundred Deathbringers, stationed in a revetment, ready to fly at a moment's notice, with their pilots camping right next to the fighters in full flight gear. With the comprehensive protec-tion provided by the enormous laser turrets, this was an unnecessary precaution; however, Maada preferred to be prepared in the unlikely event the Akakie fleet decided to take a shot at them.

Maada chuckled at the thought. As if the Akakies, or anyone else in the galaxy, would dare attack the Xortaags. *They are all sheep waiting to be slaughtered*, he thought.

The Akakies were an advanced race and could summon a lot more ships than his own fleet, but they lacked the courage to fight. He could not understand such cowardice: it was not as if running away would save them. But he did not have to understand, only take advantage. Even if they decided to attack, they would be defeated as easily as the last time. The planetary defense, including the laser turrets here, could keep the enemy fleet at bay long enough for his

Deathbringers to fly off the planet and join the fight, and that would be that.

Two trucks stopped in front of the mess hall, and soldiers started to unload them. Maada saw two of them, a man and a woman, leave the trucks and walk towards the control tower but did not pay much attention. His mind was already focused on their next campaign. In three months, their transport ships would arrive, and millions of Xortaags would complete the first phase of the colonization, at which point his fleet would be free to invade the second target on their list. That planet was more advanced than Earth, but Xortaag surveillance had marked them as an easier target. Their people had gone soft as a result of a few hundred years of peace and prosperity.

Peace! Maada smirked. They were in for a rude awakening.

Something caught his attention. The man and woman he had noticed earlier were passing by the control tower now. The man was carrying a big backpack. A corner of Maada's brain wondered what was in the bag.

All of a sudden, his warrior instinct, honed over a life-time spent as a soldier, yelled at him that something was very, *very* wrong. He tensed, jolted upright and started scanning the base, looking for a threat.

He had learned to trust his instincts, but his brain did not immediately catch up with his intuition. In his very long military career, the threat had always come from above. On a planet where all inhabitants worshiped the Xortaags as gods, being attacked on the ground was unthinkable. Maada had no frame of reference for it.

The two soldiers Maada had noticed earlier were out of his line of sight now. More out of curiosity than anything else, he decided to see where they were going. He walked to the other side of the balcony. Once he turned the corner, he saw something so unbelievable that for a second he wondered if he had been dreaming.

The pair stopped, and the man pulled something out of the bag that could only be a small missile launcher. He kneeled on one knee and aimed at the laser turret behind the control tower.

Maada's jaw dropped, and he was frozen, but just for a second. He still could not comprehend how this was possible, but that was a moot point. He drew his sidearm and shot at the man wielding the missile launcher, hitting him square in the back. The woman glanced up and fired back, forcing Maada to hide behind the railing. She picked up the missile launcher and aimed at the laser turret. By this time several other Xortaags had seen her. She was hit just before she pulled the trigger, and the missile missed its target by a small margin. The woman was severely injured and surrounded by Xortaags, but she kept trying to load another missile into her weapon. Maada admired her courage as he aimed carefully and shot her in the head. The woman died still struggling to arm the missile launcher.

Maada heaved a sigh of relief.

Then explosions and gunshots rang out behind him.

OUTSIDE SH-2 - 15:00 EST

KURT, looking through binoculars, touched his earpiece and said, "Here they come."

Wearing the Xortaag dark gray uniform, he was lying down by a tree next to a road leading to SH-2. The road passed through a dense forest. After surveilling the base for weeks, he knew a food convoy would be passing in a few minutes. There were twenty dark blue Volvo trucks in the convoy, bringing food to the ten sections of the huge fleet base.

Kurt wondered for a second what would happen if they failed in carrying out their part of the operation. He concluded it would mean a swift death or at least heavy casualties for Jim and the rest of the pilots. The picture that appeared in his mind—thousands of bloody corpses in flight gear, trapped in the wreckage of their space fighters—made him cringe. He pushed the thought out of his mind and focused on the task at hand.

Kurt put down the binoculars and picked up his suppressed M-28 Sniper Weapon System. Next to him, Sergei did the same. He knew all the two hundred Commandos in his strike force were following suit. Once the convoy reached the spot he'd designated, he shot the front tire of the first Volvo with a subsonic bullet. The vehicle came to a screeching halt. All the other trucks behind it stopped too. The four Xortaags in the Volvo got off and gathered around the flat tire. From their body language it was obvious they didn't know how to fix it. They normally depended on their human slaves to do something like this, but since the completion of the fleet base's construction, no humans had been involved in any fleet-related activities, including menial work like cleaning or preparing food. Tarq had guessed Maada didn't want his precious fleet contaminated by human presence.

The Xortaags didn't have to worry about changing the tire. Kurt took a deep breath to calm his nerves and said in his PDD, "On three. One, two, three."

A hailstorm of bullets hit the Xortaags. Kurt shot an

alien soldier and through his telescopic sight saw his head explode. The Xortaags were cut to pieces in a few seconds.

His heartbeat racing, Kurt shouted, "Let's go." He left his sniper rifle, grabbed his STG 666 assault rifle and ran towards the convoy. Sergei followed him. An injured Xortaag was crawling next to a truck, trying to draw his sidearm. Kurt leveled his gun at the alien's chest and pulled the trigger, giving him a short burst. Dark purple blood splashed from the Xortaag's body, and he stopped moving.

The rest of the Commandos dispatched all the survivors. Then they moved the Volvos out of the road and replaced them with their own, which were identical to the Xortaags' trucks except for three things: They were armored —including hidden metal plates which would cover the tires when the time came—they had a concealed compartment in the back that could hide four commandos, and they had several smaller compartments that were used to hide assault rifles, machine guns, and missile launchers. The Xortaag energy weapon small arms were fine, but the aliens were hardly experts in land warfare, which was reflected in their weaponry. As Allen had put it, "Ain't nothing wrong with some extra firepower."

Kurt climbed on one of the Volvos and concealed himself in the hidden compartment. Sergei and Oksana followed.

Right before the truck started moving, a tall, blond man joined them in the back. Sergei glanced at him; then he jumped out of his seat and yelled, "Moy bozh! What the hell is *that*?"

Matias, unrecognizable with white skin, blue eyes and blond hair, smiled. "What's up?"

"Matias didn't want to sit this one out," said Kurt, looking at his PDD. "So Tarq talked him into this. He had to spend forty-eight hours in the sickbay for his skin color to change. He's been busy running around scaring people since he got out. Tarq's insufferably pleased with himself for his new masterpiece."

"Was this necessary? He is creeping me the hell out," asked Sergei, trying not to look directly at Matias.

"*You*'re feeling hard done by?" said Oksana. "Tarq says it'll take two weeks for his normal skin color to come back, which means I have to deal with this freak show for two damned weeks."

"Says Miss Unibrow," Matias countered.

"Children," said Kurt, with the annoyed tone of a fed-up parent, "I'm trying to work in here. In case you haven't noticed, the first human versus alien guerrilla war in history has just started."

They entered the Xortaag's fleet base and drove towards their designated section without any incidents. When they reached the mess hall, the Commandos not hiding in the concealed compartments got off and started unloading the trucks. Kurt, who was following all his team members as well as the other teams converging on their respective targets in the other sections on a PDD, noticed two Commandos separate from the group to deal with the laser turret behind the control tower.

"Stop playing with your goatee," Oksana told Kurt. "You're making me nervous."

Kurt said, "Sorry," but while staring at his PDD he unconsciously kept pulling his facial hair. A few minutes later he touched his earpiece and said, "Execute."

"Cry 'Havoc' and let slip the dogs of war," said Oksana, removing the barrier to the hidden compartment.

Sergei gave her a confused look.

The Commandos already outside started mowing down

the unsuspecting Xortaags. The sound of shooting and the cries of the dying Xortaags made Kurt's heart beat faster. He and Sergei each grabbed a shoulder missile launcher and jumped out of the truck, flanked by Oksana and Matias. Kurt went down on one knee and targeted the laser turret two miles to his left using the command launch unit. The turret was the size of a five-story building. Tarq had helped the Commandos develop a special armor-piercing missile capable of destroying it, and he was positive the laser turret wouldn't be able to stop something as small as a shoulder-fired rocket. Kurt prayed Tarq was right and pulled the trigger. The missile slammed into the laser turret. The ground shook, and the Xortaag weapon disappeared behind a blinding explosion. Relief brought a satisfied smile to Kurt's face.

Bull's-eye!

He turned his head in time to see Sergei blow the second turret to bits.

Some Xortaag soldiers were shooting back. A large number of them poured out of the various buildings around the mess hall. Kurt ordered, "Back to the trucks. Time to get out of here."

While getting on the Volvo, Kurt heard Tarq say, "All teams have been successful, only Alex and Kate are down."

Kurt cursed under his breath. "And the target?"

"Still standing," Tarq answered.

Kurt taught about a full-frontal assault to the third turret. With the element of surprise gone and hundreds of Xortaags converging on them, it would be suicide, armored trucks or not. But they might still be able to pull it off.

Tarq, all the way back in Winterfell's Command Center, read his mind. "Don't even think about it. Remember we have planned for this. Get out of there."

The Volvo started moving. Kurt grabbed an STG 666 and joined Sergei, Oksana, and Matias who were pouring fire on the Xortaags. He found Oksana and Matias perching next to each other, counting loudly every time each of them dropped a Xortaag. He looked at them and said, "Really?"

Oksana, something dark and primal flickering in the back of her eyes, answered, "We're still short of seven hundred million!"

The trucks sped up, hurrying toward the fleet base exit, leaving a trail of death, hurt and mangled bodies covered in dark purple blood.

Xortaag's small arm energy bolts hit the Volvo from all directions but caused little damage. His mouth set in a hard line, Kurt scanned the truck's surroundings, forcing calm. He aimed at an enemy soldier shooting at the vehicle and pulled the trigger. The Xortaag's face disappeared behind an explosion of blood. Kurt shot another one, and a third, and a fourth, using his STG 666 with such precision it could've been a sniper rifle. This carnage partially satisfied the need for revenge that had been gnawing at his soul since the fall of Earth. He told Oksana, "You're right. Way short."

Now it's all up to you, Jim.

* * *

I was flying a golden Viper.

Tarq had some of our fighters painted in different colors. He explained to us he believed in this stupid superstition that coloring senior officers' space fighters differently would bring good luck, with gold showing the highest rank. Keiko's fighter was dark green, and Liz's—after her recent demotion, she was a major—was light blue. We had a few captains whose fighters were painted silver.

I was as excited as a teenage boy on his first date, and not with just any girl, with a girl he'd been secretly in love with for a long time. Unable to contain myself, I contacted Liz and said, "Today is a good day to die."

"Really? Now?" she said with annoyance in her voice.

Tarq contacted me. "Jim, we have a problem. One of the laser turrets is still active."

"Which one?"

"A-3."

I consulted my PDD. It was good news that there was only one left. This meant Kurt's mission had been mostly successful. I spoke over my mike. "A Squadron, you're with me. Everyone else, proceed as planned." I thought about adding something meaningful and inspirational on the verge of our first battle with the Xortaags, but all I could think of was, "Give them hell."

What would I've done without worn-out clichés?

I put my Viper in a sharp nosedive, followed by Liz, Keiko, and the rest of the A Squadron. Behind us, a hundred Vipers fired their Phoenixes at the target. The laser turret came alive, shooting down all the missiles in quick succession. This gave us time to get closer and fire our own missiles. A Squadron veered off, with only Liz, Keiko, and I pushing forward. Our missiles streaked towards the laser turret. It stopped the new threat with ease, but now I had it in my effective weapon range.

My heart racing, I firewalled the throttle and flew in, energy bolts flying from all three of my Viper's cannons. The laser turret was hard to miss—it looked to be the size of a small mountain. My laser bolts impacted the turret. Flames erupted and smoke belched from the giant weapon. Its crew tracked me and started shooting. It fired thick bolts longer than my Viper in very rapid succession, but I wasn't one of the best pilots on the planet for nothing. I swerved right in a sharp curve and kept avoiding its fire with evasive action. With each passing second, enemy fire was getting closer and closer to my Viper.

I was focused on not getting vaporized, but I had one eye on my display monitor, following Liz and Keiko's space fighters. Keiko came in right after me, spewing out a stream of laser bolts, scoring several hits. She swerved left and, zigzagging between massive laser bolts, took the enemy's fire and attention with her.

And Liz flew in on her heels, letting go of her Viper's full weaponry.

The colossal weapon exploded in a red ball of fire, big enough to cover the whole turret.

Beside myself with exhilaration, I bellowed, "Yes! That's my girl!"

"Why, Jim, I'm flattered, but you really aren't my type," answered Keiko.

* * *

Milan - 16:00 EST

Allen was crouching behind a tree, looking at the images on his through-the-wall surveillance device.

Since this was probably the only chance to mount a surprise attack against the Xortaags, Kurt and Allen had decided to use this opportunity to hit the Xortaag leadership. Maada lived in SH-2 and was out of reach, but Mushgaana lived in his private mansion, guarded by a small security force. This was where Allen and a strike force of thirty Commandos were right now. The plan was to capture Mushgaana alive if possible, assassinate him if not.

Allen's second-in-command, Tanaka, the ex-leader of Japan's Resistance, looked over his shoulder. "Is everything in order?"

"Looks like it," answered Allen. "Around fifty servants and guards, as always. You see this room here with someone inside? This is Mushgaana's office, so this should be him."

"Let's go then," said Tanaka.

Allen put on his night-vision goggles and trotted toward the mansion. Tanaka followed him. They jumped over the mansion wall and entered through its main entrance. Allen shot the three men in the first floor living room using his suppressed STG 666 and ran upstairs. The two guards stationed outside Mushgaana's office were alerted by the noise from downstairs, and one of them was talking to his PDD. Allen shot them both in the head.

Allen opened the door of the office and cautiously peered inside. He was welcomed by a hot energy bolt hitting the door frame a couple of inches from his head, burning a black hole into the frame. He growled, "We don't have time for this," and sprayed the inside of the room with bullets. A man screamed in pain, and a body fell to the floor.

A minute later, Allen and Tanaka were standing over a dead man in Mushgaana's office. The man was tall, muscular and bald. "Well, this definitely isn't him," said Tanaka.

Allen heard another Commando's nervous voice in his earpiece. "Colonel? We have a problem. Look outside the window."

Allen approached one of the room's big windows, and with a heavy feeling in his stomach, saw five Deathbringers hovering mid-air right outside, slightly higher than the mansion roof.

Allen's mouth twitched. He told Tanaka, "This can't possibly be good, eh?"

* * *

SH-2 - 16.30 EST

Maada ran to the other side of the control tower. In utter disbelief, he saw both turrets destroyed, with the trucks speeding away, killing everyone in their path.

Trembling with uncontrollable anger, he contacted the officer in charge of the Quick Response Force and shouted, "Get the fighters in the air!"

A faint sound caught his attention. He looked up trying to find the source of the sound, and his mouth fell open when he saw hundreds of missiles racing toward the hangars and the Quick Response Force fighters' revetment. The fighters were just beginning to get off the ground. If they had already been in the air, they could have easily avoided the incoming missiles, but they were sitting ducks now as they started their ascent. The missiles hit, and most Deathbringers in the Quick Response Force were annihilated by thunderous varicolored blasts before they got the chance to take off. Some of the hangars were also hit.

The worst was still to come.

Maada saw hundreds of triangular craft approaching the now defenseless air base at a low altitude.

Xortaag pilots were running towards the hangars that had survived the missile attack while the hangar rooftops were being retracted so slowly it was agonizing to watch.

Maada knew it was too late. Savage desperation crept over him. The enemy space fighters were so close. Without the laser turrets, there was nothing between them and the hundreds of Deathbringers in the hangars.

There were some fifty men and women on duty in the control tower. Maada turned to look at them. His despair was mirrored on their faces. He rubbed the scars on his face and made a decision that he knew would doom them all.

He softly said, "Join me."

No one hesitated. They all rushed out and stood next to him on the balcony. "Draw your weapons and wait for my command," said Maada.

The Xortaags followed his order.

The enemy craft opened fire on the hangars. Energy bolt after energy bolt landed, causing explosions that killed countless Xortaags and destroyed their space fighters. The ground shook beneath Maada. His ears pounding, he witnessed people under his command slaughtered, feeling utterly helpless. Some Xortaag soldiers were shooting from the ground, but the enemy pilots dispatched them with ease.

If I survive this, I will find and kill all these mother-fuckers.

The enemy fleet got closer to the tower, destroying everything in their path like an unstoppable hurricane.

It was fifty of them against a thousand space fighters. It was desperate. It was hopeless. It was suicidal.

It's magnificent.

A young, beautiful woman to his left said, "General? It has been an honor, sir," and performed a perfect salute. Everyone else followed suit.

Maada knew the woman, just like he knew all the other fighter pilots under his command. She was an off-duty

Deathbringer pilot whose name was Arminaa. Maada wondered what she was doing in the control tower. His mouth curved into a sad smile. He returned the salute and aimed his weapon. "Target the silver craft in front."

A minute later he shouted, "Fire!"

They all opened fire in unison, and with satisfaction, Maada saw thick smoke pouring from the silver fighter's engine. The fighter started losing altitude.

"The one to its left," ordered Maada. He took aim and fired his weapon.

Several enemy space fighters fired back.

The last thing Maada saw was a red and yellow explosion engulfing the control tower.

* * *

SH-2 - 16.50 EST

JOSEF COULDN'T BELIEVE his bad luck.

He'd gone toe-to-toe with the Xortaag fleet during the invasion of Earth. Not only that, he was one of only a handful of humans alive who had shot down a Deathbringer. He'd done all that, just to get hit by ground fire during their first mission.

He told himself, "Aviate. Navigate. Communicate."

He tried everything he could to save the space fighter, but all in vain. He contacted Winterfell. "I'm going down. I'll parachute out in a second."

"We are sending a Commando team to pick you up," answered Tarq.

A few seconds later, he heard Jim's voice. "Josef, take care of yourself. We'll have a beer when this is over."

Josef chuckled. "I don't drink, but I'll have one with you."

"Welcome to Martin-Baker Fan Club," Jim said.

A few minutes later, Josef parachuted from his Viper.

* * *

MILAN - 15:30 EST

MUSHGAANA, sitting in his office, was pleased with himself. He was looking at a holographic map of Kingdom of God on his desk and evaluating their progress. The construction was ahead of schedule. Soon the first phase of their colonization would complete, and he would be off to a new conquest.

All of a sudden, he sensed a group of humans moving towards his residence. What got his attention was that they were moving in close formation and were obviously trying to avoid attracting attention. He reached out for their minds and saw the intention to harm him.

This was impossible. These people should have thought of him as a god. Something had gone terribly wrong. Mushgaana tried to get control of the humans' minds, but he failed. If he concentrated on each individual, he could sense their thoughts—rage and a desire for revenge, recognizable but subtly different from how a Xortaag would think—but he could not exert any control over them.

Time to think on your feet, he thought.

He ran out of his office. On his way out, he telepathically ordered one of his men to go to the room and sit behind his desk. He ran downstairs, opened a hidden door and entered a secret passage that led to a small underground military base right next to his residence. Nobody knew this place existed because Mushgaana had had it built in complete secrecy to protect himself from a possible attempt on his life by his brothers, or even worse, Maada staging a coup d'état. The general was too loyal and honorable to do such a thing, but it was always better to be safe than sorry. On the way, he contacted the commander of the base.

"We have got company," said Mushgaana.

* * *

Milan - 16.14 EST

A SCREEN on Mushgaana's desk came to life. Allen and Tanaka heard a voice say, "You guys speak English?"

Allen approached the desk and found himself staring at the crown prince's image on the screen. Mushgaana said, "You know who I am; you have obviously come here to kill me. The problem is I have no idea who you are, and because I am getting reports of a widespread attack against my people all over the planet, I am eager to get to know you. Can you make it easy on all of us and just surrender, or do we have to come in guns blazing?" He wiggled his index finger at the screen. "I am going to count to three. There will be no four."

Allen wanted to say something snappy and shoot the screen, but something on Mushgaana's desk caught his attention. *This is interesting*, he thought and leaned over to study what he'd found on the desk more closely.

Mushgaana counted to three. When he saw no response, he said, "This is just awkward," and the screen went blank.

"Can we call out?" Allen asked Tanaka.

"All communications are jammed," Tanaka answered a few seconds later, "and even if we could call for help, there won't be enough time for anyone to come."

Allen said, "I wasn't thinking about calling for help. Come have a look at this."

* * *

I SAID, "Bandits at two o'clock low."

On my display monitor, I could see nine enemy craft that had somehow survived the attack and managed to get off the ground flying away from the fleet base.

"Let's go get them," I added.

We followed the Deathbringers. The pursuit only lasted a few minutes. They noticed our fighters, did the math and turned around to meet us.

Adrenaline coursed through my veins, and my heart vibrated with anticipation. I'd been fangs out for a while.

Laser bolts bursting from all our cannons, we zoomed in and closed the distance. I caught a fighter in my targeting scope and fired. The enemy vessel vanished in a blinding explosion. I swung my golden Viper up and around in a sharp curve and found myself behind two Deathbringers. They flew away in different directions.

I had to make a split-second decision. I said, "Eeny, meeny, miny, moe" and followed the one to my left. The gomer threw his space fighter all over the sky to shake me. I lined up my shot and squeezed the trigger. The Death-bringer disintegrated under my continuous fire.

The second Deathbringer was making a sharp curve, trying to get on my six. It lashed out at me with its cannons. Laser bolts streaked past my fighter. I released four Sparrows that made an almost 180 turn and went after it. The gomer twisted and turned and managed to avoid all four, but now I was on top of their fighter. The Deathbringer went on a twisting dive. I followed and kept firing. It erupted in angry red flames.

Sierra Hotel!

I throttled back, pumped a fist and thundered in my mike, "*Are you not entertained?*"

Caroline said in my ears, "First time I watch you in action. Gotta admit you're a lot more badass than what I'd thought."

I looked at my monitor to see what was going on with Liz and Keiko. What I saw made my eyes bulge and beads of sweat appear on my face.

On my nine o'clock high, Liz was hot on a Death-bringer's tail, spitting a deadly stream of laser bolts at the bandit. She was so focused on her target she didn't see another enemy vessel sneaking in right behind her.

I shouted, "You've got a bandit on your ass! Break right!"

Liz probably heard the urgency in my voice and imme-diately rolled right. The laser bolts fired by the Death-bringer on her six missed her by inches. I snapped my Viper's nose into a hard-climbing turn and gave the gomer who had almost killed my wife all I'd got, laser cannons *and* missiles. I obliterated the Deathbringer and then shot a few more bolts into the wreckage to make sure.

I stayed motionless for a few seconds, allowing the relief to sink in. Liz broke to the left and gave chase to her original target. "You are welcome!" I said after her. No answer.

"I got four kills," I announced.

With the tone of a teacher reproaching an overly enthu-siastic student, Keiko said, "Jim, we are a team. This isn't a competition," and then she cheekily added, "At any rate, I got four too."

Oh, for crying out loud!

* * *

SH-2 - 17.18 EST

COUGHING, Maada regained consciousness. His lungs were full of smoke, and he felt he was about to suffocate. Half of his face, as well as his left arm and shoulder, were drenched in blood, but he managed to sit up and look around.

Most of the control tower had collapsed, and the rest was on fire. There were blood and body parts everywhere. Maada recognized the burned bodies of some of the people who were standing next to him on the balcony before the attack and barely managed not to throw up. He also saw Arminaa, lying on the floor, her chest moving with shallow breaths.

At least this one has survived.

He weakly stood up, leaned on the balcony railing and looked around.

The fleet base was destroyed. The hangars were burning, and it was obvious only a miracle could save a few of the Deathbringers inside. From where he was standing, he could see hundreds of dead bodies, and he had no doubt the actual number of casualties was far greater. He had never suffered such a comprehensive defeat in all his life. It caused more anguish for him than all his injuries.

He spotted a lone, dark green enemy vessel circling the base. The pilot was probably making sure nothing worth destroying was left. Maada looked around and recovered his sidearm. He used the railing to support his mangled body, tried to wipe blood and sweat from his eyes, aimed with his good arm and started shooting at the space fighter.

* * *

IN HER COCKPIT, Keiko, joy streaking through her because of their decisive victory, saw the tiny laser bolts passing by her fighter. A few energy bolts hit the vessel without causing any damage. She looked around and saw an injured man trying to shoot her Viper down with a sidearm. She thought about shooting back, but it was difficult not to admire the defeated man's courage.

As Jim would say, David versus Goliath much? Let's not kill the stupid bastard.

She flew away and left the destroyed Xortaag base bahind.

* * *

WITH WIDE EYES, Maada watched her go and collapsed on the balcony, shivering. In what felt like a blink of an eye, their second-biggest fleet base was destroyed, more than a third of his fleet was annihilated, thousands of men and women under his command were slaughtered, and worst of all, the pilot of that damned green vessel had not even found him worthy of a warrior's death.

Only ferocious willpower and a burning desire for revenge stopped him from eating his own gun.

* * *

Milan - 17.15 EST

.   .   .

Hɪᴅɪɴɢ behind the desk in Mushgaana's office and shooting at the Xortaags massing in the corridor, Allen contemplated the ironies of life.

He'd been a soldier for nearly forty years, participating in three wars and countless black ops, and the second-in-command of the Resistance for two violent, bloody years, which brought him a reputation as a fierce warrior. He'd been in more tight situations than he cared to remember, and he'd survived all that just to die in the first encounter with an enemy who was notoriously inexperienced in ground warfare.

What a stupid way to die.

His comrades had fought hard, aided by their better weapons and body armor, but there were too many Xortaags. Of the thirty Commandos in the unit, only Allen and Tanaka were still breathing.

Allen shot a few rounds at the door and hit someone, but his STG 666 clicked empty. He drew his Glock 55 and said, "I'm almost out."

"Me too," said Tanaka. "I think they're waiting for us to run out of bullets so they can rush us."

The thought had occurred to Allen too. It couldn't happen. If they were captured alive, there was a good chance the Xortaags could find the Winterfell's location, which would spell the end for Lilly, Kurt, the other people in Winterfell, and all humanity. And there still was a minuscule chance he could get the information he'd found on Mushgaana's desk to Kurt, but he could do it only in death, assuming that Kurt would find a way to take his body back to Winterfell for burial. Knowing Kurt, he probably would.

Allen thought about the decision he was about to make. What he had to do was clear. He had no regrets: He'd lived a good life, and to be honest, he had been on borrowed time the past few years, ever since Zheng assassinated Thomas.

He only wished he could see Lilly once more.

I hope Kurt kicks the Xortaags' ass as soon as possible, so Lilly will get to have a normal life, get married, have kids, all that jazz.

Allen told Tanaka, "Sorry, buddy," and shot him in the back of the head from two inches away. Tanaka's blood spattered on Allen's hand and clothes. The Japanese man collapsed with a surprised look on his face. Allen started to turn the gun on himself. His arm suddenly stopped moving.

Allen stared at his unmoving arm in unspeakable terror as his mind screamed commands. His arm was no more responsive than that of a corpse. His stomach rolled, and his fingers went cold. The memory of Tarq having control of his body rushed to him like a horde of zombies. Someone was controlling his arm. *It must be that fucking Mushgaana.* He pushed and pushed, but his arm, shaking uncontrollably, didn't move an inch.

Several Xortaags poured into the room and ran toward him. Half-paralyzed, he could do nothing to defend himself.

The old man stopped struggling with his arm and made his mind blank. Then he said, "Fuck it," bent forward in a sudden movement, put his head in front of the gun barrel and pulled the trigger. His brains sprayed the uniform of the nearest Xortaag soldier, who was already on top of him.

* * *

Mushgaana had probed Allen's mind as soon as he shot his comrade, understood his intention and used all his mental power to stop him. He had a splitting headache, and a few drops of blood were trickling from his nose. When the human killed himself, Mushgaana's rage pierced him to the core. He was aware of the heavy casualties they had suffered, and now he had lost the only lead he had. He telepathically boomed, *"You incompetent losers!"*

All the Xortaag soldiers in the area dropped dead, blood pouring out of their nose and ears. A few moments later, the Deathbringers crashed to the ground too. The pilots' brains had melted in their skulls.

"Shit!" murmured Mushgaana. "Maada is going to kill me when he finds out."

CHAPTER ELEVEN

W hen I landed in Winterfell and got out of my cockpit, a big crowd consisting of the ground crew and everyone else around gave me a near-hysterical welcome. Word of our victory had spread, and after months of doom and gloom, people were ecstatic. Everyone was squealing, hollering or whooping. I was greeted with fist bumps and high fives from every direction.

Liz, still in her flight suit, threw herself in my arms and shouted, "We did it! We did it! It was so cool!"

It really was. Even Keiko afforded a faint smile. "Bravo Zulu," I told her.

She bowed politely. "Otsukaresama desu."

I made an exaggerated bow. "Oklahoma desu to you too."

Elizabeth hit my arm. "Aren't you even slightly curious to know what that means?"

"I know what that means," I said. "She's inviting us to sushi."

Keiko said, "Typical American cultural insensitivity,"

and told Liz, "I honestly don't know how you of all people put up with him."

"You know I'm American, right?" Liz said with a tightness in her eyes. "And me of all people? What's that supposed to mean?"

"You know, you're black, and he's obviously a racist," answered Keiko as if explaining a simple fact.

I threw my hands up in frustration. "For the last freaking time, I am not a racist!"

The three of us went to the operation room. Before entering, Keiko told me, "Can I have a word?"

Liz gave me a questioning look and left us.

Keiko stepped closer to me, looked up into my eyes and said, "You realize that the few seconds you wasted patting yourself in the back and quoting *Gladiator* nearly cost Elizabeth her life, right?"

My face burned up, but embarrassment quickly gave way to anger. "And where were you, Miss High-Horse?"

"Fighting two Deathbringers," she answered. "And I'm not the commander of the fleet, you are. If she was killed, it would've been your fault. I respectfully suggest you take your head out of your fucking movies and focus on your responsibilities the next time, *Sir*."

She turned and entered the Command Center, leaving me alone to fume for a few minutes. Then I followed her. I met Tarq and Barook, both beaming with almost childlike happiness. For the supposedly peace-loving people that they were, they'd enjoyed the carnage we'd inflicted on the Xortaags a bit too much. They updated me on everything that had been going on elsewhere.

Operation Free Earth was as comprehensive a victory as it gets. Everything had gone according to the plan Kurt had concocted with his typical German efficiency.

We'd managed to destroy the Xortaags' second biggest fleet base, the under-construction city next to it, and most of their smaller military bases and settlements in one coordinated strike, eliminating nearly forty percent of their space fighters in the process. The whole of Winterfell was dizzy with euphoria, and our success finally counteracted the despair engendered by the fall of Earth.

"Have we suffered any casualties?" I asked Tarq.

He brought up a screen on a nearby monitor and pointed at it. We'd lost nine pilots: A handful of Deathbringers that had survived the initial attack killed eight, and one was a blue-on-blue loss. A cold hand grabbed my heart and made it skip a few beats. I slumped down into the seat in front of the monitor, ran a shaking hand through my hair, and read the names. Five men and four women. I knew all of them, of course.

Liz held my hand. "I'm so sorry, Jim."

I spent the rest of the evening obsessing over our plans, wondering if I could've done something differently to avoid those deaths. I tortured myself by watching the images of each death—recorded by the other fighters and the Akakie stealth ship on orbit—a thousand times, and by replaying them in my mind a thousand more, wishing I could go back in time and change what had happened. Liz kept trying to convince me it was in no way my fault, and Kurt repeatedly mentioned losing people was a part of being a leader, but it was the first time I'd lost pilots under my command, and I took it hard. The hurt wouldn't go away, no matter how hard I tried. Regardless of what Liz and Kurt said, it was my responsibility, and I couldn't shake the feeling I'd let down those pilots.

Kurt called me the next morning. "Don't tell me you're still kicking yourself over the people we lost."

"Nope. All good here," I lied. "What's up?"

Kurt laughed. "You aren't a good liar, even over the PDD. Come to the Command Center. I have something here you should see."

I came face to face with a freaking Xortaag when I entered the Command Center.

The alien was the Conan-the-Barbarian model. He was huge, at least five inches taller than I with bulging muscles and very wide shoulders. He moved towards me with such speed I didn't have enough time to reach for the sidearm I carried after the attempted coup a few weeks ago. I didn't even have time to get scared.

He took my hand, shook it up and down, and with a huge smile that reminded me of a crocodile said, "My name is Zaart. It is an honor to meet you!"

I stood on my toes and tried to look over his shoulders. Kurt and Tarq were there, both laughing.

"Who the hell is this?" I asked.

"I am Zaart," the Xortaag helpfully answered,

"Let me guess," I told Kurt, "MICI?"

"Yep," said Kurt. "We've captured a few of these guys and threw them in MICI, and now they're nice and friendly, spilling their beans. Come on in. I'm sure you have many questions to ask our new friend."

Did I ever!

We held a wake for Allen the next evening. Despite his sour personality, a lot of people showed up. I even spotted a few of the pilots whose asses he'd kicked in what now seemed like another lifetime in the crowd. We didn't have a body, so we used an empty coffin with Allen's photo on top. Kurt showed up wearing his favorite black trench coat and not the Commando uniform. I think it was his way of emphasizing the two of them went way back and reminding everyone of their days in the Resistance.

Kurt said a few words. He told us how, after his father's assassination, Allen had taken him under his wing. Back then, Kurt was a young, idealistic politician dreaming of a peaceful and united Earth, and his whole world had been shattered all around him. Allen had thought him everything he knew about guerrilla warfare—Kurt's euphemism for terrorism—including how to use a sniper rifle or his favorite machine pistols. Mr. Hard-As-Nails, Devil-May-Care Super-Assassin was speaking like he had a frog in his throat, and I could swear I saw a tear or two in his eyes. At the end of his speech, he saluted the coffin and said, "Allen, thank you for everything. I owe you my life several times over. I am, and forever shall be, your friend."

"That was a nice touch," said Venom.

Hell, even I felt my throat tightening. Just a little bit.

After the wake, Lilly asked Kurt to let her join the Commandos. Kurt denied her request. "We have plenty of soldiers but few people with your skills."

"Plus, if he puts you in danger, Allen's ghost will follow him for the rest of his life," I added.

"Has anyone ever told you you're a bit much?" Lilly asked me.

"All the time," said Cordelia.

"It's a small consolation," Kurt told Lilly, "but I wanted to let you know I plan to bring your father's body back here for a proper burial. When we started the Resistance, we made a pact that if one of us fell the other one wouldn't leave him in enemy hands."

Kurt and I got a few bottles of Allen's favorite beer (Molson Canadian, what else?) and spent the night drinking and talking about old memories. The fact that Kurt agreed to drink Canadian beer instead of his own usual Paulaner told me how distraught he was. We mostly reminisced about happier times, when Kurt's father was the President of United Earth and Allen was his head of security.

Kurt showed me an antique six-shooter. "Allen gave it to me for my last birthday. It was a present from my dad. He said I should have it."

"Do you remember the time Allen tackled a man just because the poor fellow had 'looked funny' at the president?" I asked.

"You know, I never, ever heard him say 'sorry' in the famously cute Canadian way," said Kurt. "Or apologize for anything, for that matter."

Yeah, including that time the two of you sent half a squadron of my people to the hospital.

"Did you know he collected stamps?" Kurt asked me.

Surprised, I said, "Seriously? Who collects stamps in this day and age? I honestly don't remember having seen one in my life."

We both had a little laugh when we remembered how furious Allen was when Tarq made him quit smoking.

Kurt raised his bottle and said, "To Allen. You'll be missed."

WE STARTED phase two of Operation Free Earth as soon as phase one finished. Kurt, Tarq and I began going over the plans, and the Commandos commenced their deployment.

For three happy days, most people in Winterfell were in a celebratory mood, and with good reason. Whoever said "While seeking revenge, dig two graves, one for yourself" was dead wrong. Personally, I was with Shakespeare on this one. Even Liz confessed the biblical "Love your enemies" motto didn't apply to an alien invasion.

In our first meeting after phase one of the operation, Tarq started by saying, "I am afraid I have bad news."

He didn't try to soften the blow or anything. Stupid alien.

"Faced with their obvious inexperience in ground battles, Maada has decided to use Earth's military and security forces for protection," continued Tarq. "The Xortaags have placed thousands of human soldiers around SH-1, supported by armored vehicles, helicopters, and fighter jets. Our trick of using their uniforms will not work anymore either. They are issuing identity cards for all Xortaags and setting up voice and fingerprint scanners everywhere. Even the fleet base is now crawling with human security forces."

His words were like a bucket of ice cubes spilled over my head. With Tarq's announcement, all our plans and preparations for phase two went right out the window. I even thought I could hear Maada laughing at us through the same window.

At that point, despite the heavy losses the Xortaags had suffered, they still had more than twenty thousand space fighters to our ten. Kurt—and Matias, who had come up with the idea—had planned a World-War-II-style blitzkrieg: They wanted to use heavy tank battalions to attack SH-1 and hit the enemy fleet on the ground, hoping to destroy enough Deathbringers that my pilots could deal with the rest. The Xortaags didn't have any anti-armor weapons, so this could work, but not with human soldiers defending SF-1 now.

"Why couldn't Maada just die during our attack?" I said, rubbing my forehead.

"If it is any consolation, he appears to be rather seriously injured, so you guys got very close," answered Barook.

Tarq continued, "The Xortaags also have used OMC-BOWS to ask people if anyone has any information about us or has witnessed anything suspicious, which is how they heard about the prisonbreak and the few times you defeated Zheng's people using Vipers."

"I guess we got lucky they didn't find out about this before Operation Free Earth," I said.

"There was no real chance of that because there was basically no contact between the quote, unquote gods and the humans, other than using them as construction workers," answered Tarq. "But with all humanity on the lookout for us, our jobs are going to get harder from this point on."

"So what're we going to do now?" asked Liz.

Her question was directed at Tarq, but Kurt answered it. "We still have three months before the Xortaag colonists arrive. For now, we're going to keep observing the enemy and collecting information. Hopefully, we'll come up with a plan in time."

"And if not?" I asked, ever the optimist.

"We'll have two options," answered Kurt. "We could attack SH-1 with all our forces, or we could stay here and keep trying to hurt the Xortaags even after the colonists arrive. Both will probably end in our defeat."

This was a sobering thought. We couldn't possibly defeat the Xortaags in a full-frontal attack, and we had always known we'd be done when the colonists got here. We were screwed either way.

"There is a third option," said Tarq. "We could leave. Instead of dying pointlessly here, we could go to Kanoor and join our forces. Together we might have a chance. The

Fireflies are capable of carrying all our fifty thousand people."

I stared at him, astonished. Liz said, "And leave ten *billion* people to die?"

"Nine billion three hundred million," I corrected her. She hit me in the arm.

Tarq pointed out, "We are not helping them by sacrificing ourselves."

"Dude, have you learned nothing yet?" I asked. "Do you remember the choppers attacking the Xortaag fleet?"

Tarq shrugged and didn't push it.

I walked out of the Command Center with Kurt. "You remember the conversation we had about respect?" I asked him. "I'm finally getting some around here."

"Getting some! Ha ha!" said Cordelia.

"Didn't you recently get married?" Kurt asked.

I tried to mimic his signature pained look that he had whenever I made a stupid joke.

He patted my back. "Yeah. I've noticed."

I blinked. "What do you mean? Is it that obvious?"

"Yes. People under your command salute more firmly when they see you, and they seem to pay more attention when you talk. Things like that."

"You *are* the greatest detective in the world!" I exclaimed. "More importantly, they follow my orders without hesitation now, even Liz."

"You did save her life."

"I did, didn't I?" I said humbly. "I just hope she doesn't relapse into her old ways any time soon."

* * *

San Diego - July 24, 2078

. . .

ARMINAA OPENED her eyes and with a groan tried to sit up. She was in a hospital bed in a typical Xortaag military hospital room: small, purely functional, everything sparkling clean. There were a few pieces of medical equipment placed next to her bed.

She saw General Maada, all banged up, with bandages all over his head and face, and his right hand in a plaster cast, dozing off on a chair next to her bed.

Surprised, she unconsciously started to stand at attention, only to be overcome with blinding pain. She sunk back to bed with a moan.

Maada opened his eyes. Unlike Arminaa, he was not wearing a hospital gown but his uniform. He stood up and asked, "How are you feeling?"

Still in pain but trying hard not to appear weak in front of the general, Arminaa answered, "Like I have got first-degree burns on ninety percent of my body."

"Unfortunately, that's an accurate description of your current status," said Maada sadly. "Not to worry. You will be back to active duty in no time."

"What happened?" asked Arminaa. "I remember we started shooting at the enemy craft, and nothing after that. And who was the enemy?"

"We were attacked by the humans. We do not know why the Voice of God had no effect on them or how they got such advanced space fighters, but we will soon find out. Of the soldiers on the control tower, only you and I survived, but we managed to shoot down, eh, a few of the attacking vessels. On that note, I have recommended you for a Crimson Deathbringer Medal, for showing extreme valor in the face of certain death. All the others with us

263

SEAN ROBINS

will receive the same medal, unfortunately posthumously."

Despite her pain, Arminaa beamed with pride. The Crimson Deathbringer, inspired by General Maada's legendary craft, was the highest and most prestigious medal in the Xortaag fleet. "Thank you, General," she said.

"You have earned it," said Maada. "Now if you excuse me, I have work to do. I will send a doctor to check on you."

He was about to leave the room when Arminaa asked, "General, can I please ask you a question? Any news about my unit? Did they survive the attack?"

Maada stopped with a pained expression on his face, and for a second, he seemed lost for words. He walked to the bed, gently held the young woman's hand, and said, "Arminaa, you know your unit was stationed in the barracks closest to the hangars. They reacted fast and with courage, and tried to fly their Deathbringers off the ground, but by the time they were ready to launch, it was too late, and the enemy was right on top of them. They all died in the battle. I am really sorry."

Arminaa bit down a scream, but tears welled up in her eyes and then ran freely down her bandaged face. She was an orphan, and she had joined a military school at a very young age. Most members of her unit had graduated at the same time as she, and they had been together in the same unit ever since. They were the only family she had ever had. They had been in several campaigns together, just to die *on the ground*, on this fucking godforsaken planet.

She suspected the general knew all this, as he just stood there, holding her hands, saying nothing.

Hatred came on the heels of grief. Pure, burning hatred for humans. *All* humans, not only those who attacked them. They would all pay for taking her family away from her.

* * *

SH-1 - July 30, 2078

Mushgaana was sitting in his new office in the Xortaags' under-construction city, reading the depressing reports on the surprise attack against them. The scope of their failure was shocking. After decades of total dominance, they had lost a big part of their fleet on the ground, and to make things worse, they had no idea where the attackers had come from. All they knew for certain, based on examination of the bodies left at his former residence, as well as his personal observation, was that the attackers were human. But they still had a thousand unanswered questions.

The enemy space fighters had distinct similarities to the Akakie ships they had encountered in the past. This was not conclusive, but the only idea he could come up with was they were somehow involved. He wished he had attacked Kanoor as he had originally planned, but it was too late now. They could not leave this stupid planet until the fleet that had attacked them was destroyed.

After that, they were going straight to Kanoor.

His own ship, which had landed on a nearby base, had also been destroyed. He could have asked for another one, but there was no way he would let his father know he had managed to lose his command ship. He decided not to report the attack and have one of the transport vessels retrofitted to function as a command ship as soon as they arrived.

Lucky for them, they had already transferred the Voice of God's controls to their bigger city; otherwise, controlling nearly ten billion enraged humans would have been impossible. On the other hand, with his command ship destroyed, their only means of traveling in space was now the SDF in Kingdom of God. Fortunately, the device was well protected.

Maada walked into his office. He had a couple of new scars on his face, and his right arm was in a white plaster cast. Remarkably, he had walked out of this fiasco smelling like the proverbial rose. If anything, the story of him and a small group of Xortaags, carrying only sidearms, defying a thousand enemy ships and shooting down a few had added to his status as a living legend.

Maada went straight to the point as usual. "It has come to my attention that you have killed twenty of my pilots, whom I did not even know were here, I might add."

Mushgaana thought, *Shit!* and said, "It was an accident."

"How long have we been campaigning together, Your Highness?" asked Maada.

Mushgaana chuckled. "Since we were both very, very young."

"And in all this time, have you ever seen me make a promise and not keep it?"

Mushgaana did not like the way this conversation was going. "Nope."

Maada leaned over and looked in the crown prince's eyes. "So believe me when I say this. If you hurt another one of my pilots ever again, I will come for you. And do not think your powers can save you from me. I will come with a squadron of Deathbringers. I would like to see you try to stop us from incinerating you and everything in your ten-mile radius from orbit with your voodoo."

Mushgaana was used to Maada's fits of anger; still, the pure, unadulterated rage in the general's eyes made him flinch. He momentarily considered the idea of killing Maada on the spot, but he needed this man now more than ever; moreover, to his surprise, he was not offended. Maada was right. Mushgaana did feel guilty about slaughtering a few of his own men.

Mushgaana understood, better than the general did, that this was the main reason people under Maada's command loved him to death: Despite his legendary bad temper, he cared for them in ways no other commander would. The fact that he had led them to one glorious victory after another, bringing them all fame and fortune, was secondary. The prince did not look into the minds of ordinary people often; he was not that interested. But he kept tabs on his general's reputation, as he knew his brothers did. Maada's popularity was one of his assets.

"Do we understand each other?" asked Maada, rubbing the scars on his face.

The crown prince smiled, saluted mockingly and answered, "Perfectly, General."

Maada saluted, turned on his heel and left.

* * *

Winterfell - August 1, 2078

Elizabeth, lying on her bed in her and Jim's quarters, called Tarq. When the alien's face appeared on her PDD's screen, she said, "Hi, Tarq. I've got a question for you."

"Something intriguing, I hope," said Tarq. "I have had a boring day."

"Our second anniversary's coming up, and I want to do something special for Jim," she said. "I figured with Akakie technology, you can think of things that I can't even imagine."

Tarq beamed.

"Eh, Liz?" said Cordelia. "Tarq might not be the best person to ask for romantic advice."

He wasn't. His first three suggestions were atrocious. Elizabeth was about to hang up when Tarq said, "Okay. How about this: You slip a sleeping pill in Jim's drink. We take him to MICI and imprint a memory of the two of you having a huge fight and you leaving him in his mind. When he wakes up the next day and remembers this memory, you jump out of a hiding place and shout 'happy anniversary!' "

"How do we make that memory?" asked Elizabeth.

"Piece of cake. You act out your part, and I will film it. I will feed it into MICI, and it will do the rest based on the script I will provide. On second thought, I have a better plan: We can give him a memory of you dying in his arms."

With a sparkle in her eyes, Elizabeth thanked him and disconnected the call.

The idea itself was distasteful, but the possibilities it offered were limitless. The anniversary was still a few weeks away, but she could barely contain her excitement. It wasn't every day that you could find an ideal present for the man you loved. She called Kurt and asked, "Got a minute? I need your help with something."

Kurt answered, "It just so happens I need your help with something too."

* * *

I WAS LOOKING at The Harem's gate through my sniper rifle scope when Sergei growled, "Humanity's gone down, but these assholes are still here."

Two guards were standing outside the gate. Several men were entering and exiting the building. An unfortunate result of things continuing mostly as before the Xortaag invasion was the Russian mafia was still active, and with them, The Harem.

"Not for long," I said.

We were accompanied by Oksana, Matias, and Kurt, filling in for Allen, who would've wanted to be here on account of his young daughter. This was Oksana's plan, but my friends had to wait until after Operation Free Earth to avoid the off-chance the Xortaags got wind of a rescue operation involving a spaceship.

The plan was simple: Kill the goons and most of the clients, round the girls up in a ship, give them a load of cash and let them go in LA, asking them to lay low. Oksana had floated the idea of bringing the girls back to Winterfell. This was immediately vetoed by Kurt, who said having some fifty traumatized women in Winterfell was out of the question.

Kurt had asked Liz to fly the ship, knowing full well she was always ready to dedicate her time and energy to a worthy cause. She'd told me about it, and there was no way I'd let them go without me. Despite growing up in New York, I was a Southern gentleman at heart, and protecting women was sort of our thing.

I had very little weapons training. I certainly didn't know how to use an M-28 SWS. Kurt used MICI to give me a crash course in urban combat at both the operational and tactical level, so here I was doing something I never thought I was capable of doing: killing a man with a sniper rifle.

A man! More like a rabid dog. Plus, all the bloodshed I'd witnessed recently had thickened my skin.

The two guards went down with bullets in their skulls

without knowing what hit them. We moved in total silence. There were at least ten more security guards inside, but they were just thugs, good for controlling the girls, making sure the clients behaved and discouraging the competition. They had the proverbial snowball's chance against us, armed with tactical weapons and wearing body armor.

A few minutes later, Oksana, her eyes sparkling with glee, shot the man whom she said was in charge of The Harem; then she told me, "The sweetest morsel to the mouth that ever was cooked in hell indeed!"

I frowned. "Is that from a movie?"

We kept moving, looking for more goons to shoot.

"You know, you should try reading literature some-times," said Oksana. "It's good for your brain."

"I read literature," I said. "I have you know just last night I finished a novel."

"Let me guess: Was it about spaceships, galactic wars, and sexy alien slaves?" Kurt asked.

"No," I said triumphantly. "It was about vampires and monsters, sort of Dracula meets Frankenstein, with sexy human slaves."

Kurt shot another man. "You're hopeless."

"This is what I get for helping out with a good cause," I said, pretending to be offended.

* * *

SH-1 - August 5, 2078

As soon as the doctors opened Maada's cast and told him he could use his right hand, he went to his office, sat behind his desk, and overwhelmed with grief, stared at the list of casualties on his PDD.

Such a long list.

More than twenty-five thousand men and women under his command had died in the enemy surprise attack. He had never lost so many of his people in a single battle. He had failed them all. By being so criminally unprepared, he had played a major role in their death, even more so than the enemy. He was determined to avenge them by finding and killing every single person responsible for their slaughter; still, he would carry this on his conscience until the day he died.

Writing so many letters to the families of the fallen soldiers would take a few days. *Let this be the beginning of your punishment*, he thought.

He was about to start writing when the door to his office opened, and Mushgaana came in. Maada rose to his feet, surprised. The prince had never come to his office before. If he needed something done, he would summon the general, or send him a telepathic message.

"I had asked the doctors to inform me when they open your cast," said Mushgaana. "I thought you could use some help writing all those condolence letters."

Maada bowed his head in respect, an inch or two more than usual. The only thing more honorable than receiving a handwritten letter from the commander of the fleet was receiving one from the crown prince himself. His office was as Spartan as it got, but he had three extra chairs for the occasional visitors. He grabbed a chair and placed it next to his. Mushgaana sat down, and the two of them, shoulder to shoulder, started writing.

* * *

WINTERFELL · AUGUST 10, 2078

ELIZABETH SAID, "POPCORN'S READY."

"Where the hell did you get popcorn from?" asked Oksana.

They were in Elizabeth and Jim's quarters. Elizabeth, who had just found out neither Oksana nor Keiko had watched the movie made about Jim's life, had invited them over to watch it together. She turned on the holographic TV and told the others, "I asked Barook to change the movie's format so we could watch it on this."

When the movie started, Keiko rolled her eyes. "*Superman in a Cockpit?* Could it be any lamer?"

"The lead actor doesn't look like Jim," said Oksana. "And he doesn't sound like Jim either. What kind of an accent is that?"

"Southern," Elizabeth answered. "Jim was born in Atlanta. He can switch between his Southern and New York accent at will, but he doesn't normally talk like a Southerner."

"So the reason behind this whole you-are-a-racist gag you guys were laughing about the other day is he was born in the South?" Oksana asked.

Elizabeth laughed. "Nope. That's one of Tarq's master-pieces. Apparently, when MICI reads your mind, it can also see what your pet peeves are. Once Tarq found out Jim is overly sensitive to being called a racist, he started teasing him non-stop, and the rest of us just went with it."

Oksana smiled. "You guys are evil." She asked Elizabeth, "What is your pet peeve? Being called fat? I've noticed you barely touch your food when you eat in the mess hall."

"And yours isn't? I've noticed you spend half of your time in the gym."

They drank wine, ate popcorn and watched the movie. Keiko complained incessantly throughout. She said the whole thing was unrealistic, there were many factual errors, and, "They made it look like I shot him down by accident. I managed it because I'm a better fighter pilot than he is."

"Make sure you never repeat this in front of him," said Elizabeth. "Because he'll kill you, and it'd be such a shame now that he's finally warmed up to you."

.

* * *

Rotterdam - August 13, 2078

Arminaa, leading a group of about twenty armed, stone-faced Xortaags, walked into a shopping mall. It was early evening, and the mall was full of people, mostly families with small children. Arminaa looked at a young couple and wondered why they were sucking each other's faces. These fucking humans were so strange.

The word that the gods were visiting spread. They were soon surrounded by a big crowd, men, women, and children, bowing down and praying hysterically. A few humans knelt down in front of the Xortaags and started chanting. An old woman tried to touch Arminaa. She flinched and pushed her back.

"Disgusting, filthy animals," Arminaa murmured.

"Disgusting, filthy _dead_ animals," one of her companions answered.

They made their way to the center of the mall, where

two soldiers put down a machine they were carrying and turned it on.

It was a portable force field generator. Arminaa had always thought it was a useless device. It used an enormous amount of energy and could operate for only around twenty minutes, covering a small area. But it did one thing perfectly: It could block the Voice of God.

Killing the animals that worshipped them would not be much fun. Killing them while they were scared shitless, on the other hand, was a different story.

The praying stopped. The humans stared at them with confusion and terror on their stupid faces, probably remembering everything that had happened before the Voice of God became active. Their joyful expressions turned into masks of horror.

Arminaa told the others, "Spare the children. We are not monsters." She pulled her sidearm and shot a young woman standing in front of her, looking at her with wild eyes.

All the Xortaags started shooting. In an instant, the deafening screams of humans filled the mall. They tried to run away. With the force field surrounding them, there was nowhere to go. A lot of them were trampled in the crowd. The Xortaags took their time, walked around and killed them one by one. A few of the Xortaags, not satisfied with the carnage, holstered their weapons, drew knives and started stabbing people. Red blood spattered everywhere, its stench mixed with the smell of burned flesh.

Arminaa shot a woman who was trying to shield her two little children and begging her to stop. For a fleeting moment, she was ashamed. The general, being the honorable warrior that he was, would not approve of this. However, the humans had it coming since their cowardly attack that killed off her entire unit. Remembering her dead comrades only fueled her desire for revenge. She kept on shooting people indiscriminately, left, right and center.

* * *

SH-1 - August 16, 2078

MUSHGAANA, sitting at his desk in his office, read the report he had just received about the unauthorized massacre of humans at a shopping mall.

This was a major breach of discipline, but it gave the crown prince an idea. *Why did I not think about this before?* he asked himself.

He contacted the team in charge of running the Voice of God, "Find me a human who knows how to broadcast a video message."

* * *

HUNGOVER AND WITH A STABBING HEADACHE, I woke up when both my PDD and Liz's started beeping at the same time. Liz had thrown a wild party last night, and we might've drunk just a tad too much. Next to me, my wife groaned, "Bloody hell! What time is it?"

I looked at my PDD. "Six-thirty. Tarq's asking us to come to the Command Center for an urgent meeting."

"Six-thirty AM or PM?" asked Liz.

Definitely too many drinks.

We showed up a bit late to the Command Center, with unkempt hair and bloodshed eyes. Tarq gave us a disapproving look but said nothing. Good decision, too. Liz might've skinned him alive given the mood she was in. Kurt, Keiko, and Barook were there too, but Sergei was nowhere to be seen. I figured he was still too drunk to get out of bed.

Kurt, who was also at the party but somehow had managed to show up well-groomed and well-dressed, reeking of expensive perfume, said, "So what's the emergency?"

Tarq turned on one of the virtual reality screens in the room. "This is being broadcast in a loop on all TV channels. The video is all over the Internet."

Mushgaana appeared on the screen, looking straight into the camera. He spoke in the Xortaag language. "This is a message for the humans who attacked us a few days ago. I have got two things to tell you. One, starting today, I will kill a thousand people for every Xortaag you kill. Let me show you how."

The screen showed an aerial view of a city. I recognized it as downtown Houston. Liz and I once went there to attend a friend's wedding and came back with lots of photos and good memories. It looked like it was early evening. Thousands of people and cars moved around the city.

My mouth went dry. Liz grabbed my arm so hard her nails cut into my skin.

Mushgaana's image appeared on the corner of the screen. "I do not know the name of this city, and I do not really care. What I do care about is the fact that we estimate this city has two and a half million residents. And now, lo and behold."

He touched the screen of a PDD he was holding in his hand, and everyone in Houston dropped dead at the same time. All the vehicles in the streets went off the road or ran into each other. A city bus ran straight into a tanker and exploded. A few passenger planes fell out of the sky and caused massive explosions. One hit a skyscraper, engulfing a huge section of the building in a raging fire.

Just like that, my hangover, as well as the euphoria I'd been feeling since Operation Free Earth, evaporated, substituted with a sense of dread that locked my teeth tight together.

Mushgaana looked at the camera again. "And second, we are coming for you. And when we find you, we will kill you; we will kill your wives; we will kill your parents and your parents' friends. We will burn down the houses you live in, and the stores you work in. Mark my words and mark them well. You are all dead. You just do not know it yet."

I half expected him to do a trademark Dr. Evil laugh when he was done. This guy had watched way too many movies.

Creativity is dead, I thought.

The screen went black.

We had a very long meeting after that. I didn't say much. I was numb, and not only because of last night's drinking and Mushgaana's stunt. There is only so much a human mind could take. I was just beginning to get over the Xortaags' last massacre. That said, I suspected that had slightly desensitized us since we kept functioning in a more or less normal way, with no one losing their head, rolling on the ground and trying to scratch their own eyes out after witnessing what'd just happened. Although Keiko, who was always the very picture of stoicism, looked like she did want to scratch her Akakie-made new eye out and throw it at Tarq's face.

As for the rest of us, I started wondering if Tarq had sedated us when we were sleeping again. I wouldn't put it beyond him to gas us in our quarters.

Liz looked ghostly pale, gripping the arm of her chair, but at least she didn't faint this time.

None of us had realized Mushgaana had his finger on the trigger of the ultimate doomsday machine. Even if we defeated their fleet, he could end humanity with their damned MFM, and nobody had a clue how to stop him.

I was feeling sick to my stomach, but that didn't prevent me from trying to make light of the situation. "Look at the bright side: If he does that, it'll be up to us to repopulate the planet, and we can shape humanity in any way we desire."

Nobody paid me any attention. Again.

Kurt suggested, "If he carries the MFM's controls with him all the time, maybe we can incapacitate him and stop him from activating the machine."

Tarq and Barook looked at him in surprise, and it took a few seconds for them to understand what he meant. "You mean that PDD?" said Tarq. "That definitely was not OMC-BOWS's control. It is a satellite system, and it must be controlled from a smaller, less high-tech version of this room. He probably used that PDD just to send a message to the people controlling the system. Plus, on the subject of killing Mushgaana, we have another bad piece of news."

I rolled my eyes. "It's pouring already?"

"I do not get that reference, but I often do not understand what Jim is talking about," said Tarq. "We have a Xortaag spy working for us now. She has just arrived at Kanoor and is being debriefed as we speak. According to her, the Xortaag royal family possesses very strong telepathic powers. Apparently, Mushgaana can read people's minds from a distance, which means we cannot even get close to him."

All color disappeared from Kurt's face. "This means we sent Allen and his team to their deaths."

"If it is any consolation, we also sent many of our own spies to death. Every agent I sent to Tangaar just disappeared, and we never knew why."

"How did this Xortaag spy survive then?" Kurt asked.

"She has her own telepathic abilities. No one can read her mind."

"Do we know where the MFM control center is?" I asked. "Maybe if we destroy it, Mushgaana can't use it to kill every single human being on Earth."

"It would work," answered Barook. "Based on bits and pieces of information we gathered through our bugs, we know it is somewhere inside SH-1, but we have no idea exactly where."

Tarq stopped biting his fingernails to add, "We must make finding it a priority, but to be honest, unless we get lucky and our bugs pick something up, I do not see how we can do it. Our spy ship has flown over SH-1 several times, but there is no indication of its location or even existence."

"What about our Xortaag prisoners?" asked Kurt.

"They would have already told us if they knew, trust me," replied Tarq.

So, to recap, as if it weren't bad enough that Mushgaana had just murdered *two-and-a-half-million people* right in front of our eyes, ensuring I'd have nightmares for weeks, we'd just realized he had the power to go biblical on humanity and kill them off at whim. Not a pleasant thought. Not a pleasant thought at all. I felt much better when I thought he was just a mini-Thanos. I wondered how things could get any worse.

* * *

I was surprised when I found out someone outside of Winterfell didn't like what'd happened in Houston. It was, funnily enough, General Maada.

A few days after the attack, Tarq sent a recording of a heated argument between Maada and Mushgaana about the issue. He sent a message along with the note, saying, "The first voice is Maada; the second is Mushgaana."

He didn't need to tell us; by now we knew both their voices. Just two days ago I'd listened to a recording of Maada marching into the crown prince's office and threatening to kill him if he hurt any more of his men. I was beginning to grudgingly respect that man. And it wasn't like we were going to forget Mushgaana's message to us anytime soon.

Liz and I listened to it together. Maada argued that the senseless killing of defenseless civilians had no strategic value and made them look weak. Mushgaana pointed out they had killed a lot more people already and all "these useless, brainless animals" would be dead in a few decades anyway.

The crown prince was all heart.

"Those are both strategic decisions," said Maada. "We cannot afford to allow several hundred million of a planet's inhabitants to roam freely, and when the colonization process is complete, we cannot have them competing with us for the planet's natural resources. This? This is different. There is no honor in this." Then he added, "With all due respect, Your Highness, sometimes I think you just enjoy killing people."

"And you do not?" scoffed Mushgaana.

I could feel Maada's anger. With a shivering voice, he said, "I am a fleet general, and I serve the kingdom. I kill people because it is necessary for the future of the kingdom and our people. But no, I do *not* take any personal pleasure in it."

A genocidal, world-conquering manic with a conscience. Now I'd seen everything.

TEN DAYS after the Hudson massacre, Tarq called us to another urgent meeting. We showed up at the Command Center with "now what!" written all over our collective faces.

Tarq said, "We have recorded a conversation between Mushgaana and Maada that you all need to listen to."

Using his PDD, he played the recording.

Mushgaana: *General, come in and sit down. Let me guess. Coffee?*

He said coffee in English. They probably didn't have a word for it.

Maada: *Yes, Your Highness. Thank you.*

"Maada drinks coffee?" I whispered.

Liz shushed me.

Mushgaana: *I have wonderful news. As you know, our R & D department has been trying to develop a planet buster for years.*

Maada: *And they have always failed.*

Something stirred in the back of my mind. There was something vaguely familiar about this conversation. A single word began to form in my brain, but Mushgaana's next sentence took my breath away and my attention with it.

Mushgaana: *Until now. They have developed a proto-type, and they have decided to use it on Earth.*

We all paled and looked at each other in horror. This

was completely unexpected, and it threw a big monkey wrench into our plans.

"You were wondering how things could get any worse?" asked Venom.

Maada: *But we have spent so much time and energy building Kingdom of God here.*

Mushgaana: *Which is of no use to us. We do not know where the first attack originated, and we are vulnerable to another one. This planet is of no use to us like this, but we do have the opportunity to destroy the enemy with no risk to our forces.*

Maada: *So what is the plan?*

Mushgaana: *A convoy is scheduled to arrive in exactly sixty-four Earth hours. They will bring us the planet buster. It does not work from space. We will deploy it right here; then we will evacuate this place and watch it burn from orbit.*

Maada: *If they are already so close to Earth, they must have left Tangaar even before we conquered Earth.*

Mushgaana: *Yes. My dear father had kept it a secret even from me. At first, he was planning for us to use the planet buster on our next target, but the recent events changed his mind.*

Maada: *Should I send my fighters to escort the convoy?*

Mushgaana: *There is no need. They have a thousand Deathbringers escorting them, and any actions from your side might attract the enemy's attention. We are keeping this under wraps. They will not know what hit them.*

Oh, the irony!

Maada: *And where are we going to go, once Earth is destroyed?*

Mushgaana: *I have decided to follow our original plan and attack Kanoor. I am certain they were behind the attack on City of God. How else could humans achieve such advanced technology?*

Tarq, biting his fingernails, stopped the recording. Liz was the first to speak. "We have to stop them."

I almost said "Dah!" but bit my tongue. Who said I couldn't be diplomatic?

"Obviously. But we need to come up with a plan," said Tarq.

"Aren't we forgetting something?" said Keiko. "What about Mushgaana's threat to kill a thousand people for every Xortaag we kill?"

"We do not have a choice here," answered Tarq. "I do not want to sound heartless, but even if he kills another couple of million humans, it is better than letting him destroy the whole planet and kill everyone."

I wanted to pull a Captain America and say, "We don't trade lives," but to be honest that argument was totally stupid.

Sorry, Cap.

CHAPTER TWELVE

I was flying in space.

As a sci-fi fan, I'd read many books and watched lots of movies about being in space. Hell, I had hundreds of hours of MICI-induced memories of flying a Viper in space. Still, nothing could have prepared me for the sense of overwhelming awe when I looked at Earth from six thousand miles away. One could argue we were still in Earth's exosphere and technically not in space, but I couldn't care less. The view took my breath away in a most sensational way. I was transfixed, wonder uplifting me until I was as light as air.

I listened intently, trying to hear if anyone screamed.

"It's peaceful up here," said Venom.

Liz said in my headset, "This is breathtaking."

I shared her sentiment.

When I looked at the blue planet glowing down there, the first thing I thought was "home." Getting involved in intergalactic politics, as in forming an alliance with an alien race to fight another one, had made me fully realize that despite all our considerable differences, conflicts and wars, we were all the same species.

Our plan was simple. We knew when the convoy was scheduled to arrive. Mushgaana had mentioned "exactly sixty-four hours." We assumed he meant local time, which meant August 31, 0500 EST. We were waiting for them at that time. Tarq and Barook would track the enemy ships as soon as they arrived, and they'd send us to welcome them using the SFD. There were three thousand of us against a thousand of them, so we'd destroy them and their planet buster and disappear before help could arrive.

As I said, simple.

Tarq said, "Heads up. The convoy has just arrived."

My heart started beating faster, just a little bit.

"In a few minutes, we will send you to the new coordinates. Stand by," Tarq added.

I knew it took a few minutes for Barook to make the necessary calculation and lock on us with SFD. "Okay, boys and girls, you heard the boss," I said. "Put your game face on. The fate of the planet depends on us. But while we stand together, no invader shall pass. Let them come with the armies of Hell; they will not pass! And when this day of battle is ended, we meet again in Heaven or on the field of victory!"

I had practiced my speech several times, and I was proud of it until Liz, much to my chagrin, dissolved into laughter and ruined it for me.

"We are sending you in three, two, one," said Tarq.

I half expected to fade little by little and appear again in another location, but I didn't feel a thing. One second, we were alone in space, and the next a thousand enemy ships appeared in my targeting scope. The position of Earth had changed a bit, but you had to look for it to notice.

The enemy saw us and tried to change course and speed away. It was a futile gesture. They had to protect the cargo ship, which was much slower than our fighters.

"I see dead people," I told Liz.

I was certain she was rolling her eyes in her cockpit.

Suddenly Keiko contacted me, her voice strained, "Jim, check BT-451."

Curious, I checked the coordinates she'd mentioned, and to my surprise found a single space fighter hovering there. I zoomed in and found myself staring at a crimson Deathbringer. *The* crimson Deathbringer.

Maada's space fighter.

With a jolt, I remembered what I was thinking about when listening to the conversation between Maada and Mushgaana, and why that conversation sounded familiar.

The word that had appeared and disappeared on the back of my mind was *exposition*.

Their conversation was like a poorly written dialogue in a movie, where both characters kept talking about information they should both already have known, for the benefit of the audience. Hell, Mushy even started his line with "As you know..."

My heart started trying to leap out of my chest. I yelled in my mike, "Tarq! Get us out of here!"

In an instant, we found ourselves surrounded by some *ten thousand* Deathbringers, materializing all around us.

* * *

Earth's Exosphere - August 31, 2078, 05.15 EST

.   .   .

MAADA LOOKED at the enemy fleet, surrounded by his own much bigger force, and confidently smirked. He had been waiting at that spot for the enemy fighter pilots to fall into his trap, and they had not disappointed him. Everything had gone according to plan.

Payback time.

Three days ago, he was working in his office when the crown prince's "voice" spoke in his head. "We need to talk."

He opened his mouth to answer, but Mushgaana said, "No, don't talk. Just think about what you want to say. I can hear you loud and clear."

Maada thought, *How can I help you, Your Highness?*

"I was thinking about the attack," said Mushgaana, "and it occurred to me the enemy knew a lot about us. The only way they could pull that off with such precision was if they had detailed information on our operations around the world."

The same thought had occurred to Maada, but he could not figure out how the enemy had obtained this information.

Mushgaana continued, "Then I remembered when I first moved into my residence, I felt an independent human mind, not under the influence of the Voice of God. Also, in a movie I watched a few weeks ago, humans used something called a 'bug' to secretly obtain information about their enemy."

"A what?" Maada said out loud and bit his tongue.

"A small listening device that transmits data to the enemy," said Mushgaana. "I put two and two together and figured this is probably how the humans knew so much about us. Needless to say, I had no idea how to look for these bugs, but we found a human security expert here, and he came to my office with something called a bug detector."

Maada sat up straight. *Did he find one?*

"No," answered Mushgaana. "He found many. They are everywhere. I bet there are some in your office right now. Tiny little things. I could never have imagined something like this if I had not seen it in that movie."

Maada struggled to keep his rising anger under control. *How the hell did the enemy manage to do this?*

"You remember they wore our uniforms, spoke our language and just waltzed into our bases, right?"

Come to think of it, I vaguely remember we developed a similar tech a long time ago, thought Maada.

"We did, but it is an obsolete technology, for before the Voice of God era," said Mushgaana. "I had completely forgotten about it."

We can use this to our advantage, thought Maada.

Maada's plan had worked to perfection. These Earthers were so predictable. He savored the moment for a second; then he opened a channel to the enemy fleet.

* * *

MY MIND HAD ALREADY GONE into overdrive, trying to find a way to escape this Charlie Foxtrot, when I heard Maada's voice in my headphones, speaking English. "I am General Maada, commander of the Royal Fleet. You must have realized you have been ambushed. If you surrender now, you have my personal assurance you will be treated well, but if you resist, we will kill all of you."

I gritted my teeth. The bastard knew we'd not surrender. This was only a mind game.

Tarq's voice sounded in my ear. "Jim, we need a few minutes to lock on the fleet and get everyone out. Try to stall."

Maada was still talking, which I realized was a good thing. If I could get him to talk more, we still had a chance to get out of this with our lives.

In the movies, the bad guys always paused on the verge of victory to gloat, explaining their super complicated plans, giving the heroes the chance to turn the tables on them. All I needed was to keep Maada talking a few more minutes. How difficult would that be? I sent a message to the fleet, "Everyone, stand by and wait for my orders," and then I contacted Maada. "General Maada, my name's Colonel Jim Harrison. What guarantee do I have that if we surrender you won't kill us all?"

With anger in his voice, Maada replied like a pompous jackass, "I am General Maada, Colonel. Everyone in the universe knows I keep my word."

You got under his skin, I thought. *Good. Keep him talking. This is already going much better than I imagined.*

*　＊　＊　＊*

EARTH'S EXOSPHERE - 05.17 EST

ELIZABETH LISTENED to the exchange between Jim and Maada and thought, *Is he really going to surrender?*

It wasn't possible. Jim wasn't a coward. The exact opposite. During the war, five Japanese fighters had surprised him and killed his wingman. Jim followed them over enemy territory and didn't stop until he shot down all five, even though he knew he didn't have enough fuel to get back to his carrier. He ended up parachuting over the Pacific into the shark infested waters. He was lucky that an American destroyer found him soon after.

On the other hand, if he thought he'd save *her* life by surrendering . . .

Elizabeth was going to contact Jim and ask what was going on when she noticed something: Maada's Death-bringer was hovering in space, right on the edge of her effective weapon range.

The general might've been the best fighter pilot in the universe, but his ship still had to obey the laws of physics. It'd take him a few precious seconds to get moving from an inert position. This was too good an opportunity to miss.

Of course, if she killed Maada right in front of his pilots, she'd paint a huge target sign on the back of her Viper. She was okay with it as long as it meant saving Jim and the others.

Her acrobatic pilot brain calculated the distance and angle of attack. She didn't even need to use her onboard computer for that. Her breathing quickened, and her cheeks flushed. She wrapped her fingers around the stick.

* * *

I OPENED my mouth to say something along the lines of "Oh my God! How did you pull this genius plan off?" hoping to get him to monologue when a Viper separated from the rest of us and with fire pouring from all three of her laser cannons went straight for Maada's fighter.

Even before my eyes registered the Viper's light blue color, Venom said, "I give you three guesses who that is."

My heart jumped into my mouth, which was still open.

Freaking relapses!

Liz very nearly got the general. Maada banked right and dove "down." Liz's laser bolts missed the crimson Death-bringer by mere inches.

Several of our pilots, in all likelihood guided more by instinct than conscious thought, followed her, and a swarm of enemy ships moved in to intercept.

My mouth went dry. I thought, *Oh crap!* and shouted in my mike, "Fight's on! *Fight's on!*"

All hell broke loose.

Dante didn't know shit!

* * *

WINTERFELL - 05.20 EST

IN THE COMMAND CENTER, Kurt was looking at the images transmitted by the Akakie stealth spy ship monitoring the battle. Jim and his fighter pilots had no chance of winning this one. Tarq was standing next to him, and with Kurt pulling his goatee and Tarq biting his nails, they made a funny couple.

"How on earth did they know about our attack?" asked Tarq.

"They must've found our bugs," said Kurt, and mentally kicked himself for falling for such an obvious trap.

"How did they know where to look for the bugs to begin with?" said Tarq. "This is impossible. The Xortaags do not have a frame of reference for this sort of thing."

"It's a moot point now," said Kurt. "Can we send the rest of our space fighters for help?"

Tarq pulled up another live feed, showing the rest of the Xortaag fleet getting off the ground. "It is too late. By the time we send more ships, the battle will be over. They would walk into the same death trap."

Kurt asked, "Don't we have eyes on them? How did the

other ten thousand ships manage to leave their base without us noticing?"

Tarq threw his hands up in despair. "I have no idea. It turns out Maada has a few tricks up his sleeve."

Kurt watched the dogfight for a few more minutes. The fatalities were rising quickly. Nearly a third of the Vipers were already destroyed. The pilots were fighting with determination and skill, but at this rate, the battle would be over very soon.

"Can't we pull them out using the SFD?" asked Kurt.

Tarq answered, "No. The ships are fighting too close to each other. If we transport our fleet, many enemy vessels will come with them, and the rest will follow."

Kurt thought about this for a second. "Can't we pull them out one by one?"

Barook, who was listening to this conversation, cursed under his breath and ran towards the SFD control panel.

"It will not be much help though," Tarq told Kurt. "We will need a few minutes to make the necessary calculations, and after that, it will take around ten minutes to lock on each individual ship. We will be able to save just a few."

"Can I help with calculations?" asked Cordelia.

"No!" Tarq and Barook shouted together.

Kurt approached Barook who was working feverishly at his station and said, "Start with the senior officers."

"On it," answered Barook through clenched teeth.

* * *

OUR FLEET MET THE XORTAAGS', and thirteen thousand space fighters started to maneuver, chase each other's tails and shoot at each other, creating the biggest furball in history.

Now that's what I call a target rich environment.

"Can you take things seriously for once in your life? We're all about to die!" said Venom. He sounded really pissed.

I destroyed four Deathbringers in less than ten minutes.

For me, shooting down enemy vessels had always been one of the greatest pleasures life had to offer. It brought me little joy now. Our situation was hopeless. The enemy outnumbered us three to one. Our ace fighters—Keiko, Liz, Josef, and maybe another twenty people—could hold their own against three Deathbringers, but the rest of our people had no such hope. We were losing ships faster than I could keep track of them. Despite trying to focus on the battle, every time we lost a Viper, it was like someone stabbed me in the heart with a blunt knife. Still, I refused to believe this was the end. Engaged in a savage dogfight with an annoyingly persistent Deathbringer, I searched for a way to unfuck this mess with half of my brain, and all of a sudden I realized Liz had had it right: I had to cut off the head of the snake.

Maada was a legend among his pilots. Who knew how they'd react if I killed him right in front of their eyes? Maybe they lost heart and ran away. It was a slim chance, but a chance nonetheless. I'd always been the straw-clutching type.

I fired my remaining two Sparrows at the enemy. While the pilot was busy avoiding the missiles, I drew a bead, pulled the trigger, and unleashed a turret of laser bolts. The Deathbringer blew up brightly under my fire. Then I scanned the battlefield, looking for Maada.

I found him entangled with two of my pilots, twisting and spinning up and down, right and left. He vaporized one of my people right in front of my eyes. I didn't know who the pilot was, but a painful tightness grabbed my throat anyway.

This guy's supposed to be the biggest, baddest dude on the block. I wish I could see his face when I blow him out of the sky.

I said, "Your soul is mine," and dove in, energy bolts flashing from my cannons.

Maada swerved wildly to his left, disappeared from my view for a second, and the next thing I knew, he was on my six.

I had no idea how he'd pulled this maneuver off. What he'd done was just not possible. It was as if he had somehow teleported his space fighter.

I froze, rooted to my seat.

All those years ago in another life, when I engaged Keiko's Mitsubishi F-110 during the war, I felt for once I was dealing with a better pilot than I, and I was paralyzed by a panic attack. It was just like that, only ten times worse.

Maada started shooting at me. Laser bolts passed dangerously close to my ship.

My heart was thumping so hard I could hear my heartbeats echo inside my skull. My hands were trembling, and my vision become so blurry I could barely see the controls of my space fighter. I tried to take a deep breath to calm myself and found it impossible. I was unable to move. I couldn't even start jinking.

Red energy beams were all over my cockpit. I was dead.

Or I would've been if Keiko's Viper hadn't shown up at that moment and attacked Maada. The two ships started twisting, turning and shooting at each other. My vessel kept going straight away.

I told myself, "Jim, turn around."

Nothing happened.

I shouted like a madman, "Snap out of it! Turn around! What the fuck!"

"No!" said Venom. "Run away if you want to live. You can't fight that guy. Did you see what he just did?"

Shut the fuck up!

I might've started slapping myself in the face when my view changed. I found myself alone in space.

I heard Tarq's voice in my helmet. "Jim, we have just pulled you out using the SFD. We are going to try to save as many as we can, starting with senior officers."

I was shocked by my very close brush with death and my subsequent unexpected rescue, so it took me a few seconds to figure this out: Starting with senior officers meant only one thing.

Feeling like the cockpit closing on me like a coffin, I yelled, "*Get Liz out!*"

"We cannot right now," answered Tarq after a few seconds. "We are in the middle of locking on Keiko's ship. It will take only a few more minutes. We will go after Elizabeth next."

I wanted to ask him to send me back, but it'd be of no use, and it would waste the time we needed to save other people. So I stayed there and waited in agony for the chips to fall. An image of Liz's Viper exploding under Maada's fire appeared in my mind. It was so terrifying even Venom didn't comment on it. I closed my eyes and tried to push the image away. I told myself everything would be fine. In a few minutes, Tarq would save Liz, and she'd be here with me, safe and sound, out of Maada's deadly reach.

I even believed that for a second.

* * *

EARTH'S EXOSPHERE · 05.41 EST

MAADA RECOGNIZED the dark green vessel he had encountered a few weeks ago during the surprise attack on their fleet base. He rubbed the most recent scar on his face and smiled. This pilot was going to rue the day he humiliated Maada by not killing him.

The enemy pilot was very skillful. Countering Maada's maneuvers and shooting incessantly, they even managed to score a few hits. The general could not remember the last time something like this had happened.

Finally, a worthy opponent.

The green fighter tried to maneuver to the rear of Maada's Deathbringer. He responded by rolling right and swinging in on the enemy's six, letting loose a stream of energy bolts. The enemy vessel dove to get out of his line of fire. Maada pitched his Deathbringer's nose down and gave chase, zeroing on his opponent's ship. Trying to get a lock, he muttered, "You are good. You are very, very good. But I am Maada."

A few seconds later, the general's fingers gently touched his firing control. Energy bolts flew towards the dark green vessel. The first few hit its left wing, and the rest went through the space it had occupied a fraction of a second ago.

Maada looked at the ship disappearing into thin air without a trace and immediately knew what had happened: Someone was pulling out the trapped enemy using an SFD.

The familiar anger rose in his soul. He nearly started shouting in rage and frustration.

How dare they deprive him of his prey!

His blood boiling, he looked around for a new target

and found the light blue fighter that had started the dogfight by trying to attack him.

This will do, thought Maada, narrowing his eyes.

He flew as fast as his Deathbringer could toward his new target.

EARTH'S EXOSPHERE - 05.50 EST

ELIZABETH WAS ENGAGED in a frenzied battle with three Deathbringers when all three broke off and flew away in different directions. Then she saw the infamous crimson space fighter approaching her.

Tarq's voice pressed urgently, "Elizabeth, Maada is moving towards you. We are pulling you out. Do not engage. I repeat, do not engage. Just stay away from him for a couple of minutes."

"Like hell I will," she answered, and trembling with excitement, moved forward to meet Maada's threat head-on. This was another chance to take on the devil himself. If she killed Maada right now, thousands, even millions of lives would be saved.

Jim will be so proud, she thought, and her eyes lit up.

* * *

KURT HELD his head between his hands. *Typical Liz!*

Tarq blanched visibly. He shouted at Barook, "Pull her out. Right now!"

"Working as fast as I can here," answered Barook, his jaw set.

Kurt put his hand on Tarq's arm. "Let him concentrate. You aren't helping. And stop biting your fingernails so hard."

Come on Liz, hang in there. Just for a minute.

He told Tarq, "We should've made killing Maada a priority during Operation Free Earth."

* * *

ELIZABETH TRIED a tactic she'd learned from Jim. She fired her Sparrows at Maada, and when he banked left to avoid the missiles, she lined up her shot and opened fire with laser cannons. Maada changed direction and avoided most of the laser bolts. He rolled up his vessel and emerged on top of Elizabeth's Viper.

Elizabeth, trying to escape Maada's grasp, went into a twisting dive. She saw energy bolts shot from the crimson Deathbringer ripping her Viper apart, getting steadily closer to her cockpit. Her gut twisted in horror as she realized she was staring death in the face.

* * *

KURT, pulling his goatee so hard he plucked a few facial hairs, was staring at Barook and mentally urging him to work faster when the Akakie shouted, "Got her!" and pulled his hand across the touchscreen.

Kurt let out the breath he was holding, told Tarq, "That was close," and turned to look at the screen showing the battle.

ELIZABETH's last thought right before a laser bolt hit her cockpit was *Jim, I'm so sorry*.

* * *

"WHAT HAPPENED? WHERE'S SHE?" I shouted hysterically into my mike.

No one answered.

Mind-numbing horror grabbed my soul and didn't let go.

I yelled even harder, "*Where is she?*"

"Jim, I'm sorry," answered Kurt. "We couldn't save her. Maada got her."

My whole body started trembling. I clutched at my chest, choking on my own breath, my world collapsing all around me, until nothing was left but pain. Enough pain to break me a thousand times over. Those three words ended me. I was gone, and there was no coming back. My soul had imploded; only an empty shell was left, covered inside with a sheet of ice.

CHAPTER THIRTEEN

A s soon as I landed, I went straight to the mess hall, indiscriminately grabbed as many bottles of alcohol I could carry, and went to our—*my!*—quarters. Once there, the first thing I did was take off my wedding ring and throw it at the wall. Then I started drinking.

"Jim, I can't begin to tell you how sorry I am Liz is gone," said Cordelia. "But I don't think killing yourself with alcohol would change that."

"Yes, yes. I am such a cliché," I murmured. "Well, screw you."

Kurt walked in, saw my ring, picked it up, and put it on the bedside table. He sat next to me, saying nothing. I stared ahead and drank, rocking slightly back and forth, trying hard to keep the tears from overflowing. Kurt moved to touch my shoulder, but I pushed his hand away. Kurt sat with me for a few hours. We barely talked. Then he stood up, picked up my gun, went to the washroom, and came back holding a pair of scissors. He looked around, obviously looking for sharp objects I could kill myself with. I turned my head slightly to the left, showed him my carotid artery, and said, "I can do it with a broken bottle, you know."

He flinched. The agony in his eyes made me regret what I'd said for a second, but I immediately thought, *Boo-fucking-hoo. Cry me a river. I'm the one who's lost my wife, not him.*

"No, you can't," said Cordelia. "I'll zap you if I see you are about to hurt yourself. You won't die, but it'd hurt like a bitch."

"Zap me?" I snorted. "Who the fuck do you think you are, Zeus?"

"Funny you should ask," she said.

A lightning bolt hit the sofa next to the one I was sitting on. The sofa fell over and caught fire. A single sprinkler in the ceiling became active and put the fire out.

Kurt stared at the sofa, his mouth gaping. I didn't react at all. Kurt asked Cordelia, "How the hell did you do that?"

She sighed. "I'll tell you, but don't tell Tarq. He'll freak out, and maybe this time he has a heart attack for real. I'm in all Winterfell systems. I can do things you can't even dream of."

They were wasting their time. I had no intention of killing myself. I wanted to feel the pain.

"It's your fault," said Venom. "If you hadn't frozen and had gone back to help Keiko, the two of you might've defeated Maada, and Liz would be alive now. You killed her as much as Maada did. Because you're a coward. A freak and a coward."

I tried to argue this wasn't true. I was pulled out mere seconds after Keiko attacked Maada; there wouldn't have been enough time for me to turn back even if I'd wanted to. But it was pointless. Logic had no power over guilt.

The thought of never seeing Liz again gave me such a

heavy, leaden feeling in my chest that the mere act of breathing was difficult. I'd make myself breathe or move—just turn my head—and the action of that would flip a switch and she'd be there in my mind, showing off her flight suit, prancing like a happy child, sipping coffee in the mess hall, complaining about lack of sleep, or wearing that little grin that meant she was about to kiss me. The smell of her hair. How could she be so vivid, *so right here*, and be nowhere?

My mind went around in circles. I'd tell myself to stop thinking about her; it was too painful, and then I'd feel like I was suffocating, held underwater, unable to swim to the surface. All I wanted to do was to sit and drink until I died. And why not? My life had ended the moment I heard Liz was dead.

Kurt came to sit with me every day. At some point, he stopped trying to encourage me to shave or take a shower. Matias, Samantha, and Theresa showed up, but I refused to even open my door, even though I could hear them saying we were family and had to stay together at times like this. Josef didn't get a better reception either. One evening, Tarq accompanied Kurt, and with scientific detachment explained how MICI could erase my pain. I kicked him out. Liz's death was partly his fault anyway. If he hadn't demoted her, she'd have been pulled out ahead of Keiko, who didn't come to visit me even once. Bitch!

Liz coming out of the shower, beads of water on her hand-sized breasts. Liz the night before it all started, shivering against my arm outside the club, curls blowing in my face. Liz on our honeymoon wondering what life would be like after we won the war and humanity realized the universe was full of alien life. Liz!

Father Philip came with Kurt one night. He was

wearing his black robe, showing he was there in an official capacity as a priest, not just a friend. He sat in front of me next to Kurt and told me how sorry he was for my loss and how much everyone was missing my wife. "I know you don't really believe in God, my son, but it's exactly in times such as this you must ask Him for help. I am certain He would listen."

What he said reminded me of Tarq's prank—Liz and I in "heaven," surprise and happiness on her face. *I thought I'd never see you again.*

I rubbed my temples for a few seconds, trying to control my rising anger, and then smirked and said, "Father, you think I don't believe in God?"

Kurt murmured under his breath, "Oh-oh!"

I went on a rant. Words poured out of my mouth faster than I could consciously think them. "I'm a selfish man, Father. I spent most of my life caring about myself and nobody else. My only focus in life was having fun and enjoying myself, plus status and wealth. I didn't join the air force to answer some selfless higher calling to serve my country; I just wanted to fly and blow shit up. When my best friend here asked me to join an honorable cause, I turned him down, and I even don't really care about saving humanity from an alien invasion."

I paused to take a breath. "And despite all these, I met the kindest, warmest, most amazing woman who ever walked on this planet, and she loved me, and you know what? I loved her back. Until *your* God took her away from me. No, Father. I absolutely believe in God, and I absolutely hate the—"

Kurt jumped out of his seat. "Okay, time for Father Philip to go." He pushed the priest, who looked like he was about to have a cardiac arrest, out of the door, probably saving me from eternal damnation.

Sometimes, from a dark corner of my tortured mind, a voice would whisper, blaming Liz for getting herself and almost three thousand other people killed. I'd had a good chance of stalling. All we needed was a few short minutes, and all this could've been avoided. If she'd controlled her impulses for once in her life . . . Of course, Maada knew very well how SFD worked. He might not have fallen for my trick, but we'd never know for sure. Maybe given that their technology was inferior to the Akakies, it took longer for their SFD to track and lock onto a target. That might've made him think he had time to gloat, letting us escape from right under his nose.

But I knew what made her attack Maada. She wasn't aware of Barook's attempts to pull us out, and she'd come to the same conclusion I came to a bit later: The only chance we had to escape that trap was killing Maada himself. Liz, being Liz, had acted upon that conclusion as soon as she'd reached it.

I also had to deal with the agony of losing the three thousand pilots under my command. I should've figured out there was a trap. A superweapon capable of destroying an entire planet? Mushgaana and Maada had taken that straight from *Star Wars*. I'd been such a fool, and thousands of other people had paid the price. A better, smarter commander wouldn't have led his people into such a clear trap.

I didn't even go to Liz's memorial service. It was too much to bear.

We should really have stayed on that Island.

"By the way, just in case you didn't get it, no more jokes,

banters, or funny comebacks," I told Cordelia. "My life would be a strictly DC universe from this point on."

* * *

Winterfell - September 7, 2078

Feeling exhausted, Kurt sat behind the piano in his quarters. It'd been a rough few weeks. First Allen was killed. Then the pilots were massacred. And now, with Elizabeth's death, Jim was a broken man, on the verge of either insanity or suicide. Kurt had been watching his best friend dying little by little for days now. That had taken a toll. Kurt wondered how much more of this he could take.

He had never thought anything would affect Jim this badly, even losing Elizabeth. His OCD aside, that man had a natural capacity to take things lightly, even things that were dead serious. Kurt remembered how composed Jim was at his father's funeral. He didn't cry once, and he was only seventeen. Granted, he wasn't close to his parents, but everyone wept on such occasions. Kurt himself had locked himself in a room and cried his heart out for two straight days when his father and mother were killed. Come to think of it, he'd never seen Jim shed a tear in all the years they'd been close friends. Mr. Macho Man probably considered it unmanly.

Well, he isn't crying now either, is he?

The morale in Winterfell couldn't get any lower. Right after the euphoria of their victory, Maada had sucker-punched them hard. A lot of people had just realized how desperate their situation was. Maada's fleet outnumbered Winterfell's by a large margin, and using MFM, the

Xortaags could bring all Earth's ex-military forces against them too, as evidenced by the two hundred thousand human soldiers now guarding SH-1.

And with the Xortaag transportation ships bringing the first wave of colonists to Earth, they had only about six more weeks left to defeat the Xortaags. How they were going to do that in such a short time was anybody's guess. Kurt himself had no idea. Everything considered, it seemed certain they were going to lose, which would extinguish humanity's last hope.

Well, what else was new? It was just like the two years he was leading the Resistance with little hope of victory. The only difference was that Maada was infinitely more dangerous than Zheng could ever be. At least Zheng wasn't hell-bent on turning humanity into slaves and eventually killing them off.

He started playing Richard Wagner's *Die Meistersinger von Nurenberg*. Losing himself in playing classical music took his mind off of his problems and made him relax just a little bit.

Someone knocked on his door. It was strange that anyone would just show up here without contacting him first. He got up, opened the door, and found Keiko on the other side. Her face was as calm and stoic as ever, but her eyes were red.

"Can I come in?" she asked. "I have to show you something."

"Of course," said Kurt, and moved out of her way.

Inside the room, she gave him her PDD and played a video. "You probably know the Vipers are equipped with a camera that records everything happening during flight. This is from our attack on the Xortaag fleet base a few weeks ago."

Curious, Kurt took the PDD. The video showed an injured man shooting at Keiko's fighter with a sidearm. Keiko's Viper turned around and flew away.

Somehow, Kurt immediately guessed what was going on. The blood in his veins turned to ice.

Keiko reached over, paused and zoomed the image. Kurt found himself looking at Maada's face, leaning on the control tower's railing, completely at Keiko's mercy.

The two of them stared at each other for a long moment.

Keiko burst into tears. "It's all my fault. I could've saved them all, but I didn't. I got everyone killed!"

She threw herself into Kurt's arms. He reflexively put his arms around her, still trying to digest both what he'd just seen and the fact that Keiko, of all people, was crying uncontrollably. She hung on to him as if her life depended on it, her eyes flooding with tears. They stood like that for a couple of minutes, with Kurt trying to find something to say and failing. He felt an urge to comfort her somehow but didn't know what to do.

All of a sudden, Keiko raised her face, her lips searching for Kurt's and finding them.

The kiss caught Kurt by surprise. Suddenly, he realized how lonely he'd been. After Janet had died in his arms in an SCTU ambush, which happened right after his parents were killed, he'd built a wall around his soul and hidden behind it. The only two people he truly cared for were Allen and Jim; one was dead, the other one slowly dying.

You should pull away. Right now. Pull the hell away!

Instead, for the first time in years, Kurt lost his self-control under waves of unfamiliar, intense emotions. He couldn't deal with his mental anguish alone anymore. He kissed Keiko back. Her body loosened. Kurt loved the way her small body melted into his. For a short time, the two of them forgot the misery surrounding them, lost in each other's arms.

* * *

WINTERFELL - SEPTEMBER 8, 2078

TARQ COVERED his eyes with his hands and put his head on his desk, holographic tears running down his cheek. He had bitten his fingertips so hard now there were tiny bloodstains all over his white clothes.

Victory seemed at hand just a few short weeks ago, with the first phase of Operation Free Earth a complete success. The Xortaags had never tasted such a terrible defeat in their entire history. It had happened with such ease Tarq was confident that with humans he had found the Xortaags' match. He was certain the second phase would end Maada and Mushgaana's reign for good.

And then Maada had ruined their plans for the second phase by using humans to defend SH-1 and destroyed a third of their fleet along with their most experienced pilots.

With twenty million Xortaags and ten thousand more Deathbringers so close to Earth, Tarq knew he had lost. Everything he had done in the past few months was for nothing. All those humans who perished had died for no good reason. Worst of all, Mushgaana had decided to go straight to Kanoor as soon as Earth was dealt with, which spelled the end for his species. Tarq had sentenced not one, but two species to extinction.

His despair kept building until he felt he was about to explode. His hearts started beating faster. He pressed his lips together and swallowed down his frustration. If Maada had been there right now, Tarq would have happily chewed on his neck until his head was separated from his body.

I have doomed us all, my own people and the humans. The greatest strategist the universe has ever known, my feet! And all four of them!

His hands were moving towards his antennae when the door to his office opened and Barook rushed in, out of breath. Tarq looked at his burning red cheeks, so human-looking, and not for the first time marveled at his species' technological and scientific advances. Barook was so excited he nearly tripped over his own feet. He waved a plastic bag in the air and yelled, "Commander, you have got to see this!"

Tarq saw a USB drive inside the plastic bag.

"Why are you carrying a USB drive inside a plastic bag?" asked Tarq.

When he found out, he wished he had not asked.

SH-1 - September 9, 2078

Sipping his coffee, Maada was sitting in Mushgaana's office, reading the reports on the ongoing search to find the enemy fleet's base. Using the Voice of God, they had made humans search their own planet looking for the enemy, but they had found nothing yet.

Mushgaana was pacing around his office in deep thought. Maada asked him, "If you wanted to build a fleet base on Earth to fight us, where would you build it?"

Mushgaana shrugged. "In a cold place, to minimize the chance of us finding the base by accident."

"My thought exactly."

"I must point out this is simply a conjecture," said Mushgaana. "They could be under the sea or inside a mountain. They could even be on an invisible carrier ship, for all we know."

"There is no way to hide a ship big enough to carry several thousand space fighters and soldiers, even for the Akakies," said Maada, "and if they could do it, they would come at us with all their fleet and hit both our fleet bases at the same time. No, I am certain they have a base somewhere on Earth, and we have already seen the maximum strength of their fleet. At this point, a conjecture is better than nothing, and it is not like we have to spend any time or energy doing it ourselves."

He brought up a holographic image of Earth. "There are plenty of cold places to search. North Pole, Antarctica, Siberia, and look at this."

"What?"

The general pointed at the globe. "There is a frozen wasteland called Canada right next to City of God."

"That is just a coincidence," said Mushgaana. "There is no way for the humans to know we were planning to build a fleet base there."

"There is no way for them to do any of the things they have done, but when did that ever stop them?"

"Good point," said Mushgaana. "Have the humans go over this place, as well as the other cold places on Earth, with a fine-tooth comb, as they put it."

"Why would the humans use a comb to search through ice and snow?" asked Maada.

Mushgaana looked at him sideways. "Did you just crack a joke?"

"Maybe," said Maada, his face impassive.

"You did!" exclaimed Maada. "I am beginning to rub off on you, after all, my old friend."

Maada looked at the place called Canada on the map, scratched his beard and thought, *I have a good feeling about this.*

* * *

WINTERFELL - SEPTEMBER 9, 2078

KURT WALKED into Winterfell's cemetery. It was quiet and peaceful, covered with grass and trees. There were several rows of brand new white marble gravestones, with bouquets of fresh flowers in front of most of them. Kurt knew some pilots and Commandos were making unauthorized trips out of Winterfell just to bring in flowers. He didn't mind.

How he hated this place.

Most of the graves there were empty. They belonged to the pilots killed in Maada's ambush. Allen's grave wasn't. The Xortaags had buried him and the other members of his team in a mass grave next to Mushgaana's previous residence. A few days ago, Kurt and a group of Commandos had exhumed the graves and brought the bodies back home, to be buried properly here. Promises made, promises kept.

There were a few fresh flowers on Allen's grave too. Lilly had probably brought them. Or maybe Sergei. Kurt put two Molson Canadian bottles on the grave and said out loud, "It's good to have you back home, old friend."

He stood there, lost in his thoughts.

A few minutes later, Tarq joined him. "We need to talk, and for what I am about to tell you, this place is quite fitting."

"What's going on?" asked Kurt.

"There is no easy way to put this, so I am just going to go ahead and say it," Tarq said. "When our people were preparing Allen for burial, they found a USB drive in his rectum."

Kurt opened his mouth to ask a question, thought about it for a second, and asked another question instead, "Do I even want to know?"

Tarq, for once, managed to keep a straight face. "I am positive you do not."

"Too late," said Kurt, tugging his goatee. "That image is now burned in my mind forever."

Tarq took his PDD out of his pocket and gave it to Kurt. "This is what we found on the USB drive."

Kurt looked at the screen for a minute. "Is this what I think it is?"

"It is a holographic map of SH-1," said Tarq. "We guess Allen had found this in Mushgaana's mansion and took photos using his PDD, and he hid it in his you-know-what knowing you would recover his body. It shows the fleet base, the laser turrets, the barracks, you know, most of the things we already knew based on the information our spy ship had sent to us, but most importantly, it also shows this," and he zoomed a section of the map.

"What am I looking at?" Kurt asked.

"It's a small, invisible and undetectable force field. Similar to the one we use here, but much, much smaller. It basically protects a single building."

Kurt immediately got where he was going with this. "You think the MFM's controls are here?"

Tarq, with exaggerated patience, like he was talking to an insolent child, said, "No. we think *OMC-BOWS*'s controls are here, and that is not all. We think the Xortaags' interplanetary communication center and their SFD are here too. Before the Xortaags found out about our bugs, we had noticed people in charge of these three always talked like they all worked in the same place."

Kurt considered this information for a minute. "Are you telling me if we destroy whatever's under this force field, they can neither travel in space nor contact their home planet, and MFM will stop working?"

Tarq replied, "Better. I have come up with a way to hack into OMC-BOWS if its controls are destroyed. I am telling you if we pull this off, we can control it ourselves, and use it to send any messages we like to every single human in the world."

This was huge. It took Kurt a couple of minutes to wrap his mind around all the possibilities this piece of information presented. "How certain are you it's there?"

"Very," said Tarq. "Keeping a force field up takes a huge amount of energy, which is why they cannot be used in spaceships. There would be no reason for them to have one in SH-1 other than to protect their most vital instruments."

"But so far as I know, there're no weapons that can penetrate a force field," Kurt said. "Which is probably why the Xortaags have packed them together to begin with."

Tarq gave him a sideways look. "No, there are not. But I think you have forgotten whom you are talking to."

* * *

WINTERFELL - SEPTEMBER 17, 2078

•   •   •

His mind focused on the information Tarq had given him a few days ago, Kurt was playing with his food in the mess hall. He didn't feel hungry. He didn't notice Keiko approaching him until she sat at his table and said, "If I didn't know any better, I might think you're avoiding me."

Kurt put his fork down and looked at her. He'd been postponing this conversation. "Keiko, I'm sorry, but we can't do this," he said.

Keiko's normally stoic face became even more expressionless than usual. She gave Kurt an icy look with her blue and black eyes. "What do you mean by 'this'?"

"This. Us. You and me," said Kurt. "We can't be involved."

Keiko said nothing. She just tilted her head a bit and waited.

"Everyone I've ever loved has died since Zheng's coup d'état," continued Kurt, speaking fast. "Everyone whom I get close to dies. I pick up the mantle of defending humanity against the aliens, and seven hundred million people end up dead. With the life we're living, it could be our turn tomorrow. Look at Jim. Do you really want this to happen to you?"

Even mentioning Jim's name was painful.

"I disagree," said Keiko, after a short pause.

Kurt sank back to his seat, trying to find something to say.

"I used to fly kamikaze escort missions during the war," said Keiko. "Do you think we'd sit at home like fucking losers and whine we might die the next day? We were determined to enjoy every second of life. The fact that it's so short just makes it more precious."

She stood up and gave Kurt a contemptuous look. "But it's not like I'm going to beg you to be with me.

Enjoy the rest of your lonely, pathetic life." She walked away.

Kurt just sat there watching her go, feeling like a coward.

* * *

WINTERFELL - SEPTEMBER 18, 2078

TARQ, Kurt, Sergei, and Matias approached Jim's quarters. Kurt checked his through-the-wall device, said, "He's out," and used a key card to open the door.

"I am not so sure gassing your best friend is a good way to prove your friendship," said Tarq.

"Tomorrow would've been Jim and Liz's second anniversary. If we want to do this, it's now or never," said Kurt. "Let's just hope he'll not kill us when he wakes up."

When they entered the room, Tarq looked at the broken man with the long, unkempt hair and matted beard lying half-naked on the floor. "I don't think he is in good enough shape to take five steps in a straight line, let alone kill someone," he said, grimacing.

Matias and Sergei held Jim up and carried him out.

"Let's see if we can fix that," said Kurt.

* * *

I WAS SITTING on the captain's chair on the bridge of the Starship Enterprise.

Various crew members, wearing the old STO style uniforms, were busy working on computer consoles. There were three Klingon Birds of Prey on the display screen, and a bluish green planet behind them. Sulu and Chekov were sitting in front of me at the helm. Scotty, deep in conversation with a redshirt, sat at his station. The familiar red alert siren wailed incessantly.

This wasn't a dream. It was way too vivid and real. I could feel the weight of my body on the chair, the air I was breathing and the fine texture of my golden yellow shirt. And I wasn't surprised at all. I really did feel I was the captain of the Enterprise.

From behind my chair, Liz whispered in my ear, "Happy anniversary" with her sexy British accent. I turned my head a little bit, and her warm lips covered mine in a soft kiss. It was a short, delicate kiss, but it made the world fall away. I'd forgotten how good her lips felt pressed against my own.

I swiveled my seat and stared at her in amazement. She was wearing one of those red miniskirt uniforms, which with her long legs looked even shorter than normal, and she'd done her hair the same style as Uhura. I didn't move or say anything for a few seconds; I just sat there and stared at her. Flashing her radiant smile and playing with a curly lock, she was more beautiful than an ocean sunrise, more beautiful than the sky at night, more beautiful than...anything.

Kurt was standing behind her, looking like Mr. Spock, with a blue shirt, pointy ears, and sharply upturned eyebrows. He waved and repeated, "Happy anniversary."

No goatee, thank God. A mirror universe evil Kurt/Spock would've been scary.

"Eh, what exactly is going on in here?" I said, still feeling no surprise at all. I was on the Enterprise, my wife was alive, and Kurt was Spock. It was just an ordinary day.

"Do you see that planet on the screen?" replied Liz. "It's

XXM-150, and its population is being ravaged by a deadly plague. In two hours, all the planet's inhabitants will be dead. We have the cure, but those Klingon ships are hell-bent on stopping us. There's three of them and only one of us. So here's what you're going to do, Captain. You'll defeat the Klingons, save the planet, and"—she kissed my lips again before finishing her sentence—"you'll definitely get the girl."

"Lieutenant, this is completely inappropriate," said Kurt, raising an eyebrow. "Fraternization with a superior officer is strictly forbidden." Then he asked me, "What are your orders, Captain?"

I swiveled my chair around and looked at the screen, smiling. Liz, Kurt, and I fighting the Klingons to save a planet! Sunshine flooded my soul and warmed my heart.

"Ensign Sulu, Full speed ahead. Ensign Chekov, prepare Phaser arrays and Photon Torpedoes," I said, feeling a lightness in my chest I hadn't experienced in a long time. "Lieutenant, you come here and sit on my lap."

"Your wish is my command, Captain," said Liz. She sat on my lap and gave me another kiss.

"So unprofessional," said Kurt.

* * *

WHEN I OPENED MY EYES, I found myself in my bed. My room had been cleaned. Someone had taken out all the trash and empty bottles and changed my bed sheet and, eh, my clothes.

I looked at Liz's photo on my bed stand and savored the memory of the two of us on the Enterprise's bridge, fighting the Klingons. I'd immensely enjoyed every second of it. The corners of my mouth curled up in an unfamiliar movement, which soon turned into a full-blown smile. My first in several days.

That memory could've only been induced by MICI. I had no idea how it'd happened, and I didn't care. I was grateful I'd seen Liz one more time.

I stayed in bed and remembered Liz. The first time we met. The swimming competition. The trip to Cancun to celebrate our six-month anniversary, right after she moved in with me. Meeting her father for the first and last time, and how much he hated my guts, a feeling I happily reciprocated. That time she broke up with me because she thought I'd looked at another woman—I hadn't. My proposal. Our wedding, and the look on Tarq's face when his prank failed. The long walks on the beach during our honeymoon, hand in hand, only the two of us. Swimming in the ocean, with her on my shoulders like a kid. All the movies we watched together. The silly games we'd play. The hours we lay in bed in each other's arms, just talking. The scent of her hair after a shower. Flying Vipers together. The ten million times I got lost in her eyes. The laughs we shared. The life we built together.

Most of all, I thought about how passionately she'd made saving humanity her mission in life.

"And all you've done since she died is staying in bed and drinking, like the lazy loser you are," said Venom.

Why would I get out of bed? Liz was the center of my universe. With her gone, I had no reason to live.

" 'I have no reason to live,' " Venom mimicked me. "Mr. Masculinity. You spend your life pretending to be a man, but you turn to jelly the moment you lose the woman who was supporting you. And what about the people under your command? All those people who count on you? Should you leave them all to die, just because you lost your wife?"

I rubbed my forehead and sighed. He was right. Venom was very wise for a parasite.

"Parasite? *Parasite?*" said Venom.

Liz, who was so full of zeal and life, was gone. But the goal she believed in so much that she gave her life for was still not achieved. Her sisters were at risk. Her orphans were at risk. Would she forgive me for letting them die? Could I forgive myself? Liz might've been my favorite person in the universe, but I still had other people to protect. I had a feeling that though this didn't seem to matter now, one day it would.

I chuckled when I remembered she told me I reminded her of Peter Parker when we first met. Great power, great responsibility. Commander of the fleet and one of the best fighter pilots on the planet, not staying in the fucking bed. It was time to get back to work.

"Jim, get up. Get up. *Make it so*," I murmured.

"Wrong captain," said Venom.

I got up, showered and shaved, tried to make my long, curly hair look more respectable, and put on a uniform. I picked up my wedding ring from where Kurt had left it but hesitated to put it on. Somehow, wearing the ring when Liz wasn't with me anymore felt wrong. I pulled a necklace chain through the ring and hung it around my neck under my shirt. In a strange way, the touch of the cold metal on my skin near my heart comforted me.

"Welcome back, Boss," said Cordelia.

"No thanks to you," I said. "You haven't been much help."

"I'm an AI, not a fucking psychologist specializing in treating losers suffering from suicidal depression."

"One of these days—" I said.

Lightning struck the floor five inches from my feet. I did *not* squeal like a little girl.

I went to the Command Center.

Tarq, Kurt, and Keiko were there, huddling over a map and discussing something. They looked surprised to see me, but it didn't escape my attention that Kurt and Tarq exchanged a satisfied look.

I knew they had something to do with it!

Keiko stood straight, gave me a salute, and said, "It's good to see you, Colonel."

"What have I missed?" I asked, saluting back.

"Quite a lot, actually," said Kurt with a twinkle in his eyes.

* * *

MY TIMING WAS, in a way, perfect. There was an important meeting in the Operation Room that evening. Tarq and Barook were there, plus Keiko, Kurt, and Sergei—who was now his second-in-command—and all Commandos and pilots with the rank of lieutenant and above, which included Oksana, Joseph, and Matias.

Tarq made his grand entrance after everyone was seated, his pipe in his mouth. He wore a hip-length blue gray military uniform with cuffs coming to the mid-forearm and a five-button front. It was familiar, but I couldn't remember where I'd seen it before.

There was an embroidered eagle over the right breast pocket.

I did a facepalm. It was a Luftwaffe uniform. That idiot! No one else seemed to notice though. I decided to do him a favor and didn't mention his faux pas.

Tarq brought up a holographic image of the Xortaag

city. "We have prepared this based on the map of the city that Allen provided us, demonstrating unprecedented courage and initiative under fire, I must add," he said. "We have studied the map carefully, and we believe we have a risky but viable plan."

"Allen sent us the map of the city, allowing us to come up with a plan to defeat the bad guys?" I asked Kurt. "How very *Star Wars* of him! How exactly did he send this information?"

He looked uncomfortable and hushed me.

"Most of you have a pretty good idea what we are up against but allow me to reiterate," said Tarq. "The residential part of SH-1 is still under construction, but the fleet base and their defenses are fully operational, and there are around a million Xortaag living there. While they are not particularly efficient in land warfare, they are all armed and ready to battle. Moreover, the city is surrounded by two hundred thousand human soldiers under Xortaag command, who are armed to the teeth and are supported by jet fighters, helicopters, and light armored vehicles."

"So in order to reach the Xortaags, we have to go through our own people," I said.

Tarq continued, "Their fleet, landed in a huge multi-section fleet base inside the city, is very well protected by several dozen laser turrets. After what we pulled the last time, security around the turrets is extremely tight, and there is no way we could destroy them all. Our fleet cannot get anywhere near SH-1 as long as those turrets are active. Moreover, their fleet outnumbers ours three to one, and to make things more complicated, the first wave of their colonists, twenty million Xortaags accompanied by ten thousand Deathbringers, is about a month away from Earth. All Mushgaana and Maada need to do is to hold on for a month, and we are done for. To make things worse, the Xortaags have arranged for human search parties who are looking for our location. It is only a matter of time before one of them finds us."

"Let's not forget Mushgaana can kill every human on the planet whenever his nasty little heart desires," said Kurt.

"Well, if it was an easy problem, it wouldn't need heroes like us to fix it, right?" I said.

That brought a chuckle from the crowd. Tarq glared at me for a second. "In short, we are significantly outgunned and outnumbered. The only advantage we have is the element of surprise. Based on a similar situation in your history, I have decided to call this operation"—he paused for theatrical effect—"Operation Z."

I burst into laughter. The look on most of our people's faces was priceless. Even Keiko didn't look amused.

Tarq hurriedly said, "Just kidding! Seriously, I want to call it Operation Barbarossa."

"Not better," said Kurt.

I suggested Operation Royalty, which got me questioning looks from most people and knowing smiles from the rest. I wasn't in the mood to explain, so I said, "Google it."

Everyone admitted it was very fitting. Operation Royalty it was.

I finally got it out of Kurt how Allen sent us SH-1's map. I laughed so hard I nearly pulled a stomach muscle, despite Kurt's indignant stare. The image of Allen, who was always so menacing and intimidating, doing *that,* and right in the middle of a gunfight with the Xortaags, was just too much.

"Do you think he tried to swallow the USB drive first?" asked Venom.

I laughed harder. Allen was so lucky he was dead; otherwise, I'd have ragged on him mercilessly for the rest of his life.

"You'll probably still get the chance to do that if Operation Royalty doesn't go as planned," said Venom.

I didn't get a chance to answer him. The next thing I knew, I was sitting on my ass grabbing my painful nose, with Kurt walking away, his hands clenched into fists, his face red.

Half an hour after the meeting, Tarq sent me a message and asked to see me in his office. I went there and sat on a chair in front of his desk. He said, "I am sure you have a thousand questions about us, and I guess you might have noticed I used MICI to block your curiosity."

"Dah," I said.

"I am a shadow master," he said. "That's what you might call a master spy. Because of my profession, I have always been overly secretive. However, I have just realized something important."

I didn't say anything, just looked at him and waited.

"We are friends, and there should be no secret between friends. With this verbal command, I remove your block. The only taboo topics are our appearance and my daughter. Go ahead, ask all your questions."

His face was flushed, and his eyelids were twitching. It was obviously a difficult and emotional decision for him. Revealing the secrets he preferred to keep from an alien must've been traumatizing. I was impressed by the trust he was showing me. Friends, indeed.

"Great! Thank you so much for trusting me," I said. "First question: Are you and Barook a couple?"

* * *

WINTERFELL · SEPTEMBER 29, 2078

KURT APPROACHED KEIKO, who was sitting on the grass in a small park in a corner of Winterfell, meditating, and sat down next to her.

"What's up?" asked Keiko, still looking straight ahead.

Kurt told her about Elizabeth's anniversary present for Jim and added, "The fact that Elizabeth managed to save Jim literally from beyond the grave made me think about us."

"What do you mean 'us?' " asked Keiko, her face impossible to read.

"You know. About our relationship," answered Kurt, feeling uneasy.

"We don't have a relationship," replied Keiko coldly. "We had a one-night stand. That's it."

Kurt looked away, blood rushing to his cheeks. He hesitated for a second, and then started to get up and leave, but Keiko grabbed his arm. "I'm just messing with you. Of course, there's an 'us.' There's been one since the day I came to Winterfell for the first time, you blind idiot."

Breathing a sigh of relief, Kurt sat back down. Keiko continued, "Did the night we spent together seem like a one-night stand to you?"

"I honestly have no idea because I've never had one," answered Kurt.

Keiko sounded surprised. "Never ever?"

"I was with my high school sweetheart most of my adult life," answered Kurt, "and I've been single since she died."

"You'd been only with one woman all your life?" asked Keiko.

She sounded so astonished that Kurt couldn't help

asking, "Why're you so shocked? How many lovers have you had?"

"I was in a kamikaze unit," said Keiko. "We were the live-fast-and-die-young types, and it isn't as if we had to worry about an old man sitting on the clouds and keeping an eye on what we were doing with our sex organs. Plus, the air force is full of good-looking, fit young men and, eh, women."

"Way too much information, especially that last bit," said Kurt. "I wish I hadn't asked."

"If it makes you feel any better, I haven't been with another man since I came to Winterfell, only you," said Keiko. "Anyway, what did you want to talk about?"

Kurt wanted to ask if not being with "another man" meant she'd been with other woman but decided he didn't want to know. "I came to say you're right," he said, "and after Operation Royalty, I want to invite you to dinner one evening."

Keiko flashed a rare smile. "I'd like that." After a pause, she added, "Kurt, there's something I've wanted to tell you for a very long time."

Kurt leaned closer, thinking she was about to say something romantic. "What's that?"

Keiko pretended she was pulling a goatee she didn't have. " 'I pick the mantle of defending humanity against aliens, and seven hundred million people end up dead.' You are a real drama queen, aren't you?"

* * *

THE CRIMSON DEATHBRINGER appeared right on top of me, laser cannons blazing. My Viper exploded.

"Restart simulation," I said.

Maada's ship was on my six. My Viper exploded.

"Restart simulation," I growled through clenched teeth.

The enemy ship came down from below. I didn't even see it. My Viper exploded.

I closed my eyes and rubbed my temples, disgusted with myself. There had to be a way to make this happen.

Keiko had fed our recordings of Maada's ambush to our battle simulators and had them programmed for new dogfight scenarios. I'd devoted all my waking hours to practicing, but it was no use.

I called Keiko, "Any luck?"

"I got shot down fifty-eight times today," she said.

"Huh! I was shot down only fifty-two times. In your face!" I said triumphantly.

"I can't feel my arms anymore. Gonna call it a night."

"Yeah, me too," I said. "I must go meet an old friend."

* * *

I KNOCKED on Kurt's door, and when he opened it, I showed him the box of Paulaners I was carrying. "I've come bearing gifts," I said.

Kurt looked at me and said, "What happened to your hair?"

I ran my hand through my short hair, which I had cut military style. "I figured this is more professional. You know, it makes me more leader-like."

Kurt chuckled. "Good call if you're trying to change the movie star image you were complaining about. And what are these?" He lightly touched the black circles under my eyes.

"I'm not getting much sleep recently," I said. "Have been practicing non-stop."

We sank into his sofa, clanked our bottles and started chatting. With Operation Royalty less than forty-eight hours away, I couldn't help wondering if this would be the last time we'd drink together. A pang of loss startled me. I wanted to grab him and run for the hills—as if that would help—but I didn't show it. I figured we all were having these feelings.

He told me what was going on between Keiko and him. I approved. "Liz thought the two of you were made for each other." It didn't hurt as much to say her name now. It hurt, but in a way that was almost beautiful. She seemed close to me, not as a ghost, just a presence. A warmth.

Kurt sipped his beer. "You realize this is exactly what you and I did on the Christmas Eve when I came to hide in your place? We talked about my love life back then too. The only difference is . . ." he looked guilty and left his sentence unfinished.

"The only difference is Liz was alive," I said with a steady voice. "So was Allen. Yeah, I remember. I'll always remember." We were both quiet for a moment; then we moved on, letting the dead fade back into memory.

"Ready for the big day?" asked Kurt.

"Yep. I even have a kill list and a detailed step-by-step plan on how to do away with everyone in it. Look." I took out a piece of paper from my pocket and handed it to Kurt. There was only one name on the "list": Maada. Under his name, I'd written "Step One: find him; Step Two, kill his alien ass."

After my third beer, I asked him, "When we were teenagers, chasing girls, did you ever think we'd end up on the front lines of saving humanity?"

"First of all, we weren't chasing girls, you were. I was with Janet," he said. "Secondly, yes I did. I always thought my father and I would do something great. And thirdly, we are saving the *universe*. If we fail, who is going to stop the Xortaags?"

"The Akakies? Maybe Tarq can prank the Xortaags to death."

Kurt laughed. "Speaking of Janet, I'm going to tell you a secret I've never told you: When she and I started dating, she hated your guts."

I was horrified. Janet was the sweetest girl you could imagine, and she hated me? "How come?"

"Apparently, it had something to do with you sleeping with all her friends in high school and dumping them the next day."

I crossed my arms. "I was a teenager."

"By that criteria, you stayed a teenager until you met Liz."

"It's not my fault women kept throwing themselves at me."

Kurt laughed. "You'll never change, will you? You're planning to be annoyingly cocky until you die?"

"I'm not cocky," I said. "I'm confident, and with good reason. I'm sexy, and I know it."

Kurt laughed even harder.

We drank, teased each other, and remembered the good times, trying to forget what lay ahead.

CHAPTER FOURTEEN

S H-1 - October 5, 2078, 20.00 EST

UNDER THE COVER OF NIGHT, twenty black-clad frogmen silently swam out of the river passing through SH-1, hid behind a half-constructed building, and started taking off their diving suits.

Putting on his armor and combat helmet, Kurt saw a ring flashing on Oksana's left hand and asked, "What's this?"

Oksana, busy with her own armor, answered, "Matias proposed last night."

Sergei smiled widely. "Big boy came through."

"I guess congratulations are in order, but nobody bothered to tell me?" said Kurt.

Oksana squinted her eyes. "You've been burying yourself in the Command Center for a week now."

Kurt touched his earpiece. "We're here."

Tarq answered, "The coast is clear. You can proceed."

"Are the search parties getting closer to Winterfell?" asked Kurt.

"One is fifty kilometers away and is coming straight towards us. Please hurry up."

Kurt checked his assault rifle, gestured to his team to follow him, and walked into the street on his right. Behind him, Oksana told Sergei, "You go first. I don't want to watch him playing with his goatee all the time. It makes me nervous."

Kurt's team moved in total silence. This part of the city was still under construction. Human workers worked here in two ten-hour shifts, and it was empty during the remaining four hours. A few buildings here and there looked ready for residents to move in, but most were half-built. There were no human soldiers in the city; they were stationed either around the city or in the fleet base. There were a few small Xortaag security teams patrolling the city, but with Tarq's guidance—he could observe what was going on using the Akakie invisible spy ship—it was easy to avoid them. It was a cloudy and moonless night, which made things easier.

After half an hour, the Commandos entered an empty twenty-story building. The elevator was not installed. They used the stairs to make their way to the roof. There, they met another team that had been sent via a different route as backup, just in case Kurt's team ran into trouble on their way to the target.

"You're up," Kurt told Oksana.

Oksana opened the tactical backpack she was carrying and took out something that looked like a small, folded satellite dish. She unfolded it and put it on the roof ledge facing outward. Working with her PDD, she said, "It'll take a couple of minutes."

The device, another gadget out of Tarq's bag of magic, was called a force field penetrator. It could open a small hole in a force field. The catch was it had a maximum five-mile range, and it had to be at the line of sight with the target.

Which was exactly where Kurt's team was right now.

"I'm ready," whispered Oksana, wiping the sweat from her brow with the back of her gloved hand.

"Why're you whispering?" whispered Sergei.

Kurt, Sergei, and six other Commandos stood in one line, facing the target, and prepared their shoulder-fired missile launchers. Tarq had estimated two missiles would be enough to destroy the target, and four would be overkill. Inside the confines of the force field, the explosions would be devastating. Kurt had decided to leave nothing to chance and shoot eight missiles.

Here we go, thought Kurt, checking his watch.

For a second, Kurt pondered the enormity of that moment. Everything depended on what happened next. If the force field penetrator didn't work, or if the MFM controls weren't here, Operation Royalty was dead before it started, and with it, their last chance of saving humanity. The fate of the universe depended on the trigger he was about to pull. That thought made him breathe faster and brought a tight-lipped smile to his face. His neck and shoulder muscles tensed.

I should be freaking out right about now. What's wrong with me? he thought, using Jim's true and tested method of using humor to fight anxiety.

At exactly 0300 local time, Kurt said, "On three. One, two, three," and Oksana touched her PDD. Through his command launch unit, Kurt saw a light blue circle appear midair nearly five miles away. The force field, just like the one in Winterfell, was invisible, and it mirrored its surrounding area for perfect camouflage. Kurt targeted the blue circle, said, "Missile one away," and pulled the trigger. Next to him, Sergei counted to three, said, "Missile two away," and shot his own missile. The other Commandos followed suit.

Through his CLU, Kurt watched the missiles disappear into the blue circle. The only visible effect was that fire and smoke emitted from the circle, and some debris was thrown out. The force field itself didn't collapse, which confirmed Tarq's theory that it had a second power source outside the field itself. This worked just fine for Kurt because the missiles were a lot more effective inside a confined area.

After the last missile disappeared into the circle, Oksana touched her PDD once more, and it disappeared.

Buzzing with anticipation, Kurt asked Tarq, "Did it work?"

Tarq's answer came a few seconds later. "We are in."

Kurt clenched his right hand above his head, happiness swelling inside his chest. The hard part of their operation was still ahead, but now humanity was freed from the Xortaags' mind control machine, and they had ten billion new allies, including the two hundred thousand heavily armed soldiers surrounding SH-1. Oksana and Sergei caught him in a group hug, and there were high fives, fist bumps, and more hugs all around.

Kurt gave his team a minute to savor their victory. "Let's go. We aren't out of the woods yet."

* * *

THE ONLY THING worse than going into a battle that, if lost, would get you, your friends, your family and all of humanity killed was waiting for the said battle to freaking start.

Experience had taught me when the actual fighting started, adrenalin would be pumped into my bloodstream, and I wouldn't have the time to worry or get scared. But before that, I'd obsess over every single detail, wondering what I might've missed or what could go wrong. What made my situation worse was the fact that there was nothing I could do about our plans. Our whole strategy was based on destroying the Xortaag fleet on the ground. If that failed (and as the famous adage went, no plan survived the first contact with the enemy), Maada had around twenty-two thousand space fighters against our seven, which meant swift death for every single one of us. There was no way we could overcome those odds.

And with the Xortaag transportation ships only two short weeks away, we'd never have another shot at defeating them if we failed tonight.

Venom was busy predicting all sorts of nightmarish outcomes, driving me crazy, as usual.

I opened a channel to my fleet. "Guys, we are fencing in. You all know this already but allow me to say it out loud. If the Xortaag fleet gets off the ground, we are the only thing standing between them and the destruction of our planet. We are the last line of defense. Today we aren't fighting for ourselves, or even our families and friends. Today we fight for all humanity. If we fail, our species is finished. Think about that when you fly into battle."

I paused a second, my mouth set in a hard line, and then added, "What we do now echoes in eternity."

The last time I plagiarized a great leader I ended up getting almost everyone under my command killed. Feeling the veins pulse in my temple, I fervently hoped to do better this time.

One of the fighter pilots, a twenty-four-year-old rookie on his first mission whose name was Peter McKinley, answered, "We won't let you down, boss."

Playing with the wedding ring hanging from my neck, I thought, *I'm not worried about that, rookie. My main concern right now is I might let you down.*

We flew closer to the enemy fleet base, waiting for the battle that would determine the fate of our species.

* * *

SH-1 - 20.30 EST

TEN MILES south of the Xortaag city and behind a ridge that hid him and the force under his command from the city guards, Matias was waiting for Operation Royalty to start. In the turret of an enormous seventy-ton Leopard 3 tank.

The Leopards were multilayer armored tanks, armed with a 140 mm gun, three machine guns, and two grenade launchers. They were thirty-five feet long, fifteen feet wide and twelve feet high. The Commandos had gotten them from military bases in Holland and Germany. They'd entered the bases disguised as Xortaags and ridden away with the tanks.

This part of the operation was mostly his brainchild. Kurt was a genius when it came to guerrilla warfare, but as a US Marine, Matias was more qualified to plan conventional battlefield tactics. The Commandos had set up three small invisible force fields behind the ridge, and in the past two weeks, they'd moved the Leopards one by one late at night under cover of darkness inside the force fields. The human security forces protecting the city didn't do any recon beyond the city limits because they didn't expect a full-frontal assault—they were there to stop the Commandos from infiltrating the city.

Matias had four tank battalions, around two hundred and forty armored vehicles, under his command. The fleet base was located three miles from the southern limits of the city. When Operation Royalty started, the Leopards were supposed to enter the fleet base and destroy as many space fighters as possible on the ground.

Time passed very slowly, and with each passing minute, Matias's tension increased. Somewhere out there, Oksana, who as a member of Kurt's strike force was one of the first people entering the Xortaag city, was risking her life, and Matias could do nothing but wait.

His proposal was still fresh in his memory. Oksana had told him she wanted children. They had, half-jokingly, discussed if they should have six kids or seven.

Our kids will be gorgeous.

He giggled for a second and then wondered why that thought had passed his mind this particular moment, right before going to war.

At 02.45 local time, the tanks left the force fields and moved up the hills, stopping just before the top. At exactly 03.01, Tarq announced, "All units, Operation Royalty is a go."

Matias's heart started pounding, and his breath became fast and shallow, but he tried to sound calm and confident when talking to his units. "It's showtime, everyone. Let's go kick some Xortaag ass."

Engines roaring, the giant Leopards rolled down the

hill, moving fast toward the enemy fleet base, a trail of smoke and dust behind them.

* * *

SH-1 - 21.00 EST

BORED OUT OF HER WITS, Arminaa was sitting on a wooden chair on the twelfth floor of one of the newly constructed buildings in Kingdom of God, idly shining her Crimson Deathbringer Medal.

The injuries she had sustained a few weeks ago were mostly healed, but she was still not cleared for duty. She had been hanging out in the barracks with the rest of the fighter pilots until three nights ago when General Maada had ordered all pilots to be on a red alert until further notice, which meant the pilots were practically living and sleeping in the hangars next to their Deathbringers. Arminaa had the highest respect for the general, and the fact that the two of them had stood shoulder to shoulder against a swarm of enemy ships and survived had elevated her admiration to worship; still, even she thought the twenty-four-seven red alert was too much. Maybe the general was paranoid after what happened during the last enemy attack.

Because the barracks were now empty, Arminaa had decided to spend the evening with some of her friends who had just moved into one of the new buildings in the city. She had found it difficult to sleep in a new bed, which is why she was sitting here in the middle of the night, trying to kill some time, wishing to be cleared for active duty as soon as possible.

And all of a sudden, she saw missiles shot from a neighboring building rooftop.

Her mouth gaping, she jumped out of her chair and tried to get a better look. From where she was standing neither the shooters nor their target was visible, but missiles fired at the middle of the Kingdom of God meant only one thing: The same people who had surprised them in the other fleet base were here right now. Rage pulsed through her with such ferocity her hands started trembling.

This time they won't get out, she grimly thought, baring her teeth.

Arminaa ran out of the balcony, shouting into her PDD, alerting the rest of the Xortaags.

* * *

SH-1 - 21.03 EST

Eric Green was having a good night, just like any other time spent serving the gods.

He was standing guard outside a hangar in the fleet base, along with three other guards. Protecting the gods and their machines was a great honor, one which had been bestowed upon him several times in the past few weeks. What more could a humble servant want from his life?

In the blink of an eye, everything changed.

Into his calm consciousness crashed horrible images of an alien invasion, with Earth burning and millions of dead bodies, including women and children, everywhere. Along with the images came a clear command: *Tear them the fuck apart!*

He exchanged a look with the other guards, cocked his assault rifle, opened the hangar door and walked in.

Hundreds of Xortaags, pilots and ground crew, were sleeping on the hangar floor in sleeping bags. A few were awake, playing a card game. They turned and looked at Green and his companions with surprise in their faces, feeling no danger.

Green opened fire and sprayed the Xortaags with bullets.

The Xortaags he'd targeted had no chance. They all died without being able to draw a weapon. Green turned his attention to the ones just waking up and trying to get out of their sleeping bags.

Green and his companions threw a few grenades inside the closest Deathbringers and moved forward, leaving scores of bodies behind.

* * *

SH-1 - 21.04 EST

LYING on the hangar floor in a sleeping bag, Maada was trying to fall asleep.

He had had a bad feeling for a couple of weeks. His warrior instinct kept telling him something was wrong, and a threat was imminent. The last time he ignored his instinct, thousands of Xortaags had been slaughtered. He was not a man to make the same mistake twice.

He had spent hour after hour obsessing over their defenses. The city was surrounded by two hundred thousand heavily armed human soldiers, and both the fleet base and the laser turrets were under heavy guard. The human security experts the Xortaags had brought in assured him there was no weak point for the enemy to exploit and a repeat of the surprise attack on their other fleet base was impossible. Maada had ordered a thousand Deathbringers, accompanied by another thousand human jet fighters, to fly over the city at all times. This was definitely overkill: The strength of their aerial defense was in the laser turrets operation. The Deathbringers flying overhead were likely to get in the way. He was still not satisfied, so he had demanded the fleet to be on red alert until further notice. For the last three days, the pilots and ground crew had stayed by their fighters. True to form, Maada himself had joined them.

He was beginning to doze off when the sound of gunfire jolted him out of his sleep. He scrambled out of his sleeping bag, grabbed his sidearm, and with eyes wide in horror saw their human security guards shoot at the pilots and ground crew.

What the fuck?

All around him, his pilots grabbed their weapons and started shooting back. There were several hundred of them and only four assailants, so this encounter had only one possible outcome. Maada hid behind a Deathbringer and pulled out his PDA. Reports of attacks by human security forces were pouring in. They were in deep trouble. He opened a channel to fighter pilots and shouted, *"Get off the ground now!"*

Only one assailant was still standing. Maada shot him in the head and hurried to get on his crimson Deathbringer, fury vibrating through his being.

* * *

SH-1 - 21.04 EST

. . .

Mushgaana was doing what he had done most nights since arriving on Earth except when he had female company: sitting in his private movie theater in his residence, he was lost in a world of crime thrillers, sci-fi or fantasy stories. He had just discovered vampires and werewolves. These humans had such vivid imaginations.

He was thoroughly enjoying himself when the sound of gunfire and explosions startled him.

He reached out with his mind, and what he found made his jaw drop all the way to the floor.

After the last attempt on his life, his residence was surrounded by human security forces, just like all the vital locations in the city. Right now, there was only one thought in those humans' minds: to kill him and all other Xortaags. They had surprised his Xortaag guards and made short work out of them, and they were approaching his location. Mushgaana tried to stop them using his mind, but just like the last time, it was no use. He counted more than a hundred humans moving towards him. He wished he had had a secret exit built in this house too, but after killing the members of his security force the last time, there would be no way to keep it a secret, which would defeat its purpose.

I'll fucking kill them all! He sent a mental command to the team in charge of the Voice of God. Nobody answered.

So this is it. He thought of his favorite courtesan back home. He thought of his brothers, fighting over his place. He wondered how the vampire movie ended. Then the crown prince calmly went to his office, which was adjacent to the theater, opened a hidden panel under his desk and pushed a red button.

Mushgaana stared at the button for a second. *I hope this*

works, he thought, but he figured it probably would not. No one had ever tried something like this before. And either way, *he* would never find out.

The humans are in for a nasty surprise if it does work though. He smiled at the thought.

He could hear the enemy soldiers massing outside his office door. His PDD started buzzing. It was Maada, probably trying to launch a rescue attempt. It was way too late for that. He sent him a telepathic message. *Goodbye, old friend. I hope you get out of this triumphant, whatever this is.*

He chose an assault rifle out of his gun collection. The gun was also equipped with a grenade launcher. Remembering a scene from a movie he had watched a few weeks ago, he smirked, cocked his gun and yelled, "Say hello to my little friend!"

He shot a grenade straight at the office door, killing a bunch of humans standing right behind it. Then he walked into the smoke and dust, fire and bullets pouring out of his gun, mowing down the assailants left, right and center, killing dozens of them.

My mental powers might not work, but I am still the crown prince of the most fearsome kingdom in the universe, you cockroaches!

* * *

SH-1 - 21.10 EST

Kurt and his team were still running down the stairs, just approaching the ground floor, when Tarq contacted Kurt. "Your presence has been noticed. Two small Xortaag patrols are converging on your location. Nothing you can't handle, but...oh no!"

Out of breath after running down so many flights of stairs, Kurt didn't bother to ask what Tarq meant. The alien continued, "A large group of Xortaags is coming out of a nearby building, moving straight towards you."

Kurt asked, "How large?"

"Unknown, because they are still running out of the building, but at least several hundred," answered Tarq.

This complicates our situation, Kurt thought. He told Tarq, "Oh, good. For a moment there I thought we were in trouble."

"You should really stop hanging out with Jim," said Tarq. "That boy has a bad influence on you."

Yeah. Everyone keeps telling me that.

Kurt stopped at the building's main entrance and scanned the area. The streets were empty. He sprinted out of the building, followed by Oksana, Sergei, and the rest of the team. Less than two minutes later, a laser bolt passed by his head. A group of Xortaags was shooting at his team from inside another building. Adrenaline pouring into his bloodstream, Kurt reacted by diving to the ground, aiming his STG 666 and shooting two Xortaags, one in the belly, the second in the head. The sight of the Xortaag's head exploding gave him a slight satisfaction. The rest of the Commandos returned fire too. Kurt got up and darted toward the river, shooting as he ran, followed by his team.

* * *

WINTERFELL - 21.11 EST

. . .

TARQ HAD JUST FINISHED TALKING to Kurt when Barook announced, "The Xortaag fleet is getting off the ground."

Tarq's antennae stiffened. If Maada and his fleet flew off the fleet base, it would all be over, regardless of how the ground battle went. Biting his fingernails, he said, "How the hell did they get to their Deathbringers so fast?"

"I do not know but let me see if I can do something about it," said Barook.

* * *

SH-1 - 21.12 EST

JOHN TAYLOR WAS HIDING behind the remains of a destroyed truck, shooting at a group of Xortaags in a building in front of him.

He'd been recruited into the human security force to fly jet fighters over Kingdom of God. He was off duty when the call to kill all the "gods" came in. He initially joined the fight using his sidearm but later grabbed the assault rifle and ammunition of a fallen soldier.

He suddenly saw an image of a laser turret in his mind and "heard" a new order: *If you see one of these, try to get inside and shoot at the enemy ships leaving the fleet base.*

The message was followed by images showing how to operate the turret once inside.

Taylor had seen one of those things. He ran towards the giant weapon's location. A few minutes later he joined a group of soldiers already gathering next to the turret.

The turret had a metal hatch which the soldiers opened using explosives. They killed the four Xortaags inside. Taylor and three other soldiers slid behind the weapon controls. He looked at the laser turret's targeting scope and saw hundreds of Deathbringers getting off the ground in close formation.

The humans brought the weapon to bear and started shooting at the Deathbringers. At such close range and with the ships flying next to each other, the results were spectacular. Enormous laser bolts hit the enemy ships, destroying dozens of them. It was like shooting fish in a barrel.

Revenge is a dish best served cold.

Taylor had no idea where that thought had come from.

Shooting at close range turned out to be a double-edged sword. The Deathbringers fired back. Taylor knew he was a sitting duck, but he didn't leave his post and kept killing enemy ships until a brilliant explosion destroyed the turret.

* * *

SH-1 - 21.12 EST

MOVING at the maximum speed of sixty miles per hour, the Leopards approached the Xortaag city. Matias, following the feed transmitted by the Akakie spy ship in orbit, saw how the human security forces turned on the Xortaags. The Xortaags didn't have any anti-tank weapons. *This will be a walk in the park*, he thought.

Tarq's voice squawked in his headphones, "Be advised the Xortaag fleet is leaving its base."

Matias cursed under his breath. *I shouldn't have jinxed it!*

They were still three miles away from the city's outer limits. He contacted his people. "Time for plan B. Fire at will."

The Leopards carried duel-purpose mid-range munitions. These rounds could be shot directly at line-of-sight targets; they could also be fired in a ballistic arc and seek their own targets, in which case they had an effective range of fifteen miles.

Matias's gunner used the tank's fire-control system to fire the main gun. Each Leopard carried fifty-five rounds. With a rate of fire of nine rounds per minute, the three tank battalions unleashed their wave of death.

Looking at the information transmitted by the spy ship, Matias saw the destruction their bombardment caused, and he burned with a fierce joy. Several Deathbringer hangars went up in smoke, taking the space fighters still inside with them. Hundreds of enemy ships were hit while still trying to get off the ground. The Leopards' crew whooped and cheered excitedly.

Matias still wished their original plan had worked. The tanks' main guns would've been a lot more effective at close range and shooting directly at targets, not to mention the damage their heavy machine guns and grenade launchers could have inflicted. If they'd entered the base with the Deathbringers on the ground, chances were very few would've been able to fly off. Still, destroying so many enemy ships felt great. It was the first time in history that a fleet of space fighters was destroyed using tanks.

I FOLLOWED the battle using the spy ship feed. At first, everything went according to plan: Kurt's team hit the installations under the force field, Barook hacked into MFM, and the human security forces turned on their previous masters, killing scores of them.

I watched a short and brutal dogfight unfold over SH-1. A thousand F-44s and an equal number of Deathbringers were patrolling the Xortaag city's airspace. The jet fighters suddenly fired on their Xortaag counterparts, flying very close to them in visual range. They caught the Xortaags by total surprise and brought down more than half of the enemy fighters. The remaining Deathbringers fired back using their deadly laser cannons. The F-44 pilots didn't even try to run away. They kept fighting until every single one of them was dead.

I thought, *At least now there are a couple of hundred fewer enemy space fighters to worry about*—and immediately felt embarrassed for being so selfish. I murmured, "A thousand pilots just died, you moron."

Venom muttered, "In the grand scheme of things, that's really nothing."

One of these days, I'd get a Swiss Army knife, stand in front of a mirror, open my skull and pull Venom out, kicking and screaming.

Less than fifteen minutes into the battle, the Deathbringers started getting off the ground.

I didn't know how they managed to do that so fast, but I had no doubt Maada had something to do with it. It gave me extreme pleasure to watch so many Deathbringers shot down by their own laser turrets, and so many more destroyed by our tanks' artillery fire.

Tarq's voice was somber. "Jim, we estimate some fifteen thousand enemy ships made it, and they are coming straight towards you."

"I have eyes, you know," I snarled.

Grinding my teeth in frustration, I glowered at the image of the fast-approaching enemy fleet on my monitor. Despite our meticulous planning and flawless execution, our ground assault had failed for all intents and purposes. The Xortaag fleet still outnumbered us two to one. How could we beat a Xortaag force twice our size and walk out of it alive?

This had just turned into a suicide mission.

"You don't have to do it, you know," said Venom.

He was right. We didn't have to die today. I could order the fleet to turn around and go back to Winterfell. Then we could get on the Fireflies and go to Kanoor, joining forces with the Akakie fleet. Live to fight another day.

As the commander of the fleet, my first responsibility was protecting the people under my command. Would I be a good commander if I ushered them to their demise? And what difference would it make? Our death wouldn't change anything. Maada would kill us all and then do whatever he damned pleased with our ground forces and the rest of humanity.

All I needed to do was to leave Kurt and his Commandos in or around SH-1 to die. On top of Liz, the three thousand pilots who died in Maada's ambush, the seven hundred million humans, and everyone else I'd failed to protect. I had enough guilt for five lifetimes.

I opened a channel to my people. "Let's go save the planet. And for my pièce de résistance..."

I touched a VR screen, and Ride of the Valkyries boomed in all the Vipers' cockpits. I could imagine Liz rolling her eyes.

I flew in to meet the enemy fleet, leading the seven thousand man and women under my command to certain death.

"On the bright side, this probably means you'll join Liz sooner than later," said Venom.

"Yeah. Tonight we will dine in hell," I said. "I sure hope they don't let you in though."

* * *

SH-1 - 21. 25 EST

Feeling veins pulsing in his neck, Maada was so mad he entertained the idea of removing his flight helmet and chewing on his cockpit equipment.

Despite all his precautions, and for the second time in just a few months, the enemy had wiped out a big chunk of his fleet on the ground before they even got the chance to fly to battle. The sight of their own laser turrets shooting at the fleet they were supposed to protect was the worst thing he had ever endured in his life.

From the forty thousand space fighters under his command when they entered the orbit of this fucking planet just a few short months ago, now only fifteen thousand remained. Mushgaana was dead, and even worse, their space communication center, SFD and the Voice of God controls were all gone.

The Earth invasion had been a complete failure. Without the Voice of God, there was no way one million Xortaags could hold on to Earth against ten billion humans. Hell, the two hundred thousand humans he had tasked with protecting the city were probably enough to wipe out all the Xortaags. And without the space communication and the SFD, they were trapped here and had nowhere to go.

Everything he had achieved in a lifetime of military campaigns was decimated in less than five minutes. History would not remember him as the conqueror of the galaxy but as the fool who lost everything on a stupid backwater planet.

His hands were shaking so hard it was difficult to control his Deathbringer.

The humans were done. If the Xortaags could not have Earth, neither could they. He would massacre every last human and make their planet uninhabitable. Let it be a lesson for all the other species who might be tempted to make an alliance with the Akakies against his people.

First things first though. The enemy fleet had been spotted approaching the city. They would be the first ones to taste his wrath. Feeling his blood boiling, he led the remainder of his fleet towards the enemy.

* * *

SH-1 - 21.45 EST

Breathing laboriously, Kurt stopped running, shot a Xortaag following his team, and started running again.

It'd begun to rain, which made both running and shooting more difficult.

He repeated the stop-shoot-run sequence thirty seconds later. His situation was getting increasingly desperate.

Kurt's first plan was to make a beeline for the river where the Commandos had hidden their diving suits, but they ran into a Xortaag patrol on their way to the river. Then he decided to push towards the city borders, hoping to unite with human forces battling the Xortaags. The Xortaags had blocked their communications, and without Tarq's help, avoiding them had become impossible.

Urban warfare was the Commandos' specialty. They

were much better armed, had armor, and used military rounds that could go through a cement wall and kill the man hiding behind it. Most Xortaags in this part of the city weren't even real soldiers; they were engineers, electricians, and foremen carrying sidearms. But there were just too fucking many of them, and they outnumbered Kurt's team a hundred to one.

With two new Xortaags showing up for each one the Commandoes killed, Kurt thought, *It's beginning to feel like fighting Hydra.*

Sergei, shooting with one hand and helping an injured Commando move with the other, said, "This looks bad."

Oksana said, "Dah!" and threw a grenade inside a building where several Xortaags were shooting at them. An explosion made pieces of stone, dust and body parts fly out of the building.

"Got any bright ideas?" Sergei asked Kurt.

Wiping beads of sweat on his forehead, Kurt said, "Yeah. Don't get shot."

"I always knew there's reason everyone thinks you're military genius," said Sergei.

This must be how Colonel Faulkner felt towards the end, Kurt thought, shooting at a group of Xortaags who had just appeared behind them.

* * *

I WAS ENGAGED in a dogfight with a Deathbringer when Josef called me. "We found him."

There was no need to ask who "him" was.

I tried a new tactic I'd thought up recently: I shot at the enemy ship with my laser cannons, targeting the right side of the space fighter. Trying to avoid the laser bolts, the pilot snapped to the left, straight into the path of one of the two Sparrows I'd released five seconds ago.

I thrust my fists in the air and shouted, "Alpha Mike Foxtrot!"

How I loved fighter pilot jargons! Only we fighter pilots could pack so much emotion into such a short phrase.

I firewalled my Viper and made a beeline to the coordinates Josef had just sent me.

I will have my vengeance, in this life or the next.

Sometimes I just couldn't help myself.

I found Maada's red Deathbringer fighting three Vipers. Several enemy ships were flying or just hovering close by, protecting their commander. I was certain they were doing that on their own initiative. Maada struck me as a man confident enough to tackle a hundred enemy ships on his own without thinking about it twice.

I thought about joining the fight, and I froze.

Again!

I took off my left glove and touched the wedding ring around my neck. When the cold metal met my hand, I saw Liz putting it on my finger. I saw her as clearly as on our wedding day, the form-fitting white satin dress setting off her smooth dark skin as she flashed her dazzling smile. She was looking directly at me, her deep brown-drizzled-with-gold eyes full of joy and passion. She was the love of my life, taken from this world in her prime. There were two people on this earth responsible for her death: Maada and me, and by God, one of us would pay today.

I dove in before I could change my mind. Two Deathbringers moved to intercept me. My cannons roared to life. I fired dead center bursts into the bandits. They both lit up like enormous candles.

One of the Vipers fighting Maada exploded into flames.

I heard Josef's voice. "Good timing, boss. We could sure use your help."

I flew in, shooting my remaining two Sparrows and firing the laser cannons at the same time. Maada saw me coming, wildly twisted his ship, steered clear of the missiles, and started shooting back. His laser bolts missed my fighter by a few inches.

And then, I had an incoming message from the devil himself. Maada said in my earphones, "Colonel Harrison, welcome to my party."

"You mean your funeral, General," I corrected him.

"Such confidence. Did you not run away in a straight line as fast as you could the last time we met?" he taunted me.

Jerking the stick hard left to avoid his incoming fire, I felt my face and ears start burning, and the muscles around my mouth became so tense my teeth started to ache. I wanted to shout, "You mother-fucking son of an alien whore!" but I bit my tongue. That wouldn't have been very dignified, and I didn't want him to know he had gotten under my skin. Still, hatred poured through me like white-hot liquid metal. Intense, implacable hatred for the general who had killed Liz, who was responsible for the death of half of our pilots and countless others, who would murder every single human on Earth given the opportunity.

I pulled up and to the right, and for a glorious second managed to get him dead center in my gunsight. I pulled the trigger. Maada snapped to the left and dodged my laser bolts. I stayed on him like glue, trying to get him back in my gunsight, trying harder not to get killed.

"So, no comebacks? He walks all over us and gets away with it?" said Venom.

We couldn't have that. I hated it when others had the

last word. Still following the crimson Deathbringer, I contacted Maada. "General, what we have here is a failure to communicate."

"Seriously?" said Venom, filling in for Liz.

"How so?" he asked.

I could bring my gunsight right up to his fighter, but I couldn't get it on the Deathbringer. I kept trying to get a clean shot. My finger poised on the trigger, I said through clenched teeth, "You seem to think you have the upper hand here, sitting in that obsolete piece of junk you're flying. You're wrong. We have destroyed your precious city. You've got nowhere to go."

Maada rolled and put his fighter in a sharp curve. "I still have enough firepower to scorch Earth several times over. I will rain fire on Earth until ninety percent of humanity is slaughtered; then I will land and kill the rest up close and personal."

That was it. "*You mother-fucking son of an alien whore!*" I yelled and pulled the trigger, missing him by a mile.

* * *

WINTERFELL - 22.05 EST

BITING HIS FINGERS, Tarq thought, *We are going to lose.*

The battle on the ground was going as well as it could have been expected. The human forces, despite the Xortaags' numerical advantage, had the upper hand. The Xortaags' remaining laser turrets had easily shot down their choppers, but they still had armored cars, light artillery, and shoulder-fired missiles, for which the Xortaags had no answer. Not to mention Matias's tank battalions that were freely moving in the city, massacring the enemy soldiers by hundreds.

The more important battle, the one raging in the sky above the city, was a totally different matter.

The fleet had already lost more than two thousand space fighters. They had inflicted slightly higher casualties on the Xortaags, but that was not enough. And after this was over, Maada would not leave a blade of grass standing on Earth.

Tarq could not have another ten billion deaths on his conscience. *If we lose this battle, I must kill myself, and because I am too much of a pussy to do it, I will have to program MICI to make me commit suicide.*

Tarq asked Barook to open a channel to the enemy fleet. A few moments later, he said, "My name is Tarq. I am the commander of the Akakie Special Operations Force. It gives me extreme pleasure to let you know you have fallen into the trap I had carefully laid for you."

He took a breath and continued, "By now, you all know you have lost. We have destroyed your space communication center and your SFD. Your city is surrounded by our forces, and it will fall in the next couple of hours. We have already demolished your fleet base and all your support facilities. More importantly, with your so-called Voice-of-God-my-Ass gone, there are now ten billion humans on Earth screaming for your blood. I am well aware of your fleet's capabilities, but the fact of the matter is you cannot remain airborne forever. In a few days, your energy reserves will be depleted, and you will have to land. Regardless of what happens to the humans, I promise you this: We Akakies will hunt down every last one of you, and I will personally see to it that your death is spectacularly unpleasant."

Tarq waited a second so that the Xortaags could ponder their dilemma. "However, if you surrender now, we will treat you well. We actually do not have a choice because you captured several thousand of my people during our last encounter. We want to arrange for a POW exchange. If you surrender, you will be home with your friends and families soon. The choice is yours. Make a wise one."

Barook gave him a thumbs-up. "Well said, Commander."

Tarq left the channel open, anxiously waiting for a response that came a few seconds later. "*Fuck you and the horse!*"

It was unmistakably Maada's voice.

Tarq and Barook exchanged a confused look. "Horse? What horse?" whispered Barook.

"Sorry, General. Thanks for offering, but I'm married," said Tarq. "The horse might be interested though."

Tarq watched in horror as Maada, as if trying to make a point, hit Jim's Viper with a few laser bolts at that very moment. He gasped and waited for the golden space fighter to explode. A long second later, he heaved a sigh of relief when that did not happen.

"Not a single Xortaag will surrender as long as this guy lives," said Barook.

Tarq sighed. "I know. Let's hope someone kills him, or we are all dead." He contacted Jim. "Your space fighter is badly damaged. Disengage and return to Winterfell."

"Negative. Not as long as this motherfucker is drawing breath," Jim answered.

Tarq had a sense of déjà vu. He had had this conversation with someone else recently. When he remembered, both his hearts skipped a beat, and a sudden coldness hit him at his core. "I had a similar conversation with Elizabeth, and you know how that ended. I am giving you a direct order. You cannot possibly overcome Maada in a damaged fighter."

* * *

With confidence I didn't feel, I answered, "Watch me."

Cordelia yelled, "Listen, you! Get your ass back here. I can't lose both Liz and you."

Touching, but I had to focus on the task at hand. I ignored them both.

In the last twenty minutes, I'd used all my flying skills and mastery of dogfighting tactics trying to shoot the crimson Deathbringer, and yet not even one of my laser bolts or missiles had landed. Josef, who was one of our most experienced fighter pilots, and the third pilot, who happened to be Peter McKinley, were not faring any better. It was like the general's ship didn't abide by the laws of physics. He kept making impossible twists and turns at a very high velocity, evading our fire and repeatedly hitting us in the process.

McKinley's Viper spiraled out of sight in flames. The poor boy probably hadn't imagined himself coming up against the galaxy's deadliest fighter pilot on his maiden mission. I watched his space fighter disappear in thick black clouds over SH-1, rage and guilt competing to see which one could bite off a bigger chunk of my soul.

One more person I'd failed.

My fighter was hit a few times. A number of warning systems were flashing furious red lights, and my Viper reacted more slowly to the stick movements. The space fighter's computer engaged multiple damage control and repair systems. Still, I had to fight my equipment just to stay in the battle. I put both my hands on the stick, trying to steady it and get my space fighter under control.

I faintly smelled smoke, even though I was wearing my oxygen mask.

This can't possibly be good!

And if Maada had been in any real danger, all those Deathbringers around us wouldn't have stayed there and watched.

Josef said, "Boss, I—"

I never found out what he wanted to say. His Viper exploded with such force that the shock wave shook me inside my cockpit. The silver space fighter was completely obliterated. Maada must have hit her engine.

Up to this moment, I still had hope, just a tiny snowflake against the warm summer wind. With Josef gone, utter, profound despair washed over me, hurting so badly I felt what was in my veins now wasn't blood but molten lava.

Josef had two beautiful little children whose pictures he used to show us any chance he got. But I had more important things to worry about than my old friend and his now-orphaned kids. We were *all* doomed. It was like our last battle all over again. They had two space fighters for every one of ours, and I'd already lost more than a third of the Vipers under my command. Our pilots hadn't died cheaply. The enemy had lost at least one space fighter for every one of ours, but when the enemy fleet had twice as many ships as you, inflicting one-on-one casualties didn't win the battle.

Terror came on the heel of hopelessness and made me shudder inside my temperature-controlled flight suit. Terror of failure. Terror of losing the battle. Terror of being single-handedly responsible for the death of every man, woman, and child on the planet.

Sweat drenched my skin, and I found it difficult to breathe.

Our only way out of this was to break the Xortaags' resistance by killing Maada. Talk about doing the impossible. The guy was invincible. There was a reason he was a living legend in the galaxy. Tarq once had told me parents all across the known universe scared their children by telling them if they didn't behave Maada would take them. I'd wondered if he was serious but didn't wonder anymore.

Here I was again on the verge of certain death, and my brain kept itself busy by pulling up nonsensical memories. It had to be some sort of a defense mechanism to distract me from thinking about my impending demise. Anything not to face the truth.

Venom chose this moment to stick his ugly nose out. "Let me get this straight: As the commander of the fleet, you led your forces to three battles and got everyone killed in two of those. Well done! You make General Custer look good."

Bugger off, you useless parasite!

If I were going down, taking humanity with me, I'd go down fighting. I raised my chin and kept trying to lock on Maada's Deathbringer. Grinding my teeth so hard the sour taste of blood filled my mouth, I made my Tango Uniform Viper twist and dodge wildly, barely escaping death every second.

What do we say to the Lord of Death? Not fucking today!

"Fighting Maada in a damaged Viper, with no missiles left?" said Venom. "I'm pretty sure it's today, as in right about now."

I wished Dr. James could've seen me right now.

* * *

SH-1 - 22.25 EST

Kurt murmured to himself, "So, this is the end then."

He and the remaining members of his team were surrounded in a small, under-construction one-story building. Most of his people had been killed, and the remaining eight Commandos were injured, except for Sergei, who despite his large built was unscathed. That guy was so lucky.

What bothered him most was not dying in this godforsaken city. He wanted to know that Operation Royalty would be a success, that all of this wasn't for nothing. He'd die in peace if he knew they succeeded. But with the Xortaags blocking their communications, there was no way to know how the battle was going. All he could do was wish Jim and the others good luck. He considered praying for a second, but after all those years of ignoring God, it was unlikely the deity would listen to him now.

Oksana, shooting from behind a wall, said, "It was fine and good to be defiant to the end, but it was better not to get caught in the first place."

Sergei gave her a puzzled look. "I love you like sister, but sometimes I have no idea what the hell you're talking about."

Oksana wiped the blood pouring out of a cut above her eyebrow with her sleeve and smiled like a crazy woman. "*A sister!*"

Sergei removed his night-vision goggles and with a trembling hand rubbed his eyes to clear the sweat running down his forehead and blocking his vision. He told Kurt, "She's definitely losing it."

One of the Commandos screamed in pain and collapsed

to the ground after getting hit in the chest. The man's armor had weakened after absorbing several hits. Kurt rushed to the Commando's body, but the smoldering hole in his chest told him there was nothing he could do.

Seven, Kurt thought. He went back to his position and kept shooting his STG 666, bringing down a Xortaag with each shot, even though a wound in his right shoulder was throbbing with pain and made concentration difficult.

Sergei, finally running out of luck, was next. A laser bolt hit him squarely in the face. Oksana screamed and despite having been shot in the leg limped to his side as fast as she could, but it was obviously too late.

Kurt gripped his rifle so hard his knuckles turned white, closed his eyes for a second, and thought, *Farewell, enemy mine.*

He aimed and shot a Xortaag in the head. Then another one, and a third soldier after that. His gun clicked empty. He looked for a fresh magazine, and when found none told Oksana, "I'm out."

Oksana threw him Sergei's gun. "I'm on my last few rounds too."

"There must still be a few hundred of them out there," said Kurt. "Maybe if they all stand in one line?"

The earth beneath them started shaking.

"An earthquake? Now?" asked Oksana.

Kurt looked outside the building and smiled tiredly. "Nope. It's General Blucher, and not a second too soon."

From down the street, five gigantic Leopards rolled into view. The tanks' heavy machine guns roared, killing a dozen helpless Xortaag soldiers instantly. The Leopards' crew manning the grenade launchers joined in. Some Xortaags fled. Others started shooting at the tanks with their sidearms. Hundreds of tiny laser bolts hit the tanks, causing no damage, while the armored vehicles kept firing at the enemy and butchering scores of them. The lead tank ran over a group of alien soldiers who were still shooting at it. They all died a horrible death.

Kurt burst into uncontrollable laughter.

"What is so funny?" asked Oksana.

Kurt suppressed his laughter long enough to say, "The Xortaags are brave, but you have to question their judgment."

Oksana looked at him blankly for a second; then she started laughing too. The two of them laughed so hard they both soon found it difficult to breathe.

A tank stopped right outside the building. Its turret hatch opened, and Matias pulled half of his torso out of it. He shouted, "Kurt? You in there?"

Kurt stood up and looked outside. There were no Xortaags in sight. He waved to Matias. "Hi, Matias."

"Is Oksana with you?" asked Matias, his voice tense.

Oksana called out, "Hi, honey. Thanks for the rescue."

The former Marine, immense relief obvious in his face, said, "Sorry it took us a while. They've blocked your coms; otherwise, we would've let you know we were on the way."

Kurt helped Oksana stand up, and they both started limping out of the building towards the tank. He asked Matias, "How is the battle going?"

"Could not be going any better," said Matias. "The soldiers Maada had placed around SH-1 are slaughtering the Xortaags, and nobody can stand against my Leopards. SH-1 is ours."

Relieved, Kurt smiled, raised his free hand in a V-for-victory signal and told Oksana, "We did it. Say something epic."

Oksana let out a thin laugh. "One other such victory would utterly undo us."

* * *

ARMINAA WAS HIDING inside a building on the opposite side of the street. Soaked with rain and feeling utterly miserable, she'd watched with hate in her eyes as the huge metal monsters killed her comrades by the dozens. She'd have happily given her life to be in a Deathbringer's cockpit right now, raining fire and destruction on enemy vehicles. Since that was impossible, giving her life was all she could do.

Arminaa looked at the grenade she was holding in her hands. She had taken it from a dead Commando. She'd never seen one of those before, but she'd watched how the enemy soldiers used them, and at any rate, how difficult could it be?

Arminaa carefully cleaned her Crimson Deathbringer Medal of dirt and mud one last time, pulled the pin, and with a sidearm in one hand and the grenade in the other, ran out of the building. She was approaching the tank from behind, so none of the Leopard's crew saw her. The street was full of fog-like smoke, both from the tanks engines and the explosions, which helped her cause. So did the downpour. She ran as fast as her enhanced muscles allowed her, feeling wind and rain on her face for what certainly would be the last time.

* * *

Kurt caught a glimpse of the Xortaag woman before she disappeared behind the tank. A sudden coldness hit him at the core, and he shouted to Matias, "Watch out!"

An energy bolt hit Matias in the back of the head. He disappeared inside the tank's hatch. Kurt, still holding on to Oksana with his left hand, started shooting with Sergei's gun, but his target was mostly hidden behind the tank turret. The Xortaag woman managed to throw the grenade down the hatch a fraction of a second before Kurt shot her in her forehead. Most of her brain splashed from the back of her skull. Her blood painted the tank dark purple.

There was a dull explosion inside the tank, and smoke started coming out of the hatch.

Kurt collapsed on the ground, pulling Oksana with him, not even daring to look at her. He'd never been so dead tired in all his life. Then he forced himself to check on Oksana. Her eyes were glazed with tears. She bit her lips, got up and tried to limp towards the tank. The image of what she'd find inside turned Kurt's stomach. Feeling defeated and useless, he stood up and pulled the girl into a gentle embrace. For a second, Oksana struggled to free herself, but soon she hid her face in Kurt's chest, desperate tears spilling down her face, crying in such a desolate way that Kurt felt he himself was hanging by a thread, his own eyes wet with tears. The two of them just stood there under the rain, exhausted, hurt, and heartbroken.

* * *

SH-1 - 22.25 EST

. . .

WHILE THOUSANDS of deadly dogfights raged all around her, Keiko circled the small area where Maada was fighting Jim and his companions.

She watched the fight for a few minutes, trying to find a weakness in the general's tactics, finding none. She knew she was no match for Maada. Still, she had one final card to play.

She'd been thinking about her plan for a few days now, but she hadn't been able to make up her mind. With the moment of truth upon her, she knew what she had to do. Once she made her decision, a wave of serenity washed over her. It was how one felt when going home after a hard but rewarding day at work.

She recited the Earth prayer in her mind. *We gently caress you, Earth, our planet and our home . . .*

Keiko witnessed Maada destroying Josef's Viper, and Jim attacking the enemy craft with renewed vigor, probably born out of desperation, even though his vessel was damaged. The two space fighters started an aerial dance, fiercely twisting and turning around each other, each pilot trying to gain the upper hand.

Keiko saw her window of opportunity.

She pushed the stick and flew in without hesitation. The Viper screamed into a power dive. Two Deathbringers tried to intercept her, but she didn't engage them at all. She just evaded them and moved forward. The two enemy pilots gave chase, shooting at her from behind. They would hit her in a few seconds, but it was inconsequential.

Moving in fast, feeling the thrill of hunting the biggest hunter of all, Keiko released all her six Sparrows in pairs and let go with the laser cannons. Maada countered by making a hard turn up and to his right, avoiding the missiles and keeping himself out of her line of fire. Under normal circumstances, Keiko's Viper would fly by the crimson Deathbringer, causing little or no harm.

This is no normal circumstance, thought Keiko. *General Maada, welcome to Earth!*

* * *

MAADA, intoxicated by his most recent victory, recognized the green Viper. He smiled wolfishly and thought, *Good to see you again, old friend. You and I have unfinished business.*

With a lifetime of experience as a fighter pilot, Maada might have sensed the danger, but his attention was still focused on the golden enemy vessel, whose pilot, despite being outmatched and having taken several hits, still doggedly tried to target his Deathbringer.

Some people just do not know when to quit, Maada thought with disdain, but he felt a grudging respect for the commander of the enemy fleet who had apparently grown a gigantic pair since the last time they met in battle.

The green space fighter abruptly changed direction and charged towards Maada's ship. He understood the enemy pilot's intention and with lightning-fast reactions started maneuvering to avoid the collision, smirking confidently.

I have been dodging energy bolts all my life, and this idiot thinks he can ram my ship!

He would have succeeded, but at that very moment, a white-hot laser bolt shot by the golden space fighter ripped into his Deathbringer. This caused only minimal damage, but it delayed the execution of his maneuver by just a fraction of a second.

That was all it took.

From his cockpit, Maada saw the green vessel getting

bigger and bigger until it filled his field of view. He had only enough time to think, *Fucking humans!*

The fabled crimson Deathbringer and the green Viper turned into a tiny supernova.

* * *

Dumbfounded, I stared at the expanding ball of fire and whatever was left of Keiko and Maada's space fighters.

My vision blurred so completely I thought I was going blind until I realized my eyes were full of tears. I broke down into tears, crying as soundlessly as I could, ignoring both Tarq and Barook who were shouting in a frenzy, asking me if Maada was indeed dead, apparently not trusting their own eyes.

"This is new," said Venom.

Teardrops freely slid down my cheeks, my sobs only interrupted by the need to draw breath. The magnitude of my loss swept over me, and I felt as if my brain was being shredded from the inside. Liz was gone. Keiko was gone. Josef was gone. Allen was gone. More than half of our pilots were already dead, and only God knew how many more would join them before this day was over. For all I knew, Kurt was dead or dying. Now Maada was gone, and I couldn't even get the slight satisfaction of having my revenge. That was an unbearable torture to my soul, and I kept crying as if the depth of my sorrow would bring everyone back.

It didn't.

But I was still here, having to carry this burden for the rest of my life. And I still had a job to do.

I shook my head to clear the tears from my eyes and rejoined the battle.

Tarq contacted me. "Jim, some of your Viper's systems are dangerously close to failing. You have to return to Winterfell immediately before your space fighter falls from the sky."

"No way," I said.

"That was not a request."

"You can demote me later. Right now, I ain't gonna leave my men," I answered.

My men.

I belatedly added, "And women. My women? My people?"

The first group of enemy pilots transmitted their intention to surrender less than five minutes later. First in small groups, and then in bigger ones, almost two-thirds of the Deathbringers hoisted the figurative white flag. Despite losing their numerical advantage, the rest fought to the bitter end and took a lot of us with them.

By the conclusion of the battle, I had shot down more than a dozen enemy space fighters, but I had stopped counting.

With the Xortaag fleet out of the way, we turned our attention to the battle still raging in the city. By this point, their laser turrets had all been destroyed by human ground forces, and the Xortaags were defenseless against an air strike.

"Ants, meet boot," I murmured.

We slaughtered them by the thousands until every last Xortaag on Earth was either dead or captured.

Operation Royalty, and the Xortaags' occupation of Earth, was over.

Due to the extensive damage to my Viper, I was the last pilot to RTB, barely hanging in the air. A few of my men (*people!*) had stayed behind to escort my fighter, but they all

SEAN ROBINS

landed before I did. By the time I started my landing run, the whole space fighter was shaking so badly I was beginning to think I might not make it after all, and I pulled a deadstick at the end.

When I landed my golden Viper, all our surviving pilots were waiting for me, nearly four thousand men and women, still in flight suits, standing in formation. Someone shouted, "Commander on deck!"

All my pilots, in unison, faced me and executed a perfect military salute.

After struggling with my space fighter's flight equipment for what seemed like hours, my limbs might as well have been chained to iron shackles, but with pride welling up, I stuck out my chest and saluted back.

If only Liz was here.

* * *

THAT EVENING, Kurt, Oksana, Dr. Bob and I got together, had a few drinks and reminisced about Liz, Keiko, Sergei, Matias, and Anastasiya. The four of us looked more miserable than Dr. Gachet. Van Gogh would've had a blast drawing our portrait.

Feeling bone-weary, I murmured, "If this is how we feel in victory, I wonder how we would've felt if we'd failed."

Kurt sipped his Paulaners. "You know, Keiko was right all along. I should've cherished every second we had together. Instead, I pushed her away."

"It's better to have loved and lost than never to have loved at all," said Oksana.

"Didn't your mother teach you not to use clichés?" I asked.

Cordelia laughed. "Look who's talking."

CHAPTER FIFTEEN

There was a lot of work to do, so we decided to keep MFM running until we could deal with several urgent issues.

Nearly half a million Xortaags had surrendered. We turned what was left of SH-1 into a POW camp and kept them there under heavy guard for the time being.

We rounded up Zheng's people and put them in normal prisons. I was with Kurt when he was informed Zheng himself was found and was in custody. His eyes flashed, and a predatory smile crossed his face. I was so happy I wasn't in Zheng's shoes.

We took this opportunity to deal with the organized crime once and for all. We used MFM to send out a message, asking whoever had been involved in any criminal activity to report to their local police and confess to everything, supporting their confessions with evidence. Hundreds of crime bosses all over the world willingly went to prison, and an untold number of unsolved crimes and cold cases were closed.

With all that done, we sent out a message, asking

everyone on the planet to be in either front of a TV or online on October 14th at 12.00 EST. We stopped the MFM at that moment and broadcasted a previously prepared message by Kurt. We knew once MFM stopped, the people would remember their last memory before going under, which for most of them was the alien invasion, with incoherent bits and pieces of what'd happened ever since.

Kurt filled everyone in on the Xortaag invasion, the Akakies' help, the liberation of Earth, the whole nine yards. He asked people to go on with their normal lives and wait for a democratic election to be held in a few weeks. Until then, Earth would be governed by us, and if anyone had a problem with that, we could just turn MFM back on. He wasn't joking about that.

We did turn MFM back on, but only for a few minutes. It was Tarq's idea. We were worried about mass hysteria—it wasn't every day that you woke up from a several-months-long dream and were told you'd been living under an alien occupation that had claimed the lives of several million people. Tarq used MFM to send out soothing messages for about five minutes. He kept doing that once every hour for the next few weeks until, slowly but surely, everything went back to normal.

NEW YORK · OCTOBER 14, 2078

A VOICE in Chancellor Zheng's head kept repeating that he should be in front of a TV at 12 o'clock. There wasn't a TV in his cell, so he sat on his bed, waiting for someone to come and tell him what to do.

All of a sudden, the voice disappeared, and his half-forgotten memories came rushing back. He remembered the alien invasion and the desperate attempts to fight them off. He barely had any memories of the last few months, but it appeared he had been busy running some sort of a figurehead government.

Zheng noticed a man standing on the other side of his prison cell bars. When he recognized the man, he jumped out of his skin.

Kurt von der Hagen was standing there, wearing his trademark black trench coat, staring at him with cold, gray eyes.

Kurt took an antique six-shooter out of his pocket. It was an 1851 Colt Navy. He slowly loaded it, bullet by bullet, taking his time.

Zheng paled. Coming face to face with the infamous assassin had always been his worst fear. He'd never dreamed of it happening with him unarmed and helpless in a prison cell. With a shivering voice, he said, "Now wait a minute. I'm sure we can come to a reasonable arrangement."

Kurt cocked the hammer, pointed the gun at Zheng's head, and said, "You killed my parents. I told you you'd pay for this."

Zheng, trembling with fear, hid his head behind his hands, sobbing uncontrollably.

"Do you want a fresh pair of pants before I pull the trigger?" asked Kurt.

* * *

KIEV - OCTOBER 14, 2078

. . .

Oksana was sitting in a small, one-bedroom apartment when the door opened, an old man walked in and shouted in Ukrainian, "Maria, are you home? Did you watch the news? We've been living under an alien occupation these last few months!" Then he saw Oksana, his jaw dropped, and he stopped dead in his tracks.

Oksana raised the gun in her hand so that the old man could see it and said in the same language, "Hi, Uncle Alex."

The old man, Alex, stared at Oksana. With a trembling voice, he said, "Where's my wife?"

Oksana nodded towards the bedroom. "In there, unconscious. I'm not a monster, but I can't say the same about you."

Alex, beginning to shake, said, "I had to do it. I have a gambling problem, and I owed thousands of dollars to the mafia. They threatened to kill my wife and children. This was the only way to save my family."

Oksana pointed the gun at him. "Still, you have to answer for my sister."

The old man fell to his knees and started begging. "Please! Have mercy!"

Oksana said, "There will be killing till the score is paid," and double-tapped him through his heart.

* * *

Two weeks after Operation Royalty, I was sitting in my Viper cockpit, with all my four thousand pilots behind me, when a single Xortaag scout ship appeared in orbit.

The scout ship crew received a message from their friends on Earth. "Welcome to Earth. We have been eagerly waiting for your arrival. Everything is ready as planned. The fleet can proceed."

The message was coming through Xortaag channels and had their codes. Little did they know it was sent by the captured Xortaags turned by MICI.

I watched the exchange intently, hoping the scout ship crew didn't decide to scan Earth, and they did not. Why would they? In their entire history, there had never been a single planet freed after occupation.

"Time to chew bubblegum and kick ass," I said.

The Xortaag transport ships made the final jump after they received the all-clear signal from the scout ship. They ran straight into a salvo of our Phoenixes—eight thousand of them, to be exact. The missiles were useless against Death-bringers, but the huge and cumbersome transport ships were a different story, with ten thousand Deathbringers tucked safely in their hangars. The salvo was followed by three more, Sparrows this time, and we flew in right after them, cannons blazing, making sure not a single transport ship survived the attack.

There were twenty million Xortaags on that convoy.

We killed every single one of them.

I knew I wouldn't lose any sleep over it. By my count, if we had killed another six hundred and eighty-two million of them, we would've been even-steven.

Now I've become Death, the destroyer of worlds.

THERE WAS a public ceremony to commemorate the brave men and women who gave their lives defending Earth against the Xortaags.

A huge monument was erected, in the form of several

men and women wearing various uniforms and flight suits. In front of the monument was a pedestal where we wrote the name of the nearly six thousand Winterfell-ers who'd lost their lives, to be inscribed in stone later on.

I wrote Elizabeth's name.

Kurt wrote Keiko's name. Allen's was written by Lilly.

Oksana wrote "Anastasiya."

Theresa and Samantha wrote Matias's name, and Dr. Bob wrote Sergei's.

* * *

THREE MONTHS LATER, a delegation of the Akakie high-ranking officials traveled to Earth to sign an alliance treaty.

As the first official human-Akakie meeting, it was a historic occasion. They were supposed to meet Earth's newly elected government officials in the government head-quarters in New York. There was no real reason for Kurt, Oksana and me to be there, but we weren't going to miss this, and as Earth's mightiest heroes, we had every right to be there. Plus, Tarq said my presence would give more credibility to our government representatives because as the only person who'd gone toe-to-toe with Maada, in a damaged space fighter no less, and survived, I'd become an urban legend among his people and a lot of other species across the universe. "Your golden Viper is now as famous as Maada's crimson Deathbringer," Tarq added.

"My team shoots the missiles that brought the Xortaags to their knees, and Jim gets to become a legend?" said Kurt.

I mimicked Allen. "Commandos are pussies. A real man tests his mettle against the universe's most badass conqueror."

The three of us looked dashing in our full-dress

uniforms. We sat next to each other behind a huge desk along with the Earth officials, waiting for the Akakies to arrive. Tarq and Barook were there too. At their request, there were no reporters present, and the meeting was neither recorded nor televised.

"Do you really have to use so much cologne?" Oksana asked Kurt.

Tarq kept biting his fingers, which told me something was wrong. "What's up?" I asked him.

"You remember I told you my people had a super strong sexual appetite?" he said. "I am not sure how they will react when they meet your people. You guys are ravishing, but I think I mentioned that already."

Was he serious, or was it just another example of the Akakies' weird sense of humor? I hoped he was just trying to scare me. Then, for the first time it occurred to me, *Is Tarq even a 'he'?*

The doors opened, the Akakie delegation entered, and we finally realized why Tarq was hiding behind a hologram all this time.

Tarq was right about one thing: The Akakies indeed came in various shapes, colors, and sizes. They were also insectoid. And not just any insectoid, the type you hallucinated about after using LSD. They were so hideous that we would've probably run to the Xortaags asking for help if we'd met them in their true form first.

Allen must be rolling in his grave right about now.

The Akakies reminded me of praying mantises. They were relatively short, had three fingers and an opposing thumb on each hand, four freakishly big eyes, and a lipless mouth with several rows of tiny sharp-looking teeth. They didn't have fingernails, their arms could bend backward, and they had four legs. I wondered how Tarq and Barook managed to hide those behind a hologram. They probably taped each pair together or something.

The Earth officials were all seasoned politicians, too experienced to show their shock. Tarq introduced them to the Akakies, everyone sat down around a table, and the first human-alien official meeting in history started.

Despite their alien forms, some of the Akakies were openly drooling over Oksana. One, however, didn't pay any attention to our beauty queen and instead winked at me. I silently prayed to God this was a female, and she was only teasing.

Tarq and Barook sat with their own people on the other side of the table. Tarq was grinning from ear to ear. This was the crown jewel of his efforts. But he looked so happy that Kurt and I immediately guessed something was up. We exchanged a look and said, "Oh-oh!" at the same time.

An earsplitting siren wailed through the room.

Tarq jumped out of his seat, shouting, "It is a Xortaag attack! Their fleet has just appeared in orbit! Everyone! Run for your life!"

Chaos ensued. The Akakies, who were probably in on it, started shouting and running in every direction. Our government officials' bodyguards rushed in, weapons drawn, and tried to guide them to safety.

I opened my mouth to warn people, but in all the commotion it would've been a wasted effort. I shrugged and sat back in my seat. A little bit of fun never hurt anyone. And our officials would have to deal with the Akakies for the foreseeable future. They might as well learn why they were called "the galaxy's pranksters" the hard way.

The hopefully female Akakie was running towards me. I thought about hiding under the desk, but that was unlikely to deter her/him/it, so instead, I drew my sidearm and kept it on my lap. That gave the creature pause. The Akakie gave me a hurt look and left me alone. Captain Kirk didn't have the monopoly on breaking alien beauties' hearts.

Tarq waved at Kurt, Oksana and me, and with obvious pride said, "What was that famous saying? If you failed once, try, try again?"

EPILOGUE

"Then the crown prince calmly went to his office, which was adjacent to the theater, opened a hidden panel under his desk and pushed a red button.

Mushgaana stared at the button for a second. *I hope this works,* he thought, but he figured it probably would not. No one had ever tried something like this before. And either way, *he* would never find out.

The humans are in for a nasty surprise if it does work though. He smiled at the thought.

He could hear the enemy soldiers massing outside his office door..."

Somewhere deep in the Amazon, an automated machine that nobody but Mushgaana and Maada knew about came to life. It threw a small cylinder into space. The cylinder had a small, portable SFD with enough power to make just one jump. Once sufficiently away from Earth, the SFD sent the cylinder as close as possible to the Xortaag territory, where it activated a beacon and waited to be picked up by their fleet.

THE END

THE GOLDEN VIPER

(The Crimson Deathbringer Book Two)

Kanoor has fallen.

The Xortaags are back, and they've conquered the Akakie homeworld. If they have enough time to reverse-engineer all the advanced technology they can find on Kanoor, they'll be undefeatable, and they won't stop until they'll have colonized the rest of the galaxy, starting with Earth.

To make things worse, an even more sinister threat (yeah, more sinister than the Xortaags) is emerging 1500 years in the future. An alien scientist is trying to send a two hundred thousand strong armada back in time to exterminate all sentient life in our galaxy. Will he succeed?

Now it's up to Jim, Kurt, and Tarq to save not only humanity but also billions of other people living on hundreds of different planets.

You thought the stakes were high in *The Crimson Deathbringer* (with Earth conquered and 700 million humans killed)? You ain't seen nothing yet!

THE BLACK FLEET

(The Crimson Deathbringer Book Three)

In *The Crimson Deathbringer*, an alien race conquered Earth, and humanity faced extinction. The stakes were high.

In *The Golden Viper*, the Xortaags occupied Kanoor, planning to annihilate all their enemies—starting with the humans—using the weapons they would have found there. The stakes were higher.

Could things get any deadlier?

Yes!

In *The Black Fleet*, (spoilers—sorry guys, but a few sentences here would have spoiled the events of book 2). This is nothing like what Jim, Kurt, and Tarq have faced before—this is nothing like *anyone* in the universe has ever faced before.

"Let me make this perfectly clear: if we have to sacrifice a few billion humans in order to save a hundred trillion people in the galaxy, that is exactly what we are going to do."

Commander Tarq

This is ENDGAME.

ABOUT THE AUTHOR

This is Jim Harrison, your favorite flying ace. If you've read my trilogy, you know these books are autobiographies, and Sean Robins is just a pen name. If you haven't, well then, SURPRISE!

* * *

Sorry about that, guys. I could never resist a good meta-joke.

So, this is me. The real me, Sean Robins. Unfortunately, my life is nowhere nearly as interesting as my main protagonist's. I'm a university/college-level English teacher, and including Canada, I've lived and worked in five different countries. I've met people from all around the world, which is probably why my characters are so diverse. They look like the bridge crew from *Star Trek*. One of my female characters even impersonated Uhura once, albeit posthumously.

I'm a huge Marvel (plus *Game of Thrones*, *Star Trek* AND *Star Wars*) fan, which shows since my novels are loaded with pop culture references. If you are a sci-fi fan (I assume that you are), you'll enjoy them tremendously. I even went full Deadpool in my first draft and broke the fourth wall multiple times, until my editor told it was distracting and kept taking her out of the moment. Shame. Those fourth-wall breaks were hilarious. Still, I can guarantee a few laugh-out-loud moments. Case in point: The "good" aliens in my books are a race of pranksters, whose main goal in life is pulling other people's legs (They have four legs, hence the slight change in the idiom). My favorite author is Jim Butcher (*The Dresden Files*), which is probably how I ended up writing in a first-person POV with the same light-hearted, funny tone as he does. The fact that my MC's name is Jim is purely coincidental though.

I hope you enjoy reading my books as much as I enjoy writing them.

https://www.facebook.com/seanrobins300
    @seanrobins300
    https://seanrobins73.wixsite.com/website

AUTHOR'S NOTE

Writing a novel is hard.

Don't "Dah!" me. Think about it for a second. The amount of time that goes into research, planning and outlining the novel, preparing the character sheets, writing, re-writing, re-re-writing, editing and proofreading is ginor-mous, and if you have a day job (I am an English teacher), finding enough time to do all that on top of all your other responsibilities is almost impossible. During the nine months it took me to write *The Crimson Deathbringer*, I stopped all my hobbies (I didn't even watch movies) and most of my social activities. I even stopped going to the gym, and I ended up with a belly by the time the book was finished. Now I understand why George R. R. Martin looks the way he does.

What prompted me to take on this Herculean task then, you ask?

I've got purely obsessional OCD. What this means is a thought enters my mind—usually something negative—and doesn't leave. I end up having to think about it 5000 times a day, and once this starts, my life is ruined for a week, two weeks, a month, or six months. I'd tried a lot of different ways to get rid of this problem: therapy, medication, meditation . . . Nothing ever worked, until I read an article that said the people who had this problem had an overly active imagination, and it would help if they channeled it into something productive, like writing.

I'd always wanted to be a writer. This is literally a childhood dream, one of those you give up when you grow up. I had the story of *The Crimson Deathbringer* in my mind for years (even started writing it and stopped a few times). When I read that article, I was going through a tough time in my marriage (fighting with your wife is no fun, even for sane people), and my mind had gone into its life-destroying overdrive, so I told myself, "Well, you've tried everything else, let's give this a shot."

And then a miracle happened.

My mind put the same energy it used to put into producing BS and making my life miserable into coming up with stories. Ideas would come to me fast and furious, and I had to stop whatever I was doing several times a day to write them down. I've been OCD-free since then (I know, I sound like a recovering alcoholic). When TCD (cool, eh?) was finished, it took my out-of-control brain half a day to plan my second novel, which is about a nerdy scientist and a sexy female mercenary who use a time machine to defeat an alien invasion.

I have a confession to make: I've fallen in love with TCD's characters. Jim, with his infuriating ability to take nothing seriously, Liz, despite her occasional goody-two-shoes tendencies, Tarq and his non-stop pranks, and Kurt, who is just awesome. If you end up liking them half as much as I do, then my job here is done, until I start writing the sequel.

BOOK REVIEW REQUEST

What did you think of *The Crimson Deathbringer*?

First of all, thank you for purchasing TCD. I know you could've picked any number of books to read, but you picked this book, and for that, I am extremely grateful. I hope that it added value and quality to your everyday life, or at least made you laugh, which to be honest was my main goal to begin with. If so, it would be really nice if you could share this book with your friends and family by posting on Facebook and Twitter.

If you enjoyed this book, I'd like to hear from you and hope that you could take some time to post a review on Amazon or Goodreads. Your feedback and support will help this author to greatly improve his writing craft for future projects and make this book even better. Moreover, it will increase sales, which allows me to write the sequel. Wouldn't it be nice to meet Jim, Kurt, Tarq, and Oksana again?

I can't wait to hear your thoughts. Thank you in advance.

Lightning Source UK Ltd.
Milton Keynes UK
UKHW022047031120
372753UK00003B/246